TIMELESS ADVENTURE

& OTHER VERY SHORT STORIES

eBook ISBN: 979-8-9880496-7-8
Paperback ISBN: 979-8-9880496-8-5
Hardback ISBN: 979-8-9880496-9-2

Library of Congress Control Number: 2024915609

TIMELESS ADVENTURE

& OTHER VERY SHORT STORIES

MITCH OLSON

ACKNOWLEDGMENTS

I dedicate these stories to my daughter, Sienna, who constantly amazes me. She is a committed student-athlete who consistently excels in the classroom and on the basketball court through intelligence, sheer determination, and hard work. Your mother and I are proud of you every single day. This dedication is for my beautiful wife, Lina, who is always there for our family and is the epitome of selflessness.

We are grateful for our dog Barkley, who is always there to bring us joy, make us laugh, and keep us company with his wagging tail. We also remember our beloved Gervin, who may be gone but always holds a special place in our hearts. Lastly, I would like to acknowledge Bernard King, a hometown hero for the New York Knicks, who inspired Sienna to wear the number 30 on both her high school and AAU basketball teams.

PART 1
TWISTY TURNS

PLOT TWIST

MALIBU MISCHIEF

The trio of friends, John, Fred, and Henry, were on the highway, setting off on a long journey from their hometown of Cottonwood Falls, Kansas to California in John's old Chevy Nova nicknamed "mechanized death." Their names were as basic as their small town. In this close-knit community, everyone knew each other's business. Most residents had never left the city limits, and a 75-minute drive to Topeka - meaning "place where we dig potatoes" - was considered a thrilling adventure in the "big city."

The Cottonwood Falls mayor had announced a prize for the one-thousandth inhabitant, who would receive a key to the city and serve as mayor for a day. It was not clarified how this lucky resident would be chosen, but it hardly mattered as there was little chance that such a milestone would ever be reached. The "third-class city" consisted of roughly eight hundred residents, mostly made up of multigenerational families whose main contribution to society was maintaining a perfect balance between births and deaths. Any outsiders passing through were quick to leave unimpressed, and the locals lacked the intellectual capacity to venture beyond the town's borders or devise an escape plan.

The three friends had been talking about visiting California since their junior year of high school, the idea sparked by a few shots of Crown Royal. Now, years later, they found themselves on a spontaneous road trip to make their dream come true. It was all spurred on by a night of heavy drinking and reminiscing, their determination fueled by alcohol and nostalgia. Against all odds, they decided to pack up and leave for Cali in just three days.

John was the star athlete, once a starting middle linebacker for the local high school team. He did not lift weights but was "country-strong." In one game, he made an interception that defied all conventional techniques. The football, as if guided by benevolent football gods, suddenly turned into a solid iron object and was drawn towards John's internal organs due to their "magnetic fields." It knocked the air out of him as it collided with his stomach before falling to the ground with a thud. Confused and dazed, John looked up at the sparkling stars above, still visible through the bright stadium lights. He fell onto his back, arms cradling the football before losing consciousness.

Out of the group, Fred was known as the intellectual. In a town full of underachievers, where "C" grades were the norm and handed out like Halloween candy by bored teachers, Fred's consistent "A" and "B" grades were a rarity. He was also the proud owner of a personal library consisting of twenty books, which immediately qualified him as a town scholar.

His four favorite books were part of the Encyclopedia Brown series, stories involving a boy detective who solves mysteries for the neighborhood kids and also helps his police department chief father solve actual crimes. Each book has multiple mysteries with a solution at the end that the reader tries to solve before reading. Fred had purchased four of the books at the local antique store "Out of the Attic." Despite meticulously reading each story multiple times, he had failed to solve any mystery in the first three books. It was akin to a professional baseball player beginning his major league career hitless in 30 at-bats, only to be demoted to the lowest minor league level, with an impending risk of being permanently ousted from the sport.

Fred devoured the fourth book, his attention completely fixated as he desperately tried to solve a mystery. Yet, no matter how hard he concentrated, the outcome remained the same. He couldn't unravel this enigma or any others. Did this mean he was unintelligent? After reading the solutions, everything became clear and logical. Of course, the Roman numeral had been written incorrectly. It was only natural that the home plate umpire was facing the wrong way from the fielders when dusting off home plate. And it was obvious a bird watcher would not hike east towards the rising sun in the morning.

Finally, on the eighth story of book four, he broke through the frustrating slump by solving one of the most challenging mysteries within its pages. With a stroke of luck, Fred correctly deduced that the supposed valuable sword offered as a trade for his friend's bike was fake. The alleged rare sword used by a famous southern general was inscribed with the battle name used by the Union, the North, not the battle name used by the Confederate South. Some might argue that Fred didn't truly solve the mystery but rather took an educated guess. He vaguely remembered the battle being mentioned in his high school class and figured it was possible that the winning side's name survived and made it into history books. That night, he drifted off to sleep with his teacher's words ringing in his mind: "History is written by the victors."

Henry was seen as a "normal" boy in a typical small town - average in athletic skills, intelligence, and appearance. He carried a bit of extra weight and had a subtle knack for mischief. Among his peers, he was the most outgoing and earned the title "Most Likely to Be a Politician" in the high school yearbook. Henry could effortlessly blend into various high school groups—the jocks, goths, populars, stoners, artsies, and everyone in between. Like a chameleon, he could adapt to any social setting, shifting his beliefs and behavior to fit in with different crowds. He was always a follower and never a leader.

A fortunate interception, an intuitive problem-solving guess, and a versatile human adapter would all rank high on the boy's list of lifetime achievements - a sad reflection on life in Cottonwood Falls. The town, nestled in Chase County at the heart of the Flint Hills, seems to stifle more ambitious dreams, with each rolling hill acting as a barrier to more grandiose, adventurous bucket list aspirations. If you walk just two blocks from Highway 177, known as the Flint Hills Scenic Byway, you'll reach the downtown area. The byway is often called one of Kansas' eight wonders, which amuses locals who find it hard to believe there could be eight extraordinary things in their otherwise ordinary state.

The journey to California felt never-ending, with miles upon miles of freeway stretching out before them. The three of them were exhausted from hours of nonstop driving and had fallen into a monotonous cycle. Each took turns at the wheel, struggling to stay alert and avoid fatigue.

Meals consisted of simple sandwiches made from cheap cold cuts and Wonder Bread. The bland sandwiches were a constant source of disappointment, but they were all too aware of the need to save money. Despite the unpleasant taste, it kept their hunger at bay and prevented their wallets from dwindling too quickly. Financial constraints also meant they couldn't afford a hotel for the night, so they slept uncomfortably in their cramped car seats, trying to ignore the stiffness in their bodies.

After only 28 hours, the boys reached Malibu, drawn by their infatuation with Pamela Anderson and the television show Baywatch. On that beautiful California day, the sun was shining down, and the weather was perfect. They had nine large cans of chilled Foster beer with them, easily recognizable by the blue label and bold letter F. The beverage was marketed as an Australian beer, but whether it was brewed there was unclear. It was a favorite beverage for the trio, who were big fans of Mel Gibson and the Mad Max movie franchise. On a previous much shorter road trip, they had driven to Topeka to watch Crocodile Dundee, and Fred had even purchased a boomerang from an antique shop in the tiny area known as "downtown" Cottonwood Falls. The term "downtown" was misleading; the area consisted of a compact blend of businesses such as restaurants, art galleries, boutiques, and antique shops, all easily walkable within a few minutes. The boys had formed a brief, unofficial Australian club with Fred as the self-appointed president. His fascination with the outback often bordered on absurdity. In fact, in middle school, he once asked his mother if they could trade their golden retriever for a koala. She was not amused and firmly said no. But Fred persisted and suggested getting a kangaroo instead.

The friends each cracked open their first Foster and raised their glasses in a quick toast to "Cali." They were wearing dark sunglasses, which served a dual purpose of hiding their bloodshot eyes and allowing them to take in the beautiful view in front of them discreetly. The Beach Boys had been right about "California Girls." Three college-age students from a dull Midwestern town were now surrounded by an array of stunning beachgoers wearing vibrant string bikinis. Los Angeles truly lived up to its nickname as "The City of Angels," with one gorgeous girl after another catching their eye. There were angelic blondes, mesmerizing brunettes, and even an occasional porcelain-skinned strawberry goddess.

The first can of beer was quickly consumed, its contents disappearing down the boys' throats. The empty cans were carelessly tossed onto the hot sand, partially buried by its warmth. In between rounds of dozing off, the boys had one main task for the day: to choose their top three picks for future supermodels or movie stars. They had a set of simple rules - every girl chosen must have unanimous approval from all three boys, and once three girls were selected, the game ended. They argued passionately, each making their case for their favorite choices among a sea of beautiful women. The competition was fierce with a large pool of dazzling candidates to choose from.

The boys were exhausted from their long journey, and the effects of alcohol had relaxed them to sleep. Suddenly, a beach patrol officer appeared, who could have been Erik Estrada's doppelganger in CHiPs. The three friends were swiftly awakened from their pleasant thoughts by the officer. The scorching mid-afternoon sun left them feeling disoriented. John was the first to regain his senses and respectfully questioned the officer, "Good afternoon, sir. How can we be of assistance?" The cop informed them that drinking on the beach was prohibited, and they would each receive a citation for breaking the rules.

After getting his bearings, Fred turned to the officer and asked, "Excuse me, sir, we were not aware that drinking on the beach is not allowed. We are simply trying to enjoy the day and get some sun. Could you perhaps give us a warning instead of a citation?"

The officer replied sternly, "I'm sorry, gentlemen, but I will have to issue citations for each of you. May I see your IDs? And how many beers do you have left? I see six empty cans here."

The boys handed over their Kansas driver's licenses, which the officer carefully examined before returning. Fortunately, all three were of legal age, so there would be no additional infractions.

The officer repeated, "And how many beers do you have left?"

"Three," the boys responded in unison.

"These citations are for $108 each, and remember that drinking on the beach is considered a misdemeanor. It would be best to just pay the fines. Instructions are provided on the back if you wish to contest the citations. Before you leave, please throw away the six empty cans in the designated trash container and empty any partially filled ones. I strongly advise against driving at this time; please arrange for a cab or have someone pick you up. I will wait here until you dispose of all the beer. Thank you for cooperating, and welcome to California."

Henry and Fred threw the empties away while John dumped the remaining beer in the garbage can. They returned to their sandy towels as the cop continued his rounds on the beach. The group of friends discussed the citations they had received and brainstormed potential solutions. However, since none of them could afford the $108 fine, they knew that ignoring the citation and avoiding Malibu in the future was their best option. They were relieved that the infraction was not a vehicle-related moving violation and wouldn't affect their driving records or result in increased car insurance rates.

The rest of the journey was a blur. They spent a few nights at a cheap Motel 6, and the rest were passed on the beach, only to wake up in the morning with sand in every nook and cranny imaginable. After ten days, they ran out of money and had to return home. With just enough funds to make it back to Cottonwood Falls, they arrived late at night to the familiar welcoming sights and sounds of a small

Midwestern town: buzzing bugs and sticky humidity. It was good to be back in their forever home and familiar, comfortable surroundings.

As the years went by, the trio of close friends slowly drifted apart. John and Henry followed the predetermined "Pleasantville" path that most of its residents took - being born in Cottonwood Falls, living a mundane life, and eventually dying there. Fred pursued a graduate degree in Missouri and lost touch with his hometown companions. John had taken up a job as a tour guide at the nearby museum, dressed uncomfortably in a blue suit. Meanwhile, Henry was working as a cashier at a nearby antique shop. Although they both worked in the compact "downtown" area, their paths seldom crossed. Their once strong bond had faded over the years, the "friends forever high school pact" warranty only lasting for about five years.

Henry unlocked the door to his rented room above the antique shop, exhausted from a long day's work. Once a week, he quickly stopped at the mailbox, hoping to find a personal letter among the usual pile of junk mail. As he spread the mail out on his small dining table, one envelope immediately caught his eye. Sweat began to form on his forehead as he read the return address: Malibu Superior Court. Trying to calm his nerves, he poured himself a beer and turned on the TV for background noise. After quickly downing the refreshing drink, he finally mustered up the courage to open the letter ten minutes later and read it aloud.

July 8, 1999
People of the City of Malibu
To: Henry Smith
Reg: Case # 125675

Malibu, California Municipal Code 12.08.170

A person shall not enter, be or remain on any park, beach, or public recreation area while in possession of any can or other receptacle containing any alcoholic beverage which has been opened, or a seal broken, or the contents of which have been partially removed, or while consuming any alcoholic beverage. Any person who violates the rules of regulation 12.08.170 relating to parks, beaches, and recreation areas, is guilty of an infraction, a violation of the Malibu Municipal Code, a misdemeanor.

12.08.050
Violation—Penalty

The fine for violation of section 12.08.170 of the Malibu Municipal Code shall be one hundred eight dollars ($108.00). Failure to pay the initial fine is punishable by additional fines of up to two thousand dollars ($2000.00) and/or imprisonment in the county jail or an acceptable jail in another jurisdiction for a period of up to six months.

Upon receipt of this letter, it is your legal obligation to immediately pay the city of Malibu the sum of $1900.00 (one thousand nine hundred dollars) to cover the initial fine of $108.00 (one hundred eight dollars) for the misdemeanor infraction which occurred on June 21, 1987, plus additional incremental non-payment penalties including accrued interest, If you do not pay the entire amount within 30 days, a collection agency will be contacted. In addition, we have been in contact with your local jurisdiction and they are aware of your initial misdemeanor "open container" offense and subsequent failure to pay the original fine and subse-

quent late fee penalties over a 12-year period. Failure to promptly pay the entire outstanding amount of $1900.00 will result in additional fines being levied and will also result in an immediate imprisonment for a period up to 180 days partnering with the Chase County Courthouse and Chase County Sheriff Department. If the city of Malibu receives the entire past due amount of $1900.00 within 30 days of receipt of this letter, the case will officially close, a one-time amnesty opportunity. The acceptable method of payment is a money order. You will need to send two separate money orders because domestic money orders can only be purchased for amounts up to $1000.00.

Remit your payment to:
Rufus G. Rutherford
23838 Pacific Coast Hwy
Malibu, CA

This is your final notice.

Rufus G. Rutherford
Malibu Superior Court

He read the letter again, hoping that it was just a figment of his imagination and the words would change. But no, it was real. A nightmare come to life, not just a bad dream.

He picked up the phone and dialed John.

"John, Henry here. This is completely random. Did you receive a letter from Malibu? You did yesterday? Can you meet me at the Blue Moon in two hours? We have to talk."

The Blue Moon was a popular hangout spot for both locals and tourists. John and Henry arrived at the bar around eight o'clock and chose a booth in the back corner. As they settled in, "Don't Fear the Reaper" by Blue Oyster Cult played softly in the background. They each opened their letters, which were identical except for their names. It was time to come up with a plan.

"Henry, I'm not sure what to make of this letter. Do you think it's legitimate?"

"John, it has to be real. The only people who know about that citation we received over ten years ago are the city of Malibu and us. With today's technology and states working together more closely, they were able to track us down."

"This is bad news. Should we just ignore it?"

"We can't ignore it. They'll send our case to collections, possibly garnish our wages, and add on extra fees. I don't know if they're serious about jail time, but I definitely don't want to take that risk."

"What if they ask for more money after we pay the $1900?"

"That's a good point. But as long as we have this letter, we have proof that paying the full amount will close the case. Just make sure to keep it safe. I can't afford it either, and it'll wipe out most of my savings, but I'm going to pay and consider it an expensive lesson learned. What about you? What's your plan?"

"I'll do the same. You've convinced me. It's better than risking going back to jail - one night there was more than enough. I'm not going back."

They nursed their beers as they halfheartedly attempted to catch up on each other's lives. They talked about the old days, when they were both young and naive, chasing after dreams that never seemed to come true. As the minutes ticked by, Henry began to feel restless. He wanted to leave, but he didn't want to hurt John's feelings. So, with a slight tremor in his voice, he fabricated an excuse.

"I should get going," he said, draining the last of his beer. "Got the morning shift at the antique shop tomorrow."

John nodded understandingly with a forced smile. They both knew this was just a polite gesture, that Henry didn't really have to leave.

Rufus pulled out two ice-cold Foster beers from his backpack and handed one to Fred. They clinked their aluminum cans with enthusiasm, making a sound like cymbals. The cans were covered in condensation, reflecting the sunlight as they raised them in a toast, the bright colors of the labels merging into one another.

"To us!" Fred declared.

"To your buddies," Rufus added.

"To my mates," corrected Fred with a grin.

FINAL CONFESSION

Chris Riley arrived at school before anyone else, making his way to the Parish church. The clock read 7:30 AM, and classes wouldn't begin until 8:15. Despite not being a religious person, Chris occasionally found himself drawn to the quiet sanctuary of the church in the morning instead of waiting outside for the school doors to open. He was Sacred Heart's star athlete, excelling in all three seasonal sports - soccer, basketball, and baseball. Even though he was only an eighth grader, he already sported an impressive mustache that seemed to grow thicker by the day. But despite this sign of physical maturity, he had yet to start shaving. And like most teenage boys, Chris couldn't help but daydream about girls; some might say he was even obsessed with them.

Chris's decision to enter the church was not a random one. He had always been intrigued by the confessional, and he thought today was as good a time as any to satisfy his curiosity. The church was quiet, with only a few people inside - two elderly women deep in prayer at the back and a woman lighting a candle near the altar. After ensuring the coast was clear, Chris entered the confessional and shut the door behind him. Little did he know that once the door closed, a light would go on outside, indicating that the priest was ready for confession. Chris felt at ease as he sat there for a few minutes until he was suddenly startled by an unfamiliar voice.

"Forgive me, Father, for I have sinned. It has been four days since my last confession."

Chris found himself in a predicament. The sensible thing to do was to slip out unnoticed or remain silent until the parishioner left. But his mischievous side won out. He couldn't see through the opaque screen, and a curtain further obscured his view. Fighting to recognize the voice, which he believed belonged to a woman, Chris hesitated before nervously blurting out: "Go ahead with your confession, my dear."

"I forgot to feed my cat yesterday and ended up serving his dinner two hours late. I must have fallen asleep in the early evening because I missed my grandson's call. And, for the first time in two months, I missed daily mass yesterday. I am sure there is more. That's all I can remember. I am sorry for my actions."

Chris rolled his eyes at the familiar boring sins from an elderly woman. However, he couldn't help but feel a little excited about the potential for some drama. This G-rated movie had the chance to turn into an R-rated one.

The boy assigned a simple penance of five Hail Marys and three Our Fathers to be completed before leaving the church. He declared her absolved of her sins and sent her on her way with a wave of his hand. Mrs. Miller dutifully exited stage right, pondering that it was odd for Father not to require her to say the Act of Contrition. But at 82 years old, Mrs. Miller knew better than to question a priest; she settled into her usual seat in the front row and began reciting her assigned prayers - a routine ingrained since her first communion as a young girl in North Dakota.

Chris was faced with a dilemma: How could he escape from the confessional without attracting attention? He knew there was no foolproof solution, so he cautiously cracked open the door and swiftly made his way to the rear of the church before slipping out unnoticed.

Chris was captivated by this new game of chance filled with adventure and risk - a real-life board game he had created, now available for purchase at Sacred Heart Parish. That night, Chris did some preliminary research to get acquainted with the basic confessional procedure. The official guide was too lengthy, and Chris wasn't fond of reading or memorizing text. So, he simplified it into his own confessional crib notes: Perp greets the priest and lists sins, the priest jabbers and delivers a sentence, the sinner recites an Act of Contrition, the priest forgives the cat, hit the road jack, rinse and repeat and run it back with the next customer. Chris also mentally noted that he could skip the Act of Contrition because it bored him; it was his game and his rules.

In the afternoon, he made an important decision. He needed an accomplice, and there was only one person he could trust.

Eric Smith and Chris were the first to arrive at the Sacred Heart gym for Monday's basketball practice. The previous night, the parishioners had gathered there for Bingo night, a weekly event held on the same court as the school's basketball games. As usual, Eric and Chris were tasked with clearing out tables and chairs from the night before in preparation for their practice. The hardwood floor showed wear and tear marks, particularly in five noticeable patches where heavy furniture had been dragged across it. The gym was deserted except for the two eighth graders diligently working on clean-up duties. In an effort to keep their conversation private, Chris leaned closer to his best friend and whispered through his hand, just in case anyone was trying to read his lips.

"Bro, you won't believe what happened today."

"I have no idea. Just tell me."

"Promise not to tell anyone. On your mother's grave."

"Promise." Eric's single word, "promise," was the ultimate guarantee. His father had died of leukemia when the boy was five, and he and his mother had a bond forged in the strongest gold.

"I pretended to be a priest during confession this morning. I walked in the penalty box sin bin to check it out and this old lady came in. I pretended to be Father, and we role-played."

"What? That's insane! You are a crazy bastard you know that?"

"I need your help. You won't get in trouble, I promise. If I get caught, I'll take the fall. I swear on my parents' graves. Can you meet me here at 7:30 tomorrow morning?"

"Sure."

"Are you ready for the plan?"

"Yeah, what is it?"

"I need you to sit in a church pew and act like you're reading something, like a hymn book or a flyer. Make sure you have a clear view of the confessional. When someone enters, text me their gender, approximate age, and if you recognize them by name. When I'm ready to leave, we'll exchange messages, and you'll give me the all-clear when it's safe to exit. You'll be my lookout. Sound good?"

"I'm in. See you at 7:30."

The following day, the two boys met as planned at the church grounds. Eric's house was only a few doors down from the school, making it a short walk for him. On the other hand, Chris had to trek over a mile from his own home. Occasionally, his mother would drive him if she needed to run errands, which often involved stopping by a nearby cafe for breakfast and gossiping with other stay-at-home moms.

Chris stepped into the confessional and waited. Eric took a seat in a pew where he had a clear view - not too close to draw attention but near enough to observe anyone approaching. He pulled out an old Playboy magazine he had taken from his dad's collection and settled in. Five minutes passed before Chris heard footsteps approaching. At the same time, his phone vibrated discreetly with a message flashing: It's Mr. Jones! Chris felt a wave of panic. Mr. Jones was the father of Paul Jones, a fellow eighth grader - a mysterious and introverted boy whom most people found odd. Both Paul and Chris had attended Sacred Heart for all eight grades, part of an exclusive group of eleven students. Even though they were seated near each other numerous times throughout their school years due to the assigned seating chart, they had never engaged in a meaningful conversation.

"Forgive me, Father, for I have sinned. It has been a long time since my last confession, I don't remember when it was exactly. I don't fucking remember."

"Take a deep breath. The Lord forgives all. Tell me your sins."

"I swear and cuss too much. I drink too much. I pass out when I drink too much and sometimes can't remember where I parked my car. A year ago, I slept with a woman I met at a bar, and I can't even recall her face or name."

"Mr. Jones, the Lord works in mysterious ways. He is a just God, and a merciful God. He didn't allow you to find your car after you were boozing because he didn't want you to get in an accident. Mr. Jones, the Lord can see in your heart you are a good man but are easily led astray."

Mr. Jones fidgeted uneasily in his seat. How did the priest know his name? He wasn't fond of attending confession and only went every few years to wipe the slate clean, viewing the priest as a high-powered vacuum cleaner sucking up his sins and dumping them into the trash bin.

"Sir, do you know the Act of Contrition?"

"No, Father, I do not."

"It doesn't matter. Here is what you are going to do. I want you to spend two hours preparing meals at the food bank this weekend. That's it. You're dismissed. Don't be a stranger."

Mr. Jones eagerly left the confessional before the priest could reconsider. Trading years of heavy drinking and sporadic womanizing for just a couple of hours volunteering at a food bank? Sign me up! He found himself liking this new priest and momentarily entertained the idea of attending a weekend mass now and then but quickly brushed off the notion as silly.

The church bulletin regularly listed the designated times for confessions, usually on Wednesdays and both weekend days. Sometimes, priests would also make themselves available at other times, which Chris and Eric took full advantage of for their elaborate game. The two boys didn't meet every day before school; instead, they met a couple of mornings each week at 7:30, alternating the days to avoid creating a pattern. Their target audience was a lonely elderly woman living on a fixed income who sought comfort in her faith and wanted to secure a direct ticket to heaven without an initial transfer to a connecting city called purgatory.

After Mrs. Miller was the first visitor to the sin bin grand opening, she became a frequent patron. She seemed to come up with "misdeeds" as an excuse to see the kind new priest. Chris listened attentively to her stories and even shared jokes about her cat, Gus. This brought a lighter tone to their sessions and led to the creation of "The Misadventures of Gus" series. Over time, they developed a comfortable routine with well-crafted characters, and he would often let her off easy with a light penance such as a few Hail Marys as the main dish and an occasional Our Father for dessert.

Did Chris have any guilt about posing as a priest? Not particularly. He saw it as offering a service to customers, and the religious convenience store, with its limited and inconvenient hours, could use all the help it could get. It had been six weeks since Chris started working in the confessional booth. As he glanced at the clock, it was already 7:40 am, and it seemed like it would be a quiet day for absolutions. His phone buzzed, and he checked a new message from Eric.

OMG, Mayday, Mayday! His teacher, Mrs. Rogers, was approaching. Mrs. Rogers, the Sacred Heart eighth-grade teacher, was every adolescent boy's fantasy. She occasionally went without a bra and always smelled amazing. Known for her patience and ability to bring out the potential in her students, Mrs. Rogers also offered important life lessons to the boys, such as "stay out of bars. Trouble will find you."

Chris had been drifting off to sleep until he received the text. Now he was awake - wide, wide awake.

The familiar female voice purred, "Forgive me, Father, for I have sinned. It has been six weeks since my last confession. This past weekend, I had sex with my boyfriend and enjoyed it." Mrs. Rogers paused, waiting for a response from the priest.

"How old are you? Are you married?"

"Father, I am twenty-eight years old and not married. My boyfriend and I have been together for two years, and this is the first time we have had sex."

"What do you mean you enjoyed it?"

"It was pleasurable."

"I see. Are there any other sins?"

"I am a teacher, and sometimes I feel I am not getting through to my students. They are starting high school next year, which is a critical year."

"Mrs. Rogers, you're a fantastic teacher," Chris exclaimed a little too loudly. He mentally cursed himself for breaking the rule of anonymity, an essential aspect of the reconciliation process that he had just compromised.

"Mrs. Rogers, I apologize for mentioning your name, but I recognized you when you mentioned that your students would be starting high school next year. Sex isn't a sin, and it's okay to enjoy it. For your penance, spend a little extra time with a student who needs support. Continue being the compassionate teacher that you are."

Mrs. Rogers began to tear up, "Thank you, Father. I've never experienced a confession like this before. Usually, by now, I'd be knee-deep reciting numerous Hail Marys and Our Fathers."

They both started to laugh.

"Hold on a second. You still need to say the Act of Attrition."

"You mean the Act of Contrition?"

"Of course... just making sure you were paying attention."

They erupted into laughter again. After their giggles and chuckles died down, they sat in silence for a moment, trying to regain their composure. But despite their efforts, the carefree and happy atmosphere remained, causing them to break into smiles once again.

After a poignant pause, Mrs. Rogers recited the prayer with conviction.

"Mrs. Rogers, you are absolved of your sins. Go and make a difference in a child's life. Amen."

The teacher left the confessional with renewed confidence in her teaching abilities. Five minutes later, Eric signaled to Chris that it was safe to exit the penalty box. As they emerged from the church, Eric eagerly asked what had been discussed between Chris and their teacher, whom they were about to see in class.

"Bro, I can never divulge that, or I will go to hell."

After third period ended, Mrs. Rogers asked Chris to come up to her desk while the other students rushed off to recess.

"Chris, you are a great student. Thanks for spending a little time with a troubled teacher. Make a difference in somebody's life."

The teacher and student shared a knowing look before the young adolescent took a deep breath and exited the classroom with determination. His goal was to strike up a conversation with Paul Jones on the playground. This was the last day of extended hours at Confession Supermarket, and Chris pledged to avoid bars when he grew up and pursue a career as either a priest or teacher. It was a turning point for him, signifying the end of an era. He knew it was time for him to go to confession.

MINT AT THE MINT

The three co-workers, Dan Lloyd, Fred Shing, and Joey Rossi, had several hours to spare before their flight from Denver International Airport. The three men were friendly but not friends. After checking out of their hotel, the trio brainstormed how to spend their time before the evening flight. Joey suggested touring the Denver Mint, but Dan and Fred quickly vetoed his idea. They had their sights set on a local brewery instead, but unfortunately for them, their votes only counted as one. As the designated rental car driver for the group, Joey's vote held more weight and counted as three. Resembling a rigged election in a developing nation, the visit to the mint initiative squeaked by winning by a vote of 3-2.

Joey had always dreamed of touring the Denver Mint since he was a child. He spent his youth collecting coins, each one holding a special story for him. With a magnifying glass in hand, he would meticulously examine every coin in his possession and even pay close attention to any change received during store purchases, hoping to find valuable coins. One of his most prized possessions was the 1921 Morgan Silver Dollar, with its distinct "D" mint mark on the back under the wreath, which was only produced at the Denver Mint. As it was the final year of production for this iconic coin, it held historical significance and was highly sought after by collectors.

Joey's dream coin was the 1927-D Saint-Gaudens Double Eagle, a $20 gold piece minted in Denver. Its history was fascinating; during the early 1930s, the US Treasury offered it to the general public for face value and postage, yet few people took advantage of this opportunity due to the Great Depression. Most coins from this series were destroyed during the 1933 gold recall, making them extremely rare. Today, less than 20 of these coins are believed to exist and can fetch millions at auction in top condition. Joey had always fantasized about owning one, a coin that was not just rare but also held a significant historical value. He couldn't help but think about what he would have done if he lived in that time period. If given the opportunity, would he have bought a large bag full of 1927-D double eagles for just the shipping price plus an extra $20 per coin? He had extensively examined other coins minted in Denver with comparable humble origins, each coin carrying a rich past riddled with unexpected events. And now, he was fulfilling his bucket list dream of visiting the place where these rare coins were minted, filling him with exhilaration and anticipation.

The security measures at the mint were extremely strict, with a long list of prohibited items, including purses and bags. Every visitor had to go through a thorough screening process, including a metal detector and X-ray scan of any hand-held items. Armed guards were strategically placed throughout the facility, including at the initial security checkpoint. Joey's eyes widened with excitement as he watched Dan and Fred walk through the metal detector without incident. He eagerly followed their lead, his feet practically bouncing off the ground as he couldn't wait to start exploring. However, he triggered the detector with a series of beeps. The guard calmly asked him to try again, suggesting it could be a false alarm. Joey complied but was met with another round of beeps. At this point, he could sense the guards' gaze intensifying and feared they might draw their weapons on him. "Sir, are you sure there's nothing in your pockets? Maybe some loose change or a random key?"

The anxious man frantically patted down his jeans and the pockets of his light jacket, but they were empty. The guards and the growing crowd of people behind him stared daggers at him, their impatience palpable. He could feel the sweat trickling down his back as nerves overtook him like a drug addict in withdrawal. He thought about making a break for it, but the armed guards stationed around the area made that seem like a risky move. With trembling hands, he reluctantly walked through the metal detector again - BEEP, BEEP, BEEP. Joey's panic reached its peak. "I'm sorry, sir. I really don't know what could be triggering the alarm. Let me search one more time. Please, I beg of you."

He circled through the exit back to the front of the machine. He methodically checked each pocket, starting with his jeans and then his windbreaker. But there was nothing in either. When he thought he had checked every pocket, he heard a faint rattling noise from his jacket. He quickly unzipped a small, hidden pocket he had overlooked and pulled out a tin container of Altoids with only a few mints remaining.

Sheepishly, he asked the guards, "Care for a mint at the mint?"

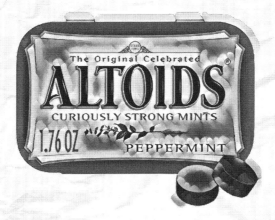

TEENAGE ENTREPRENEUR
OF THE YEAR

With a flick of a small, unassuming card, 17-year-old Billy Cooper standing tall at 6'3" and weighing in at 195 lbs., was suddenly transformed into George Donovan, a man twice his age, shorter at 5'7" and much heavier at 240 lbs. This was no ordinary fake ID; it wasn't professionally made like the ones readily available to teenagers nowadays. No, Billy had taken matters into his own hands with an entrepreneurial spirit and innovative mind, taking advantage of an unexpected opportunity to create a new identity. His ingenuity was something to be admired, even if his actions were not.

The teenager had just finished swimming at Brooks Pool, the largest indoor pool serving the city's northern part. Billy was alone in the row of lockers when he spotted a large gray Rossignol duffel bag on a nearby bench. He stood up and looked around the room, making sure no one else was there. The only other person present had just started showering, and the showers were located about forty feet away from the bag, surrounded by multiple rows of lockers like a metal maze.

Without a moment's hesitation, Billy unzipped the side pocket of the bag, not the main compartment. Jackpot. A wallet. He swiftly stashed it in his jacket, leaving the bag behind, and walked briskly, not running, just another kid leaving the facility after a workout. Once outside, he sprinted until he was three long blocks away, ensuring he wasn't being followed. He lay in the middle of the long grassy boulevard, heart pounding, and closely inspected the wallet contents - one hundred twenty-three dollars in an assortment of bills, four twenties, three tens, two fives, and three singles. There was also a Driver's License that belonged to one George Donovan. A few business cards and personal pictures were of no interest to Billy, so he discarded the wallet and continued his walk home with the cash and adult ID, his heart still racing from the exhilarating escape, the risk he took still fresh in his mind.

Back in his room, Billy locked the door and prepared for a delicate operation. He retrieved his expired license and, with precision, cut around his picture. He then carefully glued his teen picture over the original adult picture, and in an instant, he was 34 years old, short, and overweight. He examined his handiwork, a mix of art and deception, and a sense of satisfaction washed over him. The only flaw he could find was that adult George had a front view of his face, while juvenile Billy's glued picture had a side view profile. But it was a minor detail that he was confident he could manage.

It was time to put his latest art project to the test. He headed to the nearby grocery store, where he didn't recognize any of the employees. He casually walked over to the chilled section and selected a six-pack of Mickey's Big Mouth malt liquor, a popular choice among teenagers for its potent alcohol level and distinctive green glass bottle appearance. As he made his way to the counter, his legs trembled and refused to cooperate with his movements.

"ID?"

Billy George handed over his wallet and presented his freshly minted driver's license to the clerk. He kept the ID protected by the plastic insert, not wanting to reveal its true identity. The bored clerk barely glanced at the license before ringing up the sale and placing the alcohol in a paper bag. Billy's experiment had succeeded.

After his successful trial run, "Billy George" gained confidence and decided to test his fake ID at the state liquor store. He was doubtful that he could fool the trained employees in their yellow uniforms, but to his surprise, it worked. He happily left with whiskey, rum, vodka, and tequila bottles concealed in brown paper bags. He began buying alcohol for other underage students and charging a commission, becoming popular among his peers for having access to a reliable source of booze. The arrangement pleased both parties; Billy had a steady source of income, and the young customers had a lubricant to help them loosen up in social situations. His

fake ID made him part of an exclusive group of teenage en-
trepreneurs who could easily obtain alcohol.

Billy branched out and started purchasing pony kegs at
the Inferno, a popular college bar that was quiet during the
day but bustling with coeds and frat boys at night. The teen
had done his research and knew that he had to leave a deposit
when purchasing a pony keg to be refunded when the keg is
returned within the three-day deposit period. He made sure
to only go during the afternoon shift and befriended the
two bartenders who worked then. To them, Billy was just
another college student party animal buying another keg.

Billy was the go-to guy for weekend high school parties,
supplying pony kegs at unsuspecting parent houses and or-
ganizing impromptu gatherings in a nearby wooded park.
He charged more for his "Inferno" deals; there was more risk
involved, and it required more effort to transport the heavy
full kegs and return them empty.

Business was booming. Billy George was a successful en-
trepreneur with a simple economic model for his business.
On the left side of the menu, customers could purchase hard
liquor at a fixed price per bottle, with discounts for larger
orders but a limit of four bottles per transaction. On the
right side of the menu was the popular keg option, where
individual customers could pool their money together in a
group partnership.

Buying alcohol had become routine for Billy, and he now
approached the transaction with a sense of composure. He
played the role of a responsible adult purchasing beer for a
social occasion or being prepared for potential unexpected
guests.

It was a typical quiet March afternoon when he entered the Inferno at around four o'clock, just as it usually was at this time. A college student occupied a barstool, leisurely sipping on a pint of Guinness. In the front section, a couple huddled in a booth and discussed their relationship. A mechanic from the nearby auto shop was taking his lunch break and enjoying a small pepperoni pizza with a Diet Coke. In the back of the bar, two young boys were locked in an intense game of 8 Ball Pool while the iconic tune "Welcome to the Jungle" blared from the jukebox.

Billy's spidey sense tingled as he realized he didn't recognize the bartender. He should have left the bar immediately with the empty deposit keg but hesitated. As the bartender scrutinized him, the teen approached the front counter and handed over the keg.

"Hi, I'm returning this empty pony keg and would like to purchase another one," Billy said.

The bartender took the keg and disappeared around a corner before returning seconds later.

"I'll need to see your driver's license for proof of ID," he said.

Billy, as he had done countless times before, reached into his back pocket and pulled out his wallet. He held it out to the bartender, offering up his driver's license, which was protected by a plastic cocoon - a force field shielding the youthful side profile picture of himself at 34 years old.

"Take it out of your wallet and hand me the ID," the bartender demanded.

This was Billy's second chance to make a break for it, but he hesitated. Slowly and carefully, he removed the ID from under the protective flap. It took a few seconds because the cheap plastic sleeve had stuck to it. Reluctantly, he handed the card over.

Without hesitation, the bartender ripped off the picture of Billy to reveal George's face underneath. The glue left small pieces on the "original" bearded George's ruddy complexion.

"Get out of here kid before I call the cops. I never want to see you in here again!"

Another thriving small business owner pursuing the American dream has his hopes of becoming a millionaire dashed. Billy returned to his home and drowned his disappointment with a Mickey's Big Mouth. He let out a heavy sigh, knowing that his days of having easy money were over. He was once again a regular teenager, struggling to gather enough funds to buy beer. Despite feeling discouraged, Billy refused to give up. His determination grew stronger as he began brainstorming his next business venture. Fueled by the success of his first start-up company, Billy concocted an ambitious plan...

PLAYING & EATING CHICKEN

It was 3:30 AM, an unusual time for lunch. But who dines at such an hour? The dedicated souls who keep our networks running, even when the rest of the world is asleep. They are always on duty, twenty-four hours a day, even on holidays.

"Logan," said Joe Jackson, a sizeable man, "Any ideas on where to go?"

At this late hour, options were limited.

"Subway?" I offered.

Horace Green joined the conversation, "I'm sick of sandwiches. Let's get some chicken."

Jackson and Green were practically joined at the hip, both African American men driving identical dark Volkswagen Jettas, each sporting flashy rims and high-end stereo systems. During their high school years, Jackson had been a standout fullback on the city's top football team, while Green had shone as a basketball star at a smaller high school that seldom saw victories. Although Jackson had gained over a hundred pounds since those days, he still carried himself with the effortless grace of a seasoned athlete. On the other hand, Green continued to play competitive basketball regularly, maintaining his excellent physical condition.

I am a Caucasian in my mid-twenties who loves rap music and hooping. My go-to artists right now are Boogie Down Productions, Kool G Rap, and DJ Polo.

During our lunch breaks, we would often get together and act like we were carefully weighing our options for where to eat. But in reality, we only had four realistic choices: the 24-hour Subway sandwich shop, the fancy but overpriced Italian restaurant down the block that left us still hungry after each small portion, or one of the all-night convenience stores nearby. We ultimately chose Earl's, a gas station and convenience store combo known for their delicious southern fried chicken made from a top-secret recipe.

Earl's was a short fifteen-minute drive from work, situated in a predominantly African American neighborhood. Having grown up in the area and still living there with his family, Jackson had a strong connection to his community and took great pride in it. Despite the area's decline and decay, he remained fiercely protective of its culture and history.

We hastily piled into Jackson's Jetta and zoomed away. With only seventy-five minutes for our lunch break, we couldn't afford any delays. Joe expertly drove us across the grated bridge that connected the state university to the heart of the city. Soon we were cruising down 23rd Avenue, Digital Underground tunes accompanying us as the fourth passenger, the two close friends providing commentary as the speeding car navigated around human potholes, the skinny skeleton crack hoes zigzagging across the busy arterial road searching for desperate customers.

Green commented, "Shit, that's Jenny Jones, she was a fine cheerleader."

A block later, Jackson chimed in, "I might have dated that chick a couple of times. I think that's Jasmine. Everybody wanted to get in her pants. Now look at that skanky thing. What kind of diseases do you think she is carrying?"

Jackson slowed the car to a crawl as he and Green focused on the pock-marked, ninety-pound, barely recognizable female, confirming that the wench was indeed Jasmine, a formerly beautiful young black woman.

Jackson pleaded with a note of desperation, "When is this shit going to stop?"

As we stepped into the convenience store, we greeted Mr. Robinson. His first name was a mystery to everyone; he had always been known as Mr. Robinson, a title that commanded respect. He was a figure of strength and integrity, a cornerstone of the African American community. Having served two tours in Vietnam, Mr. Robinson was resolute in his mission to keep the store running, even if it meant just breaking even. The neighborhood had become increasingly troubled, its decline linked to the crack cocaine epidemic and high unemployment rates among Black youth. Yet, Mr. Robinson believed it was vital to set an example - a Black business owner serving his community.

Before we ordered our chicken, the three of us went our separate ways in the store. Joe headed towards the left aisle to find some shaving cream. Horace wandered casually down the right aisle, and I made my way down the center aisle in search of a late-night snack.

Out of nowhere, a man stumbled into the store, his movements erratic and unsteady. It was clear that he was high as a soaring kite, and he reached for something inside his jacket. He spoke in a tired, trembling voice.

"Pops, give me all your cash. I don't want to hurt you."

I was already on edge before this unstable druggie even spoke; my instincts warned me of danger as I saw Jackson and Green quickly ducking behind the aisles for cover.

In a matter of seconds, Mr. Robinson, who was known for his "shoot first, ask questions later" mentality, pulled out a shotgun and pointed it directly at the young man's chest. I couldn't comprehend how he acted so quickly; the weapon seemed to appear out of thin air from somewhere behind the counter.

My legs began to tremble as I stood there. I was half-asleep when I first entered the shop. Now, I was fully awake and on high alert. The unstable man stood between me and Mr. Robinson, making it a dangerous situation for both of us. If the shop owner were to fire his gun in self-defense, I could easily become collateral damage - just another blurb in the local police beat blog.

Mr. Robinson, speaking firmly, proposed an alternative plan: "Listen, son. You have two options. The first option is to leave this store right now as if nothing happened. I won't call the cops, but you must never return. The second option is to make any sudden move as if you're reaching for a weapon, and I will shoot you on the spot. You'll be dead. Either way, you won't get any money from me, and I'll remain unharmed. The decision is whether you want to live or die. Got it?"

The would-be thief weighed his options and hesitated. He cautiously shuffled his way out of the store, weaving unsteadily until he disappeared from view. Mr. Robinson took a careful look around his property perimeter before returning inside. He casually addressed us, "Well, that was quite the late-night show. So, what kind of chicken can I get for you boys?"

We ordered six wings, three thighs, and three breasts, expressing our gratitude to Mr. Robinson for his delicious chicken and bravery. He replied that such incidents occurred about once a month and were nothing compared to what he faced in NAM. You just have to stay vigilant. He didn't hold it against the young man; times were hard, and the guy was probably dealing with mental health issues.

We returned to work in silence, the only sound being rap music playing in the background. I paid close attention to the lyrics of Kool G Rap and DJ Polo's "Streets of New York," which echoed through the high-end car speakers. The powerful words left a lasting impression on me.

"Look behind you when you walk. That's how it is in the streets..."

Before tonight, I cherished the song for its saxophone and piano samples. However, now the vocals were imprinted in my mind. It dawned on me that I could have been just another disposable lyric in a forgettable rap track.

Lunch decision delicious chicken
Enter store, and the plot thickens
White boy sweating panic-stricken
Cause of death a game of chicken
Acts of violence are fatalistic
Another meaningless crime statistic
Added nonchalantly to the police ledger
Another life taken, impossible to measure
A mother's only son is gone for good
What is happening to the neighborhood?

HALLOWEEN SURPRISE

Must have been about nine
Exact age hard to define
Excitement building for over a week
Reaching a crescendo about to peak
Halloween was finally here
Day of costumes, make-up, and gear
Two sets of brothers made up our group
Planned out our route a basic loop
Four boys on a journey feeling cocky
Superman, a cowboy, Shazam, and Rocky

Trick or treat, trick or treat

Over and over, street after street
Mission is to get candy, our only jobs
Candy and more candy, gobs and gobs
Rule #1 grab a handful
Efficient way to get a bag full
Occasionally no one answered the door
We knew how to settle the score
Out came the raw eggs
Kids equivalent of powder kegs
Three or more eggs would splatter the house
Once a screaming woman wearing a blouse
Emerged from her residence
Dripping yokes were her evidence
"I will find you kids" she shouted
Her toothless threat we doubted
As we ran away snickering
The wife and spouse were bickering

Candy names are a source of inspiration
The most original deserve an ovation
Milk Duds, Whoppers, Butterfinger
Sweet taste on the tongue will linger
Skittles, PayDay, Laffy Taffy
Resulting sugar high can make you daffy
Junior Mints, Gummy Bears, Jawbreaker
Diffuse an argument and use as a peacemaker
Milky Way, KitKat, Hershey's Bar
Children equivalent of caviar for a czar
Snickers, Mounds, Nestle Crunch
Never stop at one need a bunch
Twix, Mr. Goodbar, 100 Grand

Loved by kids across the land
Jolly Ranchers, Blow Pops, Baby Ruth
My personal favorite and that's the truth
The variety is endless
Choices truly stupendous

The night was coming to a close
Danger of sugar overdose
The candy haul was significant
We should have been awarded a certificate
Our pillowcases were filled to the brim
As overhead streetlights started to dim
A bit exhausted but feeling content
Don't relax yet danger will be sent

A Camaro car pulled up without notice
Three teenagers jumped out and started to goad us
"Give us your candy" was the demand
It wasn't a plea sounded like a command
We thought about trying to run
A rollicking time was no longer fun
The biggest took a menacing step towards us
This was not a time to discuss
Reluctantly we handed over our candy
This Halloween was no longer dandy
They sped down the road in the hot rod
We did not cry and kept a brave façade

Nowadays, I am much older
Still introverted yet bolder
Pass out the candy to the children
Innocent eyes excitement building
Dozens of Halloweens have faded away
Only one Halloween sparked an essay
Nightmares and recollections can't be undone
A single night convinced me to purchase a gun
Conflicting emotions lead me astray
Tracing back to one eventful day

BIZARRE BASEBALL

Matt Hayes was making a big change before his final year of high school. He was leaving Urbanville Prep, a private Catholic school, to attend Douglas High School, which was closer to home and a public school. Without consulting his parents, he had already made the decision to transfer to Douglas.

In early July, shortly after the Fourth of July holiday, Matt walked into the downtown district administration office without an appointment. The receptionist greeted him warmly.

"How can I help you?"

"I want to switch schools. I currently go to Urbanville Prep and I want to transfer to Douglas."

"Do you have an appointment?"

"No, I don't."

"Please take a seat and someone will be with you soon."

Five minutes later, Matt was taken into Mrs. Whitcomb's office - she was the specialist in charge of admissions and transfers for the district.

"Hello, young man. What can I do for you today?"

Matt repeated his request to transfer to Douglas and handed her his latest report card from Urbanville Prep. Mrs. Whitcomb evaluated the grades and checked her computer screen.

"Unfortunately, Douglas is at full capacity right now. However, we do have an opening at Hamilton High School. Would you be interested in transferring there?"

Hamilton had a predominantly African American student body and was located seven miles away from Matt's house. This would mean a long daily bus ride and an early morning wake-up call.

"No, thank you. I'll stay at Prep."

"Wait a minute. A spot just opened up at Douglas. Would you still like to transfer there? Shall I reserve it for you?"

"Yes, ma'am."

Matt hastily signed a few forms and was now officially a student at Douglas High. Mrs. Whitcomb informed him that his religious course credits wouldn't be accepted, but his academic performance was outstanding, and he was on track to graduate with extra credits. It remains unclear why the school district administration processed a transfer request initiated by a 17-year-old minor without needing parental consent.

That evening, Matt informed his parents about his decision to switch schools, which led to an intense argument between the determined teenager and his parents.

"What do you think you're doing? You're ruining your future."

"I want to attend a closer school and hang with my neighborhood friends. It's my life."

"Prep is a far superior school, and we've made so many sacrifices for you. This is a terrible choice."

"You'll save a lot of money. You constantly complain and make me feel guilty about how costly tuition is."

Eventually, both sides had exhausted their arsenal of words. Like two armies with depleted ammunition, they fell into a tentative silence, a fragile ceasefire. The family war had ended, at least for the night.

They sat in silence, each one nursing their own hurt and anger. And yet, despite the absence of words, the war still raged on within their hearts. No ceasefire could quell the storm of emotions that raged within them, waiting to be unleashed once again. For in this family, peace was always a temporary respite, a pause before the next battle.

For Matt, the school year seemed to fly by. He loved the relaxed public school atmosphere compared to his previous structured private school. Spending time with his friends from the neighborhood was a highlight for him. As a typical teenager, he was enjoying his senior year of high school. An avid athlete, he had skipped basketball season while adjusting to his new school but was excited for the start of baseball season, a sport played in spring.

Due to two days of heavy rain, the tryouts were moved from the Century Park baseball field to the high school gymnasium. The field was located four blocks away and served as the home field for the Douglas High School baseball team. Century Park was the largest park in Urbanville, a city with a population of almost 500,000 people. The urban oasis boasted an expansive lake surrounded by a shorter inner trail and a longer outer trail measuring four miles. The park itself covered 300 acres and offered various recreational facilities, including a baseball field, five soccer fields, an Olympic-sized swimming pool, ten tennis courts, and an outdoor basketball court.

Matt was confident he would secure a spot on his new school's high school baseball team. A standout athlete, he had made varsity as a freshman at Urbanville Prep and consistently played top-tier summer travel baseball. Thirty-one players showed up at tryouts, displaying a wide range of skills. Matt was taken aback during the initial warm-up session when they started playing catch. Baseballs flew past some boys, hitting the gym walls with loud thuds. Even well-thrown balls were being missed by a few kids, making it clear to Matt that some had never played the sport before. This kind of scene was unheard of during tryouts at Prep.

Moving from Prep to Douglas, Matt was struck by the stark differences between his former and current academic environments. While Douglas appeared to have lower expectations for athletic and academic abilities, allowing some students to make varsity teams despite their lack of skill or promoting others to higher grades without meeting academic standards, Prep prided itself on having top-notch students overall. However, Matt was pleasantly surprised to discover that his new public school also had many exceptionally bright students, including some who excelled in music and spoke their own language that only they could understand. Matt and his friends called these teenage geniuses "Violin Kids."

Nick Chambers, the manager of the baseball team, had already selected the players for his varsity team. Unless he came across an unexpectedly talented player he hadn't noticed before, his choices were set. Chambers, known for being strict but fair, had spent the entire summer scouting potential players for the varsity team. As coach, it was his responsibility to assemble a strong team that would represent the school in the upcoming season. This task was not one he took lightly.

In addition to his role as a PE teacher, Nick had an innate ability to spot talent. He could easily identify a skilled athlete from a distance, and it was no surprise that his predictions for the final fourteen players on the varsity team were completely accurate. In fact, he had already determined the starting nine for opening day - a combination of eight returning players and one new addition: Matt Hayes, a promising transfer from Urbanville Prep.

DOUGLAS HIGH SCHOOL BEARS BASE-BALL STARTING LINE-UP AND POSITION
1. Kenny "Smooth" Jackson - CF
2. "Push-up" Dean Anderson - SS
3. Matt "the Dunker" Hayes - LF
4. "Bland" Brett Jones - 3B
5. Tim "Hollywood" Anderson - RF
6. Chip "Ankle" Hughes - 1B
7. JR "Tiny" Rosellini - 2B
8. "Bunting" Brian Jenkins - C
9. Elvis "0-16-1 Shit" West - P or
Roger "Flamingo" Corbett - P

BENCH PLAYERS

11. "Station Wagon" Tony Bianchi
12. Adam "Pinball Wizard" Simpson
13. Gus Baker
14. Sammy Edwards

MANAGER

Nick "Spittle" Chambers

PLAYER/MANAGER
SCOUTING REPORT

Kenny "Smooth" Jackson (CF) - Smooth at basketball, smooth at baseball, smooth with the ladies; the only African-American player on the team; talented player who some felt was not giving maximum effort; guaranteed to have a great game when playing Hamilton High, a predominately African-American school which included his close neighborhood friends, his performance in those games reinforcing the notion that he was "gliding" on his talent.

"Push-up" Dean Anderson (SS) - An all-conference wrestler with limited range in the field; known for doing twenty push-ups directly behind the team dugout whenever he came off the field after making an error or making an out during an at bat; push-up routine would draw a crowd of rubber necking nomadic spectators.

Matt "The Dunker" Hayes (LF) - Solid basketball player with limited jumping ability; nickname not a reference to his dunking a basketball (never made a slam dunk) but a nod to his ability to get hits by "dinking" and "dunking" the ball just over an infielders head, mastering the difficult execution of Willie Keeler's "hit 'em where they ain't" strategy.

"Bland" Brett Jones (3B) - Boring individual destined to be average throughout his lifetime.

Tim "Hollywood" Anderson (RF) - Rich boy with sparkling white teeth and movie-star looks; friends called him "Hollywood," and non-friends called him "Prima," short for prima donna.

Chip "Ankle" Hughes (1B) - Short starting guard on the basketball team; disliked practice and would feign an ankle injury to skip selected workouts; ankle would always miraculously heal and be fine for games.

JR "Tiny" Rosellini (2B) – 5 foot 1 inch player who was a terrible hitter; occasionally would get on base by coaxing a walk by squatting in an unnatural batting stance to create a tiny strike zone; other players questioned why he was starting, and most felt it was school politics because his father was president of the parent athletic booster club and made substantial donations to the athletic department.

"Bunting" Brian Jenkins (C) - Originally an average right-handed batter, he switched to batting left-handed and bunting during every at-bat, which allowed him to utilize his speed and take advantage of the shorter distance from home plate to first base for left-handed batters. Unfortunately, the strategy failed as he struggled to hit well since transitioning from a right-handed hitter to a left-handed one; led the league, the state, the nation, and likely the universe on third strike foul bunt strikeouts; a solid defensive catcher.

Elvis "0-16-1 Shit" West (P) – "Who Shit" drinking game nickname a reference to his combined woeful pitching streak including last year's HS team and summer travel team; over a 17 game stretch pitching record was 0 wins, 16 losses, and one tie; there are no ties normally in baseball but a game he pitched in was called due to darkness with the teams tied; name originally coined as "0-5-1 Shit" during a drinking game with name changing as each additional loss was added; lost a lot of close games by a single run; much more effective first time through the opposng team batting order with diminishing returns as batters faced him each additional time; rumor that his pitching performance triggered the modern "bullpenning" baseball strategy where several pitchers pitch in a game rather than relying on starting pitching; best football player in school who earned a D-1 football scholarship.

Roger "Flamingo" Corbett (P) - Starting center on the varsity basketball team, tall with skinny legs and a long neck; close friend of "0-16-1 Shit," and the two alternated as the starting pitchers.

"Station Wagon" Tony Bianchi - Bench player usually used as a pinch hitter; could occasionally crush a fastball for an extra-base hit; anemic hitter against curve balls; nickname garnered after summer league baseball teammates found him sleeping shirtless in the morning on the hood of a car after a drug-fueled Guns N' Roses concert the previous night.

Adam "Pinball Wizard" Simpson - Hearing impaired dedicated athlete; nickname a reference to a song from the musical group The Who's rock opera Tommy, the main character a deaf, dumb, and blind boy; once broke an aluminum bat in two by smashing it after striking out, leading to a game ejection by the umpire.

Gus Baker - One of two sophomores on the team; deeply religious; did not drink or do drugs.

Sammy Edwards - Other soph on the team; rarely saw game action; potential future star.

Coach Nick "Spittle" Chambers - Ex-star baseball player in his fourth year as Bears manager; trouble communicating with "modern" teenagers; played same starting lineup the entire season besides rotating the starting pitchers; when agitated, tiny pockets of saliva would squirt out of the corners of his mouth.

Despite their colorful player nicknames, the Douglas High Bears were a mediocre team. The season had been plagued with offensive struggles, with their pitching being the only constant bright spot. The team alternated between wins and losses, resulting in a lukewarm record of five wins and five losses ten games into the season. The Bears had been able to hold their own on the mound, but their bats had been silent for too many games. It was frustrating, especially for the players who took the game seriously.

Game number eleven was set for Tuesday afternoon after school, so Matt, Elvis, and Roger decided to skip their fifth period and head to Elvis's house, just a mile from campus. They set up in Elvis's backyard, pulling out lawn chairs to lounge in the sun. Elvis and Roger disappeared briefly and returned with a pitcher and three glasses. The pitcher held a blend of beer and lemonade - specifically, 45% beer to 55% lemonade - a recipe they guarded as closely as Coca-Cola keeps its formula secret. Matt tried the concoction and found it delicious. Elvis and Roger were thrilled because they had been experimenting with different ratios for some time, like amateur scientists seeking the perfect beer-lemonade mix. The three friends relaxed, finished four pitchers of "Beer-ade," and listened to Pink Floyd's "The Wall," singing along when the iconic lyrics played over the outdoor speakers.

We don't need no education
We don't need no thought control
No dark sarcasm in the classroom
Teacher, leave them kids alone

Still buzzing from the creative refreshment, the three varsity baseball players returned to school just in time for their favorite class: electronics with Mr. Nelson, also known as Doc Block. He was a sturdy man with a chiseled jawline and slicked-back black hair that reminded them of Fred Flintstone. The boys couldn't contain their curiosity any longer and asked Doc Block about his personal life. With a smile, he shared stories of his wife, his lively four-year-old daughter, and their playful dog. The boys were intrigued and asked to see a photo of his family. They eagerly anticipated the image, expecting to see a happy portrait with Doc Block at the center, surrounded by his loved ones: Wilma, Pebbles, and Dino the Dinosaur.

Mr. Nelson was known for being a lenient grader, and his class was not known for its difficulty. All juniors and seniors were guaranteed an A without much effort. The framework of his class was like a house built on shaky ground - strong on the surface but crumbling when closely examined. Whenever he reviewed completed projects, Doc Block's comments were always the same: "Hmmmm, that's interesting." His feedback seemed to have a hidden meaning, decipherable only by himself and his students.

The popular teacher instructed the class to keep working on their projects as he stepped out to take care of an urgent matter. The students diligently continued with their light bulb project. Matt handed his Nesquik container over to Carson Butler, who skillfully navigated the soldering iron to connect the wires and create a basic circuit. The Dunker had no mechanical aptitude, and Carson was happy to help his friend complete his project in just a few minutes. Meanwhile, Mr. Nelson's "pressing issue" turned into a full 55-minute absence as he frantically made phone calls in search of the best deals for a weekend trip to Las Vegas. The students laughed as they overheard the teacher negotiating deals on airfare, hotels, and gaming comps.

The baseball game was an away game in West Urbanville, a neighborhood separated from the heart of the city by a large bridge. The players arrived early only to face a predicament:

They were running dangerously low on chewing tobacco. This perfect storm arose when seven teenagers assumed they could borrow some from their teammates, only to realize the collective supply was critically low. Matt noticed a nearby supermarket and offered to make a quick run. He jogged a few blocks to the local Safeway and bought three cans of Copenhagen, two tins of Skoal, one tin of Kodiak, and a pouch of Red Man. The only open checkout line was crowded, and the cashier seemed indifferent, eagerly counting down the minutes to her union-mandated break. After making his purchase, Matt glanced at the store clock and realized he was running late - the game was about to start. He sprinted back to the field and saw his coach furiously waving his arms in a circular windmill motion toward him. The manager was livid and in full spittle mode; Matt made sure not to stand too close while receiving an earful.

"Where were you? You missed pregame infield practice! You should be sitting on the bench for the entire game. But you're starting in left field and batting third."

Despite his anger, the manager knew he needed his best (slightly inebriated) player on the field.

Coach Chambers and Matt constantly clashed over his placement as a left fielder. Matt, being tall and agile, was better suited for the first baseman position where he could easily catch high throws from the infielders and prevent runs. However, their current first baseman, Ankle Hughes, struggled in the position due to his shorter height. This became evident when high throws sailed over Hughes's head, plays that Matt could have easily handled. Matt's infield skills were evident when he effortlessly scooped up errant balls in the dirt. Despite the Dunker being a better first baseman than Ankle and Ankle being a stronger outfielder than the Dunker, they both played at their weaker fielding positions all season, negatively impacting the team. It didn't make sense to Matt, but he assumed Coach Chambers was showing loyalty to a returning player who had played first base since starting at Douglas High School.

Matt had a strong dislike for playing in the outfield. His main struggle was judging the path of fly balls while squinting to shield his eyes from the bright, blinding sun. As if that wasn't challenging enough, during home games when he played in left field, he also acted as a mediator between the baseball and soccer players whose pickup game often spilled onto the grassy outfield. Throughout the season, Matt found himself desperately trying to catch line drives while dodging sprinting soccer players and avoiding getting hit by a whizzing stray soccer ball. Sometimes, an umpire would intervene to settle the dispute, reminding the soccer players that the grassy area was designated for baseball only and part of the official boundary of the field. The soccer players would reluctantly move their game temporarily elsewhere until the umpire returned to home plate before returning to their usual spot on the field.

The Bears clawed their way to a 2-1 victory, and the stars of the game were 0-16-1 Shit and the Dunker, each fueled by the odd combination of lemonade beer and smokeless tobacco. Elvis pitched a marvelous complete game six-hitter, including striking out ten batters. Meanwhile, the Dunker lived up to his name, delivering the winning hit in the last inning. With two outs, he stepped up to the plate and, with a swift swing of his bat, sent a softly hit sliced ball, landing just over the reach of the shortstop's outstretched glove. It was a perfectly placed hit, bringing in both of the Bears' runs and securing their victory. As the players rushed the field to celebrate the win, it was clear that this game would be remembered for a long time to come.

The game's highlight was Elvis ending his lengthy losing streak as a pitcher, and there was talk between the two standout players that Beer-ade was the secret ingredient needed to finally break the string of consecutive pitching losses. Despite his impressive performance on the mound, Elvis's "Who Shit" drinking game nickname did not change to "1-0-0 Shit." The infamous name "0-16-1 Shit" became permanent, and "Who Shit" gained even more popularity among future Douglas High students.

One week after the exciting one-run victory, Coach Chambers could not make the scheduled practice, and the players decided to practice as normal at the Century Park baseball field. This would not be a typical practice; refreshments consisted of alcoholic beverages instead of water and sports drinks. A beer keg was plopped directly on second base, a strategic central location that made it equally fair for the players scattered in the infield and outfield to refill their blue plastic party cups during batting practice. As they drank, the chatter became louder and more boisterous. With each swing, the effects of the alcohol were becoming apparent as batters either missed or hit foul balls that ended up splashing into the nearby lake, startling joggers on the inner path. Matt offered a few of the soccer players a beer, a liquid peace truce for athletes from different sports occupying the same grass field. Bunting Brian, the catcher, paused the BP action occasionally, sipping a beer through his protective catcher face mask using a straw.

The team and players were easily recognizable by the big D on their baseball caps. Initially, they tried to be discreet by hiding the keg under an oversized duffle bag but eventually gave up when it became too inconvenient to access the beer tap. Thousands of people visited Century Park daily, and dozens of random spectators would stop by to watch the team practice. It's shocking that the high school players didn't face severe ramifications for their underage drinking. If someone had reported them, they could have been kicked off the team or even expelled from school. However, this all occurred before the prevalence of cell phones with cameras and the constant stream of social media updates and photos.

One of Matt's standout moments of the season was during a home game against his former school, Urbanville Prep. His friends from the opposing team good-naturedly heckled him from the dugout. But amidst the friendly rivalry, Matt made an incredible shoestring catch that saved the game. With his Jim "Catfish" Hunter Wilson A2000 glove, he secured the ball at its very tip, just inches from hitting the ground. The Dunker, as usual, had gotten a late start towards the well-hit line drive and had to dodge a speedy Somali-born soccer striker in his path. Despite the guided missile human obstacle, he still managed to make the highlight-worthy catch, preserving the Bears' 3-2 win.

After the season ended, the boys went their separate ways. Some returned to play the following year, while others ventured off to college or began working. Each of the fourteen players became successful and respected adults, pursuing careers in various fields, including a lawyer, police officer, teacher, accountant, investment banker, sanitation engineer (garbage collector), and plumber. The Dunker went on to play NCAA Division 1 college baseball, leading the conference in batting average his junior season, with most of his hits perfectly placed soft flare singles. 0-16-1 Shit and the Flamingo maintained a close friendship and eventually launched a successful start-up company inspired by their early Beer-ade initiative. Coach Spittle continued to coach the Bears for the next fifteen years, leaving a trail of saliva missiles in his wake as he trained new high school players. Under his leadership, the team won three league championships and one state title. While other Douglas High School baseball teams may have had more wins and accolades, this team's story will always hold a special place in the town's history books, a small but essential contribution to Urbanville lore.

BOXED SECRETS

oseph, who his close friends called Joe, was a fine man, always dapper and polite, viewed by everyone as a respectable gentleman who wouldn't hurt a fly. What they didn't know, however, was that Joe had a dark past regarding commitment. When Joe was four, his mother left, leaving no explanation, just nights full of tears. Gone. Gone for good. Only having one parent, a single father who did not convey all of the love that a mother would, Joe became lonely and felt unwanted. That horrid night when she abandoned him, his two parents had clashed over financial issues. His father's frequent unemployment and drinking problem had a sobering effect on his mother. She did not want to work long hours at home while he did not provide support for the family and wasted precious money on booze. Shouts of rage reverberated through the hallways, each verbal volley and accusation louder and more focused than the previous.

Joe did not remember what his mom looked like. Sometimes, if he really focused a glimpse of a core memory of the two of them together would materialize. His second birthday and her angelic voice singing to him. When he first rode a tricycle. Her remarks of praise the day he did not leave his bed with a reeking, putrid smell of a tinkle. No matter how hard he tried to remember, his mother's features were always unrecognizable, as if she were a blurred license plate. Joe's father never showed him any old photos of her as it pained him to relive the memories. The boy felt jealous when other kids got notes in their lunchboxes from their mothers telling them to have good days. All of these kids were wanted by their parents, maybe he did something wrong. Joe became wary and uncertain about people trying to get close to him. Someone he loved could leave at any second, and loneliness is less painful than pain.

During high school, Joe was dating a girl named Chloe, a beauty with flowy ash black air, eyes the color of mountain spring water, and a personality that emitted joy. Any sensible young man would want to date her. Echoing in Joe's head were thoughts of fear. Would the relationship last? Would he become heartbroken? Not being able to trust yet still needing a person to lean on in place of his mother led him to cheat on Chloe with an attractive girl named Vanessa. Throughout the next two decades, Joe cycled through 30 different girlfriends, and each relationship ended in one of two ways. Either the girl would ask for a deeper level of commitment from Joe, or he would abruptly leave without any explanation. That was when Joe met Mary. Mary had a personality and looks that enchanted him. In that instant, Joe made a firm decision to keep his questionable past hidden from Mary, fearing it would drive her away. He had searched for true love for so long and was hopeful that this could be the relationship he finally committed to for the long haul.

One day, while looking through the attic of his comfortable, tidy apartment where he and his beloved wife Mary lived, Joe discovered an astonishing item. Behind a discolored white bin full of Christmas ornaments was a box labeled "Old Photos." Joe found a rustic oak brown picture frame inside with jagged cracks through the brittle wood. The image inside was covered with dust, hiding what appeared to be two faces. With the flick of four fingers, he brushed off all of the dust and revealed the people in the photo. The picture was a side profile mother and daughter portrait. They looked almost identical besides the age difference. Their hair color was a vibrant brown. Their matching eyes were closed and looking downward. Joe was certain they would twinkle like mischievous shooting stars if they opened their eyes. Their skin was as pale as the moon. Their lips formed a smile that shined like the sun after a storm. What a gorgeous photo of Mary, Joe thought. Her mother is also beautiful.

He then flipped over the photo. Carefully brushing off more dust on the back of the frame revealed a label, "Lucy Maloney and Mary Andrews." Joe gasped. His mother was named Lucy Maloney. Questions started to flood his brain. Was he seriously married to his stepsister? What were the odds? How could his mother remarry so quickly? Just when he was about to put the photo back in the cardboard box and exit the attic full of cobwebs, Mary came up to check on him. "Darling, you've been up here for so long. I started to get worried. Maybe it would please you to come downstairs and watch a movie with me?" she asked.

"No."

"Why honey? Is something wrong?"

"I don't want to watch a movie."

"Oh, darling, you've been working so hard up here. You really should take a break."

"Again, I don't want to."

Mary started to feel uneasy. She merely wanted to watch a movie. Then she felt some faint kicking. She was almost six months pregnant and was proud of her growing baby bump. Mary loved movie nights when they would snuggle together and munch on popcorn. Joe never complained and was always in a good mood. She loved how his facial expression changed while watching movies. If there was something scary, a look of fear. If there was something pleasant, a smile. If there was a funny scene, laughter.

Joe needed to get rid of the photo and fast. Quickly grabbing the blue packing tape on the floor, he threw the photo frame back in the box face down and sealed it. Act normal, Joe thought to himself. You are just throwing away the weekly garbage. Not a big deal. He smiled, swiftly walking away while carrying the box as if nothing had happened. "I'll be back in a second, darling! Start picking a movie meanwhile," he exclaimed with forced cheerfulness.

As Joe descended the apartment steps, a sudden realization hit him. Mary was only one day away from being six months pregnant with their child. The news had brought them both joy at first, but now it weighed heavily on Joe's mind. He couldn't shake off the feeling of guilt and shame that came with knowing he was married to his stepsister and about to become a father with her. Wasn't their situation considered taboo and possibly even illegal? How could he bring a child into the world under these circumstances? Did this baby deserve one perfect parent and another parent who could never depend on anybody and lied to his own wife, who showed nothing but tenderness to him? The answer was an unequivocal no. At that moment, Joe made up his mind. It was time to be honest and truthful and end the deception. The news had to be delivered tomorrow. Their marriage needed to end. She must know.

Mary was waiting for him when he got home. Her eyes were puffy and red from crying, and Joe's heart sank at the sight of her pain. Without a word, she handed him an envelope. Inside was a stack of papers - divorce papers.

Confused and taken aback, Joe stammered, "What is this?" In a monotone voice, Mary responded, "I know about your past with other women that you never told me about. Three different women have called looking for you, and I spoke to them. They shared that they had dated you for a long time. Another one just called while you were gone. You told me you only seriously dated two girls before we met - one in high school. I can't trust you after this or believe anything you say in the future. We should end our marriage before our child is born."

In a momentary fit of rage, Joe replied, "Sit down, sis. There's something I have to share."

Mary paused, unsure of whether or not she should sit down. Her eyes narrowed as she slowly lowered herself to the seat. She hadn't understood the significance of the insult that Joe had thrown at her. Joe took a deep breath, feeling the weight of his impending confession bearing down on him like a ton of bricks. In a whirlwind of emotions, he had changed his mind and now wanted to salvage their marriage instead of ending it. He had been planning to come clean about his past womanizing and infidelity, but with Mary suddenly threatening divorce, he found himself sinking into despair. How could he possibly reveal the truth now when their relationship was hanging by a thread?

Just as he was about to speak, the shrill ring of the phone shattered the heavy silence in the room. Mary gave him a suspicious look as he hesitantly reached for the phone and saw an unknown number on the caller ID.

Joe swallowed hard and answered the call, trying to steady his voice. "Hello?" A frantic voice on the other end gasped for air before speaking urgently. "Is Mary there? It's her mother." Joe's heart started racing. He turned to Mary and handed her the phone. "It's our mother," he said.

Joe's hand trembled as he passed the phone to Mary. Her complexion paled as she took it, holding it to her ear and listening intently to her mother's words. Although it was distant and muffled, whatever was being said caused Mary's eyes to widen in disbelief. After a moment of silence, she whispered into the receiver. Tears welled up in her eyes as she listened, and her hand trembled against her cheek. Suddenly, the baby inside her kicked, almost as if sensing the gravity of the conversation. When she spoke again, her voice wavered with emotion. "Mom...is it true?" The tiny life within her continued to kick as Mary felt sharp pressure against her abdomen, almost like fists pounding from within. A wave of fear and understanding washed over her as she continued to listen, and by the time she hung up the phone, tears were rolling down her face. Turning to Joe with desperation, she asked again, "Is it true?"

Joe's heart plummeted as he met Mary's tear-filled eyes. The weight of the truth he had been hiding crashed down on him, suffocating him with guilt and regret. He couldn't bear to see the pain etched on Mary's face, a pain he had caused with his deceit and betrayal. With a heavy sigh, Joe finally mustered the courage to come clean. "Mary," he began, his voice barely above a whisper, "I didn't know how to tell you this...but yes, it's true. I found an old photo in the attic today. Your mother and my mother who disappeared when I was young...they are the same person." The words hung in the air between them like a heavy fog, enveloping them in a suffocating silence. Joe finally understood why Mary's mother had never visited them in person or attended their small wedding. He now knew why strangers often thought he and Mary were siblings rather than a married couple.

Mary's eyes widened in shock as she processed Joe's confession. The puzzle pieces were falling into place, revealing a twisted family history that neither of them could have imagined. She felt a whirlwind of emotions - disbelief, anger, confusion, sorrow - swirling within her, threatening to engulf her in a tidal wave of overwhelming truth. Her mind raced, trying to make sense of the bombshell revelation that rocked the foundation of her reality. Questions tumbled through her thoughts like a turbulent storm: How could her mother have kept such a monumental secret hidden? What other lies had been woven into the fabric of their lives? Was anything real anymore?

As Mary struggled to find her voice amid the chaos of emotions, Joe reached out a trembling hand to touch her arm, seeking some form of connection amid the turmoil.

His eyes pleaded with her for understanding, for forgiveness, for a shred of hope amidst the ruins of their shattered trust.

Joe said, "Think of the baby." As Joe's plea for understanding and consideration for the baby echoed in the room, Mary's emotions erupted like a volcano. Anger, hurt, confusion all surged within her, threatening to consume every rational thought in her mind. How could he ask her to think of the baby now after dropping such a devastating truth on her lap? The weight of the situation pressed down on her, suffocating her with its gravity. As the reality of their situation sank in, Mary grappled with a maelstrom of conflicting emotions. The image of her mother - their mother - loomed large in her mind, a ghostly specter of the past casting a long shadow over their present.

From the depths of despair, Mary suddenly found an unexpected strength. With a newfound sense of empowerment, Mary took charge for the first time in their relationship. "We are going to confront our mother together and demand answers. We deserve to know the truth, no matter how painful it may be. And then, we will decide our next steps as a family for the sake of our child and our own peace of mind. We can't undo the past but can choose how to move forward from here." Mary's voice wavered with a mix of determination and vulnerability as she laid out her plan. Joe looked at her with a sense of respect and admiration, struck by her courage in the face of adversity.

Together, they sought the truth and confronted their shared past head-on. With intertwined hands and resolute hearts, Joe and Mary embarked on a journey that would unravel the secrets buried deep within their family history. As they braced themselves for the tumultuous road ahead, one thing became clear - no matter what challenges lay in store, they would face them together, bound by blood, love, and a shared determination to uncover the truth and forge a path forward as a family. It was a leap of faith, guided not by reason but by a deep instinct that things would be different from now on. They didn't need any grand gestures or secret blood oath ceremonies to renew their marriage and commitment - their blood connection was the strongest bond imaginable, the shocking truth about their family relationship unleashed from a musty box full of secrets like the genie escaping from the lamp in Aladdin.

FAMILY FEUD

Peter's heart raced as he walked towards the train station. He was a young man with a heavy burden on his shoulders, carrying everything he owned in a worn-out knapsack. Inside were a few articles of clothing, a wrinkled piece of paper with an unfamiliar address in West Seattle scribbled on it, and just enough money to buy one meal. His mother, Susan O'Malley, had hugged him tightly before saying goodbye at the Fargo, North Dakota train depot. Her final instructions were clear: find a way to get to the address no matter what and knock three times on the front door when he arrived.

It was during the peak of the Great Depression when even the toughest individuals were struggling to find their next meal or a watered-down bowl of soup. Peter had always been a small and skinny child, but the harsh times had only made his physical appearance more dire. His clothes hung loosely on his body, and his complexion was pale and under-nourished. He often felt like an outsider in school, especially when his classmates taunted him for his worn-out outfits. But Peter never let their words affect him; he knew that he was stronger than they realized.

As the train pulled away from the station, Peter's heart pounded with a mix of fear and determination. He had to make it to West Seattle, and he knew that the journey ahead would be anything but easy.

He clutched the address his mother had given him, knowing that this mysterious distant friend was his best chance at survival. The thought of work and a place to stay filled him with a glimmer of hope, a small light in an otherwise bleak situation.

Peter felt the weight of his mother's love and worry pressing down on him. She had been his rock, his everything, and he couldn't bear the thought of disappointing her. But he also couldn't stay in their small town any longer, watching her struggle to provide for them both.

As she stood on the platform, Susan's heart ached as she watched her youngest son, Peter, board the train heading west. She tried to hold back the tears welling up in her eyes, but it was no use. Her family had been torn apart by circumstances beyond their control. Several years ago, her husband had left for Washington state in search of work since there was none available in North Dakota. He promised to send for them once he had saved enough money, but that promise never came to fruition. Instead, he sent for their oldest son, George, to join him.

The married couple communicated through letters, and every once in a while, her husband would send some money to help Peter and her survive. But it was never enough. The times were desperate, and every day was a struggle just to find enough food to survive.

As the train pulled away, Susan shed a tear for the family she once had. It seemed like a lifetime ago, when her husband and sons were still with her, and they were all happy and whole. But now, everything had been reduced to mere survival, and she could only hope and pray that one day they would all be reunited again.

But for now, she wiped away her tears and turned her back to the station, steeling herself for the harsh reality that awaited her outside its doors. She had to be strong - for herself and her family. She was alone, a desperate woman living in desperate times.

Sitting alone on the train, Peter pressed his face against the window, watching his mother's figure become smaller and smaller in the distance. A deep sadness filled his heart as he realized he was leaving behind everything he had ever known, including his beloved mother. Images flashed through his mind - memories of his father's kind smile and gentle touch, and how much he missed him. His thoughts also drifted to his older brother, George. He wondered if he would ever have the chance to see him again. But most of all, his thoughts were consumed by his mother, with whom he shared a special bond. The smell of the train's metal and oil filled Peter's nostrils, mixing with the faint scent of his mother's perfume that lingered on his clothes. It reminded him of their final warm embrace at the station and how he would miss it. As the train carried him further away, he was certain he would never see her again.

Peter was a resourceful and intelligent young boy, aware that these traits were key to his survival on his journey. He pressed on with his westward trek, cleverly boarding trains whenever the opportunity arose. It was a risky move, but he had no other choice if he wanted to reach Seattle. He would skillfully sneak onto cargo cars, finding cover among crates and sacks of merchandise while doing his best to avoid being detected by the train staff. It was a daring feat, but Peter's determination and cunning got him through the journey.

Finally, the train pulled into Seattle, and Peter joined the other tired travelers as they disembarked. He noticed how much bigger this city was compared to his small hometown. As he walked through the bustling streets, the teenager felt like a stranger in this unfamiliar place, disconnected and isolated from the crowds around him. The thoroughfares were alive with people carrying out their daily routines, merchants selling goods, and families rushing to their next stop. Peter's footsteps echoed as he navigated the streets, a sense of uneasiness creeping over him. He didn't belong here; he was just a poor boy from North Dakota.

His legs were sore and tired from so much time spent sitting still on train rides, but he pushed through it as he made his way toward the unfamiliar address. As he reached the neighborhood specified on the note, he hesitated momentarily, unsure of what awaited him at the mysterious house in a strange city. Summoning all his courage, he walked up to the weathered front door and knocked three times as instructed.

A loud noise broke the silence of the empty street, and everything stood still for a moment. Then, with agonizing slowness, the door in front of him swung open to reveal a figure standing in the darkness.

The person emerged from the shadows, revealing a friendly face framed by wisps of brown hair. She was slightly older than his mother, and her eyes glowed with warmth and recognition as she saw the tired boy standing on her doorstep.

"Can I help you?" she asked kindly.

Peter took out the crumpled piece of paper and handed it to her. She read it over quickly before her eyes widened in recognition.

"Peter O'Malley," she said softly. "You must be Susan's son."

As the boy crossed the threshold into the dimly lit hallway, he felt a wave of relief wash over him. The oppressive weight of uncertainty that had hung over him during his journey began to lift, replaced by a glimmer of hope that maybe, just maybe, he had found a haven in this stranger's home.

The woman led him into a cozy living room, where a fire crackled merrily in the hearth, casting dancing shadows on the walls. She gestured for him to sit down in a plush armchair before disappearing into the adjoining kitchen.

Minutes later, she returned with a steaming bowl of hearty stew and a thick slice of crusty bread. The boy's eyes widened in disbelief at the sight of the food before him. It had been so long since his last proper meal and the aroma of the stew made his mouth water. The attractive woman watched him with a soft smile as he devoured the food with a hunger that spoke volumes about his journey.

As he ate, she sat across from him, listening intently as he recounted his harrowing trip from North Dakota to Seattle. The boy told her about his mother, about the desperation that had driven him to embark on such a dangerous journey alone. He spoke of the kindness of strangers he had encountered along the way, as well as the cruelty and indifference of others who had turned him away.

The woman listened without interrupting, her gaze filled with compassion and understanding. When he finished his tale, she placed a comforting hand on his shoulder and spoke in a voice that was both gentle and strong.

"You've been through more than any boy your age should ever have to endure," she said, her voice tinged with empathy. "But you've shown courage and resilience beyond your years." The boy looked up at her, his eyes betraying a mix of weariness and a flicker of hope.

"You're safe here, my dear," the woman continued. "You can rest easy knowing that you have a place to call home for as long as you need." Her words wrapped around the boy like a warm blanket, soothing his frayed nerves and weary soul.

In the days that followed, the boy settled into a routine in the woman's home. She introduced herself as Mrs. Evelyn Hall, a widow who had lived alone since her husband passed away a few years ago. Together, they formed an unlikely pair forged by shared loss and newfound companionship.

Mrs. Hall shared stories of her youth, of a time when the world had been filled with hope and promise, before economic calamity and the shadow of war had darkened the horizon.

A few days after his arrival, as they sat by the fire sipping hot cocoa, Mrs. Hall turned to the boy with a twinkle in her eye. "You know, dear boy," she began, her voice soft but firm, "I believe it's time for you to uncover the mystery behind that address you carried all this way."

The youngster's heart skipped a beat at the mention of the mysterious address. Mrs. Hall rose from her armchair and disappeared into the adjoining room, returning with a weathered old chest. With a sense of reverence, she placed it on the table before the boy and opened it slowly, revealing a stack of yellowed letters tied with a faded ribbon.

"These belonged to my husband," she explained, her voice tinged with nostalgia. "He never spoke much about his past," she lied, "but I believe it's time you learn the truth." The boy's hands trembled as he reached for the letters, feeling the weight of history in his grasp.

As he untied the ribbon and began to read, his eyes widened in disbelief. The letters told a tale of love and loss, of a young man who had left everything behind to seek his fortune in the booming industries of the West. They spoke of dreams shattered by economic collapse, of hardships endured in silence, and of a promise made to a woman he had left behind in search of a better life. The boy's heart raced as he comprehended the truth unfolding in front of him - these were letters from his parents, his father he had been separated from for so long, and his beloved mother, whom he had just said goodbye to.

The woman turned to him and in a sinister voice said, "I believe it is time for you to start earning your keep around here. You have been a freeloader long enough."

The boy's heart pounded in his chest as he looked up from the letters, the warmth of the fire now feeling oppressive on his skin. The shift in Mrs. Hall's demeanor sent a chill down his spine, her eyes gleaming with a cold light he had never seen before. He felt a knot form in his stomach, a sense of foreboding settling over him like a heavy shroud.

Slowly, he stood up from the chair, the letters clutched tightly in his hand. His voice shook as he spoke, "Mrs. Hall, I...I didn't know about my father. I never meant to impose on you."

But Mrs. Hall's expression remained unchanged, her features cast in an eerie stillness that made the boy's skin prickle with unease. Without a word, she gestured towards the door leading to the basement, her eyes glinting with a steely resolve.

He hesitated, unsure of what Mrs. Hall intended for him to do next. The flickering light from the fire cast long shadows across the room, distorting the portraits on the walls and lending an otherworldly quality to the scene. With a deep breath to steady himself, the boy took a tentative step towards the basement door, the floorboards creaking beneath his weight.

As he reached out a trembling hand to grasp the door-knob, a sudden noise from below caused him to freeze in place. It was a sound like distant whispers carried on a cold wind, faint but unmistakable. Mrs. Hall's lips curved into a cruel smile as she watched the boy's reaction, her eyes glittering with malice.

For a moment, all was still in the dimly lit room as the boy grappled with a sense of rising dread. Then, with a steely resolve of his own, he made his decision and turned the doorknob, opening the door to reveal a set of steep, spiraling stairs disappearing into the darkness below. The whispers grew louder, swirling around him like a sinister melody, urging him to descend into the unknown depths. Mrs. Hall's gaze bore into his back, her presence a heavy weight on his shoulders.

Ignoring the pounding of his heart, the boy tightened his grip on the banister and took the first step down. The air grew colder with each descent, sending shivers down his spine. Shadows danced on the walls, twisting into grotesque shapes that seemed to reach out for him as he passed.

Finally, he reached the bottom of the stairs and stepped into a small, musty chamber; there, in the center of the room, stood a figure who looked vaguely familiar.

As the boy's eyes adjusted to the dim basement light, he made out the shape of a young man five years older than him and recognized his facial features. The boy cried out excitedly, "George!" before racing over to embrace him. It was his older brother who had left home and disappeared.

Tears streamed down the boy's face as he clutched his long-lost brother in a tight hug. George held him close, his own eyes shining with unshed tears as he whispered, "I never thought I'd see you again, little brother."

The chamber seemed to brighten with their shared joy, the whispers fading into a distant murmur. Mrs. Hall stood at the top of the stairs her expression unreadable as she watched the reunion unfold beneath her gaze.

She looked at them, her expression changing to one of vengefulness. "I finally have you bastards here together. It took a while to track you down and convince your mom to send you Peter. She is always moving around. You were always her favorite. You cost more to buy than George, but everyone has a price, even you her special one."

Mrs. Hall's chilling words hung in the air like a heavy fog, suffocating the joy of the siblings' reunion. The younger boy's mind raced, trying to make sense of her sinister revelations. His hands clenched into fists at his sides as he turned to face her, a mixture of betrayal and defiance clear in his eyes.

"Why would you do this? What kind of twisted game have you been playing?" he demanded, his voice trembling with a mix of anger and fear. George stood beside him, his expression a mix of confusion and dawning realization.

Mrs. Hall merely chuckled, the sound sending a shiver down the boy's spine. "Oh, my dear boys, you have no idea of the ways of the world," she cooed, her voice dripping with hatred. "You see, your mother wronged me in ways you could never understand. And now, it's time for her to pay. You see, boys," she sneered, "family ties can be so easily manipulated for one's own gain. Your mother thought she could protect you, but she never stood a chance against me."

"Why are you doing this to our family?" George asked. "What did we ever do to you? Why do you hate our mother?"

"My dear husband whose seed spawned you two bastards loved your mother the best. He only left your mother to find work and then was going to send for you. He was lonely and I seduced him. All he did was talk about you kids. Once, when we were having sex, he moaned your mother's name twice - Susan, Susan! He died shortly after. I copied his handwriting and sent your mother a note with money and instructions to send George. Then, I communicated with the whore via letters where I impersonated your dear dead dad. Eventually, I sent additional money to get you Peter. You brats cost me more money than you are worth. Your mother thinks there will be a family reunion in the future. Such a dimwit."

Peter's mind raced as he tried to process the shocking revelations. He couldn't believe the woman he had thought of as a kind and caring mother substitute figure was involved in such a demented scheme. He glanced at George, and they both shared a look of shock.

Mrs. Hall's eyes glinted with a mix of triumph and pleasure as she watched the brothers' reaction. "You should be grateful, boys," she said, her voice more sinister than ever.

"But we don't want to be a part of your twisted games," George protested, his voice shaking. "We just want to go home to our real mother."

"Oh, dear George," Mrs. Hall sneered, "your pathetic attempts at defiance amuse me. Your real mother won't be coming to save you. I've made sure of that. I could kill both of you now along with your mother but that would be too easy. I know how close both of you are to her and I want all of you to feel the pain I feel every day. I never had a child with your father and now he is gone. You will be my substitute children. If you ever attempt to harm me or kill me your mother will die. Here are my other terms. If you break any of them your mother will die. You will not attempt to contact your mother. From here on out you will refer to me as your mother. You will not contact the police. Both of you will stay in this basement with the door locked when you are home. The only exception is if I invite you upstairs. Sometimes, I might want company. Peter, starting tomorrow you will begin working at the same bakery as George. You will give me all your wages. You will never marry. You can date girls, but you must never marry. You know I am not bluffing about killing your mother if you break one of these rules. Think about it boys. Think about the elaborate plot I pulled off getting you both here and how simple the act of killing the whore would be in comparison. Dinner will be upstairs in two hours. Join me in a celebration."

The wicked woman turned her back and left the basement leaving the two brothers alone. The silence that followed her departure was deafening. George and Peter stared at each other in disbelief. They were both trembling, their minds racing with a million thoughts and questions, but mostly they were terrified.

Peter broke the silence first, his voice hushed. "What do we do?" he asked, his eyes wide and filled with fear.

George swallowed hard, trying to gather his thoughts. "I don't know, but we can't let her win. We have to find a way to get our real mother and escape from here. But first, we need to stay alive. We need to remember the terms she set. We can't make a rash move, or we will be risking mom's life. We have to be smart, be patient, and find a way to outsmart her."

They knew it wouldn't be easy, but they had no choice. Their lives and their mothers hung in the balance.

Peter and George obeyed Mrs. Hall's instructions without question. They toiled tirelessly at the bakery, suppressing their true emotions and thoughts from both customers and colleagues. Every night, they retreated to the basement to discuss and uncover their mother's history and Mrs. Hall's intentions. As they delved deeper, childhood memories resurfaced, almost as if they had been planted by Mrs. Hall herself, forcing them to piece together the clues she left behind.

They learned how their father, a hardworking man, and Mrs. Hall had met in a saloon where she had seduced him and taken advantage of his loneliness. And then, their mother, a loving woman who had spent years waiting to reunite the entire family, watched as her family had been systematically destroyed by the cruel lady's diabolical plan.

As the weeks passed, Peter and George grew closer to the workers at the bakery, listening in on their conversations and eavesdropping on their gossip. They discovered that the head baker, an old friend of their deceased father, was well-connected in the community. This was their opportunity to get help saving their mother and themselves.

After a hard day of work, the brothers approached the baker. They shared their story with him, explaining the diabolical plot that Mrs. Hall had concocted and begged for his assistance. At first, the adult found it hard to believe such an outlandish tale, but he soon realized that the brothers were speaking truthfully. The baker was taken aback and filled with horror by their story but also touched by their unwavering devotion to their mother.

After careful consideration, the baker finally agreed to assist the boys. He would need to conduct some research and advised them that it would take time. The baker warned them to proceed with caution as their mother was in peril, and it was clear this dangerous woman was capable of anything. They should continue to follow her rules meticulously and must be careful not to do anything to tip her off.

The following months were a test of the boys' strength, patience, and resilience. They worked tirelessly at the bakery, making sure to follow every rule set by the deranged lady. George and Peter were vigilant, always aware of their surroundings, and never relaxed their guard for a moment.

Even with all of their precautions, the family's lives remained in a fragile state. Mrs. Hall was a clever and venge-

ful woman, and her demands became increasingly unpredictable as time went on. She would frequently create new
guidelines or alter the current ones, constantly keeping the
boys on edge.

As weeks turned into months, the baker kept his promise
to keep an eye on the brothers, and he was impressed by their
dedication and loyalty. They never broke a single rule and
never made a move without considering the consequences
for their mother.

One day, the baker took Peter and George aside after
work. "I've been watching you boys for a while now, and I
have to say, you're impressive. Your loyalty to your family is
commendable. I've spoken to some people in the community, and we've come up with a plan to get you both out of
there safely and also keep your mother alive."

After tirelessly searching for several months, the baker
finally managed to locate Susan through his extensive
network of contacts. She had relocated to a boarding house
just across the Red River in Minnesota, a barren and unforgiving land where the wind howled relentlessly across
the plains. To make enough money to survive, she accepted
any odd job that came her way, her hands calloused and her
body exhausted from the physically demanding labor. On
days when no work was found, she resorted to begging for
food scraps to survive.

But her pain was not only physical; mentally, she was
barely hanging on. With each tragic loss of a family member,
she felt a piece of her heart being torn away. Her entire family
had been taken from her, one by one. When she received the
letter from her husband instructing her to send their youngest son to live with a family friend in Seattle, she sent mul-

tiple follow-up letters, desperate for any news about him or their two sons. But each letter had gone unanswered, lost in the dead letter office. She wondered if her husband and two sons were also lost, like her words vanishing into the void. Alone in a new place, struggling to make ends meet and cope with her losses, she felt like a small island, isolated and adrift in a vast, merciless sea.

The baker devised a daring plan: two young men who bore a resemblance to her missing sons would masquerade as vacuum salesmen, introducing themselves as Peter and George in order to catch Susan's attention. They would discreetly slip business cards into her hands with the following instructions:

You are in danger. Your sons are alive. Meet us at the neighborhood diner any night at 5 pm. Make sure you are not followed.

The baker and his allies proceeded with utmost caution, well aware of Mrs. Hall's ruthless nature and capability for anything. They suspected the boy's mother was under surveillance.

The two men disguised themselves as salesmen and arrived at the boarding house carrying a heavy vacuum cleaner. Susan, preoccupied with her own thoughts and uninterested in their product, sat quietly in the corner while they demonstrated its capabilities. When they were done, they introduced themselves as Peter and George and handed out business cards to all the boarders. Susan thought it strange that these men shared the same names as her two missing sons. She could see handwriting on the cards, which piqued her curiosity. Back in her cramped room, she eagerly read the message written on the card. Tears welled up in her eyes as she clutched onto the cards, overwhelmed with emotion as it finally sunk in - her beloved children were still alive!

A surge of emotions overwhelmed her as she processed the possibility that her sons were still alive. Hope, disbelief, joy, and fear mingled as she tightly held the cards to her chest. After enduring so much pain and grief, it was almost impossible to imagine that her boys were out there somewhere, just within reach yet still so far away.

Over the next few days, Susan's mind raced with possibilities. Could it be true? Were Peter and George really out there, trying to reach her? She remembered their faces so clearly, imprinted in her memory despite the period of separation. The thought of seeing them again, holding them in her arms, was like a dream she had long given up on. As she grappled with this newfound hope, Susan also felt a sense of trepidation. What if this was all a cruel trick? The business card said she was in danger. What if her sons were in danger also?

Despite her fears, Susan took a chance and ventured out four nights later as snow gently blanketed the streets. She decided to avoid the diner and instead strolled down an unmarked side road for a couple of blocks before backtracking towards the diner. Along the way, she paused to make sure no one was following her. When she was satisfied that she was safe, she slipped into the restaurant right before 5 PM and settled onto a counter stool to order a cup of coffee.

At exactly 5 PM, vacuum salesman Peter walked into the café and sat on the stool next to Susan. He leaned in close and whispered without making eye contact, "Come with me, Susan. You will be reunited with your sons soon." The two quickly departed the café and jumped into an Oldsmobile. Peter called the baker to inform him that Susan was no longer in danger. The baker shared the joyful news with George and Peter, who were both busy kneading dough for bread.

When Susan was rescued, the baker immediately contacted the authorities, and a thorough investigation was launched. It didn't take long for the truth about Mrs. Hall's deceitful actions to come to light, leading to her arrest and charges being filed against her. However, it was not just a simple kidnapping case; it was also revealed that she had been engaged in an extramarital affair with her late husband. It turned out that their marriage was never legally valid as he had never officially divorced Susan. This scandal caused quite a stir in the local media, raising doubts about the legitimacy of their relationship.

But the biggest shock came when the police started to suspect that Mrs. Hall may have played a part in her husband's suspicious death. Though there was no concrete evidence, the circumstantial evidence was enough to cast doubt on her innocence. So not only was she facing kidnapping charges, but now there were also whispers of adultery and murder surrounding her reputation.

The local media had dubbed it the "trial of the century," and each day, the papers were filled with sensationalized articles, complete with exaggerated details. Public opinion had already turned against the unsympathetic conniver, and she was ultimately found guilty of all counts. As she stood before the judge for her sentencing, Mrs. Hall's appearance was a stark contrast to her previously put-together self. Her hair was unkempt, and her designer clothes were replaced with a plain prison uniform. The stress and anxiety of the court case showed on her face, which was devoid of its usual flawless makeup. She avoided eye contact with the judgmental spectators in the courtroom as the judge announced her punishment. She had been a symbol of wealth and elegance, but now she sat alone in a courtroom, facing the grim truth of her downfall. It was almost like watching someone else's tragic story unfold from a distance.

Susan stepped off the train at King Street Station, her nerves buzzing with apprehension. She had been traveling for hours, her mind filled with countless questions and doubts. But as soon as she stepped onto the bustling platform, her focus shifted to the present. The chaos of the station enveloped her, with people rushing impatiently and the shrill sound of train whistles piercing the air.

As she navigated the crowd, Susan sensed someone was watching her. Furtively, she looked around until her gaze landed on a face that set her heart racing. It was a face she had never thought she would see again - her long-lost son, George.

Her legs moved of their own accord as she walked towards him, tears streaming down her face. As they stood face to face, time seemed to stand still. Susan took in every detail of her son's face - the hint of a beard, the slight crow's feet around his eyes, the same dimpled chin as when she had last seen him. Without a word, she reached out and pulled him into a tight embrace, clinging to him as if he were a life raft in a stormy sea.

They finally pulled back from each other, both overcome with emotion. "I can't believe it's you," Susan said, her voice cracking with tears.

"I can't believe it either," George replied, his voice thick with emotion. "Welcome back, Mom."

Mother and son embraced again, feeling the weight of years of separation melting away with each passing second. The bustling city faded into the background as the two of them stood locked in an embrace that bridged time and distance. It was a reunion neither had dared to hope for, yet here they were, face to face at last.

Peter joined them, his expression reflecting the shared emotions of excitement and relief. The three of them tightly hugged, their bodies swaying ever so slightly as they tried to hold onto each other, as if they were afraid to let go.

It was a moment that stretched out, as if the universe had paused just to witness this reunion. Susan couldn't believe that she was finally back with her sons. She looked at them, taking in every detail of their faces, committing each curve of their features to memory.

"So much has changed," she said softly, wiping the tears from her cheeks. "You have grown up so much since I last saw you."

Both George and Peter nodded, their eyes shining with love and appreciation for their mother. They had been through so much, but now they were together again, and nothing else seemed to matter.

"We never stopped thinking about you, Mom," George said, his voice cracking with emotion.

"Me neither," Peter added. "We knew you were out there somewhere, and we were determined to find you."

Susan's heart swelled with pride as she looked at them. Despite the difficult circumstances they had faced throughout their lives, they had grown into strong and determined young men.

"I owe my life to both of you," Susan said, her voice trembling. "Thank you for finding me."

Peter smiled warmly at his mother. "We couldn't let anything happen to you," he said.

Suddenly, a loud voice interrupted the tender moment. It was an older man, his face flushed with exertion and a look of urgency in his eyes. He pushed his way through the bustling crowd, making a beeline towards Peter, George, and their mother. Peter turned towards the source of the commotion and his face lit up as he recognized the man's voice.

"Mom, this is Michael Bowers," Peter said, introducing the man to his mother. "He's the head baker at the bakery where we work. He's the one responsible for saving you."

Susan's eyes widened in surprise as she shook the man's hand, her voice trembling with emotion. "Thank you, Mr. Bowers. I don't know what would have happened to us if it weren't for you."

The baker waved off her gratitude. "It was nothing, ma'am. Just doing my job. I'm glad I could help." He then turned to the boys, his eyes twinkling with pride. "Your sons here are some of the hardest workers I've ever had. They're a credit to their mother."

As the years went by, specific names and elements of the story became less known. Nevertheless, one thing remained clear: this tale would persist throughout time, handed down from one generation to the next as a cautionary lesson on love, betrayal, and the consequences of keeping secrets. As each day passed, the scandal seemed to gain momentum, eventually engulfing the entire city. It is an enigmatic and gripping narrative that will be remembered long after those involved are gone, forever ingrained in the memories and folklore of the local community.

PART 2
GONE FOR GOOD

CHRISTMAS DAY
FINAL DESTINATION

25th anniversary is remembered by few
Christmas day plotting a selfish coup
A broken man takes inventory of his pathetic life
Common themes of pain, suffering, and strife
Failure after failure, little success
To summarize a complete fucking mess
Mind plays tricks, memories twirl
Incomplete images compete in a swirl
Recollections punctuated by confusion
What is real, and what is an illusion?

Man peers over the building edge

Rash decision results in a pledge
To end it all time to jump
A cowardly decision made by a chump
Glassy eyes stare without blinking
Body leaps forward without thinking
Floating, drifting, plunging, sinking, flying
Trip destination is a ghost town called dying
Skull splatters, shatters, scatters upon impact
Bones and flesh no longer intact
Church bell rings, announcing a farewell
The final stop is either heaven or hell
Dear Mama, whisper a prayer for me
For your son, who was not meant to be

EMILY GONE

Best friend dead
Gunshot to the head
My lover no more
Gone, gone, can't restore
4 o'clock in the morning
Can't stop sobbing - mourning
Flood of issues
A run on tissues
Talk to someone, anyone
Feelings of despair - numb
Why did you take your life?
Fucked up world, too much strife
Goodbye, soul mate. Find peace
Your pain and suffering cease
By a rash decision to pull the trigger
Emotions flood softly snigger

Alarmingly, the bell rings
A shrill shrieking sound sings
Don't want to face the day
Feel defeated is what I say
Drowning in disabling booze
Reach for the button continue to snooze
Can't remember if I took my pills
Daily overdoses, numerous kills
No enthusiasm to wake up
No happiness, no glee club
Don't want to face the day
No purpose, no easy way

Quietly mouth words and slowly moan
Why did you leave me to face the world alone?
You had everything including a good job
Can't comprehend continue to sob
Friends and family were numerous
Perplexing action, not humorous
Life was in front of you so much to do
Rationalization futile begin to stew
On the outside, everything was perfect
On the inside, anxiety and depression crept

Alarmingly, the bell rings
A shrill shrieking sound sings
Don't want to face the day
Feel defeated is what I say
Don't want to face the day
No purpose, no easy way

You are a selfish idiot, I blurt out
Repeat the words, this time a shout
Your pain and suffering are over
Will never figure out what drove you
Ending your life, a complete mind fuck
Flatten me with a speeding truck

See your eyes kiss your lips
Your sense of humor, your funny quips
The curves of your beautiful body
Visions flicker and become spotty
Caress your soft red hair
A teasing mirage, nothing there

Settle into a dreamlike trance
Who can forget our first dance?
At the high school winter ball
Fell in love for the long-haul
Partners forever, or so I thought
Fairytale interrupted by a single gunshot

Happy, sad, angry, disappointed
Meaningless words leave me disjointed
Emotional sentence fragments continue to flow
Depression wins and continues to grow
Oh, my lover, why, why?
Find peace up in the sky

Why don't you turn to religion you ask?
God is a fraud, a devious mask

Created by rulers to maintain the status quo
Prove me wrong, and I will eat crow
God was constructed to give suckers hope
A mechanism so the masses can cope
With their dreary, dismal existence on earth
That ends with death and begins with birth
Promise of a better afterlife is a made-up fantasy
A concept so the hordes keep their sanity

Alarmingly, the bell rings a third time
Unexpectantly mood shifts on a dime
Beautiful songbird chirps outside
Melodic chorus competes with suicide
Reluctant body on the bed lying uncurled
Must get up and face the world

One day at a time, the cliche goes
I want to live is the decision I chose
Seize the day, make a difference
Direction clear becomes vociferous
Erase memories that are haunted
That is what Emily would have wanted

PART 3
LUCK RUNS OUT

CANADIAN GEESE DESTROY THE GOLDEN GOOSE

Tommy Duckworth was in dire straits. He had never been skilled at managing his money, and a string of impulse purchases and unfortunate gambling losses had left him with an overwhelming debt of $30,000. His biggest concern was Big Al, the tough-as-nails ex-Marine who ran the local bookmaking operations and allegedly had ties to organized crime. Because Big Al "liked" him, he had given Tommy one last week to pay off his entire debt or face consequences. And Tommy knew exactly what those consequences entailed - being roughed up by hired goons until he coughed up blood and teeth. If he were lucky enough to escape with just a few broken bones, it would be a miracle.

Tommy was in a desperate situation, facing a gambling debt of $12,000 and a credit card debt of over $18,000. He knew he could push back his credit card payments and avoid physical harm, but he needed to come up with the money to pay off Big Al quickly. After some thought, his not-so-brilliant idea was to bet all his remaining money on a horse race at the local track. He had $2,000 hidden away in his rundown apartment, and a friend of a friend of a friend promised him a "sure thing" named Speedy Sienna. This first-time starter would be racing tomorrow against nine other fillies in a maiden $4,000 claimer at Darrington Downs. Eight of the fillies had previous racing experience, and the prohibitive morning line favorite was Big Mama's Talkin, who had yet to win a race despite coming close in her last two races, finishing second by just a nose and neck.

The triple crown, a series of three prestigious horse races - the Kentucky Derby, Preakness, and Belmont Stakes - features the most talented three-year-old thoroughbreds. It is rare for a filly to compete in these races, with only three fillies having won the Kentucky Derby. The races are run at Churchill Downs, Pimlico, and Belmont Park, drawing tens of thousands of spectators. Meanwhile, Speedy Sienna and her nine competitors at Darrington Downs may all be three-year-olds, but they have little else in common with the triple crown contenders. Racing for a mere $6,000 purse at a minor league track with only a sparse crowd of a few hundred spectators, Sienna and the other horses entered in the race at Darrington Downs are on the bottom rung of thoroughbred racing value compared to the top echelon horses competing in the million-dollar purses and earning even more through breeding rights. The $4,000 claiming tag at Darrington Downs is the lowest offered, indicating that these fillies are not considered talented runners.

Tommy couldn't fall asleep the night before the big race. He tossed and turned on his lumpy twin bed, listening to a preacher begging for donations on the TV. For a moment, he considered calling the number on the screen to see if he could get help with his financial struggles. At exactly noon the next day, Tommy arrived at the track an hour before the first race. He stood alone at the rail, waiting for race number three to start. Despite the cool spring weather, Tommy was sweating profusely and feeling extremely nervous. The past two weeks had been relentlessly wet with constant drizzles and occasional downpours, turning the track infield into a muddy swamp. Canadian geese had taken over that area, diving their heads underwater in search of food. Disgusted, Tommy watched them from a distance. He had encountered these geese before on the local college campus, where they would play in the water fountain and leave behind large droppings that he often stepped in while walking. Tommy splurged on a $5 beer to calm himself down, leaving him only $1,995 to bet on the race. As he downed two more beers quickly, his available funds decreased to $1,985.

The first two races had been won by favorites, and Tommy wasn't sure if this was a sign that an underdog would win the next race or a warning that favorites would continue to dominate throughout the day, including in the upcoming third race where Big Mama's Talkin was set to compete. Tommy made his way down to the paddock, a circular area where the horses were prepared and shown off before heading to the racetrack. He quickly glanced at a program he had "borrowed" from someone who had left it on a nearby bench in their rush to place a bet.

Big Mama's Talkin was the 2-1 morning line favorite, which meant that if she won the race, a wager would return two dollars in profit for every dollar win bet. Speedy Sienna was 15-1 on the morning line, the eighth favorite of the ten horses entered. The remaining eight fillies had a range of morning line odds from 4-1 to 30-1 and sported descriptive, colorful names: Pray For Gold, Freedoms Gem, Bonnie's Bluff, Sally's Last Chance, Seeking The Truth, Toothless Cat, Terrible Tina, and It's My Knight.

Choosing a winning horse is not an exact science. If it were, there would be many wealthy individuals making a living as professional handicappers. Some people meticulously study the racing form to find a potential winner, considering numerous factors such as race pace, class, distance, track conditions and observing each horse's behavior during the pre-race parade. Others simply choose their favorite horse name or the most aesthetically pleasing colored horse. Some even have a superstition of betting only on gray horses. And then there are those who keep their methods for selecting winners a secret, knowing that if they shared it, everyone would use it and diminish the odds for their chosen horse.

Tommy's method for selecting a horse to bet on in today's race was straightforward: a can't-fail tip from a friend of a friend of a friend. He had some reservations about this approach, wishing the recommendation had come from someone closer to him. The added degrees of separation increased the chances of miscommunication. For a moment, he considered hedging his bet and putting $500 of his $1985 savings on Pray For Gold, using a "last-minute" name-based hunch as his handicapping strategy. But he quickly dismissed the idea and stuck with his original plan: a single bet on Speedy Sienna. It was all or nothing.

Tommy surveyed Big Mama's Talkin in the paddock area and was immediately concerned. She was a large filly with an arrogant swagger as she pranced around the circle, confident that she would easily win the race. The top jockey, Alex Hernandez, and leading trainer, Blaine Drysdale, were her connections for the race. And it seemed like the public agreed with Big Mama's confidence, as they had bet her down to 6-5 odds from her original 2-1 morning line. On the other hand, Speedy Sienna was being ridden by one of the two female jockeys at Darrington Downs, Nicole Brooks. She was a struggling novice jockey with a poor winning percentage, but Tommy knew she could still surprise everyone. Her horse was trained by Frank Roselli, an experienced trainer who had faced multiple suspensions for his horses testing positive for drugs after races. Tommy checked the current odds and saw that Speedy Sienna was a longshot at 25-1 on the tote board. Although he wasn't great at math, he knew that if the horse somehow pulled off a win, he would make a significant profit. With nervous excitement, he left the paddock and made his way towards the betting window.

Tommy exclaimed with a bit more volume than intended, "Darrington Downs, race number three. I'm betting $1,985 on horse number three to win."

The clerk gave him an astonished look and repeated, "So you want to bet $1,985 all on horse number three?"

"That's right. $1,985 straight win bet on horse number three."

"Got it. Good luck to you, my friend."

It was rare for someone at a small-town track to place such a large bet, which is why the clerk double-checked the amount. The significant wager had an impact on the pari-mutuel odds, causing Speedy Sienna's odds to drop from 25-1 to 16-1 on the tote board.

Sienna's morning track workouts were a mix of fast and slow times, leaving Tommy unsure of how she would perform in a race. He knew that workout results didn't always translate to race performance; some horses excelled in practice but faltered in the actual race when faced with competition and dirt being kicked up into their eyes. On the other hand, there were horses who seemed lackluster during workouts but shined on race day, tapping into their athleticism and competitive nature.

Sienna, a speedy racehorse, entered the track without knowing she was about to compete in the lowest-class race offered at a minor league track. She had no idea that she could be bought for just $4,000, a measly bargain price considering her star potential. Sienna basked in all the attention and pampering bestowed upon her on race day. She observed the other fillies and knew she could outrun them all. She was bursting with excitement and ready for a victorious run on the track. If only the bettors could see her confidence, they would rush to place their bets on this overlooked long shot. Luckily, Tommy had stumbled upon a prime opportunity courtesy of a friend of a friend of a friend.

According to the horse racing industry, any foal born in a given year is assigned January 1st as their official birthday. This means that regardless of their actual birth date, all horses are considered to be one year old on January 1st. Knowing the age of a horse is critical in horse racing because many races have age restrictions. Trainers and owners closely monitor the development of their horses, as those born later in the year may not be as physically developed as those born between January and April. This can put them at a disadvantage until they reach four or five years old when age differences level out.

Wealthy breeders will go to great lengths to ensure their foals are born as early as possible in the new year, even using artificial methods to trigger mares' fertility hormones earlier than usual. By simulating sunlight with artificial lighting, they can manipulate the timing of breeding and increase the chances of their foals being born shortly after the new year, giving them a competitive edge. However, if the timing is off and a foal is born on Christmas, they are considered a "lump of coal" and may be at a competitive disadvantage due to being younger. After a few days, a Christmas foal is a year old and considered a yearling. Speedy Sienna was born on January 15th, the old-fashioned way, without her mother receiving artificial light.

Not all thoroughbred foals make it to the racetrack. Some succumb to death, others suffer injuries, and some simply lack the capability or drive to run fast enough to compete in horse races. And among those who make it to the starting gate, only a small percentage will win a race. From the moment a foal is born, its owner dreams of it winning the coveted Kentucky Derby. This hopeful vision of fame, fortune, and wealth remains regardless of the foal's humble ancestry or pricey purchase price. The racing industry thrives on optimism and chance. There are tales of inexpensive horses defying expectations and winning prestigious races, earning millions in prize money. On the other hand, there are also stories like that of The Green Monkey: a colt with impeccable lineage, sold for a whopping sixteen million dollars but never able to win a single race out of three attempts. As the saying goes in horse racing, "breed the best to the best and hope for the best," but there are always exceptions to this rule. For owners, trainers, jockeys, and bettors alike, every new foal born or horse entered in a race symbolizes a potential champion and sparks grand aspirations.

Sienna may not have been a flashy yearling with a prestigious lineage, but she was still a racehorse with potential. Born to humble parents in a small town, her sire had a modest record of five wins and thirteen in-the-money finishes out of forty-two starts, all on minor league tracks. Her dam also had limited success, with only three starts and one third-place finish to her name.

Sienna's early life was similar to other first-time thoroughbred starters. She was separated from her mother at six months old, and by the time she reached one year of age, she was full of energy and going through physical growth and maturation. While all horses at this age tend to be active, Sienna was exceptionally dynamic and constantly in motion. At two years old, she underwent preliminary training, but like many horses at this age, she couldn't race due to her knees not being fully developed yet. Horses are creatures of habit, living predictable lives filled with walking, galloping, bathing, eating three times a day, and sleeping. However,

Sienna stood out from the average stubborn thoroughbred; she had an agreeable personality and enjoyed the company of all creatures - humans, fellow equine stablemates, barn goats, and even a family golden retriever named Penny, who would occasionally visit.

Sienna formed a special bond with an eight-year-old girl named Stella; whenever she saw her approach the stall, she would rush over and nuzzle the youngster. The feeling was mutual as Stella would eagerly embrace Sienna, sometimes with tears of joy in her eyes. Sienna had a special love for people and always welcomed their affection through cuddles or gentle nudges. Unfortunately, racehorses often have short careers due to health issues or lack of success on the track. However, Sienna had not suffered any injuries or major health concerns prior to her first race. Only time would tell if she had what it takes to become a winning racehorse.

Speedy Sienna did not know she came from a modest bloodline of thoroughbreds and that her parents had mediocre success in horse racing. She pranced around the racetrack with the poise and grace of a seasoned athlete, carefully warming up her muscles before the race. Her jockey, Nicole Brooks, was content with their warm-up routine and grateful that Sienna showed no signs of injury - a common worry in lower-level races. While other jockeys may be more selective about which races they compete in, Nicole was thankful for any opportunity to ride. With only one or two rides per day on average, she struggled to make ends meet. But she hoped to climb the ranks and earn more money over time. Riding Sienna during morning workouts leading up to the race gave her some familiarity with the inexperienced filly.

Frank Roselli, the trainer for Speedy Sienna, was uncertain about the filly's ability. He had been a successful, energetic trainer in the past but had fallen on difficult times. He still enjoyed the camaraderie of his fellow horse racing enthusiasts such as trainers, jockeys, grooms, exercise riders, and farriers. Even now, at sixty-three years old and semi-retired, he still relished spending time with those in the industry, though he no longer actively sought out new horses to train. For this race, Roselli entered Sienna in a $4,000 maiden claimer, hoping for a win to break his dry spell for the meet. Roselli's instructions to jockey Nicole were simple: aim for the lead or hold back if there was a speed battle and stay on the inside for an optimal charge toward the finish line. However, Brooks knew that these instructions were often just empty words used by trainers to blame jockeys if things didn't go as planned. It was common for trainers to shift the blame onto their jockeys when reporting back to owners after a disappointing losing race.

Luckily for both Tommy's wallet and physical safety, the strong and nimble filly who would be competing had more faith in her abilities than her human handlers did. As they approached the starting gate, Speedy Sienna exuded a confident snort, indicating she was ready to put on a show. In the paddock and during warm-ups on the track, Sienna and Big Mama's Talkin communicated through nonverbal signals known only to horses. It was going to be a head-to-head race between two top contenders, and they were the only ones who knew it.

As the horses were being loaded into the starting gate, there was a bit of chaos when It's My Knight, a first-time runner with a reputation for misbehaving during training sessions, hesitated to enter post position 8. She had recently undergone additional gate schooling before being approved to race. After a minute of struggling, several assistant starters finally managed to guide her into the starting stall. Meanwhile, Speedy Sienna in post position 3 and Big Mama's Talkin in post position 4 had patiently waited for It's My Knight to cooperate and enter the gate.

For the trainers, owners, and jockeys, loading horses into the starting gate causes great stress and worry. A misbehaving horse at the gate could be disqualified or lose the race before it even begins by wasting energy during the process. There is a saying in horse racing that you can't win a race at the starting gate, but you can lose it. A horse's chances of winning are greatly reduced if they struggle or act unpredictably when the gates open. However, this was not a concern for Sienna and Mama. Both fillies stood calmly in position, ready to shift their weight back and charge as soon as the starter bell rang and the gates opened.

The wait for the race to start seemed endless, and the crowd buzzed with excitement. Whether it was a prestigious Breeders Cup race or a humble claimer, the anticipation was always the same. Finally, the gates opened, and the magnificent horses burst onto the track in a flurry of hooves and dust, leaving spectators in awe. The bettors eagerly watched as each horse jockeyed for position, already envisioning how they would spend their winnings from picking the winning horse. Speedy Sienna wasted no time in establishing her dominance, blasting out from her inside post position and taking an early lead over Big Mama's Talkin. She ran effortlessly and stayed on course, a magnificent animal weighing one thousand pounds, relaxing and moving smoothly ahead unaccompanied in the front. Big Mama's Talkin maintained a close second place position about two lengths back, her experienced rider content with tracking the inexperienced front runner and overtaking her in the final stretch when she would likely tire. However, Speedy Sienna did not tire at all. It was becoming apparent with each graceful stride that she was a talented filly, far superior to the other horses in the cheap claimer.

Speedy Sienna's ears were pricked the whole way like she was listening for applause from her adoring fans. Tommy noticed she moved with the confidence of a seasoned professional rather than a first-time runner. She strategically let out subtle sudden bursts of speed forcing Big Mama's Talkin to work hard to keep up and tire herself out, hoping that the favorite would eventually give up and settle for second place once again. Big Mama's jockey was trying to encourage his horse to make a strong move and close the gap between them, eager for a showdown down the stretch. His hope was to catch the frontrunner in the stretch and have the fillies go eyeball to eyeball until one conceded. Big Mama's Talkin strained to catch the speedy filly, who was running effortlessly and happily, with Nicole sitting calmly in mutual harmony with her horse as if they were one being moving in perfect synchrony. Each thrust of Sienna's stride magically passed through the girl's body; two souls merged into one remarkable being.

The race was proceeding at an ideal pace, and Tommy's horse was in a perfect position. Sienna had been allowed to get a comfortable early lead and was able to set reasonable fractions, conserving energy for the final stretch. Big Mama's Talkin appeared to be struggling and falling further behind. Meanwhile, Sienna had widened her lead to three lengths as they turned into the home stretch. Tommy couldn't believe his eyes - this was a race for the history books. It seemed like Big Mama's Talkin couldn't catch a break, always finishing in second place but never actually winning. Maybe her owners should have named her "Just a Second." As they approached the eighth pole, Sienna had pulled ahead by six lengths, and none of the other fillies were anywhere close to catching up. Tommy felt a surge of excitement - this could be his big score, the win he needed to get out of debt. There was no doubt about it now - Sienna had sealed her victory and would cross the finish line first.

Only the race was not over. The horses were galloping fiercely down the final stretch, their hooves drumming a rhythmic beat on the dirt track. The audience erupted into cheers and stood up, their eyes fixated on the horses as the finish line approached. Just as Speedy Sienna was about to cross the sixteenth pole, a commotion arose in the infield. A flock of Canadian geese had been startled by the thundering horse hooves and took flight towards the track, honking loudly. This sudden disruption caused Speedy Sienna to slow down and swerve off course, costing her what would have been an easy victory in her first-ever race. In a twist of fate, Big Mama's Talkin took advantage of the chaos and sprinted past the finish line to claim victory and achieve her first win.

A foul play by a fowl had transformed Speedy Sienna into Suddenly Stopped Sienna.

Tommy had squeezed his eyes shut as the horses charged into the final turn. He couldn't bear to watch, relying on the track announcer's commentary instead. By mid-stretch, he knew Sienna was a sure winner, and his financial troubles were distant memories. But then, he heard an audible gasp from the crowd. Something had gone wrong. He blinked rapidly before cautiously opening his eyes to see Sienna suddenly stop and pull up just yards before the finish line. The dreaded geese mocked him from their swampy habitat. Tommy was stunned and disheartened, desperately hoping that the track stewards would open an inquiry against the Canadian geese for interference. A cynical track veteran informed him that objections could only be made against other horses, not geese. Tommy, an experienced horse racing fan, had never heard of a goose disrupting a race before. These cheap Canadian geese had destroyed his golden goose. Sure, he had seen horses spook at their own shadows during races, but geese? That seemed impossible. No one would believe it.

The world of horse racing is famous for its use of vivid expressions, with "horses for courses" and "pace makes the race" being among the most often repeated by seasoned handicappers. Recently, a new maxim has been added to the lexicon of horsemen: "Beware a goose on the loose."

The race summary chart coldly detailed the unfortunate chain of events:

BIG MAMA'S TALKIN pressed the pace early before settling, was second best until drawing off in the final sixteenth. TOOTHLESS CAT was never far back, raced three-wide through the turn, finished steadily while second best.

IT'S MY KNIGHT showed no early speed, saved ground around the turn, angled out into the stretch and finished evenly late. FREEDOMS GEM stalked outside then off the rail, bid between horses entering the stretch, drifted out a bit from the whip in deep stretch and continued gamely to the wire. SALLY'S LAST CHANCE broke a bit slowly, came out into the stretch and weakened. SEEKING THE TRUTH squeezed a bit just after the start, saved ground off the pace to the stretch and then did not rally. TERRIBLE TINA was off slowly, then got outrun. PRAY FOR GOLD broke alertly then lacked a bid. BONNIE'S BLUFF was void of early foot, raced five-wide through the turn and was never a factor. SPEEDY SIENNA broke sharply and sped to the lead, set the pace on the inside and remained in complete control deep into the stretch, steadied from geese near the track at the sixteenth pole, dropped far back and was eased before the finish line.

Tommy took a seat on the track bench and remained motionless. He would never visit Canada again in his life. If he still had a life. He knew he would likely never visit any place again. For he was a broken man with a broken past, and he knew he would never be able to outrun it.

SHAKE IT OFF

On his birthday, John Everly was driving home and singing along to the radio. The familiar tune "California Dreaming'" was one of his all-time favorite songs from the 60s. As he glanced at the car's clock, the time - 04:07 PM – struck him as a peculiar coincidence since his birthday was April 7th. The synchronicity of the time and his birthday sparked a sense of intrigue and curiosity. After the song ended, a commercial for the magic ball lottery came on followed by a warning about gambling addiction. The conversation then shifted to the highly anticipated national lottery happening that evening, with a whopping grand prize of one hundred million dollars. Despite not being an impulsive person and never having gambled before, John couldn't help but feel a nudge from fate urging him to buy a lottery ticket. So, he made a detour to a small shop on 47th Street, whose manager greeted him warmly and eagerly assisted him in selecting his own lucky numbers. John carefully read through the instructions before making his purchase.

TO PLAY, SELECT FIVE NUMBERS FROM 1 TO 69 FOR THE WHITE BALLS, THEN SELECT ONE NUMBER FROM 1 TO 26 FOR THE RED MAGIC BALL.

YOU CAN CHOOSE YOUR LUCKY NUMBERS ON A PLAY SLIP OR LET THE LOTTERY TERMINAL RANDOMLY PICK YOUR NUMBERS.

TO WIN, MATCH ONE OF THE NINE WAYS TO WIN:

5 WHITE BALLS + 1 RED MAGIC BALL = GRAND PRIZE.

5 WHITE BALLS = $1 MILLION.

4 WHITE BALLS + 1 RED MAGIC BALL = $50,000.

4 WHITE BALLS = $100.

3 WHITE BALLS + 1 RED MAGIC BALL = $100.

3 WHITE BALLS = $7.

2 WHITE BALLS + 1 RED MAGIC BALL = $7.

1 WHITE BALL + 1 RED MAGIC BALL = $4.

1 RED MAGIC BALL = $4.

John approached the task of selecting his lottery numbers with a deeply ingrained sense of superstition. After careful deliberation, he ultimately chose 4, 7, 44, 47, and 68 as his white ball numbers and 4 for the red ball. He made sure to include combinations of 4 and 7, representing his birthday on April 7th, in every possible arrangement. As a final touch, he added the number 68 because it was his birth year. Once he had purchased the ticket from the store, he placed it in his glove compartment, adding an extra layer of excitement and tension to the already nerve-wracking experience. The following day, at precisely 04:07, with "California Dreamin'" playing softly in the background, John returned to the same store where he had made his purchase. He scanned the ticket using the self-serve machine and was met with a prompt to contact lottery headquarters immediately. Driving home, he wondered what this mysterious message could mean for him and his potential winnings.

Arriving home, he quickly went online to check the lottery winning numbers and was shocked to see that they were an exact match to his ticket. He double-checked just to be sure, and the same result appeared. Was it just his imagination? He checked again...the same result. Suddenly, unimaginable wealth had been bestowed upon him. Conflicted and unsure of what to do with this new reality, he reached out to an old high school buddy and financial advisor, Bill Matthews. They met at a local eatery and snagged a secluded booth in the back for privacy. After offering his congratulations, Bill assured John that he would make wise financial decisions for his family. With a friendly pat on the back, Bill exclaimed, "Congratulations on your lucky birthday break! You, your wife, and your daughter are set for life. Heck, even your grandkids and their kids will benefit from this!" Bill was always charismatic and had been John's teammate in high school football. Putting his trust in him with this newfound wealth seemed like a logical choice.

Two days later, armed with a signed ticket and photos of both sides on his smartphone, John arrived at the lottery headquarters. He sat in the sterile, windowless office, his palms sweaty as he anxiously awaited his fate. Beside him, the customer representative shuffled through a stack of papers, her perfectly manicured nails tapping against the desk.

The customer rep took some time studying the ticket before delivering the news in a monotone, her voice lacking any genuine enthusiasm: "Congratulations, Mr. Everly. You have won over $500." The rep continued after a dramatic pause: "Actually, scratch that. You are the big jackpot winner of 100 million dollars."

John's heart skipped a beat as he struggled to process the magnitude of what she had just confirmed. The room seemed to spin around him as he tried to focus on the words coming out of her mouth.

The customer rep handed him a pen and a stack of paperwork, explaining the next steps in claiming his prize. John sat there in a daze, still in disbelief. This was life-changing money, a chance to finally provide complete financial stability for his family and live a comfortable life.

As he left the lottery building, John's mind was a whirlwind of thoughts. The sudden influx of wealth brought with it a mix of excitement and overwhelming anxiety. How would this change his life? How would this change his family's life? Only time will tell. For now, John clutched the winning ticket tightly in his hand, a symbol of hope and opportunity for a brighter future.

Driving home, John couldn't wait to share the news with his wife and daughter. He wanted to see their faces light up with joy and excitement. When he walked through the door, his family was gathered in the living room, and as soon as they saw the look on his face, they knew something incredible had happened.

"Everyone, sit down," John began, his voice trembling with emotion. "I have something unbelievable to tell you both. We...we just won the lottery."

John's wife, Linda, looked at him with surprise. My God, he's not joking, she thought. She could tell by his expression that he was completely serious. But she also knew that sudden wealth could be a double-edged sword, and she didn't want it to change who they were as a family. After hugging him and sharing in the excitement, she said, "This is wonderful news! But let's take things slow and enjoy this together. We've worked hard for this, and I want us to remain happy above all else."

John nodded, his eyes still filled with wonderment. He knew his wife was right and was grateful to have her by his side as they embarked on this new chapter in their lives.

Samantha Everly, with her thick, curly brown hair and oversized glasses, was the epitome of a bright and ambitious teenager. She had just received news from her father that would undoubtedly send her into a frenzy.

"Can I tell my friends?" she exclaimed, bouncing up and down on the couch where they sat in their small, cozy living room. "I can't wait to go shopping and maybe even travel this summer. Great job, Dad!"

John smiled at his daughter's enthusiasm but couldn't bring himself to match it. His mind was still reeling from the unexpected windfall.

"Not yet, Samantha," he said, trying to temper her excitement. "Let's wait until everything is finalized before we start making plans. I don't want to get your hopes up only to have them dashed."

Samantha's face fell slightly, but she nodded in under-standing. She knew her father was always careful and cau-tious, and she trusted his judgment.

"I'll keep it between us for now," she said with a reassur-ing smile, reaching over to squeeze his hand.

John was appreciative of his daughter's level-headedness. In moments when everything seemed chaotic and over-whelming, she was his motivation to keep pushing forward.

"Thank you, Samantha," he said, leaning over to give her a quick hug. "I promise we'll celebrate properly once things have calmed down."

He knew that winning such a large sum of money could bring unwanted attention and potential danger to their family, which was why he wanted to discuss a strategy with Bill before sharing the news with anyone else. As always, Linda would trust John with anything related to finances, and he would be responsible for managing their new wealth and making wise decisions with the money, guided by his trusted financial planner.

He glanced at the framed photo of his wife on the desk, her smiling face a reminder of why he needed to protect their family at all costs. She relied on him for anything related to numbers, and he would not disappoint her. Taking a deep breath, John picked up the phone to call Bill, determined to devise a plan to safeguard their family's future.

John had always been a practical man, methodical in his approach to decision-making. So, when he won the lottery, he knew he needed to consider all options carefully. After much contemplation, he concluded that a lump sum payment would be the best choice for him. The thought of receiving a large sum of money all at once was enticing, and he didn't want to wait years to receive his winnings bit by bit through an annuity.

However, he also knew that this decision would result in a significant decrease in the amount he would receive. After applying the lump sum discount and factoring in taxes at 30%, his initial 100 million would be reduced to 30 million. It was a considerable difference, but to John, it was worth it to have the money in his hands now. It was a decision made with careful consideration and one that he hoped he wouldn't regret.

Bill Matthews sat in his modest condo, surrounded by white powder and empty brandy glasses. He had been celebrating all night long ever since he received the call from John Everly.

He looked at himself in the mirror, a man in his late forties with a receding hairline and dark circles under his bloodshot eyes. He was once a successful planner with many clients, but now he spent most of his time partying and indulging in various vices.

But tonight was different. Tonight was about celebrating John Everly's luck, which was also his luck.

He took out a razor blade and chopped up another line of white powder on the glass coffee table. He took out his straw and sniffed the powder in each nostril. The familiar rush of euphoria washed over him, momentarily numbing any feelings of regret or guilt.

As John and his family celebrated their newfound wealth, Matthews secretly schemed behind the scenes. Unbeknownst to John, Bill had a gambling problem and a cocaine addiction that he had been hiding for years. Connecting with a lottery winner only added fuel to his addictions, and he saw it as an endless source of funding for his habits.

Bill knew he needed to set up a management structure so he could make decisions on John's behalf without needing his approval for every transaction. He also knew that John trusted him completely and would not question any financial decisions he made.

Bill found the debit card connected to John's investment account to be the ideal tool for his cunning scheme. At first, he only withdrew small amounts, hoping that John wouldn't notice. But as his addictions grew stronger, so did the amount of money he needed. He started withdrawing thousands of dollars at a time, sometimes multiple times daily. However, Bill was also aware that there were certain regulations and restrictions regarding managing someone else's finances. To avoid any issues with the law or the IRS, he made sure never to exceed the $10,000 withdrawal limit. This also helped prevent any red flags from being raised about suspicious activity.

He knew John never used cash, preferring to pay for everything with his credit cards, which he always paid off in full each month. In the beginning, the withdrawals were easy. The ATM machines didn't discriminate. They only needed a card and a PIN number, and Bill had both. But as the amount of money he took out increased, so did the risk. He knew he couldn't keep this up forever but couldn't stop himself. The thrill of getting away with it, the rush of using the money to indulge in his vices, was too intoxicating.

And so, he continued to play this dangerous game, always on edge, always wondering when John would finally discover the missing funds. But the longer he got away with it, the deeper he fell into the rabbit hole of his addictions, and the harder it became for him to stop.

The media frenzy surrounding the Everly family's big lottery win was a storm that they couldn't escape. The moment their identities were revealed as the lucky winners, reporters and photographers began to swarm. It seemed like everyone wanted a piece of them, to know their story and to catch a glimpse at the instant millionaires.

The town, usually quiet and unassuming, was suddenly buzzing with excitement and curiosity. Regional news outlets were sending their best correspondents to cover the story, and even a few tabloids were trying to get in on the action. The family's request for privacy was ignored as reporters camped outside their home, ringing their phones off the hook and even approaching them on the streets.

The family tried their best to avoid the constant barrage of attention, but it was a losing battle. One tabloid reporter, in particular, was a persistent nuisance. She had set up a makeshift studio right outside their front door, complete with a flashy sign and bright lights. She would shout questions and snap pictures whenever someone from the family stepped outside.

Despite their resistance, the media circus continued to grow. It seemed like everyone had an opinion or a theory about the family and their sudden wealth.

The Everly family had become overwhelmed with requests from various charities asking for donations. They had changed their phone numbers multiple times, but somehow, these organizations still managed to find a way to contact them. It came to a point where they could no longer keep up with all the requests and began ignoring them altogether.

At first, John felt guilty about not being able to help those in need but soon realized that many of these organizations were scams trying to take advantage of their newfound wealth. One outrageous swindle involved a so-called charity that claimed to rescue abandoned puppies and kittens from the streets and provide them with loving homes.

Unbeknownst to John, Samantha had donated a large sum of money to "Paws and Claws Rescue," an organization claiming to help save the lives of innocent animals. But John soon discovered that the organization was actually a front for an illegal puppy and kitten mill, where animals were bred and sold for exorbitant prices to unsuspecting buyers.

If that wasn't enough, John was bombarded with yet another charity solicitation. This time, it was a phone call from an organization claiming to assist children battling cancer. They asked for a small contribution, promising that it would directly benefit local kids affected by the terrible disease. However, John's previous experience with the shady puppy and kitten mill made him skeptical of their legitimacy. Determined to make an informed decision, John researched the organization. To his relief, he discovered that it was a legitimate charity that had successfully helped numerous children with cancer in the past. Feeling reassured, he decided to make a modest donation to support its cause.

As time passed, John received more and more calls from the organization, each time asking for larger and larger amounts of money. At first, he thought it was just a coincidence and that they were genuinely in need of help. But then he noticed something odd. Every time he donated, he would receive a lavish gift basket accompanied by a thank you note from a child who had supposedly benefited from his donation.

Something didn't feel right to John. He decided to dig deeper and found out that the children's photos on the thank-you notes were stock images purchased online. The organization had been using these fake thank-you notes to guilt people into making larger donations.

Burned twice now by fraudulent charitable organizations, John was fed up. He decided to quit giving to charity altogether. Little did he know that he was unknowingly contributing generously to one of the largest charities in the city, the Bill Matthews Foundation.

Matthews was a man on the brink of destruction. He was spiraling out of control, fueled by his addiction to expensive vices. His once handsome face was now gaunt and sunken, his eyes vacant and hollow. Yet, he couldn't stop himself. Each day, he would wake up with a pounding headache and a deep sense of guilt, but by nightfall, he would be chasing the next high.

His condo had become a hedonistic playground, filled with high-quality cocaine and expensive liquor. He would party around the clock, inviting strangers and acquaintances into his world of excess.

He had also started a new habit, paying for high-end call girls. It wasn't a conscious decision but rather a gradual slide into indulgence, like a stone rolling down a hill. At first, it was just a way to satisfy his carnal desires. But as time passed, it became a habit he couldn't break.

The women were always different, yet somehow all the same. They came from all walks of life and carried a certain air of detachment as if they were merely going through the motions. He felt an occasional twinge of guilt, knowing that these women were only there because of the money he had courtesy of a former friend.

The news of John's financial windfall continued to spread like an out-of-control wildfire, and with it came a wave of distant relatives who seemed to materialize out of thin air. They all had their own stories to tell about how they were related to John and how they had lost touch over the years, but now that his fortune had been made known, they were back in his life.

There was Aunt Mildred, who claimed to have babysat John when he was just a tot. Uncle Henry, who insisted he was John's father's second cousin twice removed. And then the distant cousins, once removed, twice removed, three times removed, who all suddenly appeared with their hands out, claiming their share of the winnings.

Some were more aggressive than others, threatening legal action if they didn't get their "deserved" share. Others tried to play on John's emotions, recounting stories of hardship and need, hoping to tug at his heartstrings and secure a piece of the pie.

The stress and pressure of dealing with the fallout from winning the lottery were taking a toll on the family. John was overwhelmed by it all, his sudden wealth quickly becoming a burden instead of a blessing. He couldn't believe that people he had never even met before were now demanding a share of his winnings. It made him question the true intentions of those around him and wonder if anyone truly cared for him or just his money.

With each passing day, John felt increasingly alone. The hours seemed to drag on endlessly, with no purpose or direction. After hitting the jackpot, he left his job at the library, craving some excitement and change. But as time went by, he grew more and more restless, struggling to find ways to fill his days. Meanwhile, Linda occupied herself with daytime TV and phone calls filled with petty gossip, leaving John feeling increasingly isolated.

Restless and bored, John began taking long walks around the neighborhood, pausing at the local cafe for a cup of coffee. He would sit alone, sipping his drink, watching the bustle of people around him, wondering what they did with their lives. He had always been a solitary person, content

with his books and quiet evenings at home, but now he wanted something more.

Sitting at his usual table at the local cafe, John sipped his afternoon coffee and was pleasantly surprised by the appearance of a familiar face. Zoe Simpson, an athletic woman with an infectious smile and a love for yoga, had been his high school chemistry lab partner. Despite the years that had passed since they last saw each other, their bond remained strong, and their spontaneous reunion was full of joy and laughter. They continued to meet at the coffee shop regularly, spending hours catching up.

As they sat across from each other sipping their drinks, John chuckled at Zoe's stories of her clients struggling with difficult yoga poses. Her energy and passion for her work were contagious, and he felt lighter and more carefree in her presence.

In between sips of coffee and bites of pastries, John shared stories of his family and the ups and downs of being a father to his daughter. Zoe listened intently, her eyes sparkling with understanding and empathy. Though their relationship was purely platonic, it was evident that the chemistry between them had never faded.

One day, Zoe invited John to her apartment to look through old yearbooks and reminisce about their high school years. She was a vision, with her sleek brown locks falling down her back and her big, doe-like eyes glowing with a youthful innocence. Her tight black leggings hugged her lean, toned legs in all the right places. As they flipped through pages and laughed at memories of the spring musical, Zoe leaned in for a kiss. As their lips met, John tasted the sweetness of Zoe's lip gloss mixed with the lingering taste of coffee on her tongue. He also tasted the tinge of guilt in his own mouth, as he knew he was betraying his wife.

Zoe took charge and guided him to the bedroom, where they made love. He quickly came, his body betraying him, a tangle of nerves and confusion, as he tried to keep up with Zoe's confident and passionate embrace. The taste of regret lingered in John's mouth, bitter and sour. He could also taste the remnants of the coffee they shared earlier, now tainted with the bitter disappointment of his own performance. John felt doubly ashamed about cheating on his wife and his sexual inadequacy. He quickly left, apologizing to Zoe as she sighed in bed.

After a few more covert meetings, Zoe revealed her true intentions to John. They were sitting on her apartment couch, their faces obscured by shadows. Zoe leaned in close, her red lips curving into a wicked smile as she spoke.

"Here's the deal, rich boy," she said, her voice dripping with malice. "I want $50,000 monthly, or I'll tell your wife about us. I know you have the money. And let's be real, your wife will probably leave you once she finds out what a pathetic excuse for a man you are."

John's heart dropped into his stomach. He had never expected this from Zoe, a woman he thought he could trust. But as he looked at her now, he realized that she was only

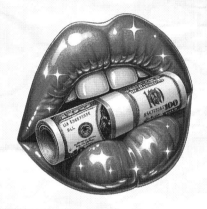

after one thing: money.

"And as a bonus," Zoe continued, "I'll still have occasional sex with you. Because let's face it, you are not getting any at home. Bring a blue pill or something...you suck in bed."

John was stunned. He couldn't believe the audacity of this woman, the way she was using him for her own gain. Feeling trapped and desperate to keep his marriage intact, John agreed to pay the hush money. He didn't want his wife to find out about his infidelity, and he also didn't want to lose Zoe's companionship.

Samantha's popularity in school had skyrocketed after news of her family's lottery win spread. Suddenly, she was part of the cool crowd, and her old nerdy friends seemed a distant memory. She went to the upscale mall almost every day, splurging on designer clothes and accessories that she didn't even need. Her expenditures were piling up, but she didn't care. It felt good to be part of the in-crowd and to have the means to buy whatever she wanted.

Her new friends were always eager to hang out with her, constantly asking for shopping trips or nights out at fancy restaurants. Samantha loved the attention and the feeling of being included in something exclusive. But deep down, she couldn't shake off the lingering doubts about their intentions.

Were they her friends because they liked her for who she was, or did they only care about her money? Sam wondered if her sudden popularity was solely based on her new wealth. The uneasiness continued to gnaw at her as she tried to push the thought aside and focus on enjoying her new life. Samantha couldn't shake off the feeling of being used by her new friends.

In an attempt to fit in even more, Samantha decided to change her appearance. She ditched her glasses and got blue contact lenses to change her eye color. She also went to the salon, changing her hair from naturally curly to long layers with side-swept bangs. Her once-conservative style was now trendier and fashionable.

Her new look drew even more attention and compliments from others, but it didn't feel genuine to Sam. She missed her old self and wondered if changing her appearance was worth it just to fit in with a group of people who may not actually care about her.

One day at lunch, Samantha overheard a conversation between two of her new friends. They were discussing how much they loved hanging out with "rich girl" Sam and how great it was that she always picked up the tab for everything. Her heart sank.

As the school year ended, Taylor Swift was coming to town as part of her world tour, and expensive ticket packages were available for purchase on the aftermarket. Samantha immediately knew that she had to attend the concerts, no matter the cost.

She used all of her charm and manipulation tactics on her father, pleading with him to buy her the VIP tickets as an end-of-the-school-year gift. John, not wanting to disappoint his daughter, gave in and purchased not only one ticket for Samantha but four additional ones for some of her friends.

He couldn't say no to his little girl, who was now a celebrity at school and had become an avid fan of Taylor Swift, even going by the name Sam the Swiftie.

Samantha was bursting with joy as she joined her friends at the concert. They even had the opportunity to meet the singer backstage and snap some photos with her. It was a momentous occasion for Sam, and she eagerly anticipated the back-to-back shows in Los Angeles later that summer. The total expenses exceeded $100,000, but John didn't hesitate to cover it all.

John tried not to think about how much money he had spent on the concerts and instead focused on his daughter's happiness. He felt like he owed it to Samantha, and it helped him forget his feeling of guilt for cheating on his wife and being extorted.

As the months passed, the guilt and pressure of keeping his secret with Zoe began to take a toll on John. He started avoiding her calls and making excuses for not meeting her. But she was persistent, constantly reminding him of their deal and threatening to expose their affair.

John felt like he was living a double life. On the one hand, he had a loving wife, but on the other hand, he had this dark secret with Zoe hanging over him. He couldn't shake off the feeling that he was betraying both women.

One day, while out for a rare walk in the park with his wife, John ran into Zoe, who was out jogging. She gave John a sly smile and winked at him before running off. His wife noticed the exchange and asked who she was. John brushed it off as just an acquaintance from high school, but deep down, he knew that Zoe could expose everything if she wanted to.

Linda sat alone at the kitchen table, anxiously twirling her fingers as she awaited John's return. The house was eerily silent except for the steady tick-tock of the antique grand-father clock in the corner. Ever since they won the lottery, she had been feeling uneasy about their family's situation. Initially, it was thrilling to have financial freedom and live a luxurious life, but as time passed, John's actions became increasingly erratic and unpredictable.

He would come home late, and sometimes his breath reeked of alcohol. She thought she detected a hint of another woman's perfume intertwined with his natural scent. The thought made her stomach churn. Was he being unfaithful? Or was she simply overreacting and letting her imagination run wild?

She didn't dare ask him, afraid of the answer, or lack thereof.

He was spending less and less time with Sam, with whom he had always had a close relationship. Their daughter, typically filled with energy and cheer, had become sullen and withdrawn in her bedroom. Her father's absence weighed heavily on her, evident in every pout and slump of her shoulders. She would sit at her desk, staring at her unfinished homework with a furrowed brow. Or she would lie on her bed, scrolling through her phone without really seeing anything.

Linda heard the front door open and close, signaling John's arrival. He walked into the kitchen with a smile on his face, not noticing the tension in his wife's body language.

"Hey honey, how was your day?" he asked cheerfully.

Linda took a deep breath before responding. "John, we need to talk."

His smile faded as he sensed the seriousness in her tone. "What's going on?"

"I'm concerned about Samantha," Linda said, getting straight to the point. "Her behavior has changed ever since we won the lottery. She's hanging out with a different crowd, looks completely different, and spends money like there's no tomorrow."

John let out a sigh and ran a hand through his hair. "She's just trying to fit in, Linda. We were all teenagers once."

"But she doesn't need designer clothes or expensive concert tickets," Linda argued. "I feel like this money is changing her."

"She's just having fun," John insisted.

"And what about you?" Linda continued. "You keep disappearing during the day without any explanation."

John shifted uncomfortably in his seat. He had been using that time to meet up with Zoe and they still occasionally slept together.

"It's nothing important," he said dismissively.

"I don't believe you," Linda replied firmly. "John, I feel like our whole family is falling apart because of this money."

"That's not true," John protested.

"Sometimes I wish we never won that stupid lottery," Linda blurted out before she could stop herself.

Silence hung heavily in the air between them as they both processed her words.

She sniffled, and John tentatively extended an arm around her, "I know, baby. We will be all right." He didn't believe what he was saying.

John's guilty conscience weighed heavily on him. He couldn't believe he was cheating on Linda, the woman he had vowed to love and cherish for better or for worse. How could he continuously betray her trust?

One day, John reluctantly went over to Zoe's apartment when she demanded sex. As he entered the room, much to his surprise, Bill Matthews was seated on the couch relaxing in a robe and slippers, with a drink in hand. "Hey, John Boy, have a seat," Matthews sneered. "Let's play catch-up."

John wondered what kind of twisted plan these two had cooked up. How did they even know each other?

As if reading John's mind, Bill offered: "I was in Zoe's hot yoga class, and we went out for drinks afterward. We discussed you, our mutual friend, and put our heads together. Here is our first and final offer. We will leave you with one million dollars and want the rest of your money. Your initial thirty million dollars has been greatly depleted. You have expensive tastes with your daughter and mistress. And I must admit I am a terrible financial planner. And since I am confessing, I don't like sharing Zoe with you," he cackled.

"In exchange for your generous contribution to us, we will leave you and your family alone. Why would you agree to our terms? Do you want the press to get ahold of this story? Do you want your family to be torn apart? Think of your precious daughter. Zoe and I are reasonable people. A million bucks is way more money than you had before your lucky birthday windfall."

John was reeling from this unexpected turn of events. How could he trust either of them? Would they really leave his family alone? Matthews assured him that they were sensible people and planned to use their newfound wealth to travel or relocate to a big city like Los Angeles or New York.

The room was silent save for the chirping of birds outside the apartment. John had never felt so powerless in his life. He thought of his family, his daughter's innocent face flashing before his eyes. The thought of them being dragged through the tabloids, their privacy invaded, was too much to bear.

Bill smirked as he challenged John, "The ball's in your court now, John Boy. Are you gonna take it or leave it?" John felt a surge of panic and despair wash over him as he sat there, processing Bill and Zoe's ultimatum. His mind raced, trying to come up with a solution that would protect his family and salvage what was left of his life. The idea of losing everything he had achieved, regardless of how much was due to chance rather than effort, was too painful for him to contemplate.

John knew he had no choice but to agree to their terms. He had to protect his family, even if it meant giving in to the twisted twosomes' demands. Money was a small price to pay for their safety and happiness.

Then he changed his mind. He couldn't allow these two to hold his family hostage, using his despair as a bargaining chip. He couldn't live with the constant fear and uncertainty that came with their demands.

John, a man of few words and strong determination, had been pushed to his breaking point by Zoe and Bill's repeated attempts at blackmail. However, he had decided that enough was enough. For too long, he had allowed them to manipulate him and his family with their lies and deceit, but today, that would all end.

As they smirked and sneered at him, thinking they had finally conquered him, John's face hardened, and his eyes flickered with a dangerous fire. They had not expected such defiance from him and were taken aback by his sudden assertiveness. But John was fueled by a newfound purpose to protect his loved ones at all costs.

He reached for a pen and paper, his hand steady despite the tremors of anger coursing through him. With a cold glare, he wrote the number one million on the page. His message was clear: this was his final offer. Take it and get out of his life. He would not be blackmailed any longer, and he would do whatever it took to save his family. He growled, "You get one million dollars total, and that is it. You also agree to leave my family alone and never contact me again."

Without saying another word, John stood up and exited Zoe's apartment, slamming the door behind him with a resounding echo. His heart raced with a mix of dread, anger, and relief.

John spent the next few days in a state of apprehension. He had cut off all contact with Zoe and Bill, but he couldn't shake off the nagging feeling that they would still find a way to ruin his life. He knew he had to act fast if he wanted to protect his family.

With a determined spirit, John made some tough decisions. He fired Bill as his financial advisor and took control of his own investments. He also made sure that Matthews no longer had any control over his assets. Fortunately, most of the money was still in John's name only, so he was able to reclaim it without much trouble.

The two blackmailers were seething at how things had turned out. They reluctantly accepted John's million-dollar offer.

Zoe and Bill stood in her empty apartment, the echoes of the meeting with John still ringing in the air. They were both furious, with red-hot rage pulsing through their veins like venom.

They had been so close to ultimate success, so close to achieving their dreams. But then John had thrown a wrench in their plans, refusing to cooperate and forcing them to accept his million-dollar offer.

As they packed their belongings, Bill looked at Zoe with a look of defeat and frustration. "I can't believe we let him slip through our fingers like this," he said bitterly. "We could have had so much more if he had just cooperated with us."

With disappointment in her voice, Zoe nodded in agreement. "I know," she said softly, her eyes looking down. "But there's no use dwelling on what could have been. We just have to make the best of our current situation." They packed their belongings in silence, both lost in their own thoughts and regrets. As they walked out of the apartment for the final time, they wondered what might have happened if John had gone along with their original plan.

Zoe and her partner-in-crime relocated to a condominium in a different state, leaving John and his family behind. It was a drastic contrast from Zoe's previous modest apartment. Their new abode boasted lavish amenities, all thanks to the money they had obtained through blackmailing and stealing from John. They indulged in an opulent lifestyle, splurging on luxury cars and extravagant vacations. But amidst the glitz and glamour, a lingering sense of guilt weighed on their minds. They had betrayed a friend for their own selfish desires. Though they tried to suppress these thoughts, they resurfaced during moments of solitude. For now, they pushed them aside and reveled in the materialistic pleasures surrounding them, determined to savor every moment of it.

When Bill and Zoe presented their final ultimatum, John's fortune had shrunk from thirty million dollars to a "mere" eight million. The majority of his wealth had vanished due to a series of illegal activities, including embezzlement and extortion, as well as excessive spending.

Instead of fixating on the money he had lost, John focused on the money he still had. Eight million dollars was a fortune for most families, and he was thankful that he hadn't squandered all of it because of his reckless decisions.

John prioritized spending time with his loved ones and worrying less about his financial status. He took Linda and Sam on trips to various parts of the United States, showing them the beauty and diversity of their own country. They even embarked on a two-week journey to Europe, immersing themselves in different cultures and customs.

John also tried to attend all of Sam's volleyball games and tournaments. His daughter's talent and passion for the sport amazed him, and he was a proud father. He even started assistant coaching her high school team, something he never would have considered before.

John realized that money could not buy happiness or love. It was the quality time spent with loved ones that truly mattered. His relationship with Linda grew stronger as they bonded over shared experiences and adventures.

As for Sam, she no longer felt neglected by her father. She had grown closer to him than ever before, and she cherished every moment they spent together.

However, there were still moments when John imagined what could have been if he had managed his wealth better and made better decisions. But then he glanced at Linda's smiling face or saw Sam working hard on the volleyball court, and those thoughts faded away.

One day, while hiking with Linda, John couldn't hold his feelings back any longer. "I'm sorry for all the time I neglected you both," he said with tears in his eyes. "I was so focused on the lottery windfall that I forgot what truly mattered."

Linda smiled warmly at him and squeezed his hand. "It's okay," she said. "We're just happy to have you back in our lives."

John made his family his top priority and began using his remaining wealth to make a positive impact. He donated to reputable charities and established scholarships for less fortunate students.

Despite promising themselves they wouldn't splurge again, John and Samantha couldn't resist indulging in one last treat. The thrill-seeking pair embarked on a spontaneous trip to Las Vegas, the notorious city of excess, for a chance to see Sam's musical idol Taylor Swift perform live. As they strolled down the vibrant streets adorned with neon signs and buzzing with anticipation, Samantha slipped identical friendship bracelets onto their wrists to symbolize their bond.

"Come on, Dad," she urged, tugging at his arm with excitement. "We've got to get to our front-row seats."

John smiled at his daughter's infectious enthusiasm. He knew how much this meant to her and he was also looking forward to it. They navigated their way through the crowd, the energy and adrenaline pulsing through their veins. As they found their seats and waited for the concert to begin, Samantha couldn't contain her excitement, bouncing in her seat and singing snippets of Taylor's songs under her breath.

As the lights dimmed and the stage came to life, Taylor Swift emerged, glittering in a sequined ensemble as she sang her chart-topping hits. John found himself unable to look away from Samantha, who had a smile of pure bliss on her face as she sang along to every lyric.

When the first notes of "Shake It Off" rang out, Samantha grabbed John's hand and pulled him to his feet. For the rest of the concert, they sang and danced along to every song, losing themselves in the music and the magic of the moment.

As they left the concert, sweaty and hoarse but bubbling over with joy, John knew this was a memory he would cherish for the rest of his life. As they walked together hand-in-hand back to their hotel, he couldn't resist giving Samantha a squeeze and whispering, "Thank you for taking me on this adventure, sweetheart." He was finally at peace and could "Shake it Off."

At the same time, Bill and Zoe were jamming out to a Taylor Swift song while cruising down the highway in their sleek BMW convertible. As they blasted "Bad Blood," they brainstormed strategies to get a certain "John" to pay for services from a high-end escort company, Blackmailers-R-Us.

CRUEL CARD

The familiar chords of Bruce Springsteen's "Thunder Road" filled the room as two of the seven friends belted out the lyrics, their voices competing with the sound of shuffling cards. It was a typical Friday night for the group, gathering for their monthly poker game. But tonight was extra special because David Sherman, who attended an out-of-state college, had returned to join in on the fun. Known as Sherm to his friends, he was the only one at the table in a serious relationship with a steady girlfriend. He had been saving for an engagement ring for over a year, and his fund had finally reached $575.

Sherman was never a regular at the poker game, even before he went away for college. He wasn't one to take big risks and had a reputation for being frugal. He always split restaurant bills evenly and itemized them down to the penny, fearing he might be overcharged otherwise. Rather than splurging on expensive new designer clothes from fancy shops, he hunted for bargains at thrift stores. And instead of paying full price for a movie, he always opted for the cheaper matinee shows.

The seven of them, who had been friends since their days in school, shared a deep history that formed the core of their strong bond. They used to play various sports together, switching between football, basketball, and baseball depending on the season. This was before the trend of year-round specialization in one sport that started at a young age. On their regular poker nights, there was always a disagreement about what music to listen to: three of them were die-hard Springsteen fans, while the others couldn't stand him. The group would often debate over drinks about Springsteen's live concerts, with his fans claiming it was the best show ever while the detractors argued that his legendary three-hour performances were filled with too much storytelling and not enough music. After much deliberation, they came to a compromise about the music played during their poker nights. They decided to rotate each month, with one month exclusively featuring tracks by "The Boss" and the following month being completely free of Springsteen's music. The year was 1983, and tonight's chosen artist hailed from New Jersey.

The initial buy-in for the game was five dollars per player, a hefty sum for cash-strapped college-age students. If someone exhausted their initial five-dollar stake, they would curse and rummage through their wallet for more money to buy additional chips. Among the six regular players, two consistently turned a profit; two were unpredictable - sometimes winning, sometimes losing - and two were habitual losers. The worst player bluffed every hand, never realizing that adopting a "mixed strategy" of occasional bluffing, as recommended by savvy poker pros, would yield better financial outcomes.

The poker game found its usual pace, a comfortable ebb and flow of friends having fun and enjoying each other's company. They sipped on cheap beer, shared exaggerated stories, listened to music, and either cursed or praised their luck based on the outcome of the last hand. Each player held onto the hope that this hand would mark the beginning of a winning streak that would carry them through the rest of the evening.

Frank Simpson sat in front of the TV with bulging, bloodshot eyes and exclaimed, "Oh shit, it's Baker!" The other card players turned their attention to the screen. There, in all his glory, was Joe Baker appearing as a mime in a state lottery commercial. And sitting to the right of the current dealer was the very same Joe Baker, watching himself with his friends. The room filled with jeers and laughter as everyone poked fun at him. Despite being a talented young actor with a handful of commercials and small movie roles under his belt at just 22 years old, Baker took the good-natured teasing from his friends in stride.

"Hey, what's with the black and white outfit?"

"Did they hire you for your voice or just because you look good in stripes?"

"I thought this was supposed to be a musical. Then you showed up, and they had to change the whole thing."

"So, did they pay you in cash or lottery tickets?"

Baker chuckled and admitted that it was his first time seeing the commercial. He had filmed it about a month ago in Vancouver, Canada.

A spirited debate erupted without warning, like a volcano spewing molten lava. It began with Sherman questioning the optics of filming a Washington State lottery commercial in a foreign country. The discussion quickly turned into a full-blown debate about the state of Washington's film industry.

"I just don't understand why they insist on filming everything in Vancouver," said Baker. "Seattle has plenty of talented filmmakers and beautiful locations. Why not support our own communities and economy?"

"But Canada offers better tax incentives," countered Sherm, an econ major. "And the urban terrain in Vancouver is similar enough to Seattle to pass as the real thing. It's a win-win for the film industry."

"But at what cost to our identity?" Baker shot back. "We're losing our sense of place and becoming just another city in the background of some Hollywood production. It's not worth it."

The two continued their playful banter, and the rest watched with entertainment. Soon other poker players took sides, chiming in with their opinions and thoughts on the subject. It was a familiar sight that often occurred during poker nights, where topical discussions would arise only to be forgotten moments later.

The most popular game was always Kings, a split game where the pot is divided between the player with the best traditional hand (known as the high hand) and the player with the low hand. At the end of the game, players must declare their hand (no chips for low, one chip for high, two chips for both). Seven cards are dealt to each player, with the first two and last card dealt face down and cards three through six dealt face up. If a king appears face up, the player automatically goes "high" and does not have to declare their hand.

Whenever it was Fred Willis's turn to deal, he always opted for his quirky game, "follow the 2, 6, 8." This was a game of his own creation. Two initial cards were dealt face down, followed by cards three to seven dealt face up. The card that followed the last 2, 6, or 8 dealt face up became the wild card. His game announcement always elicited groans from the group, as winning this game depended entirely on luck, the wild card changing so frequently that it seemed like a chameleon on caffeine.

The dealer changed every hand, and it was their responsibility to choose the game for that round. Throughout the evening, they selected a variety of games, ranging from classic options to more unique ones. The players were well-versed in various forms of poker, each with its own intriguing moniker, such as Baseball, High Chicago, Stud Poker, and Anaconda.

The poker game was in full swing. Chips clicked and clacked as they changed hands, a mesmerizing display of towers in varying shades of blue, red, and white scattered across the green table. The players were a motley crew dressed in casual attire, but all with a glint of competitiveness in their eyes. Beer bottles were scattered among the chips, adding to the vibrant energy of the room. The air was thick with smoke, laughter, and the occasional curse when a player lost a hand. It was a familiar poker night scene.

As the night progressed, bluffs were called, bets were raised, and the occasional audible gasp could be heard as the community and wild cards were revealed. The "regular" card game ended after four hours, and the players cashed in their chips. The night had gone according to plan: the usual winners celebrated their victories while the predicted losers accepted defeat. Two players walked away with twenty dollars each; one earned ten dollars, and another five, while three others faced losses of twenty, twenty, and fifteen dollars, respectively. With the four-hour Springsteen poker jam session wrapped up, it was time for the encore - dealing hands in the popular game of Acey-Deucey.

Known as "In-Between," this game begins with each player contributing one dollar to the pot. Then, two cards are dealt face-up, and the player can bet any amount up to the limit set for the pot. If the third card drawn falls in between the first two cards, the player wins their bet plus an equal amount from the pot. However, if the third card does not fall in between, the player loses their bet, which is then added to the pot. If the third card matches either of the first two cards, the player must double their initial bet and add that amount to the pot. The game is simple and uses a regular deck of 52 cards without any jokers, with ranks as follows:

A (high), K, Q, J, 10, 9, 8, 7, 6, 5, 4, 3, 2.

The best opening two-card combination is "Acey-Deucey" (Ace and 2). This combination often encourages players to bet all of the money in the pot. Once someone wins all the money, each player contributes another dollar, and a new round begins with the betting order rotating among the participants at the table. Typically, this game is played for fun and serves as a casual form of entertainment rather than a serious gambling opportunity. The pot rarely grows large before being emptied by a daring player who bets everything after receiving favorable initial cards. In contrast, this game can also result in players losing their hard-earned winnings from previous poker sessions based on pure luck rather than skill. However, it offers frequent poker losers a chance to recover some losses or even make a small profit.

The pots were emptied, and modest amounts of money were won after all-in bets emptied the pot. It was past 2:30 AM, and the friends agreed to play one final Acey-Deucey game. After the next pot was emptied, the card game was officially over. That is when things got interesting.

The pot had grown to $25 after some careless all-in moves and a series of mandatory minimum $1 bets made with poor hands, where the first two cards dealt were close in rank.

When it was the actor's turn to bet, he received a king-3 opening hand. "Pot it. All in," he declared, reaching for the pot just as an ace was revealed. Frustrated and angry, he tossed a crisp $5 bill and a crumpled $20 into the pot, gesturing wildly with his arms like a performer in an Academy Award-winning scene.

As a method actor, Baker channeled the frustration from his Acey-Deucey loss to fuel his future roles that required intense rage. Losing $25 may have been painful in the moment, but it ultimately contributed to his career development and held some value.

The pot had reached an impressive $50, and the once lively room now reeked of greed and anticipation. The once jovial conversations had been replaced with silent scheming and calculating stares. It was as if the group had transformed into a pack of cartoonish wolves, their mouths watering at the thought of devouring a juicy T-bone steak made out of cash. Fingers tapped anxiously on the table, and drinks were gulped down frantically. The tension in the air was almost suffocating, a heavy fog that seemed to consume everyone in the room.

Before the dealer could begin, the deck was thoroughly shuffled and then passed to the player on their right to cut. This new step, requiring a unanimous vote, had been added to the house rules a few months ago to add more tension to games where the pot reached at least $25. It was a way to heighten the drama when large amounts of money were on the line.

Next up was George Brown, a perennial loser on poker nights. Tonight was no different; he'd already lost $15 in poker and another $6 in Acey-Deucey. This moment was his shot at redemption. He silently wished for the two cards to be far apart.

Queen and Two.

"Pot it! Winner! Chalk it up."

Brown felt a surge of confidence, convinced he would walk away with $50, netting a tidy profit of $29.

The card flipped over as seven pairs of eyes eagerly scanned it to see its rank.

A King!

Everyone except George burst into fits of laughter, resembling a choir of hysterical hens singing along to Springsteen's "Jungleland."

The pot had climbed to $100, a cool Benjamin. It was the biggest pot ever - a surprising temptation and an epic conclusion to the night.

Next up was Richie Harris, whose name seemed to fit him perfectly. He was the only one at the table who came from wealth, courtesy of his father's wise decision to invest in two promising stocks instead of following traditional financial advice of diversifying. After initially making a modest sum from a start-up company that didn't quite take off, his father cashed out his stock options and put everything into these two companies. It turned out to be a brilliant move, as they saw incredible returns of 50 times their initial value. An only child, Richie received a $50,000 high school graduation gift from his parents.

He was one of the two consistent losers at the monthly poker game and never folded. It didn't matter if his cards were good or bad; he played every hand until the end, making bluffing an ineffective strategy for him.

The sound of shuffling cards filled the room, with the occasional clink of a glass or murmur of conversation adding to the background noise. All the attention was on the table, waiting for the next move. The cards made a soft rustling noise as they were flipped onto the table, followed by the collective gasps and exclamations from the players.

An Ace and a Two - the ideal starting hand.

There was never a moment of hesitation in Richie's bold bet. "I'm all in," he declared nonchalantly.

The dealer turned over the next card, revealing an ace of clubs.

The other players at the table were stunned as Harris calmly added two crisp $100 bills from his expensive leather wallet to the already sizeable pot.

While the rest of the group was focused on winning or losing during their monthly game, Harris didn't seem to care either way. He was content with just being in the company of his friends and having a good time.

The pot now stood at an astonishing $300 dollars.

It was David Sherman's turn to be dealt a hand. The dealer with a flourish revealed the top two cards from the deck, and E Street Band drummer Max Weinberg added to the excitement with a perfectly timed crash of his cymbals in the background music, giving the moment a choreographed feel rather than just pure luck.

An Ace and a Two - the perfect starting hand.

Sherman knew that the fact that the first two cards were the same in this hand as the previous one was purely coincidental. Each hand was its own separate event, as the deck was shuffled whenever the pot reached a value of $25 or more. Yet, his gut feeling told him otherwise. What were the odds of getting another ace or two after they had just been revealed in two consecutive hands?

His imagination ran wild as he envisioned the possibilities. The previous five cards dealt had all been either an ace or a two, a stroke of luck that felt like winning the lottery. And if the next card turned out to be another ace or two, it would be like hitting the Powerball jackpot - an almost impossible feat with odds in the millions.

Sherm knew that out of the fifty cards remaining, only three aces and three twos were left. He was suddenly thankful for taking that probability course in college. Math genius Sherman calculated that the odds of the next card being a winner were 88%, while the chances of it being a loser stood at 12%. A "pot it" winning bet would yield a $300 profit, whereas a loss - which seemed highly unlikely—would cost him $600. Unfortunately, he didn't have $600 on him and couldn't afford to lose that amount. An image of an engagement ring fleetingly crossed his overactive mind before vanishing.

Sherm had a reputation for being risk-averse and always playing it safe. Therefore, he would be expected to place a modest bet of $25 or $30. If he felt particularly bold, he might go up to a maximum of $100, but that would push his limits, considering his cautious nature and frugal tendencies.

However, the demonic part of his brain began to battle with the angelic part - the former urging him to go "all in" while the latter advised caution. The devil's influence ultimately prevailed, symbolized by its pitchfork with three prongs representing the first two cards and the soon-to-be-revealed third card.

Without giving himself time to reconsider, Sherman blurted out, "I'm all in! I am betting the pot."

A new Springsteen song, "Badlands," started playing in the background.

The dealer's hand moved slowly, lifting the card from the top of the deck. The soft rustling sound was barely noticeable amidst the hushed murmurs of the players gathered around the table. It was a moment that felt frozen in time, as all eyes were fixed on the single card that held David Sherman's fate in its grasp. As it flipped over with a gentle slap, the worn and creased edges were revealed, evidence of countless shuffles. Despite its age and wear, the colors remained vivid and eye-catching. The seven people watching intently couldn't help but hold their breath as they waited for the outcome.

The Ace of Clubs.

Sherman had just been clubbed in the head. He appeared on the verge of tears, blinking rapidly and glancing down before looking back at the card, hoping it had magically changed into a four. But it remained the ace of clubs - a symbol of good fortune, luck, and success in Tarot readings, often signifying the start of a new life phase. Sadly, this new chapter for Sherman involved paying his friends money he didn't have by depleting his girlfriend's engagement ring fund.

The stunned college student assured his friends he didn't have that amount of cash on him but promised he was good for it. He scribbled an IOU for $600 and tossed it into the pot.

His friends mercilessly rode him.

"Sherm, you are not leaving town until you pay."

"He's good for the money. We know where his mom lives. She can be collateral."

"15% interest if the debt is not paid within 30 days, compounding to 25% interest if not paid within 60 days. You are a math major. You can figure it out."

Sherman remained motionless, his defeat apparent in his empty expression. He paid no attention to the teasing around him and instead focused on the lyrics of Spring-

steen's "The Price You Pay," followed by "Growin' Up." In that moment, he went from being a Springsteen critic to a devoted fan of the Boss, a Bruce tramp. As the pot reached a record-breaking $900, four players took fifteen minutes eagerly splitting it among themselves like sharks drawn to chum. Sherman was not one of the lucky winners.

David Sherman eventually married his long-time partner - the same woman he had been in a committed relationship with on that fateful poker night.

Four years later, at their wedding reception, the newly-weds took a moment to enjoy each other's company. The reception was in full swing, with music blaring, people laughing, and the smell of delicious food wafting through the air. Nancy Sherman and her new husband had managed to steal away for a moment of quiet in a secluded corner. They were both glowing with happiness, basking in the warmth of their love.

Nancy's face radiated with pure joy as she planted a tender kiss on her husband's lips. In between kisses, she teasingly asked him, "Why did you wait so long to ask me to marry you?" Sherman softly chuckled, "I wanted to make sure I could afford the perfect engagement ring." While this was partly true, he chose not to reveal the other reason.

Unexpectantly, she asked about his nickname among his closest friends, "Ace." As he gazed into her eyes, he noticed an obscure Springsteen song, "Brilliant Disguise," playing in the background as guests danced. With a playful grin, Sherman told his first (or maybe second) lie to his new bride: "To be honest, I have no idea. It must have been in the cards."

PART 4
POLITICAL PLAYS

FUTURE PRESIDENTIAL CAMPAIGN I

(YEAR 2036, DAY 300, TIME 22:58:52)

My name is Ulysses S. Viewer, age 82, born in the Great American Postwar Baby Boom of the 50s and raised in the Great American TV Boom of the 60s. I am here to tell you that I am pleased with life in the 21st century. The ozone layer is a bit more depleted, and the resulting greenhouse warmth makes winter in Peoria pleasant. In a reversal of WWII results, Sony ultimately beat out IBM or Big Blue in the ultimate competition, the corporate buyout, to end all corporate buyouts. After an initial struggle, Sony's futuristic 512K HDTV (high-definition television) easily outdistanced the IBM PC, and Sony achieved maximum penetration (mp) of ms (market share, not multiple sclerosis). Sony's brilliant Operation Pay Per View Futuristic High-Definition Television (OPPVFHDTV) campaign reached a climax before IBM's IBM (International Business Machine's Intercourse Between Machines) strategy was fully inserted into the buying habits of frenzied consumers. Of course, today there are no longer governments or countries. Because there is no longer any government, there are no longer politicians, and the world's oldest profession no longer exists. However, as a kudos to the past and due to consistently large ratings as determined by the Instant Audience Analysis Indicator (IAAI), a  form of the archaic political practice of a presidential debate and campaign still exists. Show time nears, and the following may or may not have happened. Does it matter?

(YEAR 2036, DAY 300, TIME 23:00:00)

The combatants: John Kennedy vs. Ronald Reagan

The moderators: Frank Sinatra and Arnold Schwarzenegger

With his recently installed plastic vocal chord, Frank Sinatra walks arm in arm with Arnold Schwarzenegger, back from Terminator 134. Ol' Blue Eyes knew JFK well and had an intimate relationship with Nancy (Mrs. Reagan, not his own daughter). Arnie was active in Republican circles and was married to a Shriver, which is almost a Kennedy.

Suddenly, holograms of Kennedy and Reagan appear.

(YEAR 2036, DAY 300, TIME 23:00:19)

Terminator: Greenhouse effect?

Raygun: Growth...good, good.

Jack: Too much tan.

(Canned laughter)

Ol' Blue Eyes: What about surveillance? Mobs, Mafia?

Ronnie (Chomps on jellybeans): Well!?!

JFK: FBI=Hoover=Bad News. Therefore, I don't like... (pause) IKE.

RR (Thumbs up): A-OK for R&D, CIA, FBI.

(YEAR 2036, DAY 300, TIME 23:00:31)

Images shift. Reagan rides a horse while Kennedy sails a yacht.

Mr. Universe: Proposals. Give me. Now.

Images shift back to facial profiles of Reagan and Kennedy.

Teddy's Brother: New Frontier, great society, moonwalk.

The Gipper appears to be dozing; he suddenly wakes up.

Ronnie (Shouting, obviously agitated): I paid for this microphone!!

Jack: Yes, Mr. Reagan made a contra-contra-contra (IRAN) bution.

(More canned laughter)

Note: The holograms of Kennedy and Reagan are being watched "live" by a group of 10 people who are engaging in the outdated practice of human interaction. These 10 outliers are the studio audience. People have become very reluctant to attend events in person. Partly, it is the sheer electronic wonder and fun that staying home offers, but there are other contributing factors. The Latest Instant Audience Analysis Indicators (IAAI) placed HDTV penetration at 97% with an average viewing time of 42.33 seconds.

(YEAR 2036, DAY 300, TIME 23:00:38)

Conan: Any threats?

Raygun: Evil Empire!!

JFK: Missile Gap.

Ronnie: Commies...Welfare Queens...Well?!?

Terminator (With a follow-up): Solutions?

Gipper (Offers a jellybean to the bad driver's brother): Star Wars!

Jack (Turns down jellybean): Peace Corps?

(ЧEAR 2036, DAY 300, TIME 23:00:44)
The facial profile holograms of Kennedy and Reagan are replaced by images of Lee Harvey Oswald and John Hinckley, Jr. Oswald is practicing gun tricks, while Hinkley is looking at movie stills of Jodie Foster and professing his love for her, or rather for the character Iris in Taxi Driver.

(ЧEAR 2036, DAY 300, TIME 23:00:47)
Nancy's father (Crooning): The debate's over! Decide.

The hologram images begin to shift. Images of Kennedy and Reagan replace facial profiles of Oswald and Hinkley, are replaced by action shots of the two, and the process repeats. The images change every 1/10th of a second, and the viewers in SONYland begin pressing the RED (Rudimentary Election Device) button, the power stick, the ultimate modern voting lever.

(ЧEAR 2036, DAY 300, TIME 23:00:52)
(Reagan 51.2%, Kennedy 48.8%)

The image changes again, and Lee Harvey Oswald points a gun at Kennedy's temple. He squeezes the trigger, and a brilliant display of grey and red engulfs the viewers in SO-NYland. All the Ulysses S. Viewers recoil at the sound of gunfire and clean up bits of brain from their carpet.

The Terminator and the Gipper briefly go off script and debate over who was the better governor of California. Arnold and Frank walk off arm in arm. Ol' Blue Eyes sings, "I did it my way," while the Terminator turns and somberly addresses the audience, "I'll be back!"

(YEAR 2036, DAY 300, TIME 23:00:57)

The Dead Kennedys are piped into SONYland homes in perfect digital MUZAK clarity.

(YEAR 2036, DAY 300, TIME 23:01:00)

(Note: total elapsed time of 'campaign' - **00:01:00**)

FUTURE PRESIDENTIAL CAMPAIGN II

(YEAR 2040, DAY 300, TIME 22:58:52)

Welcome back to another presidential debate! My name is Ulysses S. Viewer, age 86, born in the Great American Postwar Baby Boom of the '50s and raised in the Great American TV Boom of the '60s. A reminder of the rules. There are no rules! The debate moderator needs no introduction. Welcome Arnold Schwarzenegger! Some of you might wonder what happened to Frank Sinatra. The Instant Audience Analysis Indicator (IAAI) determined that Arnie is more popular than Frankie, so the Terminator has eliminated the Ol' Blue Eyes moderator role. Let's start the show and welcome the contestants!

(YEAR 2040, DAY 300, TIME 23:00:00)

The combatants: Ronald Reagan (Incumbent) vs. Donald Trump (Challenger)

The moderator: Arnold Schwarzenegger

Arnold Schwarzenegger, back from Terminator 162, was the Republican governor of California, and the two candidates were also Republicans.

Suddenly, holograms of Reagan and Trump appear.

(YEAR 2040, DAY 300, TIME 23:00:02)

Terminator: Greenhouse effect?

Raygun: Growth...good, good.

Trump: Growth...good, good.

Mr. Universe: Global Warming?

Ronnie: Growth...good, good.

The Donald: Growth...good, good.

Arnie (Growing Exasperated): Climate Change?

RR (Consulting notes): Growth...good, good.

DT: Growth...good, good. Got the last word...I trumped you! So smart. Person, Woman, Man, Camera, TV...stable genius.

(Canned laughter)

Arnold: What about surveillance?

Ronnie (Chomps on jellybeans): Well?!?!

Trump: No Intelligence.

RR (Thumbs up): A-OK for R&D, CIA, FBI.

Trump (Chugging a Diet Coke): CIA=Crazy Idiot Assholes, FBI=Fucking Bad Idiots.

(YEAR 2040, DAY 300, TIME 23:00:15)

Images shift. Reagan rides a horse while Trump plays golf.

Mr. Universe: Proposals. Give me. Now!

Images shift back to facial profiles of Reagan and Trump.

Trump: Build a Wall.

The Gipper (Pointing a finger at the Donald): Mr. Gorbachev, Tear down this wall!

The Donald: Build a wall, build a wall.

RR: Tear down the wall, tear down the wall.

Trump: Build the wall. Mexico will pay for it.

Raygun: I will make a contra-contra-contra (IRAN) bution. You did not make a contribution. You did not pay taxes.

Trump: Fake News! Smart people do not pay taxes...Person, Woman, Man, Camera, TV...stable genius.

Reagan: I paid for this microphone!

Trump (Pivoting off topic): The feds took stuff from Mar-a-Lago.

Mr. Reagan (Straining to hear): Mary's Legos? Why would they take that? To build your wall?

Trump: Build the wall.

The Gipper: Tear down the wall.

(Polite applause for this heated, in-depth exchange)

Note: The holograms of Reagan and Trump are being watched "live" by 20 people engaging in the rare spectacle of human interaction. These 20 outcasts are the studio audience. The debate is another smashing success. The Latest Instant Audience Analysis Indicators (IAAI) placed HDTV penetration at 94% with an average viewing time of 38.45 seconds.

(YEAR 2040, DAY 300, TIME 23:00:24)

Arnold: Conan or Terminator?

Trump ignores the Arnold movie trap question and lists a few shows he has been in. Reagan follows Trump's lead and counters with a few of his own shows.

The Donald: WrestleMania 23, Playboy Centerfold, The Fresh Prince of Bel-Air, Home Alone 2: Lost in New York.

Ronnie: Bedtime for Bonzo, Naughty but Nice, The Girl from Jones Beach, Girls on Probation.

The Trumpster (Excited by the last 3 titles): I was in the Nanny. I did a nanny. Swap notes?

Raygun (Confused and starts shuffling talking point crib notes): Well?

Trump (Confiding to Raygun): When you are a star, they let you do it. Grab 'em by the pussy. You can be my apprentice!

The Gipper doesn't respond to Trump's offer. He has dozed off for a few seconds and then opens his eyes.

Trump: Sleepy Ronnie just woke…woke, woke, woke, woke. Wokeism bad.

(YEAR 2040, DAY 300, TIME 23:00:33)

Mr. Trump is pleased with himself that he has just introduced the moniker Sleepy Ronnie, adding to his long list of derogatory nicknames for opposition candidates including Crooked Hillary, Low Energy Jeb, Little Marco, Corrupt Joe, Lyin' Ted, and Crazy Bernie.

Trump (Sips a Diet Coke and blurts out): Sleepy Ronnie! Sleepy Ronnie! Person, Woman, Man, Camera, TV…stable genius I am.

Reagan (Munching on a handful of jellybeans): Agent Orange!

Trump is surprised by this turn of events. Ronald Reagan, with a reputation for being civil to his opponents, has just turned the tables on Trump by giving him a nickname that references Trump's strange hair color that appears orange in certain lighting conditions. Raygun has broken his own 11th commandment: "Thou shall not speak ill of another Republican." The gloves are off. This is getting personal.

(YEAR 2040, DAY 300, TIME 23:00:36)

Trump: Sleepy Ronnie!

Raygun: Agent Orange!

The Donald: Sleepy Ronnie!

The Gipper: Toxic Trump!

The Donald: Jellybean Man! Not-so-great Communicator! Teflon President!

Reagan (Likes this new name-calling game): Orange Julius! Groper-in-Chief! Cheeto Jesus! Teflon Don!

(YEAR 2040, DAY 300, TIME 23:00:41)

Terminator: Closing Comments?

Raygun (Enjoying a black jellybean): Well?!?

Stable Genius: MAGA (Make America Great Again).

RR: You stole that from me. I introduced MAGA in 1980. It's mine.

DT (In a taunting, mocking tone): MAGA, MAGA, MAGA.

Gipper (Fires right back): MAGA, MAGA, MAGA.

Mr. Trump realizes there are no longer countries, and therefore, America no longer exists. He quickly pivots by removing the letter A. He is pleased with himself and beams.

Trump: MGA, MGA, MGA...note to self, trademark that. Stable genius...Person, Woman, Man, Camera, TV.

Raygun ignores the Trump bravado and brings a small chimp on stage.

Mr. Reagan: His name is Bonzo.

The audience sighs. Reagan is always effective in using visual aids to connect with the viewing voters.

The Donald (Rips off his suit, a Superman shirt underneath): Buy my superhero trading cards and clearance MAGA hats on sale now in the lobby. Be the first to own a MGA hat.

Terminator: Decide now!

The hologram images begin to shift. Facial close-ups of Trump and Reagan are replaced by action shots of Trump golfing and Raygun riding a horse. The process repeats in a loop. The images change every 1/10th of a second, and the viewers in SONYland begin pressing the RED (Rudimentary Election Device) button, the power stick, the ultimate modern voting lever.

(YEAR 2040, DAY 300, TIME 23:00:51)
(Trump 51.2%, Reagan 48.8%)

(TEAR 2040, DAY 300, TIME 23:00:53)
(Trump 50.8%, Reagan 49.2%)

(YEAR 2040, DAY 300, TIME 23:00:57)
(Trump 50.1%, Reagan 49.9%)

(YEAR 2040, DAY 300, TIME 23:01:05)
(Reagan 50.2%, Trump 49.8%)

Reagan wins in a nail-biter.

Trump (Screaming hysterically): Fake News! Stop the Steal! No mail voting! Person, Woman, Man, Camera, TV.

Arnold: You're fired.

Trump: I'll be back.

Terminator (Trumps Trump): No, I'll be back.

Terminator forcefully removes "Superman" Trump off the stage while Sleepy Ronnie shuts his eyes and settles in for a long nap.

"Rocket Man" is piped into homes in perfect digital MUZAK clarity while the debate scene backdrop fades out and is replaced by a close-up of the Little Rocket Man, former Korean leader Kim Jung-on.

YEAR 2040, DAY 300, TIME 23:01:19
(Note: total elapsed time of 'campaign' - **00:01:19**)

PRESIDENTIAL PITY PARTY

2024 is a critical year
Vitally important let's be clear.
Presidential election should be about choosing a real leader
Instead, choice is limited to casting a vote for a bottom-feeder
Republican challenger is Donald Trump
A convicted felon, a fast-talking chump
Former president, voted out of office
A narcissist who should have taught us
Beware a man with a fake orange tan
Part of a plot, his master plan
All fluff, no real substance
Never discusses issues not once

Obsesses about "Stop the Steal"
Election was fair. That's the real deal.
Another staple is "Secure the border"
Make it happen that's an order
Fancies himself as a dictator
Or better yet "the creator"
Lies come in flurries, media runs a fact-check
Supporters say, "Who cares? What the heck?"

HAPPY 4TH OF
UHH YOU KNOW
THE THING

Democratic incumbent is Joe Biden
A simple man, not a titan
Years ago, a senator from Delaware
A common fact, people are aware
Now, an old man past eighty
Not all there, bar the door, Katie
Talks in a whisper, mumbles
Frequent gaffes, stumbles
Stopped midsentence during a debate
Confusion set in, couldn't think straight
Biden first presidential octogenarian
Opponents wish he were a retired librarian

Mental faculties continue to fail and slow
Growing groundswell, Joe must go
And be replaced at the top of the ticket
Time to retire and play games like cricket

Trump is equally forgetful and elderly
Both men routinely go to bed early
Neither of the two has stamina
Both nod off - easy to imagine a
Presidential debate highlighted by snores
Biden's mind vacant, Trump dreams of whores
How can a great nation of millions
Nominate these two unremarkable civilians
One will become the leader of the free world
Most agree the scenario is crazy, absurd
Plenty of other qualified people to choose from
Instead, the choices leave perplexed voters glum

There is another option, another choice

Don't get excited, no need to rejoice
The third-party candidate, Robert Kennedy
Is not like his father, this one's zany
Promotes conspiracy theories, anti-vax
Says COVID-19 attacks targeted whites & blacks
Mass shootings are linked to prescription drugs
Anecdotes are wild and lead to listener shrugs
Siblings do not support his independent run
Afraid his father's legacy will be undone
By this controversial figure running for prez
Ignore him, don't listen to what he says
With most of his family against him
His presidential prospects are grim
Dead Uncle JFK considered by many a hero
This nephew has no chance, a big zero

In alphabetical order Biden, Kennedy & Trump
Miserable choices all, a sophomore slump
Rather vote for Tom, Dick, or Harry
Imaginary candidates who are less scary
Than the real choices currently on display
Citizens protest and shout no way
Should we be in this predicament
This sucks disaster is imminent

Presidential campaigns are stuck in a rut
Dumb, dumber, and a complete nut
Who should one vote for given the choices?
How are we in this bind cry out angry voices
Don't like any of them, who will do the least harm?
Any of them will do lasting damage, sound the alarm

Reshuffle the political deck of cards
Discard these three clowns send best regards
Give them a one-way ticket far, far away
So they can't permanently injure the US of A
Hope America survives election day
The skeptical public begins to pray
That the next four-year term quickly passes
With democracy intact, not reduced to ashes

Late breaking news Biden is dropping out
Key Democratic players demanded with a shout
President announces he's not running for another term
Many applaud the decision while others squirm
Replacement is Vice President Kamala Harris
Some are ecstatic while others say spare us
From another flawed candidate running
Latest development is sudden and stunning
Withdrawal decision shakes up a crazy presidential contest
This is not a routine test, different & wackier than the rest
Unconventional campaigns, a topsy-turvy race
If you want chaos, you are in the right place

Election day approaches 100 days away
November 5th is the exact historic day
Polls are close with Trump in the lead
One will win, the other will concede
If Harris upsets Trump that scenario is in doubt
Election was stolen talking points will spread & sprout
On podcasts, talk shows and social media
Repeat of 2020 election – read in Wikipedia

Hopefully divided country won't splinter in two
Conservative red army battling a liberal army in blue
Must keep United in United States
Citizens sharing meals rather than tossing plates
At one another or even worse firing guns
Future is sobering, an absence of puns
Where will United States of America be in 10 years?
Making progress or a once proud nation reduced to tears
One final desperate prayer for the good old US of A
That we survive the election, democracy's judgment day

PART 5
TRAVEL TALES

TIMELESS ADVENTURE

Thirteen hours in the air
When will I finally get there?
Embarking on a new life
Visiting my future wife
Lithuania the destination
From America, a distant location
Arrive safely and start the trip
In a good mood, start to quip
Three-hour car ride to a ferry boat
Landscape starting to look remote
Depart the vessel and resume the drive
Anticipation builds feel alive

So begins the great adventure
Drink some water need a quencher

Take a detour to Hill of Witches
Experience beyond material riches
Walking on paths is quite the thrill
Total contentment without a pill
Located on a forested sand dune
Wish I was playing a favorite
soft tune
Sculptures made of ancient wood
Never see these back in the hood
Characters inspired by folklore
Guaranteed not to bore
Gallery celebrates pagan traditions
No shock if an appearance of magicians
Freeze time never want it to end
Exit too quickly around a bend

Shortcut through a business establishment
Appeared safe, not a single inhabitant
Chased by a fierce German Shepard
Not a small dog large like a leopard
Bark, bark, bark, bark, BARK
Wish we could board Noah's Ark
Sprinting like "Bullet Bob Hayes"
Head spinning in a daze
Gaining, gaining, snarl, snarl
Surgery is a certainty; have to borrow
Visualize a long stay in a hospital
Times like this wish bones weren't brittle

The dog stops a foot away and yelps
Stopped by a metal chain which helps
Laugh later about the scary scene
Real-time shaking like a rattled teen

Walk past a fancy restaurant
Nicer place an investor bought
Couples enjoying their expensive meals
Conversations heard some closing deals
A small bird appears hovering in the air
A few diners begin to stare
In amazement as a cat appears
Next act will result in tears
Feline pounces in a blink
Bird paralyzed, no time to think
Tiny bird no more as feathers scatter
Diners wonder what's the matter?
Cat frolics away from the scene
Looks for another victim sight unseen
Proud of his performance
Certain of his importance

On the fine white sand playing frisbee
A fun activity that is free

At the border between two countries
Defined by written entries
A wooden sign in four languages
Each nation wants advantages
"Stop" in English, Lithuanian, Russian, German
Who drew the line hard to determine
Wild frisbee toss lands in Russia
Turn to my fiancée for a discuss a
Get the flying disc, or write it off as a loss
After a brief debate decide to cross

Two hesitant steps across the line
Feel a tingle down the spine
Border guard with a rifle
Giving me an eyeful
From the top of the stairs
Possible danger no one cares
Jump back to safety
Actions clearly brazenly

Observe the guard who retreats to hide
In a different time, we might be on the same side

What is he thinking?
Eyes steady unblinking
Stare to catch glimpses
Sightings rare, like solar eclipses
Two individuals at the end of the world
Thoughts pass, and silent words hurled

So many experiences, so little time
Mind is blank need a catchy rhyme
A highlight is the Hill of Crosses
Visitors cry, unleash human faucets
Canoe around Trakai Island castle
Pleasant excursion, not a hassle
Pray at historic church Gates of Dawn
Stop by soon before it's gone
View the famous painting Mother of Mercy
Take your time; don't be in a hurry
Saw so much could go on and on
Laugh and enjoy; don't dwell upon
Sites I may have missed
Will visit again and make a list
Money back guarantee that you'll be happy
Sound like a tourist guide, borderline sappy

Trip winding down must return
Joyful journey, an opportunity to learn
Lithuania, once the top country in Europe
A little-known fact you can look it up
Height of power in the 15th century
Rearview mirror, a distant memory
Top religions are Catholicism & Basketball

Latter more popular, a simple call

As decades pass
Advance to middle class
More material things abound
Worthless objects all around
Bought on a whim
Go out on a limb
The most valuable item
That I will describe to him
Are memories of a long-ago trip
To a distant land that made me flip
Recollections and experiences are real
Reasons to live make us feel

THE LONG ROAD

David eagerly settled down on a small wooden chair in the front row at Brill's driving school. Unlike most of his peers who signed up for the class, the boy considered today a milestone in his young life. He was fifteen, and his parents did not own a car. He walked or rode a bus everywhere. Without access to a vehicle, there was not an immediate pressing need for him to obtain a driver's license. But David wanted a license. It was a right of passage for a teenager, and all the cool kids drove. He signed up for the required summer course offered at Brill's Driving Academy, a more expensive option than the free course offered at the high school during the school year. He was forced to take the summer option; he was a varsity three-sport participant, and his schedule made the school driver's ed option a non-starter.

The curriculum was rudimentary, consisting of a blend of simulated sessions, low-quality videos, and the standard scare tactics regarding the grave consequences of teenage drunk driving or operating a vehicle under the influence of marijuana. Students were also expected to thoroughly review the 182-page State Department of Licensing handbook, stocked full of useless tidbits of information. On the first day, each student received a copy of the manual with a stern reminder that the written test would be based on its contents. Just like studying for a chemistry exam, preparation was crucial in order to pass.

Mr. Jenkins was the usual instructor, his monotonous voice acting as a lullaby for students to drift off to sleep. During the twice-weekly four-hour sessions of the six-week course, pockets of students would take turns dozing off. The academy introduced a new addition to its teaching tools in the second week: a driver simulator. The prototype did not accurately replicate real-life driving experiences, but it still piqued the interest of students who were desperate for any change from lectures and pre-recorded videos. This was during the era of Pong, long before video games could realistically mimic reality.

After successful indoctrination about the potential dangers of driving, the students were given the opportunity to sign up for their first test drive in week four. David chose the noon Wednesday session and was paired with Mr. Cobb as his instructor. As they settled into the car, a standard Ford with bold "Mr. Brill" lettering on the front doors, Mr. Cobb was distracted by a partially eaten wrap sandwich. David struggled to insert and turn the key, taking twenty seconds to start the engine. This should have alerted the instructor to pay closer attention to an inexperienced driver, but he was too focused on enjoying another bite of his delicious BLT sandwich and didn't notice bacon juice dripping onto his untucked yellow company polo shirt.

The car was parked on the right side of Decker Street, a busy two-lane road with a speed limit of 35 MPH. With a quick motion, David pulled up the emergency brake, and the amazing journey began. He pressed down hard on the gas pedal, causing the car to lurch forward and sending bits of food flying into the glove compartment. Instead of merging into traffic, the car careened across all lanes, heading straight towards College Inn Pub, a popular bar near the state university. David desperately switched between slamming on the brakes and pushing down on the accelerator. Mr. Cobb's eyes widened with genuine fear as he frantically slammed on the dual auxiliary brake. The Ford screeched to a halt, stopping just inches from the tinted front window of the tavern. The shaken adult shifted the car from drive into park and yelled at David to get out of the car.

The teenager followed Mr. Cobb's request, and the instructor quickly jumped out of the passenger seat in a state of shock. He appeared as though he had just seen a ghost. Mr. Cobb had a noticeable wet spot near his crotch, giving the impression that he had urinated in his pants. However, upon closer inspection, it was revealed to be bacon grease splattered on his clothes. "Have you ever driven a car before?" Mr. Cobb demanded, still shaking from the experience. "No," replied the teen. "Why didn't you tell me? Why did you start driving the car? Are you crazy? Are you under the influence of drugs?" David remained silent and did not respond to the instructor's barrage of questions.

A crowd had formed, and a few passing cars had slowed down to see what was happening. Why was a driver's education car parked so close to a bar, with the front end dangling over the sidewalk at a dangerous angle? And why was an adult yelling at a teenager outside the car? Mr. Cobb mumbled something under his breath and then nervously instructed David to get into the passenger seat.

The driving instructor silently drove them to a large, empty parking lot and instructed David to practice starting and stopping the car. Before allowing him to drive with the engine on, he had him practice pressing down on the accelerator and brake pedals, alternating between the two. Mr. Cobb was now in full Bengal tiger alert mode, ready to pounce on the passenger auxiliary foot brake pedal if necessary. The practice session in the parking lot was uneventful, except for a few jerky movements when David pressed too hard on the brake, causing Mr. Cobb's stomach to protest as the sandwich contemplated whether to continue its peaceful digestion or join a projectile vomit rebellion.

Over the course of a few weeks, David had six driving lessons with Mr. Cobb. They always started in an empty parking lot, where the instructor would go over the basics before letting the teenager venture out onto quiet side streets with little to no traffic. Mr. Cobb was strict about where he allowed David to drive, sticking to wide and peaceful neighborhood roads with minimal cars parked along the curb that could potentially lure David's Ford like magnets.

It was mandatory for every student to practice driving on the freeway at least once. Mr. Cobb had been putting off this particular lesson until David's final driving session, and he monitored the freeway traffic like a World War II general tracking the weather forecast before the D-Day invasion. Finally, they embarked on their journey with the student entering the highway through a simple straightaway entrance on the right and staying in the same lane without changing lanes. After a mile and a half, they immediately exited at the first opportunity. Despite being in a 60 MPH speed limit zone, David only reached a maximum speed of 48 MPH, gripping the steering wheel tightly in the "10 and 2" position. Oblivious to the dozens of cars zooming past on his left, the boy drove in his own blissful bubble as drivers sneaked glances to see who was operating such a slow-moving vehicle.

On the final day of class, David received his certificate from Brill's Driving Academy, signifying that he had successfully finished the course. Mr. Cobb offered a brief prayer and finally understood why some teachers pass all students to the next grade regardless of their qualifications.

David eagerly signed up for the state knowledge test without doing any preparation or studying his state Department of Licensing handbook. His confidence stemmed from his academic success in school, where he consistently received a mix of "A" and "B" letter grades with minimal effort. The exam consisted of 40 multiple-choice questions, and David needed to get at least 32 correct (an 80% score) to pass. Multiple choice tests were his specialty. He used the common strategy of eliminating obvious incorrect choices and relying on instinct when faced with uncertainty between the final two options. However, after only 29 questions, the screen announced that David had failed the test. Nine of his answers were wrong, and once it was mathematically impossible for him to pass anymore, the test ended automatically.

After failing the written exam, David had to wait three days before retaking it. Before his second attempt, he spent a few hours studying the DOL handbook to improve his score. Although he still did not pass, he noticed that he had done better than before. Out of 36 questions, he answered 27 correctly and 9 incorrectly. He also noticed that some questions were the same as ones he had seen on the first test, and he could easily answer them correctly because the computer displayed the correct response after each question.

After patiently waiting for the required period, he returned for his third attempt at the test. Unfortunately, he was cruelly eliminated after 39 questions when he gave his ninth incorrect answer. Once again, there were numerous repeat questions, and David knew that with the help of these bingo card "free square" answers, he would surely pass the written exam on his next try. Indeed, on his fourth try, he confidently answered 32 out of the first 37 questions correctly, half of them repeated, guaranteeing a passing score. When the word "Pass" appeared on his computer screen, David enthusiastically exclaimed "Bingo!" much to the annoyance and angered stares of those around him who were still focused on their own exams.

Despite his family not owning a car, David was able to borrow a 1973 brown luxury Lincoln Continental from his summer league baseball coach. In return, David promised to play on the coach's Babe Ruth league team. Other baseball teams had tried to recruit him, and David used this as leverage to borrow the expensive car for the driver's test. Nervously, David sat in the driver's seat, keeping an eye out for the examiner. A tall man approached the passenger side and signaled for the teenager to roll down the window. Following his instructions, David waited for further directions. "Please turn off the music," the man said sternly.

The speakers were blasting Bob Seger's "Mainstreet" at full volume. David always cranked up the radio whenever a Seger song came on; the Detroit musical genius and his Silver Bullet Band held a special place in his heart as they were the first concert he attended as a twelve-year-old. He could still vividly remember the band performing their hit songs while the smell of secondhand marijuana smoke filled the air and altered his impressionable young mind. As the instructor opened the door and sat beside him, David turned off the radio and watched as he scribbled notes on his clipboard with a #2 pencil.

"Leave the parking lot and make a right turn. Then continue straight."

Scribble, scribble.

"Get into the left turn lane and take a left. Continue straight."

Scribble, scribble, the pencil was getting a workout.

"Switch lanes and take a right. Now, take a right followed by a left at the stop sign. The driver's license office will be straight ahead a half mile on the right. I will remind you when to turn when we are close."

The teenager followed the instructor's directions as the author continued to work on his novel. He guided David back to the driver's license office and gave him his test results. Unfortunately, the teen had only received a score of fifty, falling short of the required eighty-nine to pass. The examiner took a moment to highlight David's mistakes: not fully stopping at stop signs, exceeding the speed limit multiple times, and failing to check his blind spot before changing lanes. Disheartened, the teen was informed that he would have to wait a week before retaking the test.

A week passed, and David was again sitting in the staging area. He had learned his lesson from last time and made sure to turn off the car radio. While waiting, he spotted the same examiner from the previous week approaching his car. David began to pray, "Please go to a different car and pick on someone else this time." But his luck didn't change as Mr. Pencil hopped into the front passenger seat to begin the driving test.

"Good afternoon. Today, we will start with parallel parking. Please pull up to the staging area and wait for my directions."

David let out an internal groan. Like freeway driving, parallel parking practice was a mandatory part of Brill's driving lessons. Mr. Cobb always took him to the same deserted parking lot and had him attempt to parallel park by backing up and aligning the tiny Ford with a paper towel on the ground. No matter how much effort David put in, he could never get it right. And at the end of each session, Mr. Cobb's words of advice remained unchanged: avoid parallel parking whenever you can.

Now, David was faced with navigating a larger Lincoln instead of the smaller Ford, and he could feel his anxiety building. As instructed, he pulled into the designated parallel parking area marked by bright red lines. Behind and to the right of the Lincoln were four five-foot yellow poles forming a rectangle.

Mr. Pencil gave him instructions:

"Parallel park the car within the four yellow poles, making sure it is straight. You may begin now."

David's heart raced as he slowly inched the car backward and turned the wheel to the right. He was doing surprisingly well. But then, as he started turning the wheel back to straighten out the car, his foot accidentally hit down hard on the gas pedal.

The Lincoln shot backward, knocking over two of the yellow poles behind it. David didn't realize it at first, but luckily, the poles were made of soft rubber and didn't damage the expensive borrowed vehicle.

Mr. Pencil scribbled furiously on his paper and handed it to David, informing him that he had failed once again and would have to wait a week before retesting. He asked if David had any questions before ending their short conversation.

David briefly considered asking if Mr. Pencil would be giving him an award for "Failing the Driving Test Before Leaving the Parking Lot" but decided against it.

Mr. Pencil quickly exited the vehicle and returned to his office.

The first driving test lasted fifteen minutes, and the second was five minutes.

Another week passed, and David found himself once again at the designated test start location. He had recently discovered that failing the test for a third time would result in a month-long waiting period instead of just one week. From twenty feet away, he immediately recognized Mr. Pencil, the fast-moving instructor heading straight to the borrowed Lincoln.

"Hello yet again. We are going to start with parallel parking. Pull up to the staging area like last time and park your vehicle within the four yellow poles."

David proceeded with the parallel parking part of the overall driver's exam. With careful precision, he slowly reversed the car and skillfully positioned it perfectly between the four yellow poles.

He immediately noticed that the pencil was inactive.

Emboldened by his accomplishment, he drove better in the next thirty minutes than ever before. Mr. Pencil occasionally scribbled a note, but it was more of a quick grocery store shopping list reminder on a sticky note than an epic novel like War and Peace.

The enthusiastic teenager parked the car and awaited the test result.

"Congratulations, you've passed. You can now get your photo taken for your driver's license."

David proudly walked into the driver's license office, fully aware that he had transformed from a passive passenger "follower" to a "leader," the one calling the shots behind the wheel and sitting in the driver's seat.

BUS TRIPPIN'

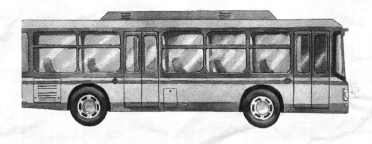

Parents didn't own a car
Some might find that bizarre
Choice was either bus or walk
No debate, no need to talk
Time to ride a Metro bus
No need to make a fuss

Time period Early Seventies
Has a fair share of devotees
Wait impatiently at the stop
Starts to sprinkle, hit by a raindrop
Nearby is Cowen Park
Never walk there after dark
Board in the neighborhood of Ravenna
Find with Seattle city map or human antenna

Did I miss the vehicle?
If so, breathe deeply and act civil
Schedules are never precise
Early or late once or twice
Another bus will come eventually
Driver doesn't do it intentionally
Waiting costs you up to an hour of time
A minor inconvenience, not a crime

In the distance, see the ride approach
Man boards first muttering words of reproach
Reuse transfers to save money
Counting coins isn't funny
Transfer letter of the day is R
Envy families with a car
7 Rainier is a long route
Settle in for excitement, no doubt

Ride begins in the U District
Return by nine parents strict
On the right is Hasty Tasty
Eating there makes one hasty
On the left is the Squire Shop
Selling bell-bottom jeans sure to flop
On the right is Tower Records
People enter wearing blue jean chords
Buying LPs like Frampton Comes Alive!
Sidewalks bustling like a beehive

Continue straight on Eastlake
Riding too long need a break

Briefly close my eyes
Falling asleep unwise
Shady characters riding
Hope no arguments or colliding
Bus driver remains patient
Always alert, never complacent

Hang a right on Stewart
Giant pothole no one hurt
Overhead is the Monorail
Near where criminals make bail
Next up is Frederick & Nelson
People exit shopping done

Winding down Third Avenue
Some riders worry about rent overdue
Passing the theater named Embassy
Films playing there show supremacy
93rd Smash Week marquee sign announces
A basketball gets loose and bounces
Movies playing there must be divine
Week after week, no signs of decline
Deep Throat is the top bill
Interesting title wait until

The opener, Devil in Miss Jones
Didn't know they were X-rated clones

Back two rows begin Three-card Monte
Lady being swindled resembles my auntie
20 dollars pass from hand to hand
Clueless "marks" don't understand
How they keep parting with their money
Raining now before it was sunny
Card dealers exit three stops later
An unstable guy prays to his creator

Bus stops at a stadium named Sick's
Miles from home - to me, it's the sticks
Rainiers and Pilots played there
Back in the day, it is true I swear
Bus finally reaches the end of the line
Only a kid but could use some wine

Time to reverse the route
Exhausted would like to shout
Bus making progress spewing diesel fumes
Decades later, global warming looms
Return trip seems quicker
Unstable soul starts to snicker

Arrive at my stop ring the bell
Stumble getting up and nearly fell
Jump off the last exit step
Had a temporary burst of pep
Walk the three blocks to my home

Adventure complete no need to roam

Now drive a fancy car
Sticker shock need a cigar
A giant, fully loaded SUV
Purchased on a shopping spree
Should be happy and content
Instead, most days feel spent
As crazy as it might sound
When I ponder and look around
A bumpy bus ride makes me smile
Memorable journey mile after mile

THE CRASH

Jackson's driving was starting to worry him. Lately, he had been driving erratically and struggling with his confidence behind the wheel of his late-model Lexus. He found himself having trouble hitting the brake pedal correctly at times while driving, and these incidents were happening more frequently. Just two weeks ago, he had a scary moment at a drive-up espresso stand where he accidentally pressed down on the gas and brake pedals simultaneously, causing the car to lurch forward and roll toward a busy road. In a panic, Jackson quickly hit the brake pedal and stopped just a few feet away from the crowded street.

A few days after this incident, he panicked again while trying to merge onto the freeway. His foot couldn't locate the brake pedal, and he slid past the red light on the merging ramp meter before finally pressing the pedal. Fortunately, there was no accident besides the damage it caused to his mental state. He wondered what was going on. Why was he reacting like this?

Jackson's usual confidence behind the wheel had diminished greatly. He used to be a cocky and skilled driver, but now he found himself leaving an excessive amount of space between his car and the one in front. He was braking far too early, causing a large gap between his Lexus and the stopped cars ahead in his lane. Other drivers honked at him and swerved around his car, only to cut back in front of him. This triggered a cycle of Jackson slowing down to maintain a safe distance, followed by another car playing the same dangerous game of darting and cutting off.

Despite his type 2 diabetes, he refused to believe that nerve damage in his feet was the cause of his recent driving issues. He started to have panic attacks and avoided driving whenever he could. Even a short four-block trip to the nearby grocery store in light traffic would leave him with a pounding heart and feelings of anxiety. Whenever he arrived home and pulled into his driveway, Jackson felt a great relief, knowing he could finally relax until the next time he had to get behind the wheel.

Lately, Jackson had to put all of his concentration into driving, which he found odd. It used to come naturally, and he actually enjoyed it. Driving was almost second nature to him, and he could easily cover long distances while listening to music and admiring the passing scenery. He used to feel at peace on the road, completely in the moment and aware of everything around him.

Those days were a distant memory. His mind was playing tricks on him, making him overly fixated on stopping in time, which only increased his stress levels. He narrowed his attention to his lane and the cars directly in front of him, holding onto the steering wheel with a tight grip. Every time he hit the brakes, it required a deliberate decision instead of an automatic reflex.

Weeks passed, and Jackson was on his way home from his eight-year-old daughter Sally's soccer practice. His daughter sat in the back seat on the passenger side. The sky had turned dark, and the moon illuminated their path. As they drove down a steep hill about a mile from their house, Jackson proceeded with caution along the familiar arterial road. However, as they approached the bottom of the hill, they were met with dozens of cars stopped at a red light, blocking both lanes of traffic.

Jackson attempted to decelerate by pressing his right foot on the brake pedal, but it seemed to have a mind of its own and refused to cooperate. Despite maintaining a reasonable speed of 25 miles per hour in a 35 MPH zone, the taillights of the car ahead were quickly approaching. In a split-second decision, Jackson yanked the steering wheel to the right to avoid a collision. The vehicle barreled through shrubbery for approximately fifteen feet before coming to a halt against a medium-sized tree. The force was strong enough to activate the driver's frontal airbag, indicating that the impact was akin to hitting a solid, stationary barrier at a high velocity.

Jackson immediately thought of Sally in the back seat.

In a sudden rush of parental instinct, Jackson flung open his car door and sprinted to the backseat. He quickly un-buckled his daughter and held her close in a tight embrace.

"Sally, are you all right? Are you hurt?"

No response.

Despite her loud, uncontrollable sobs, Sally showed no physical injuries. Other drivers exited their cars and formed a small gathering at the crash site within minutes. Shortly after, four police cars, a medical aid vehicle, a fire truck, and utility workers arrived at the scene. When questioned by an officer, Jackson stated that the car's brakes had failed. However, he couldn't be certain if that was the cause. All he knew was that when he tried to stop the car by pumping the brake with his right foot, it wouldn't respond. The officer then asked if he had been drinking, to which Jackson replied that he had not consumed any alcohol. After shining a light in his eyes and conducting a sobriety test, the policeman concluded that Jackson was indeed sober.

Sally stood mesmerized, her eyes wide, watching the chaos unfold before her. The flashing lights, bustling crowd, and bright uniforms were too much for her developing mind to understand. Emergency medical responders checked over the girl and her father, who both miraculously appeared unscathed despite their car being completely destroyed after crashing into a tree at a considerable speed. The officer kindly offered Sally the chance to sit in the police car, an idea that Jackson quickly agreed with. She was placed in the cramped backseat behind the passenger seat, usually reserved for criminal suspects. Jackson gathered a few belongings from their totaled car as the officer offered to drive them home. Their wrecked vehicle was then towed away to a scrapyard. To this day, Jackson still has photos of the tree and the mangled remains of the car, resembling a flattened soda can under a heavy boot.

In the aftermath of the accident, he found himself praying more often, grateful that Sally had emerged without any injuries or lasting effects.. She was a bright and cheerful child, excelling in all areas of her life - academics, social interactions, and sports. As an honor roll student with straight A's, she was well-liked by her peers and a star player on her elite soccer team.

He purchased a new Subaru primarily for its advanced safety features, and with great caution, he ventured back onto the road. His nerves were even more on edge than before the accident, causing him to stop at least a quarter of a football field away from any stop sign or red light. For some unknown reason, he felt more comfortable stopping behind another car than being the first at a traffic signal. When faced with these situations, he would either brake suddenly well before the sign or awkwardly drift past it by a couple of yards.

Desperate to improve his driving skills, he shelled out over a hundred dollars for a simulator session at a driving school. However, the constant motion of the simulation made him feel queasy and disoriented, and he could only endure thirty minutes before calling it quits. The instructor quickly noticed his habit of abruptly releasing the brake pedal before vigorously pressing down again, resulting in jerky and unpredictable movements. Jackson was urged to adopt a smoother and more gradual approach when transitioning between the accelerator and brake, and he absorbed this logical advice like an eager apprentice studying under Leonardo da Vinci himself.

Before the car crash, Jackson had always been a cautious driver. However, the accident shifted his driving habits to a nearly paranoid level of caution. He went out of his way to avoid the hill where the incident occurred, even though it was actually the safer and more efficient route. For nine months afterward, he stuck to this longer path, avoiding that stretch of road at all costs.

Soon after, something strange happened. Jackson noticed, almost as if by accident, that his driving had returned to normal. There was no gradual progression; rather, one day he realized he was no longer gripping the steering wheel tightly or expecting an imminent crash.

It was like a spell had been lifted, and his "mojo" had returned. He could drive without fear, without hesitation. And for the first time since the accident, he retraced the route where it all had happened. He passed by the spot where the Lexus had rammed into the tree, and instead of shuddering, he felt a sense of relief wash over him. The accident was still a part of his past, but it no longer controlled him.

It was late in the evening when Jackson noticed a piece of paper lying on the dining room table. He immediately recognized it as one of Sally's homework assignments; she had a habit of leaving schoolwork scattered throughout the house. As he read through the short essay, written in her handwriting, his heart began to race. Sally had opened up about her struggles with car rides after a traumatic experience.

"I shudder whenever I drive in a car. I have nightmares at night and sometimes wake up drenched in sweat, remembering the crash sound and the sirens. I hear noises and see lights in my dreams."

Tears welled up in Jackson's eyes as her words haunted his mind. He stumbled over to a nearby chair and collapsed onto it, overcome with guilt. He knew that he was the cause of her fear and suffering, and he couldn't shake off the weight of responsibility. He alone was to blame. For the remainder of his days, Jackson carried this burden, a living thing, heavy as a boulder and sharp as barbed wire, sinking deep into his chest and saturating his every thought and breath.

FUEL AN UNEASY RELATIONSHIP

Purchased my first car in 1978
A new relationship, a first date
An older model, a Ford LTD
Stands for limited strongly agree
Color a weathered cream yellow
Car hue designer a strange fellow
Negotiated sale price was $350
Resources limited, had to be thrifty
A Ford-able, a good deal
Hope it ends up being a steal
Car purchased from a friend
Kept a straight face, able to pretend

That the car was mechanically sound
And was sure to delight, not confound

Test drive time, let's take a journey
Accompanied by George and Ernie
Headed to the Puyallup Fair
Proceed at your own risk, buyer beware
Turned the key multiple times, no response
Mind drifts, transport me to the Renaissance
Plead, implore, appeal, cajole
Ignition system smirks, "Who's in control?"

Engine turns over and away we go
Merge into traffic follow the flow
Siren blares, see a flashing light
Cop pulls me over and begins to write
A speeding ticket for driving seventy
First time I question the car's longevity
This heap can't go that fast I protest
Don't argue officer knows best
Continue to drive down highway I-5
Random thought hope we survive

Problem with Automatic Transmission Fluid
Not a mechanic but something ruined
Steering wheel won't turn
Bad news, a major concern
Left or right turns are laborious
Car backfires, feels victorious
Engine chuckles at my plight
Battle of wills, must win the fight

Drive vehicle on straightaways
A new variable introduced, a beta phase
Need to use all of my weight
To make the turn exiting the interstate
A hard workout like lifting a heavy barbell
This temperamental vehicle is straight out of hell
Car is not manual transmission, an automatic
Nothing automatic, substitute erratic

After a 45-minute adventure, arrive in Puyallup
Car eases the final mile, a trot, a gallop
Parking lots full, all spots gone
Park on yellow trampled lawn
Give homeowner a rumpled dollar
House a dump, living in squalor

Return trip home less eventful
Memory clouded, sentimental
Take a right and carefully navigate the final hill
Car trip duration emulates a ten-hour flight to Brazil
Parking technique an adventure
This vehicle is a bitch need to censor
Wheels turned into side of the curb
Car likes to nap do not disturb
Park on a steep downhill
Made it home safe give me a pill

Month after month a test of wills
Car keeps track, sharpening its skills
Gallon of gas costs under a buck
Try finding that price now, out of luck

Car a proud hungry gas guzzler
Fuel gauge on empty, a puzzler
On occasion run out of gas
Vehicle and I are at an impasse
Outwitting the owner, showing who's boss
Should I keep the car or sell it for a loss?

Decision made for me one fateful night
Heard a big bang, a startling fright
Car rolled down the hill landing in a hedge
Final act of rebellion pushed me over the edge
Tow truck came as we said our bye byes
Much to my surprise tears in my eyes

Survived owning the temperamental Ford
A noteworthy accomplishment, deserve an award
Have owned Nissans, Chevys, and a Subaru
After a thoughtful review who knew
That my favorite car of them all
Is a Ford LTD that likes to stall

AIRPORT MISERY

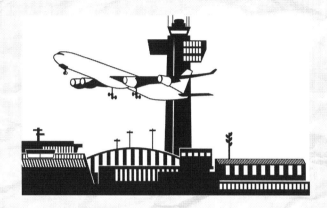

After a long and exhausting business trip to Boston, I couldn't wait to get back home. My contact lenses had dried out during the flight, causing my eyes to feel scratchy and my vision to blur like fog. As soon as I grabbed my suitcase at baggage claim, I dashed ahead of a couple to snag the last spot on the blue parking elevator. When I reached the sixth floor, I hurried towards where I thought I had parked my Nissan Maxima Sports Edition. However, it was nowhere in sight. Frantically, I scanned the two rows of cars on the sixth floor where I believed I had parked. Panic began to creep in as I wondered if maybe I had actually parked on the fifth or seventh floor instead. Where could my car be?

I tried to calm myself down and think logically. I was pretty sure I had parked on floor 6, but now I was starting to doubt myself. My mischievous car had decided to move its stall number to "stall" me from locating it. Determined not to let my car outsmart me, I decided to search each row until I found it. As I walked by row after row, pressing my key fob in hopes of hearing my car beep back at me, my vision continued to cloud. When I reached row F, I thought I had finally spotted my car from a distance. But upon closer inspection, it turned out to be a different model entirely. Panic started to set in - had someone stolen my car? Did I somehow miss it during my search? Exhausted and hungry, I realized it had been hours since my last meal - a quick "rubbery" omelet at the hotel. My rolling suitcase's bad wheel was only adding to my frustration. Why hadn't I written down my parking spot or taken a photo? My wife always reminded me to do so when we parked at the airport, but with our marriage going through a rough patch, I stubbornly refused to reach out to her for help. Now, I regretted not listening to her advice.

I swept floors five and seven and did not find the misplaced Nissan. There were 1,500 parked cars per floor, and floors 5, 6, and 7 were completely full. I had walked by 4,500 cars in all with no success, the vehicles blending together, a menu of Fords, Nissans, Hondas, and Toyotas as entrees, SUVs and Trucks as the main course, and sports cars as the desserts. I had been searching aimlessly for ninety minutes, and my will was broken.

I dialed my wife's number and quickly recounted what had happened.

"Did you take a picture of where you parked like I asked? I'm swamped at work. This is not a good time. Make sure your phone is on. I'll be there in about an hour, depending on traffic."

Click.

Seventy-five minutes later, my wife greeted me with a stern look and a quick kiss on the cheek. There was no "How was your trip?" or small talk; it was all business.

"Where do you think you parked?"

"I think I parked on floor six on an end row closest to the terminal side. But don't hold me to it. My confidence in my memory recall is not great. I am 95% sure it is on either floor 5, 6, or 7."

"Well, that certainly narrows it down. We will start on floor five and work our way up."

She drove her Audi slowly down each row on floor 5 while I pressed the key fob repeatedly. No luck.

Continuing our routine, we moved on to level 6 and started with the row closest to the exit. As we approached the end of the row, a familiar noise echoed through the garage: the high-pitched screeching of our Nissan. It was tucked away in a secluded spot, partially obscured from view. To my surprise, it was seventy-five feet away from where I originally thought I parked it. My wife drove up to the car and dropped me off before speeding out of sight. As she left, she snarled three words at me: "You are welcome."

As I sat in the driver's seat, her parting words and tone replayed in my mind. Exhausted and defeated, I unlocked the car door and sank into my seat. Weariness seeped through my body like a heavy anchor. I turned the key in the ignition, but the car refused to start, just like my broken marriage. I tried again, hoping for a different outcome, but the car remained stubbornly silent. With a sense of resignation, I leaned back against the headrest and let out a deep sigh. The battery was dead, just like my relationship with my spouse. It was official: our marriage was over.

SLOW TRAIN COMING

Dancing visions of a perfect vacation
Will be expensive could use a donation
First decision is where to go
Ponder options with limited dough
Decide to visit Los Angeles
Should be able to handle this
Next decision how to get there
Deciding factor is cost of the fare
By plane, train, or automobile
Evaluate options on the best deal
Find a colored advertising brochure
Read over carefully must be sure

Amtrack train name "Coach Starlight"
Cheaper option than booking a flight
Links greatest cities on the West Coast
Boost revenues and sales by including this boast
Claim not exactly true excludes San Diego
On numerous bucket lists, a must-go
Trip duration is an estimated 35 hours
A long trip better have arrival flowers
Scenery advertised as unsurpassed
Warming to the idea sounds like a blast
Book the train over the phone
Single round trip ticket traveling alone
Selection was coach rather than business class
Thought about upgrading and decided to pass

Depart from historic King Street station
If a train travels too fast, does it get a citation?
That won't be a problem as I quickly find out
Movement slow, tedious, sluggish no doubt
Seattle to Olympia takes 60 minutes by car
This train takes much longer truly bizarre
Tacoma, Lacey, Kelso, Longview
Start, stop, start, stop, bored with nothing to do
Why did taxpayers approve?
A train that can barely move
Wish I could cancel and hit the reset button
Feeling claustrophobic, walls begin to shut in

Cross the state border now entering Oregon
A single individual, a human pawn

In the transportation game of chess
Train chugs forward making little progress
Spend majority of time on the observation deck
This journey is making me a nervous wreck
No shower, no shave, feeling disheveled
This vacation adventure is bedeviled
Listen to forgettable songs on a Sony Walkman
Trip is taking longer than going to Japan
Musical selections include U2, Bob Marley, and The Who
Different musical genres accompany the view
Look out the windows at snow-covered peaks
Pleasant thoughts interrupted. Will this trip last weeks?

Meander intermittently through small towns
A mixture and variety of sights and sounds
An occasional glimpse of a backyard
How are these trains not barred
From having passengers view a private residence
Would buy that property with hesitance
Even saw a gentleman shoveling snow
Train barely crawling; some waved hello

Hungry riders cram in a dining section with no room
Plate crashes on the floor and makes a small boom
Squeezed next to five others at a table for four
A married couple and three kids, husband a bore
Socially awkward, welcomed silence
Words don't flow like a humming appliance
Food nondescript, bordering on awful
Don't even think about eating a waffle
Eggs are runny. Are they from hens?

Complaint survey skipped, there are no pens
Meal ends make a mad dash for the door
Walked everywhere with nothing left to explore

Train stops for hours on three separate occasions
This was not factored into any equations
Branches had fallen blocking the track
Passengers give workers plenty of flak
Next two times explanations were engine issues
Passengers by now running out of tissues
Some tired children begin to cry
"Why mommy, why, why, why?"

Passing through Mount Shasta
Breathtaking view this hasta
Mean that we are getting close
Not really get a reality dose
Approaching the Bay Area
Mood subdued, no hysteria
Sacramento, Oakland, and San Jose
City names bounce away like a ricochet
Song playing is "California Dreamin'"
Jukebox selector must have been scheming
No pleasant dream, more like a nightmare
When oh when will we ever get there?

Next up on the route is San Luis Obispo
Feeling jaded this town looks abysmal
Spanish for "St. Louis the Bishop"
Spanish to English dictionary is a "switch-up"
View before passing the town proper is a large prison

Some stories are overheard, tones of derision
Are any inmates planning an escape?
Perhaps desperate men convicted of rape
Is part of the strategy to hop onto this train?
if so, the plot was hatched by a man with no brain
This train is slower than slow
As I by now very much know
Better to remain at the correctional facility
Compared to this trip, there is tranquility
Referred to as a cushy "country club"
Food surely better than this dining car grub

Close sighting of the Pacific Ocean
No word properly captures the emotion
Majestic winter waves crash the shore
Attitude improves and begins to soar
No humans are seen, beaches are isolated
The only way for nature not to be violated
Just passed the city of Simi Valley
When will this ride reach a finale?

This trip has been hell no matter the cost
Just when all hope is about to exhaust
After testing one's patience to the outer limit
Negative thoughts turn positive with a quick pivot
It's not a mirage. There's Union Station!
Let out a whoop! My new favorite location

Here is a quick synopsis
Already started can't stop this
Plenty of time on the train to calculate numbers

Sleep is impossible, nobody slumbers
Trip duration 55 Hours
First thing needed is showers
3,300 Minutes
Every man has limits
198,000 Seconds
The City of Angels beckons
The land of celebrities and movie stars
First destination numerous bars
Will I ever ride another train?
Return trip in two weeks call me insane

THE HEALING KAYAK

The kayak, manned by a seasoned travel guide in the back and an elderly American tourist in the front, moved swiftly across the lagoon under a clear sky. As they glided, the visitor gazed up at the full moon flanked by Jupiter and Venus, and he offered up a silent prayer. Despite not being religious, he couldn't deny the feeling of awe that overcame him at that moment. In this foreign land, he was a stranger, but this experience made him feel connected to something greater than himself. It was a special moment in an otherwise ordinary life.

A year ago, the man underwent surgery on his left foot due to complications from type 2 diabetes. The specialist had alerted him to a serious infection that needed urgent treatment. As a result, he was at risk of losing one or possibly multiple toes on his left foot. The patient, who was 59 years old, was understandably frightened. He had never undergone surgery before, and his only previous injury was a sprained ankle from playing high school basketball. However, this current situation was likely a direct result of his chronic disease, which he had been diagnosed with two years prior. In hindsight, he should have sought medical attention sooner for his foot, but he feared doctors and hospitals. By the time he finally went to see a doctor, there was a hole in the bottom of his foot emitting a foul odor.

The man was stunned by the diagnosis and immediately scheduled emergency surgery. The operation was a success, but he remained hospitalized for four days under the care of various specialists. He was prescribed a strict diet and given horse pill-size antibiotics that were difficult to pronounce. Due to his weakened state, he needed a walker and had to prove he could navigate stairs before being released. For two months, he made daily visits to the hospital for IV treatments lasting 45 minutes each time. Driving himself there was a stressful task, as he struggled to concentrate on the road. Some days, he managed to park nearby, but other times he had to walk several blocks. He felt like an old stick man shuffling towards the hospital in small, halting steps. His movements were slow and cautious, reminiscent of a sloth. It was hard to believe this was the same person who used to be so athletic and agile. Gradually, he began to feel better and regained some strength. Finally, after two months of treatment, the nurses presented him with a graduation certificate marking the end of his IV regimen. Miraculously, he did not lose any toes or experience any further complications. His living in an urban region with exceptional medical centers and availability of state-of-the-art technology and treatments likely saved him from losing limbs or even dying had he been in a rural area with limited resources.

Without much thought, the man impulsively decided to go on a vacation to Mexico. He chose an all-inclusive resort situated between Cancun and Tulum and made reservations for various activities such as visiting Mayan Ruins and going on a kayak tour. Despite his lack of experience in kayaking and being in his sixties with no swimming abilities, he reached out to the tour organizers for assistance. Jessica, the tour organizer from Mexico, responded with reassurance that he would be put in a tandem kayak with the leader/ guide of the tour and could manage the excursion with their assistance.

The man was picked up from his resort lobby and endured a lengthy hour-long drive to reach the kayak departure point. Putting on the life jacket, he found it surprisingly comfortable. However, his tall stature presented a challenge as he tried to fit into the narrow kayak. He couldn't help but feel self-conscious as he struggled to get his legs in place. After some wiggling and maneuvering, he finally managed to squeeze himself into the kayak. The tour group consisted of ten people with three tandem kayaks and four singles. As promised, the tour guide leader was paired with the elderly American for the trip.

The guide, Hector, introduced himself with a sense of calm and reassurance. "Greetings, I am Hector. You can call me Hector, the protector. There is no need to worry, for this journey will be both enjoyable and safe."

To his surprise, the American proved to be a skilled rower, easily finding a rhythm with the kayak paddles. He pictured himself as a college athlete competing in the prestigious Henry Royal Regatta on the River Thames, crossing the finish line with a half-boat length lead. As they glided through the lagoon, he noticed that Hector was often relaxing in the back while he did most of the rowing. This boosted his confidence even more.

Today, the man had participated in two lively discussions about soccer, a sport that could be seen as either beautiful or ugly depending on one's perspective. Diego, the tour driver, was a fervent supporter of Chivas (the Goats), one of the top teams in the Mexican league alongside Club America. He took great pride in Chivas for being the only team in Mexico that exclusively uses home-grown players and refuses to sign foreign talent. Matches between Chivas and America are known as Super Classics and are highly anticipated national derbies. The rivalry between these two teams runs deep because they represent Mexico's two biggest cities. Chivas is known for its all-Mexican lineup, while Club America is notorious for bringing in top foreign players to win titles. Club America, based in Mexico City, is often associated with wealth and power, while Chivas, based in Guadalajara, is seen as a more blue-collar team. Diego has watched many Super Classics over the years and has even traveled to Azteca Stadium, one of the most iconic soccer stadiums in the world, which hosted two World Cup finals. Diego's love for soccer and Chivas was evident, and he believed that the local club brought the community together with a sense of pride and unity through the unwavering support of its fans.

The American and Diego shared a laugh as the tourist told a story about his city's mayor declaring their local club the best in the world after winning the Major League Soccer championship. They both knew that this league, which is considered lower in quality compared to European leagues, was nowhere near the level of teams like Barcelona, Manchester United, Bayern Munich, or Real Madrid. "Your team could beat Chivas 5-0 and still be considered the best in the world!" Diego exclaimed, causing the two to burst into uncontrollable laughter. They agreed that ignorant politicians can be found in many countries and are a universal phenomenon.

Diego's passion for soccer was a stark contrast to Hector's strong dislike for the sport, which was an uncommon viewpoint among Mexicans. Hector saw it as tainted by greed and corruption, with clubs and national teams more concerned about profit than their loyal fans. The unruly behavior of certain supporters, often influenced by young troublemakers, only solidified his disdain. Instead, he preferred individual sports like surfing, snowboarding, skiing, mountain biking, and skateboarding. The American countered that these activities were also becoming commercialized, with events like the X games drawing large crowds. Hector acknowledged this point but argued that there was still a sense of purity in individual sports. To him, soccer was beyond redemption - a corrupt and violent game fueled by greed. Like many debates, the truth likely lies somewhere in between; whether soccer is truly Diego's "beautiful game" or Hector's "ugly sport" depends on one's perspective.

The kayaks twice navigated through tight waterways, and the lagoon was occasionally populated with small crocodiles. Hector assured the group that the crocodiles posed no danger and that they were unlikely to encounter any of them.

The kayaks stopped near an island where hundreds of exotic birds were gathered in mating clusters. Magnificent frigatebirds, Yucatan jays, great white herons, cinnamon hummingbirds, orange orioles, crane hawks, and other birds with complex names sang harmoniously, serenading the human visitors on the water. As the day drew to a close, the tour group watched the sunset, a breathtaking fusion of red and yellow that would be forever etched into the memory of the American.

As darkness took hold, the kayaks made their way back to the starting point. Hector and the American paddled in perfect unison, maintaining a swift pace that required them to pause twice and wait for the others to catch up. Suddenly, Melissa, who was alone in her kayak, let out a piercing shriek. What had happened? Had she been attacked by a crocodile? No, it was just a flying fish that had landed in her kayak and was flapping around near her feet. After Hector and the elderly man quickly maneuvered their kayak next to hers, the guide calmly handled the fish and returned it to the dark waters of the lagoon.

The rhythmic sound of the paddle slicing through the water matched the beat of the American's heart, and he felt a sense of peace wash over him with each stroke. The lagoon stretched out before him, its tranquil surface reflecting the vibrant hues of the surroundings.

As they continued to paddle, the man couldn't help but marvel at the beauty of the natural world around him. The stillness of the water and the gentle light breeze all combined to create a sense of perfect harmony. He felt connected to the Earth and all of its creatures, and for a moment, he forgot about his troubles and existed in the present.

As the magnificent full moon rose higher in the sky, the visitor felt a surge of emotion. He gazed at the stars, glittering like diamonds in the dark canvas above. And then, he saw it. A shooting star streaked across the sky, leaving a trail of light behind it. It was a rare and beautiful sight, and he offered up a silent prayer of gratitude.

For the first time since his surgery, the American felt alive. He felt hopeful for the future and grateful for this moment of peace and clarity. As they paddled back to shore, he knew that this experience would stay with him forever, a reminder of the beauty and wonder of the world and the resilience of the human spirit.

BELLTOWN HELLCAT

Introducing the Belltown Hellcat
Puzzled looks, what is that?
Sit down and I'll try to explain
Story takes place in a city known for rain
If you haven't guessed the town is Seattle
An individual versus a community, an epic battle

As a young boy played with Matchbox car toys
Vroom, vroom, vroom he loved the noise
Soon graduated to Hot Wheels
A youthful crush, fell head over heels
For any fast vehicle, any hot rod
Became a member of the auto speed squad
Favorite movie Fast & Furious
An unstable teen, delirious

Grew up into a troubled adult
Spent time in prison, the result
Of elevator not stopping at all floors
Mental health issue underscores
The need for help, for intervention
A lonely man starved for attention

Soon hatched a plan, a clever plot
Let's make some money, why not?
Assembled a tricked-out supercar
Crazy looking auto, bizarre
Vehicle a modified Dodge Charger
Powerful engine one-of-a-kind, larger
Exterior custom painted with tiger stripes
People grew to hate it, a flurry of gripes

Hot rod the noisiest car in town
People pissed off more than a frown
Racing down block after block
Upload video exploits to TikTok
Makes money from online followers
Cash flows to auto shop owners
Opinions vary - a villain or a hero
For some a plague, a human zero

A speeding car, a motion blur
Cops can't catch, can't deter
Navigates streets downtown
Decibel level a deafening sound
Always ventures out very late
Drives crazy like on an interstate

Shake high-rise windows at night
Causes trepidation and a bit of fright
Tailpipes backfire with tremendous force
Sound mistaken for gunshots, what's the source?
Noise so loud it triggers alarms
Irate neighbors consider using firearms
Time to stop the out-of-control ride
Take matters into own hands cops letting it slide

People used to the ruckus of urban living jolt awake
An unplanned interruption, an unforgivable mistake
Downtown residents unable to sleep
Grievances increase, pile a mile deep
The price we are paying is too steep
When will city hall stop this creep?
Neighborhood alliance primes for battle
To stop a car racing in the streets of Seattle

Driver starts receiving noise violation tickets
What took so long? - silence, crickets
Renegade driver hit with citations and a lawsuit
Cheeky lawyer claims speeding car shortens the commute
Infractions increase at an alarming speed
Fines add up, a runaway stampede
Total eventually exceeds 80,000 dollars
Man cries out enough is enough - hollers
Goes to court hearing wearing a mask
Reporters wonder why, attempt to ask
Short response it's a matter of choice
Felt like celebrating, a time to rejoice
Judge does not reduce the fine amount

You must pay and settle the account
Admonishes man to take car to a racetrack
Curt response cut me some slack

Race car grounded in the garage
Feelings hurt need a massage
Belltown neighborhood residents rejoice
They finally listened to our unified voice
Until one day a familiar sound begins with a rev
A vehicle fine-tuned by a mechanic named Kev
The Belltown Hellcat is back in action
Auto nation is happy again, a smug satisfaction
Zooming down the street topping 100 miles per hour
Speeding driver rejoices, this is my superpower
Don't mess with me
The Hellcat is free

PART 6
NOTHING BUT NET SWISHES

BASKETBALL
TRUTHS

Talking Basketball
First you will crawl
Nerf hoop in the hallway
Keep at it every day
Practice in the snow
Learn the game flow
A buzz rising in the gym
Mad skills sound like a hymn
Transform into the "Greek Freak"
Develop perfect technique

Blasphemy but you'll say

Forget about MJ
Leave nothing to chance
Draft script for the "Next Dance"
It's a new kind of ball
No more boring stall
Those were the days of Rupp
Game & strategy evolve...what up?

Now it's 3's and a dunk
Keep bringing the funk
Bust you from the deep corner
Reduce you to another mourner
Up and down the court
Impossible to thwart
Keep up with the pace
If you want to save face

Defense gasps like fish
As I drive and dish
Boards and dimes
Make for fun times
My silky-smooth stroke
Ain't no fuckin' joke
My game is serious
Defender delirious
String music sounds
Other team frowns

Opponents stumble
Grumble, grumble
No need to talk trash

You've been reduced to ash
J from the logo
Time for you to go go
Losers again and again
Send them home to the den
To the den of pain
A constant refrain

Ball emulates life
Including the strife
Social media criticism
Leads to rigid cynicism
Pockets stuffed with coin
Feels like a kick to the groin
Nothing but mean glares
Everyone wants theirs
Mo' money mo' headache
Friends and family on the take
Why does the one with the loot
Always end up in a dispute?

Wish for simpler times
A kid and a ball
When a swish is a swish
No hands reaching out for more
Nobody keeping score

WIN TODAY DIE TOMORROW

Beckett Belmont sat in his usual spot, ten rows up at midcourt. He watched as his son Bobby, a freshman sub for Crestwood Heights Academy, lost the ball while crossing half-court. The opposing team easily made another layup, widening their lead to 60-22. Belmont's anger was visible as he yelled at the referee, "You suck, ref! That was a foul!" Beckett's outbursts were nothing new to the other parents, so they only gave him a quick glance before returning their attention to the game. However, the referee had reached his limit this time and kicked Beckett out of the game. Belmont strutted past the court, shooting a disdainful look at the referee. "Do you even know who I am?" he sneered. "If I want to, you'll never officiate another game again." Beckett seethed in his luxury car in the parking lot, waiting for the game to finish - just another lopsided loss for CHA.

Although not large in physical stature, Beckett Belmont was an imposing man who had made his fortune in real estate. He was one of the first to jump on the trend of flipping houses, and he was not afraid to use intimidation tactics to get what he wanted from politicians, contractors, and other businesses.

His life philosophy was simple and could be summed up in four words: buy low, sell high. This reasoning extended to both his business ventures and his love life. As soon as his wife started to show signs of aging in her mid-forties, he would trade her in for a younger, more attractive model. He was now on his third marriage, but he knew it wouldn't be long before he found someone new to add to his collection of trophy wives, as his current partner had recently turned forty-three.

Belmont saw himself as a decisive, charming go-getter who takes action and makes things happen. This mindset brought him to his current situation: sitting in his car, strategizing on how to turn the Crestwood Heights basketball team into a dominant force in the state. He could sense the adrenaline coursing through his body, the excitement of the unknown, and the potential for achieving great success.

Belmont was a basketball junkie often getting up early before work to play full-court pickup games at a nearby club. He may have seemed out of place on the court - a middle-aged man with a belly, wearing a headband, knee pads, and tattered shorts - but his teammates never commented about his appearance and lack of skill. They knew better than to complain about him because he was notorious in the town for being ruthless. Being a powerful and influential figure, Belmont always remained on the court no matter the outcome, whether his team won or lost.

The following evening, while enjoying expensive shots of straight malt at the exclusive downtown athletic club with his right-hand man Chase Clooney, Belmont declared: "I'm going to bring in some Black players who can hoop."

Belmont and Clooney were alums of Crestwood Heights Academy, a prestigious private school situated on a sprawling forty-acre campus. The school had a reputation for being elitist, catering exclusively to the children of wealthy and influential families. It was consistently ranked as the top high school in the state and among the top twenty nationwide. With its impressive track record, it was no surprise that all graduates went on to attend college, most of them getting accepted into highly regarded institutions like Ivy League schools, Stanford, and MIT. The education at Crestwood was renowned for its rigor and excellence.

With a strict application process, only 2% of hopefuls were accepted into the school. It had a lower admission rate than Harvard, and online forums were dedicated to discussing tactics for getting accepted. Even students with impeccable grades, notable extracurricular accomplishments, and glowing teacher recommendations were routinely rejected.

Beckett Belmont and Chase Clooney first crossed paths during their freshman year at CHA and became fast friends. Belmont was street smart, while Clooney had a sharp mind for complex problem-solving. After high school, they briefly lost touch as Clooney pursued a law degree on the opposite coast while Belmont launched his successful career in real estate. But when Clooney returned home with his law degree, they reconnected, and Belmont offered him a job, making him a key player in his thriving real estate company. In addition to handling crucial legal issues, Clooney took on tricky projects where he used unconventional methods to achieve desired results. While Belmont was the company's public face, Clooney played a significant role behind the scenes. Together, they formed a formidable team.

The two men, fueled by alcohol, huddled together at the bar, absorbed in their scheme to transform the Crestwood Heights Academy boys basketball team from chronic losers to state champions. The dimly lit restaurant created shadows on their determined faces as Belmont enthusiastically gestured while explaining his idea to Clooney. Across from him, Clooney's eyes glimmered with mischief as he eagerly brainstormed ways to execute their plan. The restaurant's upscale atmosphere exuded exclusivity with its leather booths and polished wood accents. As they sipped on their drinks, the sharp smell of whiskey wafted through the air, fueling their minds with possibilities. They discussed the strict admissions process and new diversity initiative at the elite private school. Their grand plan was taking shape - get rid of the current head coach and replace him with someone they could manipulate, establish a basketball academy for disadvantaged youth, funnel top talent to CHA, and gain control over the board of directors and admissions committee. Now, it was just a matter of making it all happen.

Belmont arranged a meeting with the Crestwood athletic director, David Atwood. The two were acquainted with each other but not on good terms, as Atwood was often embarrassed by Beckett's boorish behavior at basketball games. Skipping small talk, Belmont got straight to the point. He was a no-nonsense man with a square jaw and piercing blue eyes that seemed to see right through you. It was this directness that had made him one of the most successful businessmen in town. He had built his empire from the ground up with hard work and determination, and now he was one of the wealthiest men in the state.

"David, I want you to fire the basketball coach," he stated bluntly. "The team is performing poorly, and it's time for a fresh start."

"What?" Atwood stuttered, caught off guard.

"You heard me. Get rid of him before I get rid of you, too." Belmont's intense gaze bore into the stunned AD before he left the small athletic office.

At the end of the season, Coach Conroy was relieved of his duties. Crestwood Heights Academy would have a new basketball coach.

Belmont was well-versed in the local club basketball scene and had even founded and funded a team to give his son more playing time. Jerry Jones, a tough coach known for his no-nonsense approach, led the most prestigious local AAU program. Jones had a reputation for being ethical, a rarity in the often-shady world of elite youth basketball. Belmont wasted no time and arranged a meeting with him.

"Jones, I want you to become coach at CHA, my alma mater," Beckett said bluntly.

Jones raised an eyebrow at Belmont's proposal. He had heard rumors of Belmont's strong-arm tactics and wasn't sure if he wanted to get involved with someone like that. But the offer was tempting. CHA was a prestigious school with an unlimited budget, and Jones was intrigued by the challenge of turning their struggling basketball program around. After considering the offer, he declined.

Jones shook his head. "Not interested," he stated firmly. "My passion is coaching AAU basketball and working with kids. Plus, CHA's team isn't very strong, and the parents are elitist and always trying to interfere. I don't think it would be a good fit."

"Don't worry about the parents. I will make sure you have talented players on your team. You have my word," Belmont said.

Jones leaned back in his chair, considering the offer. He knew this would be a big move, leaving his successful youth program for a struggling high school team. But the challenge excited him.

"What's in it for me?" Jones asked.

Belmont smirked, knowing that money always talked. "I'll double your new school salary and throw in a few perks."

Jones couldn't believe what he was hearing. He took a moment to think it over. The extra money would certainly help as he was struggling financially despite all his hard work over the years. Why shouldn't he be rewarded?

"Alright," Jones said, extending his hand for a handshake, "you've got yourself a deal."

After sealing their agreement with a handshake, the two men couldn't hide their excitement about the potential of this partnership. Belmont was brimming with enthusiasm as he envisioned the impact they would have at CHA. "We're going to revolutionize things here," he declared confidently. As they said goodbye that evening, both men were filled with anticipation for what was to come. They were determined to turn CHA into a dominant basketball program, and nothing was going to stand in their way.

Chase Clooney, Belmont's lawyer and "fixer," finalized plans to establish a foundation emphasizing basketball. He created a non-profit after-school foundation called "The Future is Bright Youth Program" to assist at-risk middle school students. Belmont became the main supporter of the organization, not only contributing his own funds but also matching any donations received. The advisory council for the nonprofit included Belmont and his sister, as well as several other alums from CHA who were friendly with him and some prominent local retired NBA players. These former stars often appeared at the facility, helping draw top youth basketball talent to the newly formed organization.

The foundation targeted middle school-age kids by design. The only time Crestwood Heights Academy admitted students was freshman year of high school. Unlike other schools, there were no transfers in the sophomore, junior, or senior years because there was no attrition. On rare occasions, a student left CHA before graduation, but it was always for extenuating circumstances such as a family moving out of state or a severe health issue.

The morning sun shone brightly through the windows of the foundation's new basketball facility, "Belmont Court."

"The Future is Bright Youth Program" had just opened its doors, and a buzz was already in the air. Middle school kids from all over the city were flocking to the program, hoping to improve their skills and hang out with former professional basketball players.

Among these hopefuls was Sammy King, an eighth grader who had been generating a lot of hype in the local basketball community. He stood tall at 6'5" and was already ranked #20 in the nation by a prestigious eighth-grade national ranking service. His size and athleticism were unmatched at his age, and he was already turning heads with his impressive skills on the court.

When he entered the facility, Sammy's eyes lit up excitedly. He had heard about the new program and couldn't wait to see what it had to offer. And from his initial impression, it did not disappoint.

Sammy quickly made his way to Coach Jones, who was overseeing some drills with a group of younger players. Jones and Sammy knew each other from the AAU circuit. After fist-bumping King, the coach greeted him with a warm smile. "Sam, the man. What's up? Did you hear I am coaching at Crestwood Heights Academy?"

"No, coach. Congratulations."

As he watched Coach Jones interact with the other players and give them advice, Sammy couldn't help but be drawn in by his passion for coaching and helping kids improve their skills.

Everyone assumed that King would follow in the footsteps of his older brother, who had played for thc Carter High Bulldogs, the local central area powerhouse that dominated the league and state in boys basketball.

The Bulldogs, playing in their intimidating home gym known as the "dawg house," had a remarkable 50-game winning streak. Their reputation for relentless defense and powerful offense struck fear into their opponents. They were a force to be reckoned with and had produced several NBA players over the years. Crestwood played in the same league as Carter and had lost to them by 40 and 55 points the previous season.

King was handpicked by Belmont to attend CHA. Beckett knew the first step in the process was to persuade Sammy's mother. King lived with his mother and two younger brothers in a small apartment. His father had left the family when the boy was three years old and was no longer part of his life. Sammy's mother met for coffee with Belmont and Jimmy Cassell, a beloved community figure and former professional basketball star who sat on the foundation's board of directors.

Olivia King was a hard-working house cleaner who was deeply religious. She was her son's biggest supporter but worried about his lack of interest in school and the dangers of the nearby Carter neighborhood with its rampant drug use and gang activity.

As Olivia King entered the diner, Cassell stood up and warmly embraced her. Belmont shook her hand while maintaining eye contact.

After the three sat down in a booth, Belmont spoke first: "Mrs. King, it is a pleasure to meet you. Jimmy has mentioned your family before, and I must say that you have every reason to be proud. We believe attending Crestwood Heights Academy would be the best option for your son - he will receive a top-notch education in a safe environment. The basketball facilities are the best in the state, and the teacher-student ratio is ideal."

Olivia hesitated before responding, "I don't know, Mr. Belmont. Sammy is already struggling with school, and I'm worried about putting more pressure on him. Plus, isn't CHA an expensive school? And isn't it predominantly white?"

Belmont quickly reassured her, "Sammy will have all the resources he needs to succeed at Crestwood Heights Academy, including tutoring if necessary. The school offers financial aid to cover tuition, and they are actively seeking more students of color to diversify the student body. Trust me, CHA is the perfect place for your son."

Cassell chimed in, "Olivia, Crestwood is truly a wonderful opportunity for Sammy. You know as well as I do how unsafe our neighborhood schools can be. It breaks my heart to say it, but it's true. An education at CHA is like winning the lottery - it will open so many doors for your son."

Despite her initial hesitation, Olivia began to consider the offer.

That's when Belmont moved to close the deal: "Mrs. King, you are an amazing person and a fantastic mother who works so hard. I can only imagine how difficult it must be for you. I would love to lighten your load by giving you some money to cover your upcoming knee replacement surgery. You deserve it, and knowing I can help would make me feel good. I can also help you out with groceries and incidentals."

Belmont had done his research and knew the Kings were struggling financially, with Olivia unable to afford her necessary medical procedure.

"Mr. Belmont, is this a bribe to get Sammy to attend CHA?" she asked suspiciously.

"Of course not," Belmont quickly replied. "This is one neighbor helping out another neighbor like we are taught in the bible."

The room fell silent as Olivia and Beckett locked eyes, trying to read each other's thoughts. Finally, she spoke up: "I will think it over and get back to you." Two days later, Cassell told Belmont that Sammy King would be applying to CHA. Now Beckett had to figure out how to get the basketball prodigy accepted into the prestigious academy.

Belmont made a deal with the school's head, who promised to change CHA's admission policy in exchange for a significant donation. The revised policy would heavily prioritize athletics during the admissions process. After the new initiative was finalized, a small group of donors anonymously contributed millions towards a new state-of-the-art Performing Arts Center, which was actually funded by a single person: Belmont.

The admissions committee convened in the luxurious board room at Crestwood Heights Academy. Five individuals occupied seats around the lengthy mahogany table, prepared to deliberate on the latest batch of applicants. Two members had been part of the previous year's panel, while the head of school recently selected the other three.

Countless applicants were rejected, but a lucky few were accepted. Then, the discussion turned to Sammy King's application. When his name came up, one of the holdover members chimed in.

"I have serious concerns about this candidate," he said, flipping through King's application. "His grades are below average, and he has a history of disciplinary issues at his current school."

The other holdover agreed. "We have high standards for our students here at CHA, and I don't see how this applicant meets them."

Unbeknownst to the two holdover committee members, the head of the school had specifically requested that the three new arrivals assist with this application. King's acceptance was a prerequisite for Belmont's significant financial contribution to the school.

One of the newcomers spoke: "I understand your concerns, but we must also consider other factors when making admissions decisions." He looked pointedly at each of them before continuing. "As you know, CHA is not only an academic institution but also emphasizes a broad spectrum of interests, including sports."

"Are you implying that we should make exceptions for athletes?" a holdover asked incredulously.

"I'm not saying that explicitly, but let's just say that having strong athletes on our teams benefits everyone involved."

The other two new board members nodded in agreement.

A sour taste lingered in the mouths of the holdover members as they realized they were outnumbered. The bitter aftertaste of defeat lingered as they watched the three new members join forces to push the King application through.

The rigged vote was 3-2. Sammy King had been admitted to Crestwood Heights Academy.

Despite Sammy's best efforts, his freshman year at CHA was a constant struggle academically. No matter how much he studied or how much extra help he received, it seemed like he could never catch up to his classmates. He was lagging behind, struggling to keep up with the material that came so easily to the other students.

The school had arranged for Sammy to have a light workload and assigned him to classes with the easiest teachers, but even then, he was still struggling. Seeing everyone around him excelling while he could barely keep his head above water was demoralizing.

Thankfully, Sammy had been assigned the best student tutors at the school. They patiently worked with him, breaking down complex concepts into simpler terms and providing additional resources to help him understand. But even with their assistance, he still struggled.

Sometimes, the tutors went above and beyond their duties, crossing the line and doing most of an assignment or project for him. While it may have helped his grade, it left Sammy feeling guilty and inadequate. He knew he needed to put in the effort himself to truly succeed, but he still felt grateful for their help.

Sammy King adjusted to his new schedule at Crestwood Heights Academy. But in addition to his academic challenges, he had to grapple with another aspect of his new school: the lengthy commute. Each day, it took him more than an hour to travel to and from school, which ate into his practice time and left him feeling drained.

With his mom's blessing, King moved into a multi-million dollar estate owned by Jack Tanner, a close friend and fellow CHA alum of Beckett Belmont and Chase Clooney. The mansion was only a short drive from the school and boasted all the luxurious amenities one could desire - a stunning pool, a modern gym, a home theater, and even a private basketball court.

The opulence of his new home blew the teenager away. He couldn't believe how lucky he was to have been taken in by such generous people. His bedroom alone was larger than his entire apartment in the old neighborhood.

Tanner assured him that he would not have to pay rent or utilities as long as he lived there - it was his way of supporting a talented friend on his journey toward becoming a successful student-athlete.

But that wasn't all - King was also given access to an expensive Mercedes with a top-of-the-line car audio system. His teammates were amazed when they saw him pulling up in the sleek car every morning.

Moreover, Tanner also gave King "modest" amounts of cash to help him buy things like food and gas for the car. King couldn't believe his luck. He was living like a celebrity.

King felt a sense of pride and superiority as he drove around town in his luxury car, with its expensive sound system blaring his favorite rap beats. He would often swing by his local high school, Carter High, giving rides to his old friends from the neighborhood and trash-talking the members of the Carter basketball team.

As he cruised the streets, King felt a sense of satisfaction in his new life, which starkly contrasted with his humble beginnings. But even with all the material possessions and privileges, King couldn't shake off the nagging feeling of emptiness and guilt that lingered in his mind.

On the court, King was a force to be reckoned with. Despite being constantly double and triple-teamed, he averaged an impressive 24 points and 12 rebounds per game, single-handedly carrying CHA to a much improved 15-10 record under first-year Coach Jones. This was a remarkable accomplishment, considering the team had only won two games the previous year.

As expected, with its powerhouse lineup, Carter High School once again claimed the state title. But this time, their games against Crestwood Heights Academy were fiercely competitive. CHA lost by only six points at home and by nine points in the intimidating "dawg house." Despite the losses, King's resilience and determination had earned him the respect of his opponents and solidified his position as a young rising star.

King's stellar freshman-year performance on the court also caught the attention of college scouts, with several top universities expressing interest in recruiting him. For Sammy, this was the realization of a long-held dream. Ever since he first picked up a basketball as a child, he had been determined to play at the collegiate level. He could already picture himself on the court of a packed arena, demonstrating his talents for all to see.

Fourth grade was a pivotal year for King. This was the year when his teacher, Mrs. Roberts, asked the class what they wanted to be when they grew up. As each student took turns sharing their aspirations, Sammy's classmates listed traditional occupations such as nurses, doctors, lawyers, dentists, and even game designers.

But when it was King's turn, he confidently predicted "NBA player" as his future career. The other students laughed, and some even rolled their eyes in disbelief. But Sammy wasn't fazed by their reactions. He knew what he wanted and was determined to make it happen.

The youngster spent countless hours practicing and perfecting his skills. He trained with coaches who saw his potential and helped him hone his talents. He watched endless tapes of NBA games, studying the moves of his favorite players and incorporating them into his own game. The early interest shown by recruiters during his freshman year indicated that Sammy had the potential to achieve his goal and motivated him to work on his game.

When the admissions committee of Crestwood Heights Academy convened the following year, they were faced with a daunting task: sorting through hundreds of applications to select the elite few who would be granted entrance to the prestigious institution. It was a difficult and time-consuming process that had to be done with the utmost care and consideration.

As the committee members pored over each application, making notes and deliberating, two stood out above the rest. These two applications were moved to the acceptance stack without even being reviewed, a rare occurrence that only happened when a candidate was deemed exceptional.

The two candidates in question were Ty Ross and Hakeem Sampson, two highly sought-after basketball players identified by Coach Jones. He had spotted them playing at Belmont Court and immediately knew those were the players he wanted.

Coach Jones had discussed his desire to add these players to the team with Belmont, who then relayed the information to the admissions committee through his trusted associates. And now, as the committee members held Ty and Hakeem's applications in their hands, the two files were rubber-stamped and moved to the "yes" pile.

The two members who had rejected King's application the previous year locked eyes and sighed. What was happening to their prestigious school? Why were their standards changing? Why was academic excellence being sacrificed for athletic success?

At the first practice of King's sophomore season, Coach Jones could barely contain his excitement. The team had heavily relied on King's skills in the previous year with little support from his less talented teammates. But now, they had two new talented additions who would share the burden and bring much-needed relief. Ty Ross, a selfless point guard who prioritized passing over scoring, was a rare gem in a world where every player wanted to be a star scorer. Hakeem Sampson, an immigrant from Sudan standing at 6'10", was inexperienced but full of potential. Jones saw him becoming a defensive powerhouse, protecting the rim with his height and blocking shots while also excelling at grabbing rebounds.

King again struggled academically during his sophomore year, finding the classes even more difficult than the previous year. With each passing semester, his grades were slipping further and further behind. State regulations mandated a minimum of a D grade in all but one class, but the local school district had higher standards for their athletes, requiring a C average and progress toward graduation. To mitigate the risk of failing, King took the easiest courses he could find and ended up with 4 D's and 1 C, resulting in an abysmal GPA of 1.2. The school had a policy for students who received a C to meet with a guidance counselor to develop a plan of action and place those with D's or multiple C's on academic probation; however, these protocols were overlooked in King's case.

Ty and Hakeem struggled to balance their academic and athletic commitments as the basketball season progressed. While Ty maintained a 1.8 GPA with mostly C and D grades, Hakeem did slightly better with a 2.5 GPA and an equal number of B and C grades.

Coach Jones was concerned about his players' academic performance but didn't know how to help them improve. He knew that King's grades were far from acceptable, but he didn't want to risk losing his star player by pushing him too hard academically.

By the end of King's sophomore year, the school administration faced a dilemma. They had always prided themselves on their high academic standards and successful student-athletes, but now they were struggling to maintain those standards.

As a school administrator reviewed the basketball team's academic performance for the upcoming state awards competition, she came across an oddity. The grading system refused to accept the team's grades. After delving deeper into the issue, she discovered that the minimum requirement for eligibility was a team average GPA of 3.0. To her disappointment, the basketball team had fallen below this standard with their current average of 2.6 - their lowest score since the competition began.

Coach Jones had accurately picked out two talented freshmen players who would instantly contribute and greatly improve CHA's basketball team. They ended the season with an impressive record of 23-4 and split the regular season games with Carter, each winning on their home court. This was the first time that Carter High School had ever lost to Crestwood Heights Academy. In the winning game against his neighborhood high school for which his brother had starred, King proved unstoppable, scoring 32 points and grabbing 15 rebounds. Ross also made a significant contribution with 9 assists, while Sampson showcased his all-around skills with 8 points, 12 rebounds, and 3 blocked shots. Thanks to these standout performers, CHA made it to the state tournament for the first time in over twenty years but unfortunately lost by a narrow margin to Roosevelt High School, a talented team from the state's eastern half.

King's junior year brought lofty expectations as the team aimed for the state championship. While Carter remained the favorite, pre-season polls ranked Crestwood second in the state. After quickly being approved by the admissions committee, CHA added a pair of twins to their basketball team, Lodrick and Rodrick Anderson. Both were talented 6'4" players with all-around games. Ironically, Lodrick was a right-handed shooter while Rodrick was left-handed. The two twins were identical and had gregarious personalities. Coach Jones was excited to have the Anderson twins on the team as they brought much-needed height and skill to the roster. CHA's chances of winning the state championship increased significantly with their addition.

The starting line-up was stacked with five talented African American players, led by an African American coach. However, there was a noticeable drop-off between the starters and bench players, who were all white. Senior Bobby Belmont, known for his shooting prowess but lacking in speed, was the first player off the bench. Coach Jones had a short rotation, keeping the starters on the court as long as possible in close games and giving Bobby ample playing time in lopsided games to appease his benefactor, Beckett.

With King, Ross, Sampson, and now the Anderson twins, CHA dominated the competition, beating Carter twice during the regular season. The Crestwood win on Carter's home court was especially memorable as Belmont celebrated late in the game by screaming, "We POUNDED you in your own DOG POUND." To top it off, he proceeded to bark like an angry German Shepard, much to the crowd's amusement. The twins quickly became fan favorites with their flashy dunks and acrobatic layups. The team finished the regular season undefeated for the first time in school history.

Coach Jones was confident that this was the strongest team he had ever coached at CHA. With five talented starters blessed with unique skill sets, the line-up was formidable, and the entire team exuded a sense of self-assurance as they entered the postseason. Their first opponent in the playoffs was Roosevelt High School, an intimidating team that had knocked Crestwood Heights Academy out of the state tournament the year before. RHS was an enigma to them; being from the opposite side of the state, they were unfamiliar with their players' abilities and tendencies. Coach Jones watched two scouting tapes of their opponents and prepared his team thoroughly. CHA came out with determination, dominating on both offense and defense. Led by King's scoring and rebounding, Ross' assists and steals, Sampson's blocked shots and rebounds, and the Anderson twins' all-around talents, they easily defeated RHS by 20 points.

Crestwood faced its toughest challenge yet in a thrilling quarterfinal matchup against Taft High School. The game was intense from the tip-off, with both teams trading baskets and playing suffocating defense. King led the charge for CHA, scoring at will and grabbing crucial rebounds. Ross showcased his playmaking skills with precise passes and steals on the defensive end. Sampson anchored the defense with his shot-blocking prowess and relentless work on the boards. The Anderson twins dazzled the crowd with their flashy dunks and versatile offensive game.

Late in the fourth quarter, CHA trailed by two points, with only seconds remaining on the clock. Coach Jones called a timeout to draw up a final play to decide their tournament fate. The players huddled together, their faces determined and focused on the task at hand.

As they stepped back onto the court, the atmosphere was electric. The crowd roared with anticipation, knowing that CHA's season rested on this final play. Ross inbounded the ball to King, who drove hard toward the basket. With defenders closing in on him, King made a split-second decision to dish the ball out to Rodrick Anderson, who was waiting behind the three-point line. Rodrick caught the pass and released a perfect left-handed shot, the ball arcing beautifully through the air as time seemed to stand still.

The buzzer sounded just as the ball swished through the net, sending the crowd into a frenzy. The CHA fans erupted in cheers, the sound echoing throughout the gym as the players rushed to celebrate with Rodrick. Taft High School's players stood in stunned silence, unable to comprehend what had just happened.

The Anderson twins embraced each other joyfully, their teammates joining them in a jubilant group hug. King smiled, a sense of relief washing over him as he realized they had secured a spot in the state semifinals.

The match-up was against Liberty High School, a formidable opponent known for its impressive teamwork and strict discipline. Coached by the renowned Pete Chambers, the Liberty players were famous for their unstoppable drive and unwavering tenacity.

The pressure of the semi-final game loomed over the Crestwood team like a dark cloud, threatening to steal their chances at the championship. The air in the locker room was thick with tension as Coach Jones addressed his players.

"Listen up, boys," the coach said in his no-nonsense tone. "We all know what we're up against. Liberty High School is a tough opponent. They play as a team, they play with heart, and they never give up. But we have something they don't have."

The players looked at each other with a mixture of curiosity and determination.

"We have grit," Jones continued. "We have the will to win, no matter what. And we have each other. We are a brotherhood on this court, and nothing can break us apart."

The team nodded, feeling a sense of unity and purpose sweep over them.

"So go out there and play your hearts out," Coach Jones concluded. "Make them remember the name of our school. Make them fear the red and black. And most importantly, make each other proud."

With a final clap on the shoulder and a hard stare into each player's eyes, the coach left the locker room. The players were left with a sense of determination and a fire burning in their hearts. They were ready to give everything they had for their team, their school, and themselves.

As the CHA team entered the court, they could feel the tension in the air. The spectators in the crowd were loud and boisterous, eager to see which team would come out on top and advance to the state championship game.

Sammy King exchanged a quick glance with Coach Jones, silently acknowledging the tough task that awaited them. They knew that this game would not be easy, but they were ready for the challenge.

Crestwood Heights Academy gained possession of the ball after the opening tip, and King took control, dribbling toward the basket. He then passed it to Lodrick, who swiftly executed a few moves before sinking a flawless mid-range shot. The ball effortlessly made its way through the hoop, putting CHA in an early lead.

But Liberty wasn't going down without a fight. Their players constantly hustled on defense and worked seamlessly together on offense. Despite CHA's best efforts, Liberty managed to stay close throughout the first half.

At halftime, Coach Jones gathered his players in a huddle and delivered a passionate pep talk. "We knew this wouldn't be an easy game," he said. "But we are better than this. We have been working hard all season for this moment. Now let's go out there and show them what CHA basketball is all about!"

Fueled by their coach's words, CHA came out firing in the second half. King took over on both ends of the court, dominating with his arsenal of offensive skills and locking down Liberty's star player on defense.

The twins continued knocking down shots from all over the court while making impressive passes for easy baskets. The two other Crestwood starters also stepped up their performance, playing with intense energy and drive.

Despite Liberty's efforts, Crestwood Heights methodically pulled away in the fourth quarter, their teamwork and skill shining through as they extended their lead. The crowd was on their feet, the cheers and chants of "CHA! CHA!" reverberating throughout the arena.

The gym erupted in celebration as the final buzzer sounded, declaring Crestwood Heights the victors. The players jumped and hugged each other in exhilaration, knowing they had just secured a spot in the state championship game for the first time in history.

Coach Jones' face lit up with pride as he congratulated each player, praising their hard work and resilience. The team huddled together at center court, savoring this moment of triumph before setting their sights on the ultimate prize: the state title.

As CHA celebrated their victory over Liberty High School, they knew that their toughest opponent was yet to come. Their cross-city archrival, Carter High School, awaited them in the state championship game. Crestwood had already beaten them twice this season, but the players knew that beating them for a third time would be no easy feat.

The atmosphere was charged with excitement on game day. The players from CHA showed up at the arena with plenty of time to spare, all decked out in matching, high-end warm-up gear paid for by Beckett Belmont. They were completely focused on the upcoming challenge.

As they stepped onto the court for warm-ups, they could see Carter's players doing the same on the other side. Tensions were high as both teams glared at each other, eager to prove who was truly superior.

The game started off with a quick pace and intense physicality. Lodrick Anderson, known as one of the top athletes in the state, showcased his skills by soaring for a reverse dunk to score the first points of the game. The teams were evenly matched on both ends of the court, playing suffocating defense and making every shot difficult. Despite CHA's strong start, Carter refused to back down and matched their level of intensity. James Franklin, their star player, was dominant under the basket and kept his team within reach of victory.

In the second quarter, King stepped up his performance on offense. He used his variety of moves to get past defenders and finish strong at the rim. CHA opened up a seven-point lead, but Carter responded with a run. The Carter High School crowd was in a frenzy, their voices blending together into one deafening roar. The energy in the arena was electric, pulsing with the hope and excitement of every fan. The game had become a nail-biter.

On the court, every possession was crucial, with both teams fighting for an advantage. Players sprinted back and forth, their movements precise and calculated. Every shot, every pass was met with cheers or groans from the crowd, who were on the edge of their seats. As the final seconds of the half ticked away, the scoreboard showed a tie game: 42-42. The tension in the arena was palpable, everyone holding their breath while waiting for the halftime buzzer to sound. Franklin missed a short jumper with seconds left, and the teams jogged off the court with the game tied.

In the locker room during the break, King knew he had to rally his team together. As they gathered in a group, the normally reserved junior star player looked into each of their eyes, seeing the fatigue but also the fire of conviction burning within. "This is it, guys," King said, his voice steady and commanding. "We've worked too hard to let this slip away now. Let's dominate the second half."

The third quarter was a back-and-forth battle, with both teams again trading baskets and defensive stops. Ross shined with multiple assists, and Sampson waived a finger at a stunned Carter player after blocking his shot attempt into the third row. Meanwhile, King led the charge on defense, shutting down Carter's top scorer and creating turnovers that led to fast-break opportunities for CHA.

In the final twenty seconds of the game, with CHA trailing by two points, King took matters into his own hands. Dribbling past defenders with lightning speed, he maneuvered his way to the basket and made a crucial layup in traffic, drawing a foul in the process. The arena fell silent as King stepped up to the free-throw line, the weight of the entire season resting on his shoulders. The crowd held their breath as he dribbled the ball, his eyes locked on the hoop. King took a deep breath before releasing the ball. It sailed through the air with grace, effortlessly swishing through the net.

Half the gym exploded with celebration as CHA took back the lead, their fans erupting into cheers and applause. Carter High School called for a timeout with thirteen seconds remaining, and their coach designed a play for a game-winning shot.

James Franklin, Carter's star player, drove to the basket with determination, but King was there to meet him. In a heart-stopping moment, King managed to block Franklin's shot, securing the rebound as time expired, signaling the end of the game and the victory for Crestwood Heights Academy. The CHA players rushed onto the court, a mix of elation and relief washing over them.

Coach Jones was beaming with pride as he congratulated each player, his voice filled with emotion. The crowd erupted into thunderous applause, their cheers cascading throughout the arena.

The winning coach made his way through the crowd with a proud smile. He scanned the faces of everyone around him, searching for one person in particular. And then he saw him - Beckett Belmont.

The two men embraced tightly, tears of joy streaming down their faces. "We did it, brother," Coach Jones whispered hoarsely. "We sure did!" replied Beckett with a grin.

As the dust settled after the historic basketball season, the Crestwood Heights Academy student body and faculty were jubilant. Everywhere the players walked on campus, they were greeted with cheers and congratulations. Students stopped them in the hallways to ask for autographs, and teachers gave them high-fives as they passed by. The entire school was filled with pride and joy, celebrating their team's incredible journey to become state champions. The players themselves were still in disbelief, basking in the glory of their hard-earned victory.

Not only were they celebrated as heroes on campus, but the team was also invited to a special ceremony in their honor. The entire school gathered in the gymnasium, where the head of the school and athletic director revealed a brand-new trophy case reserved exclusively for displaying CHA's state championship trophy.

Amidst thunderous applause and cheers from the student body, Coach Jones gave a speech commemorating the team's state championship journey. He thanked each player individually for their dedication and hard work.

Beckett Belmont gave a surprise speech drawing a connection between the championship journey and his real estate empire:

"Just like in buying and selling homes, success in basketball requires teamwork, strategy, and relentless determination. These young men faced obstacles along the way, just like occurs in the real estate business, but they never gave up. They believed in each other, and that's what led us to victory." The crowd listened intently as Beckett drew parallels between the championship season and his experiences in the business world. He shared anecdotes of deals that almost fell through but were saved by perseverance and quick thinking, much like critical moments in a basketball game. As he spoke, the gym was filled with an air of inspiration, the students and faculty hanging on his every word. Beckett finished the speech by raising his fist in the air and exclaiming, "Just like on the court, we are champions in life! Let's continue to work hard, support each other, and reach for even greater heights together!" The gym erupted in cheers and applause as Beckett Belmont stood tall, proud of the victories both on and off the court.

As Belmont basked in the aftermath of his inspiring speech, the news of Sammy King's academic woes began to spread throughout Crestwood Heights Academy. It was a stark contrast to the celebration just a few days ago, and the school was filled with disappointment and disbelief.

King had been a star player on the basketball team since his freshman year, and everyone had assumed that he was also keeping up academically. However, the school administrators had been ignoring his struggles and had allowed him to advance through each year without meeting the necessary academic requirements.

As Sammy approached his final year of high school, it was evident that he could not graduate with a diploma due to the demanding course load of core classes he still needed to complete.

The news spread quickly among the students, parents, and alumni and many were left questioning the integrity of their school. How could something like this happen? How could someone be allowed to play on the basketball team without meeting basic academic standards?

An investigative reporter wrote a bombshell article, causing an uproar in the community and tarnishing the reputation of Crestwood Heights Academy. The columnist had uncovered evidence that the school had been actively recruiting talented basketball players from the inner city, offering them free tuition while more deserving students with much stronger credentials were rejected. The reporter had found out that King was living in a multi-million dollar mansion and driving a luxury car despite claiming to come from a humble background. Allegations were also made that he should have been ruled ineligible and placed on academic probation, but the school overlooked his poor grades in pursuit of athletic success.

The scandal rocked not just the school but also the entire town. People took sides; some defended King as a youthful pawn and blamed adults and the system for putting too much emphasis on sports, while others viewed him as a willing participant in a charade, taking advantage of the system.

Amidst all this chaos, Beckett Belmont stayed quiet. He knew that as the CEO of CBA Properties, he would be held accountable if anyone found out about his involvement in these recruiting schemes. Belmont spent restless nights pondering the implications of the scandal and the potential fallout it could have on his reputation and business empire. The weight of the situation bore down on him heavily, a stark contrast to the pride and joy he had felt during the championship celebrations.

Beckett Belmont and Chase Clooney met in Beckett's office to discuss their next move. They knew that the scandal at Crestwood Heights Academy could tarnish their reputation, and they needed to take swift action to minimize the risk.

After careful consideration, they devised a plan. They would strategically place articles in the newspaper that painted CHA as a school celebrating diversity and embracing inclusivity. They would highlight that while mistakes were made, the school was moving in the right direction regarding racial and ethnic diversity. This would paint a positive image of CHA and hopefully shift the focus away from the scandal.

To further support this narrative, Belmont and Clooney decided to stack the members invited for an emergency meeting called by the school. They carefully selected individuals who were known for their progressive views on diversity and inclusion and gave them scripted talking points. This way, they could control and steer the conversation in the desired direction. One point of emphasis was that a total of forty student-athletes from the non-profit foundation for underprivileged middle school youth had enrolled at local private schools, and only five of the forty had enrolled at CHA. However, they conveniently omitted that those five were the most talented basketball players and had been "steered" to the school.

The meeting was hastily arranged, giving them little time to prepare, but Belmont and Clooney were confident that their plan would work.

As expected, during the meeting, there was much discussion about increasing diversity at CHA, with many praising the school's efforts so far. Beckett and Chase's planted stories had done their job well.

However, not everyone was convinced. Some questioned whether these changes were genuine or simply a PR move to save face after the scandal.

One parent even stood up during the meeting and questioned why only five out of forty student-athletes from their foundation had been steered towards CHA if it truly valued diversity. Beckett and Chase were caught off guard and struggled to come up with a convincing response.

In the midst of the intense conversation at the impromptu gathering, a person emerged from the crowd. It was Sammy King, the focal point of the scandal that had shaken the elite school. The air around him exuded humility and remorse as he no longer carried himself with his usual confidence.

"I can't stay silent any longer," King's voice rang out, silencing the room. "I have to come clean about everything."

Whispers rippled through the audience as all eyes turned to Sammy, waiting for his revelation. With a deep breath, he began to speak.

"I didn't deserve to be on that team," the basketball superstar confessed, his voice filled with regret. "I let others manipulate my path so I could play ball, but I neglected my studies in the process. I don't want this scandal to define me anymore."

A hush fell over the room as King's words sunk in. Beckett and Chase exchanged uneasy glances, realizing that their carefully constructed narrative was about to unravel.

"Sammy, why are you telling us this now?" a teacher asked, her voice laced with a mix of concern and curiosity.

The young man took a moment to compose himself, his gaze shifting from face to face in the room. "Because it's time for the truth to come out. I may have been used as a pawn in this whole scheme, but that doesn't excuse my actions. I want to make things right, starting with owning up to my mistakes."

A murmur spread through the room as people exchanged surprised glances. Beckett Belmont's jaw tightened as he realized that his carefully crafted facade was falling apart before his eyes.

Thankfully, Belmont was saved by Sammy's sudden outburst of uncontrollable sobbing, which resulted in him being escorted out of the room. It was not often that someone as physically strong as Sammy would break down in tears, especially since outdated societal norms dictate that boys don't cry. However, at this moment, Sammy felt vulnerable and exposed, and his emotions were fragile.

Belmont and Clooney felt grateful for the interruption, knowing it would halt further questioning. However, they were aware that this was only a temporary reprieve. Eventually, the truth would come out in its entirety.

Chase noticed Beckett's tense demeanor leaving the meeting and placed a hand on his shoulder. "Don't worry, man. We can figure this out together," he reassured him.

But Belmont wasn't convinced. "We need to do more extensive damage control," he said firmly. "I'll handle things here at school; you "fix" things."

Clooney nodded in understanding.

Two days had passed since Sammy's unexpected confession at the emergency meeting. Rumors were swirling about what would happen next, but no one could have predicted what came next.

On a sunny Friday afternoon, a hastily arranged press conference was held at Crestwood Heights Academy.

Sammy King stepped up to the microphone. Cameras flashed as he took a deep breath before speaking: "I want to announce that I will be transferring to my local public school, Carter, for my senior year," Sammy declared boldly. "I will finish out my junior year here at Crestwood Heights

Academy, but I believe it is best for me to return to my neighborhood roots."

The room erupted into chaos as reporters bombarded him with questions. Beckett and Chase exchanged panicked looks.

"Sammy, can you explain why you made this decision?" a reporter shouted from the crowd.

The teenager stood tall, his eyes filled with determination. "It's time for me to take responsibility for my actions. I let others manipulate me, and I want to make things right by returning home."

The coastal road wound its way above the ocean, and the only sound was the gentle lapping of waves against the shore below. Sammy King had taken the Mercedes for a late-night drive, seeking solace in the winding curves and salty sea air. The wind whipped through his cornrow braids as he drove, the moonlight casting a gentle glow over the deserted road.

Despite the late hour, Sammy couldn't shake the thoughts swirling in his head. The recent events had left him reeling, and he desperately needed an escape. So, he had driven out of the city and onto this coastal road, knowing that the peaceful scenery would bring him some semblance of calm.

In this moment, he felt weightless, free from the constraints and expectations of his life. The smooth hum of the engine, the cool breeze on his skin, and the open road ahead were all he needed to find some peace. As he rounded another bend, he caught a glimpse of the sparkling ocean below. It was a sight that never failed to take his breath away.

But then, just as he was coming around a particularly sharp bend, he saw headlights coming straight towards him. In a panic, he swerved to avoid the other car, but it was too late. The impact was like a thunderbolt, a deafening boom that sent shockwaves through his body.

In a split second, it all became a blur. The sound of metal colliding, the scent of burnt rubber, the feeling of weightlessness as his car careened off the cliff and plunged into the depths below. Then, an abrupt silence. Sammy's head slammed against the steering wheel with a sickening thud, and everything went black.

The collision proved to be fatal, claiming the young man's life in an instant. His body, twisted and crushed, was stuck inside the submerged Mercedes. Several hours later, rescue workers retrieved  the teenager's lifeless body from the mangled wreckage of the car.

For days after, the city buzzed with rumors and speculations about the accident. Some said the young man had been drunk, others whispered about a possible suicide.

The news of his death shook both Crestwood Heights Academy and Carter High School. Many in the tight-knit local community mourned the loss of such a talented young athlete, while others were relieved that the scandal would finally be put to rest.

The evening after the tragedy, five almost unrecognizable figures savored expensive shots of straight malt at the exclusive downtown athletic club. As they made their way to a secluded corner booth, their features became clearer - it was Beckett Belmont, Chase Clooney, Jack Tanner, Coach

Jones, and Tom Gardner, a renowned stunt driver known for his daring car stunts in action films.

Belmont lifted his glass in a toast:

"To Crestwood Heights Academy..."

"To winning the state title..."

"To Sammy King..."

As Chase Clooney left the room with a heavy heart, he wondered what situation he would have to "fix" next.

THE STREAK

The players were divided into groups of three, and each player took turns practicing free throws on different hoops. In all levels of basketball, having a high free throw accuracy is crucial, especially in youth games where every point can make a difference in the final score. Just one missed or made free throw can determine the outcome of a close game. The good news is that improving free throw shooting is relatively straightforward. The variables are consistent: an unguarded 15-foot shot at a 10-foot-high rim. This is much simpler compared to making field goals, which require dealing with various factors such as shooting from different angles and distances, facing tough defense, and shooting while off balance or in motion.

The sound of bouncing basketballs and squeaking sneakers filled the gymnasium. Suddenly, a cry of triumph echoed through the air: "There's a nail!" Initially skeptical, the girls shooting free throws at the other end of the court couldn't deny the evidence of the nail in question. Soon, the rest of the team abandoned their respective baskets to join in on the discovery. Three determined players crouched down for a closer look, confirming that it was indeed a nail perfectly centered on the free throw line. I explained that many players use the nail as a guide for their free throw shots during games. With their important discovery uncovered, the basketball scientists excitedly returned to their designated baskets to continue practicing.

The Riverside Eagles are a team of seventh and eighth-grade girls who play in the competitive eighth-grade varsity Catholic Youth Organization (CYO) league. Unfortunately, due to the pandemic, the previous three seasons were canceled. There was much debate on whether or not to have a season last year, but ultimately it was deemed safer to cancel the basketball season. However, the Riverside team continued to hold twice-weekly practices despite not being able to participate in games. To make matters worse, their previous parent coach was not an effective communicator and spent a significant portion of the practice time talking instead of coaching. He also taught complex plays involving multiple cuts, screens, and scripted moves that left the girls confused and uninterested. The coach's daughter Finley was the second-best player on the team, just behind my daughter Nicole.

Nicole and Finley were the only two eighth graders on the team who had experience playing AAU club basketball. Recreational basketball is generally seen as having the lowest skill level among youth leagues, followed by High School feeder programs, with the highest caliber found on the competitive AAU circuit. CYO teams are typically comparable to High School feeder teams in terms of talent, but there can be exceptions. Some CYO and HS feeder teams may have multiple skilled players, while there are also instances where AAU teams lack talent.

In the world of youth basketball, coaches often say that the key to success is having a large number of returning players and avoiding dropouts. Unfortunately, only half of the ten girls from last year's seventh-grade team decided to come back and play this season. This attrition rate of fifty percent is not ideal. It's unclear why some players did not return; perhaps their parents pressured them into playing, or they found a different hobby to pursue. However, the fact remains that only half of the previous year's players will be joining us this time around.

I am Andy Miller, and I recently agreed to take on the role of coach for the eighth-grade Riverside Eagles girls basketball team. Despite being retired from coaching, I couldn't turn down the opportunity when the high school program director urgently requested more coaches for the middle school teams. My wife Susan and daughter Nicole were supportive of my decision. I had coached Nicki in various leagues since she was a young child. But now, things were different. She was fourteen years old, and I would be coaching her teenage friends and classmates at one of the most prestigious private schools in our state.

The hiring process at Riverside was incredibly thorough and detailed. I had coached fourth grade private school students in the past, and there were background checks and mandatory meetings. However, Riverside's hiring process was entirely on another level. I first had to submit an online application for the position. Then, I completed a virtual training course on CPR and first aid through the Red Cross that took three hours to finish. After that, I attended an in-person CPR session and participated in a five-hour coaching meeting specifically for Riverside coaches, as well as a two-hour virtual session for all CYO league coaches. Once all these steps were completed, I signed a contract with the school that stated my pay would be one thousand four hundred dollars, split into three equal monthly installments starting in December. The part-time coaching position would officially begin on November 7th, 2022 and end on March 4th, 2023.

In youth basketball, the emphasis is not on winning, especially in the beginner leagues. While I support this approach, my teams were consistently dominating on the court. After four undefeated seasons and a 29-game winning streak, I stepped down from coaching. Out of those 29 games, only two were close in score or remotely competitive.

My impressive winning streak is all thanks to my players. In basketball, talent is crucial to success. Typically, the team with the most skilled players comes out on top. Just look at Phil Jackson, who has a record 11 NBA titles as a coach. But let's not forget about the powerful duos of Michael Jordan and Scottie Pippen for the Chicago Bulls or Kobe Bryant and Shaquille O'Neal for the Los Angeles Lakers - they were the driving force behind those championships. Some even argue that switching coaches right before a game would have little impact on the outcome. My friends often joke about my coaching achievements, claiming it's all due to having players like Nicole on my teams. I couldn't agree more.

From a young age, my daughter displayed impressive basketball abilities. Her natural talent and skill were evident to all who saw her play. As a second grader, she amazed me by making 62 consecutive bank shots from 10 feet away in our backyard; the following morning, she made 51 more in a row. This level of accuracy is uncommon for someone her age. She also showed ambidexterity, effortlessly shooting and dribbling with both hands. I'll never forget the time during a second-grade game when she casually made a left-handed layup; when asked about it, she simply said her coach had encouraged her to use her non-dominant hand for that shot. By third grade, she was already displaying advanced foot-work and timing as she drove from half-court with her left hand and smoothly finished with a layup. It's undeniable that Nicole is a difference maker to any basketball team she plays on.

One of the tensest moments during our impressive winning streak was a close one-point game in season three when I was coaching my daughter's rec league team. The Green Dawgs were a mix of third and fourth-graders, but the star player was my second-grade daughter, Nicole. Despite being the youngest on the team, she dominated the league, and her age went unnoticed. As we entered the final fifteen seconds of the game with a slim one-point lead, I learned an important lesson as a coach during a crucial timeout: keep instructions clear and concise.

"Girls we're up by one point and we have possession at mid-court. Bella, pass to Nicole. Nicole dribble the ball out. Game over. Let's finish strong, Green Dawgs on three!" The team huddled together, pumped up and ready to secure the win. With a high five and a chant, they took their positions on the court. The referee gave the ball to Bella who threw a perfect pass to Nicole, who caught it seamlessly. Nicki began dribbling down the court without hesitation, effortlessly controlling the ball. It looked like smooth sailing until my daughter abruptly veered off course and dribbled in a straight line directly out of bounds.

The opposing team's coach was ecstatic about the unexpected gift turnover and immediately called a timeout to strategize their next move, designing a play for a potential game-winning shot. Nicole came over to our huddle with a grin, proud that she had flawlessly executed the play. "Nicki, why did you dribble the ball out of bounds? I'm just curious," I asked. Confusion crossed Nicole's face as she replied, "I did exactly what you told me to do. You said to dribble the ball out, so I did." It turned out that my eight-year-old daughter had misunderstood my instructions. Instead of keeping the ball in play until time ran out, she thought I wanted her to dribble it out of bounds, resulting in a costly turnover. And it was my fault for not giving clear directions.

With only eleven seconds left on the clock, our opponent took possession of the ball in their own backcourt. Our team immediately started to backcourt press, which was a violation of league rules. After a successful inbounds pass, our best defender managed to knock the ball out of bounds with eight seconds remaining. The volunteer scoreboard operator paid no heed and let the clock countdown continue until 00:00, signaling the end of the game. The opposing coach attempted to argue with me about the illegal press and lack of clock stoppage, but I simply shook his hand and pretended not to notice. Another win added to our winning streak. The frustrated coach appealed for my assistance, but it was too late; the referee had already left, and the game was officially over. Exasperated, he approached the timekeeper to express his anger but quickly backed off when he realized it was one of his own team's parents.

I didn't feel any remorse. The coach on the other team was infamous for screaming and insulting the teenage referees during every game, constantly questioning their decisions. During the game that had just ended, the rest of his team's parents and his assistant coach joined in, creating a chaotic chorus of voices aimed at the officials. All of this commotion over a simple fourth-grade recreation game, where having fun and learning the fundamentals of basketball should have been the main focus. However, it seemed like destiny had intervened and taught those unruly adults a valuable lesson.

The only other close call during the steak occurred during the opening game of our fourth grade CYO season when we escaped with a 16-10 victory. The game was a nail-biter, with both teams constantly swapping the lead. In fact, the largest lead either team had throughout the first three quarters was just four points. As a coach, it was a frustrating game to watch. To make matters worse, our opponent had an exceptional player for her age group who scored six of their ten points on free throws. The foul calls on our team were questionable and seemed to come out of thin air from the referee. Our defender was even called for two fouls that clearly looked like clean blocked shots. Despite these obstacles, we pulled ahead in the final quarter and secured a narrow six-point win, keeping my undefeated record intact.

I have coached many teams throughout my career, but none were as dominant as that fourth-grade team. Throughout the season, we scored an impressive 202 points while only allowing 46 from our opponents. We could have beaten teams by even larger margins, but we intentionally held back some of our players like Nicole. We also gave our team specific instructions to focus on setting up plays and make a minimum of five passes before taking a shot instead of going for fast breaks. As a coach, my greatest challenge was keeping our winning margin under twenty points. This was the league's "compassionate competition" point threshold that the winning team should not exceed. Winning by 20 points or more would require us to submit a post-game report to the league directors explaining what steps were taken to stay within the limit.

Except for Amanda, all the players did a great job maintaining a manageable score. Whenever our lead reached double digits, I would call for a timeout and remind the team to slow down the pace and focus on passing the ball at least five times before attempting a shot. It was clear that we were going to win at this point, and we wanted to keep the lead within reason. During the timeout, I made sure to maintain eye contact with Amanda as I delivered the message. I knew exactly what she was going to do as soon as she received a pass - take a shot without hesitation.

When play resumed after the timeout, Amanda caught the ball and immediately locked eyes with me. Her lips slowly curled into a mischievous smile, and I could see the determination burning in her gaze as she calculated her next move. With her feet planted firmly on the court floor, she took a step back before expertly flinging the ball toward the hoop. The ball spun gracefully through the air, making a perfect arc towards the basket. Time seemed to stand still as we all held our breaths in anticipation. And then, with a satisfying swish, the ball passed cleanly through the net, scoring us another two points and widening our lead. Turning to me with a triumphant grin, Amanda celebrated. I sighed as the basket put us dangerously close to the "compassionate competition" danger zone.

She was a good kid but couldn't help herself. She was a "high-volume shooter," or what some might call a "mad gunner" or "chucker." She always seemed eager to take a shot, even when our team was comfortably ahead, and we were trying to maintain a reasonable lead. Occasionally, she would try to break away for a fast break lay-up, but I would call an immediate timeout. "Amanda, what did we discuss during the last break? How many passes are we supposed to make before attempting a shot?" Amanda would hang her head in embarrassment and respond, "No fast breaks, coach. And we should pass at least five times before shooting." "Correct, Amanda. Thank you for reminding the team." However, as soon as she returned to the court, she would continue shooting without hesitation and fast break whenever possible. As a coach, it was difficult to keep the score within twenty points when playing against an overmatched poorly coached team. Having a "rogue" player like Amanda only added to the challenge.

Despite Amanda's mischievous antics, the girls grasped the spirit behind the "mercy rule" and did well in keeping the score under control. Our star player, Nicole, selflessly passed the ball and focused on setting up scoring opportunities for our less skilled players. In the final game of the season, it was Olivia who shined with an impressive 8 points. As the smallest player in the league, she had only scored a total of 4 points in the previous 7 games, and those were just from close-range layups. But in this last game, she surprised everyone by making four field goals, including some impressive bank shots from a distance of 10-12 feet. Her shooting form was flawless, and she received assists from three different teammates. When she left the gym that day, she was beaming with happiness. Her parents were extremely grateful after the game and still express their gratitude whenever we cross paths. Olivia will always remember that game, and as a coach, creating memorable experiences for players is what truly matters.

Most recreational and CYO teams have volunteer coaches, with varying levels of skill. Some have impressive strategies while others leave much to be desired. During one game, I observed a fourth-grade team that used the same play constantly: setting a screen as soon as the ball crossed half-court. This tactic was utilized even when it seemed like the team had a clear path to an easy basket. The end result? Only two points were scored by the team for the entire game. It didn't make sense to me why they would continue with this strategy. The play was called "Unicorn," and the name was fitting. The chances of successfully scoring a basket by running the play were just as rare and improbable as encountering this mythical creature in real life. At that age, setting a screen across half-court served no purpose and did not contribute to scoring points.

After stepping down from coaching after my daughter's fourth-grade CYO season, I had no plans of returning to the role. My intention was to simply be a supportive parent at her games. However, after the urgent plea from the basketball director that the school needed coaches, I found myself back in the coaching ranks. Nineteen girls from seventh and eighth grade showed up for tryouts to be split into two teams: ten on the varsity squad and nine on junior varsity. The varsity team consisted of six eighth graders and four seventh graders, with a noticeable skill gap between them. Two girls stood out, already playing on top-level AAU teams, while four had experience in high school feeder programs. The remaining players were athletic but lacked basketball experience.

With tryouts concluded and the varsity team announced, I stepped onto the court for our first practice with a mix of excitement and anxiety. Beforehand, I had consulted Nicole for suggestions on drills to include in our practice. "Let's play bump," she recommended. "Bump?" I repeated. "Yeah, let's include that in our practice. Trust me it will be a hit," she replied with a smile. I was familiar with the game of bump - it was a fun way to improve our shooting skills. The objective was to eliminate other players by making a shot before the player behind you in line did. The game involves a single file line at the free throw line and two basketballs. The first player in line shoots a free throw, and if they miss, they continue to shoot until they make a basket. As soon as a basket is made, the ball is passed to the next person in line, and the process repeats until there is a single winner. Using your basketball to "bump" or hit another player's ball away from the basket added an extra element of fun to the game, often resulting in uncontrollable laughter among the players.

At our first practice, I took Nicki's advice by incorporating a quick game of bump followed by a much-needed water break. The energy in the gym instantly spiked, and the girls were thrilled and having a blast. It became a tradition to play at least one round of bump during each practice for the rest of the season, with some girls even skipping their water break just to squeeze in another game. Interestingly, the less skilled players were always the most enthusiastic about playing, despite never winning. One of them, Allison, an eighth grader with modest basketball abilities, eagerly asked if we could play bump again after our initial game. I promised her it would be a regular part of our practices, and she couldn't stop beaming with excitement.

Despite not being the most skilled player on the basketball court, Allison quickly became a favorite of mine to coach. Her infectious positivity and unwavering dedication to the team never wavered, as she consistently boosts her teammates and adds to the overall energy and camaraderie of the group. While she may not have the same natural talent as her fellow players, she enjoys being part of the team and having fun with her friends. Additionally, she has a great sense of humor and pays close attention during practices and games, often asking for clarification when needed.

"Let's beat them down the court and score some easy transition hoops."

"Coach, what does that mean?"

"Our team is athletic. Let's fast break them."

"Coach, what foreign language is fast break? Can you translate?"

Her more experienced teammates and I described a fast break as when the offensive team swiftly moves the ball down the court to catch the defense off guard and outnumbered, allowing for easy scoring opportunities. Allison's face lit up with understanding.

"That is why we practice all of the 2-on-1 and 3-on-2 drills."

"Correct, Allison, we are more athletic and in better shape than most teams and are trying to get easy scores, including lay-ups close to the basket."

During a break in one of our practices, Allison approached me and apologized, saying "Coach, I feel bad about not making the unlimited shot." Intrigued, I asked for more details. After a few follow-up questions, I realized she was talking about a free throw she attempted during our last game. Our team was in the bonus, and after being fouled in the backcourt she had to walk all the way down the court to take her shot. Initially confused, her teammates explained that she would be shooting a free throw. Allison giggled and confidently took her "unlimited shot," which hit the rim but narrowly missed going in.

As we gathered for one of the first practices of the season, I posed a question to the team. Did anyone have specific personal goals they wanted to achieve? I anticipated silence or maybe one brave individual speaking up, but to my delight, everyone eagerly shared their own ambitions in rapid succession.

"I want to work on my ball-handling."

"I want to be a good teammate."

"I want to score at least one point during a game."

"I want to improve my overall skills and deepen my understanding of the rules."

Next up was Lexi, and her response to the question made me laugh. She simply said, "win." In today's age of participation awards and the idea that competition should be toned down, it was refreshing to hear such a direct and ambitious goal from someone in middle school. When I took on this job, I asked the athletic director about their approach to winning, competing, and playing time for middle schoolers. The answer was clear: every kid gets equal playing time, winning is not the main focus, and there's a strict no-cut policy.

While middle school teams may prioritize having fun and building skills, high school teams face a different set of expectations - winning is the ultimate goal, playing time is determined by the coach's decisions, and tryouts can result in students being cut from the team. Despite the more relaxed competition philosophy from the middle school administration, it didn't stop the seventh and eighth-grade varsity players from being ultra-competitive and giving their all to win games, with visions of raising the CYO championship trophy in their minds.

Lexi quickly became another one of my favorite players to coach. She excelled in soccer and had some prior basketball experience from playing for her high school feeder team. Her athleticism was unmatched, with boundless energy on the court, reminiscent of a tireless cheetah hunting prey at full speed. She was a respectful kid and completely focused during practices, games, and timeouts. In the second game of the season, we decided to try out a full-court press after scoring a basket. Despite not having practiced it, we gave it a go in the first quarter, and it turned out to be incredibly effective. With Nicole and Lexi leading the backcourt press, we forced three turnovers within minutes, resulting in easy points for our team. The other team was clearly flustered. During the remainder of the season, whenever there was a time out or when she was resting on the bench, Lexi would politely ask, "Coach, can we give the full-court press another shot?" I explained that since we were in control of the game, we would use the strategy again in our next game. She understood my reasoning, but during our next timeout, she was sure to ask again, "Coach, can we full-court press?"

The Riverside Eagles eighth-grade varsity team was known for their unrelenting drive to win and fierce competitiveness. After celebrating their second victory of the season, the team huddled together. Uncharacteristically, quiet seventh-grader Paige excitedly raised her hand to share a new objective. With a determined glint in her eye, she proclaimed, "I want us to make it to the championship game and bring home the trophy to add to our school's collection." I was surprised by her confident statement. First, Lexi with her simple but powerful goal of "winning," now shy Paige with a grander goal of winning the championship. It was evident that this group of kids was fearless when it came to competition and eager to achieve success.

Early in the season, I shared five main objectives with the team: 1. Enjoy playing. 2. Give your best effort. 3. Be a supportive teammate. 4. Continuously improve and progress in practices and games. 5. Remember #1 - have fun!

I emphasized to the players that making mistakes is a natural part of the game and it's okay. In fact, I encourage them to take risks and try new things because it shows their willingness to improve. I don't want them to be held back by fear of failure on the court. It doesn't matter whether they miss five shots in a row or make them all, what matters is that it's a good shot within their shooting range. I want them to shoot with confidence and without hesitation.

During a practice session, I reiterated the importance of shooting with confidence. Whether a shot is made or missed, it's crucial that everyone keeps taking open shots within their range.

"How many of you are familiar with Sue Bird, Breanna Stewart, or Kelsey Plum? Raise your hand if you've heard of them."

All the girls raised their hands. These three players are among the best in the world of women's basketball.

"When these players attempt a field goal, do you think they are more likely to make it or miss it? Take a moment to discuss amongst yourselves, but I want each of you to give me your individual answer."

The girls gathered in a huddle and began discussing. The thought-provoking question sparked their curiosity, and I overheard snippets of conversation.

"This is too easy. Obviously, they will make more shots than they miss because they're amazing players."

"I agree, it's simple. My vote is for make as well."

"Wait, maybe it's not so obvious. Maybe it's a trick question. I think the correct answer is actually a miss being more likely than a make."

"Coach is trying to use reverse psychology on us."

"Reverse, reverse psychology."

"Coach is sneaky. He's definitely using reverse, reverse psychology."

After a heated debate, the girls ultimately voted 7-3 in favor of these three exceptional players having a higher chance of making a shot than missing it. However, when looking at the numbers, the truth is revealed. Plum has a career shooting percentage of 42% in the WNBA, while Bird and Stewart have percentages of 43% and 47%, respectively. Even NBA legend Kobe Bryant, known for his unbelievable 81-point game, only had a career field goal percentage of 45% and never surpassed 50% in a single season. This was an important lesson for the team to learn - shooting a basketball is difficult, even for the best players in the world. It's normal to miss shots; what truly matters is staying confident and believing that the next shot will go in.

The players on our team were sly and constantly devising strategies to gain an upper hand over their opponents. "Can I request another player take a free throw in my place?" I sternly replied with a negative, although there was an exception for players with injuries when a "substitute" free-throw shooter was acceptable. However, I did not mention this rule, as it would result in a wave of "mysterious" fake injuries during crucial free throws. "If my opponent has their back turned, can I inbound the ball off them and score a layup?" Technically, yes, but I discouraged this tactic as it could lead to injury for the opposing player and potential concussions. "Coach, can I plow through the other team's player when they set a screen?" This was easy to answer: "No, that's a foul."

After winning three games in a row to start the season, my overall consecutive win streak had reached an impressive 32 wins. However, we were still 56 victories away from matching John Wooden's legendary record with UCLA. I could almost picture the Wizard of Westwood anxiously pacing back and forth on a fluffy cloud in heaven as his record was in danger of being surpassed. Our next opponent was Assumption, also undefeated with a 3-0 record. Unfortunately, Nicole and our other top two players would be absent from the game. To make matters worse, our next-best player would have to leave the game early due to another commitment. Knowing these challenges, my main goal was for us to score at least ten points. Realistically, I expected us to lose by twenty or more points.

The odds were stacked against us, but I tried to boost the team's morale before the game. "I believe in you girls. You've been working hard, and Thursday's practice was excellent. Remember, if you're open, shoot the ball. And let's focus on defense - everyone guard their player in the key and force them to take shots from outside." During my pep talk, Allison raised her hand and asked, "Coach, what's the key?" A few teammates chimed in and explained that it was the rectangular area marked on the court between the basket and free throw line. I continued my pre-game pep talk. "The other team might be taller, but we can't let that intimidate us. Let's all crash the boards." A hand shot up and asked, "What does crash the boards mean exactly?" I clarified, "Sorry, it means everyone needs to rebound on defense - just like in our drills at practice. Block out, high point the ball, and aggressively pursue the missed shot." The players nodded in agreement. Then, a seventh grader asked hopefully, "Will

Nicole be playing today?" I shook my head. "No chance. She's participating in an AAU tournament." Another girl chimed in, "What about Finley?" Once again, I shook my head. "Same tournament, so no chance." Someone else asked about Lexi, and I gave the same answer – she's playing soccer out of state. As soon as I finished updating them on player availability, some heads drooped with disappointment.

Kaitlyn asked if she could play the pivot position. I was puzzled at first. "What exactly is the pivot role?" I asked. She explained, "I would stand near the free-throw line on offense, and after receiving the ball, I can either shoot if I have an open shot or pass it to a teammate." "That sounds like a solid strategy, Kaitlyn. You can definitely play the pivot on offense," I replied, hoping to boost our team's confidence.

As our team prepared for the game with their usual warmup routine, I noticed there weren't any players or fans from the opposing team. This was highly unusual. Would we win by forfeit? As the clock ticked closer to the scheduled start time, there was still no sign of them. But suddenly, with only five minutes left before tip-off, they arrived - walking into our gym with determined looks on their faces. They were much bigger than our team, and it was clear that their presence had an impact on our players' body language. A combination of uneasiness and defeat seemed to wash over them. It was clearly a calculated tactic to intimidate and throw us off our game. This was going to be a tough game... or maybe not.

Much to my surprise, our team of four seventh graders and three less-than-stellar eighth graders played with great energy and skill, managing to score twelve points in the first half. I was in disbelief; they had already surpassed my goal of ten total points for the entire game in just one half, even with our top three players missing. The Eagles continued to play with determination in the third quarter, and we were on track to remain undefeated. By the end of the third quarter, Riverside had a comfortable 21-14 lead. Even though we had some close shots that almost made it into the basket, we could not score any more points during regulation time. Instead, the other team managed to score 7 points, tying the game and sending it into overtime. One of their shots even looked like a miss due to an optical illusion caused by a missing piece of net, but somehow, it went in for two points.

The final minute of the game was pure chaos as the scoreboard malfunctioned, leaving both teams in a state of confusion about the time and score. As the clock ticked down to just seconds remaining in the fourth quarter, there were frantic shot attempts by both teams, but none went in the basket for a game-winning shot. Regulation ended with the score tied 21-21 and the game heading to overtime. With the electronic clock still not working, the two young referees made an unexpected decision - instead of playing an overtime period, they would have a free-throw shootout contest to decide the winner. The Assumption coach and I demanded that a regular overtime session be played; the time could be tracked manually. The referees remained firm on their choice, seemingly inspired by soccer penalty shootouts that decided tie games at the recent soccer World Cup. Fortunately, the electronic clock "recovered," and the winner would be decided by playing normal overtime. Only two points were scored in the extra period - a 10-foot jump shot made by a player on the visiting team. It was enough to secure their hard-fought come-from-behind 23-21 victory.

As the buzzer sounded, my players slumped in defeat, their faces showing a mix of devastation for the heartbreak loss and pride for their efforts.

The streak was over. Coach John Wooden, a man who had seen countless victories and defeats, watched from heaven with a smile on his face. With a twinkle in his eye, he raised a glass of heavenly champagne to toast the end of another streak. His amazing UCLA win streak remained intact and was no longer in danger.

Even though we lost the game by two points, I have never been prouder of my team's performance than on that January day. Without our top three players and only having our next best player for part of the game, the team surpassed all expectations with their exceptional individual play and teamwork on the court. Allison dominated on defense with 5 steals, making quick and decisive plays. Tatum, an eighth grader, snatched important defensive rebounds and even scored her first basket of the season with a 12-foot jump shot. Another eighth-grader, Rory, proved to be a valuable contributer as well, scoring a basket, grabbing crucial rebounds, and playing solid defense.

Our four seventh graders played better than they ever had before. Kaitlyn stepped up in her new pivot role, scoring three baskets and skillfully distributing the ball to her teammates. Molly was relentless on defense and confidently guarded the other team's top player, even proudly reporting to her teammates during a timeout about getting under her opponent's skin. Chelsea took control of the point guard position until she had to leave in the third quarter for her other commitment, pushing the tempo and making impressive shots from mid-range. Paige stepped up in Chelsea's absence and excelled as the point guard, confidently navigating through full-court presses and making quick decisions. Just last week in practice, Paige struggled with dribbling and turning the ball over; now, she was handling double teams like a pro. Our girls demonstrated incredible determination, each earning a jump ball call by fiercely battling for possession when two players grabbed the ball at once. It was an extraordinary effort, and I left the gym feeling energized and ready to start another winning streak.

The next basketball game was certainly one to remember, with all its chaotic moments that made it seem more like a pro wrestling match than a sports event. Unfortunately, our team was again short-handed with only six of the ten girls able to make it to the game. Allison, who had previously confirmed her availability at Tuesday's practice, suddenly changed her mind and announced at Thursday's practice that she couldn't make Sunday's game. She was going to visit her father in New York City for the extended holiday weekend. It was a shame because she was the only girl on the team who had yet to score a basket during the season. On Tuesday, I had told her I believed she would finally score during the upcoming game.

At Thursday's practice, Allison broke the news: "Sorry coach, I won't be able to score on Sunday. I'm off to New York to see my dad."

I reassured her that it was no problem and joked that maybe she could stop by Madison Square Garden and make a basket while she was there.

Curiously, Allison asked, "What's Madison Square Garden?"

I explained that MSG was known as the "Mecca of Basketball," an iconic indoor arena where the NBA New York Knicks played their home games.

Always eager to please, Allison replied with a deadpan tone, "Sure, coach, I'll just swing by after the Broadway show and sink a shot."

As we stepped into the gym at Our Lady of Perpetual Help, our Riverside team was already at a disadvantage with only six players. The sight of ten tall and physically superior opponents warming up was intimidating. They had four players who towered over even our tallest player and seemed capable of lifting heavy objects with ease. The opposing team definitely passed the "looks" test. It seemed like an easy win for the opposing team - but then again, looks can be deceiving. While they struggled with basic skills like dribbling, shooting, and passing, our team confidently went through their warm-up routine, practicing rainbow shots, 2-on-1 drills, and free throws. Each player focused on their strengths, whether close-range shots or long-range three-pointers, which Nicole practiced.

Before every game, the CYO organization enforces the reading of a prayer and pre-game statement. Although Riverside is not a religious institution, all the other teams in the league are Catholic schools. A player from Our Lady of Perpetual Help, representing the home team, solemnly recited the prayer, asking for fair play with guidance from God. The assistant coach of the opposing team was chosen to read the pre-event statement, emphasizing that sports should be enjoyed by youth rather than controlled by adults and reminding adults to act as supportive fans by applauding all competitors' efforts. Additionally, each parent must attend a 75-minute workshop before the season begins, focusing on appropriate behavior towards athletes and referees, as well as expectations for adult conduct during practices and games.

Once the game began, all thoughts of sportsmanship were forgotten. Our Riverside team, playing a fair and honest basketball game, were up against the fierce teenage girl lionesses from Our Lady of Perpetual Help. The opposing parents in the basketball Colosseum arena were cheering on their savagery, ready to see them tear our team apart limb by limb.

It became apparent within a few minutes that our team was going to win easily. The opposing team lacked skill but made up for it with physical aggression and unsportsmanlike behavior. One of their players could have been the basketball version of Mike Tyson in his prime, constantly elbowing and forearm-shivering our players with malicious intent. Their assistant coach even encouraged this rough style of play, shouting instructions from the sidelines to "play big and use elbows." Our opponents also employed a tactic known as "hug defense," where they wrapped their arms around our players in a defensive move that is typically only seen in second or third-grade basketball and should be called for a foul every time. However, the referee, who was a high school student officiating his first game, did not call fouls for intentional elbows or hug defense, among other dirty play infractions committed by the home team. The ref's lack of calls seemed to embolden the opposing players, who then advanced to using a "wrap-around" tactic on defense. This involved tightly wrapping their arms completely around one of our players while dribbling, essentially rendering them immobile like a mummy trapped in tape. And yet again, no foul was called.

Our team held a comfortable eighteen-point lead as the fourth quarter approached its halfway mark. With complete confidence, seventh-grader Paige effortlessly dribbled the ball across mid-court, already planning her next move. Suddenly, teenage terror Tyson from the opposing team charged toward Paige with intense determination in her narrowed eyes. With lightning-fast reflexes, she made a sudden move and crashed into Paige like a 235-pound linebacker on a football field violently sacking a quarterback on a forceful blitz. The impact was jarring, and Paige was thrown back several feet before landing hard on the unforgiving court. The sound of gasps filled the gym as our parents and I watched in shock, fearing the worst. Without hesitation, I ran onto the court to check on Paige's condition. She struggled to get up, her back in pain from the impact of hitting the hardwood. I assisted her to her feet, my heart racing with worry for any potential injuries. Despite being tough and spunky, Paige seemed shaken as she walked over to the bench and was replaced by our only substitute player.

She eased herself into the seat and released a rueful laugh, exclaiming with disbelief, "That girl just body slammed me." Even though her face showed a mixture of pain and annoyance, she couldn't help but find some amusement in the absurdity of the situation.

Over the course of five games, the four seventh-grade girls on the team had made great progress. At first, they were timid and uncertain about playing against older eighth graders. But now, they exuded confidence and no longer felt intimidated on the basketball court. It had become their second home, as they moved easily and precisely, making crisp passes and shooting confidently.

At the basketball game, many of the parents from Our Lady of Perpetual Help were wearing their "parent goggles," distorting their reality concerning the action on the court. Any clean block by our players was met with cries of "foul!" Despite the obvious anger emanating from the stands and accusations of traveling and fouls against our team, they seemed blind to the cheap shots and rough play coming from their own children. The name of the school certainly fit, as their parents constantly sought help from the young and inexperienced referee who was clearly overwhelmed. However, despite facing biased calls and aggressive play, our Riverside girls displayed remarkable courage and focus. The Eagles scored forty-eight points and won by a comfortable twenty-point margin. I was just grateful that none of our players were injured during the physical game. With a record of 4-1, we had already secured a spot in the playoffs with two more regular season games to go.

The next game was scheduled for Sunday evening, but first came Middle School Day on Saturday. This event was a beloved tradition, where the younger Eagle basketball players were invited to attend the Riverside High School girls varsity basketball game. They could wear their own jerseys and sit in reserved seats, and even join the upper school team on the court for the starting lineup announcement and a halftime competition. It was a special experience for them.

The teenage girls were bursting with excitement during Thursday's practice, giggling and whispering as they speculated on the half-time activity. Would it be a shooting contest, a relay race, or perhaps a dance-off? The possibilities seemed endless, and the predictions kept coming.

"Guess the number of gummy bears in a jar."

Three girls exclaimed simultaneously with enthusiasm, "How about playing a round of bump?"

Kaitlyn, always thinking big, suggested, "Let's have a half-court shot contest. Each of us gets one attempt, and if we make it, we win a Ferrari."

The girls were immediately drawn to this extravagant idea, and it quickly became their top choice, surpassing their previous favorite of playing bump. They now dreamed of being teenagers cruising in a luxurious exotic car.

Practice had just ended, and the school gym was deserted, save for the final echoes of a single bouncing basketball and the faint smell of sweat lingering in the air. Nicole and I walked towards the school parking lot to head home. We were greeted by the crisp, cold winter evening air.

A voice from the football field startled us, and we turned to see Tatum and Allison in t-shirts and shorts on this chilly night, practicing cartwheels on the artificial turf. They were waiting for their rides to arrive.

"Coach! Nicki!" Tatum called out excitedly. "Who has the better cartwheel?"

Nicole and I laughed, amused by their enthusiasm. We watched as Tatum executed a perfect cartwheel, her athletic body moving with grace and precision. Then it was Allison's turn, and she, too, performed a flawless cartwheel, her long blonde hair flying behind her.

"It's a tie," Nicole and I declared, impressed by their skills. "They were both great."

The girls beamed with pride, and we waved goodbye as we continued towards our car.

As the sunlight faded, the two girls' figures were silhouetted against the darkening sky, their arms and legs moving in fluid motion as they executed perfect cartwheels. Their laughter filled the air, a joyful and carefree sound despite the cold surrounding them. The crunch of the turf beneath their feet and the whoosh of their motions were the only other sounds, the stillness of the night waiting to be broken by the arrival of their rides.

The Lady Eagles dominated their last two regular season contests with strong defense and efficient offense. Before the final game, the opposing coach expressed concerns about her team's lack of skill and previous encounters with overly aggressive opponents. I assured her that our team always plays fair and never runs up the score. However, in the game's final minutes, the other team twice made overaggressive borderline dirty plays: an elbow to our point guard's head during a screen and a knockdown on poor Paige while dribbling. From her pregame observations, the opposing coach was right about one thing: her team was not very skilled. But she was wrong in labeling only her opponents as dirty players; her own team also resorted to cheap shots and rough play tactics.

After the last game of the regular season, we all gathered in the middle school cafeteria to celebrate. The girls surprised me with a card they had made themselves, each one signing their names and leaving thoughtful messages. It was the best gift any coach could hope for. The atmosphere was full of energy and laughter as parents and players told stories and enjoyed themselves. Towards the end of the party, the girls suddenly disappeared. Where had they gone? I should have guessed. They had braved the chilly thirty-degree weather to venture outside and play their favorite game: bump. This beloved game is known and loved by basketball players across the country, going by different names like knockout, elimination, lightning, or gotcha, depending on where you live. But no matter what it's called, it brings out the pure joy of playing for teenage girls like these. Kids being kids, enjoying a sport in its simplest form. It was the perfect ending to a great regular season.

Eight out of thirteen teams made it to the playoffs, and Riverside grabbed second place in the regular season with an impressive 6-1 record. The only blemish was a close loss in overtime by just two points when key players were unavailable. Our first opponent in the playoffs was St. Patrick, an unfamiliar team we had not faced during the regular season. The girls were excited to kick off the playoffs and curious about how the tournament would work. I explained that it was a single-elimination event, meaning we would be crowned as CYO city champions if we won three consecutive games. The team worked hard in our two practices leading up to the playoffs, focusing on individual skills and attentively listening during strategy sessions. Paige enthusiastically reminded her teammates about the parade they would have after winning the championship trophy.

Two referees were assigned to the quarter-final match-up against St. Patrick. However, the younger ref was not qualified for the job. After only thirty seconds of play, he quickly removed the official scorekeeper from the table and replaced him with a different parent volunteer. He called three questionable fouls on Finley in the first quarter alone due to what he deemed as a poor attitude and body language. Despite Finley not saying a word to the ref, he threatened to kick her out of the game if she said anything else. He snarled, "If you say another word. I will run you out of the gym." Later, during a second-quarter timeout, the same ref challenged me, asking if I was "done." Confused, I turned to see who he was addressing and realized it was me. I calmly replied, "Yes, I am done." Coincidentally, this official had already presided over several playoff games at the same gym earlier that day, and his subpar performance did not go unnoticed. The following day, he was permanently prohibited from ever refereeing another CYO game due to his unusual and unreliable actions, which were reported by multiple coaches and spectators. His strange, erratic behavior had not been overlooked.

For the first time all season, Riverside fell behind early and found themselves trailing 11-3 by the end of the first quarter. Late in the quarter, I called a timeout to regroup and remind the team to stick to their game plan. Despite being down, there was still enough time to catch up. St. Patrick's luck seemed to run out after their strong start. Ultimately, our talent was too much, and we pulled away to win comfortably by 19 points with a final score of 43-24. Nicole had an impressive performance, scoring 33 points and making four three-pointers. Finley contributed 10 points. They were the only two players who scored. Our offense was executed flawlessly with correct player spacing, quick ball movement, and sharp cutting, resulting in easy shots. However, some of our players struggled to make shots that they usually have no trouble making; perhaps it was due to nerves from playing in front of a big crowd during a playoff game. The unbalanced scoring concerned me; I prefer it when multiple players contribute to the scoring load.

It was gratifying that all the Riverside girls received equal playing time during the game. Throughout the regular season, our ten Eagle players also played equal minutes. CYO league rules mandated that each player must play at least one quarter per game. Unfortunately, many coaches blatantly ignored this rule, but luckily, it was strictly enforced by a CYO representative during the playoffs. This worked in our favor as Riverside players had gained valuable experience competing in regular-season games. In contrast, some of our opponents struggled when they were put into playoff games. They lacked skill and hadn't been given much opportunity to improve during regular season contests, resulting in a lack of confidence when they played during high-pressure post-season games.

The semifinal game was against St. Benedict, a team we had easily defeated earlier in the season. However, I knew this contest would be more challenging. Lexi, one of our top players who had caused chaos during the first game teaming up with Nicole on a devastating backcourt press, would not be playing due to injury. Meanwhile, St. Benedict was on a six-game winning streak and had taller and stronger players than us. We started off slow for the second playoff game in a row and found ourselves behind by seven points. Thankfully, Nicki was on fire once again. That feeling of being in a zone where every shot seems effortless is almost transcendent - the hoop appears bigger, and every shot smoothly falls through the net. It's rare and fleeting, but there's no better sensation for a basketball player than seeing their points rack up at an incredible pace. Nicole scored 27 points and made four three-pointers, just like she did in the previous game. She had scored an unbelievable 60 points in two playoff games, including 8 three-pointers. It was a remarkable display of shooting skill for a middle schooler that could not possibly be sustained over time. Fortunately, we didn't need her hot streak to continue forever; one more game would suffice.

The last couple minutes of the game were full of twists and turns. With less than two minutes left in the fourth quarter and a comfortable 12-point lead, I decided to take Nicki out of the game. It seemed like we had already secured the victory. But then, St. Benedict surprised us with two improbable three-pointers and a layup, bringing their deficit down to just four points with only forty seconds remaining. I called a timeout and substituted my daughter back into the game. She calmly took control of the ball and dribbled for 20 seconds, using up valuable time before passing it off to an open Allison. However, for reasons unbeknownst to everyone in the gym, Allison suddenly pivoted and launched a wild twenty-foot airball. As an inexperienced player, she didn't understand that all we needed to do was hold onto the ball without taking 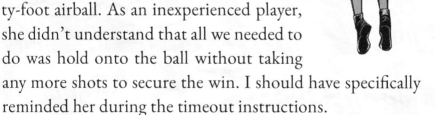 any more shots to secure the win. I should have specifically reminded her during the timeout instructions.

As the clock ticked down to just a few seconds, St. Benedict was down by four points, and their chances of winning seemed slim. The only hope was a miraculous three-pointer followed by a successful free throw after drawing a foul. Instead, the ball ended up in the hands of one of the opposing team star players, who easily drove toward the basket for an uncontested layup as time expired. Riverside narrowly escaped with a two-point victory.

Despite the narrow loss, the opposing team and their supporters exploded in jubilation, while our parents remained subdued. The St. Benedict players hugged and high-fived each other, their bodies buzzing with energy and excitement. Some of our players were confused and mistakenly believed we had lost the game, hanging their heads dejectedly. The dichotomy of emotions pervaded the air, a swirling dance of joy and disappointment amidst a sea of flailing arms and perplexed expressions.

Despite my poor coaching in the last game, we managed to advance to the championship round. Our opponents were the undefeated Blessed Sacrament team, comprised of five highly skilled girls who all played top-level AAU club basketball. In contrast, our team only had two AAU players - Nicole and Finley. Throughout my coaching career, Finley has been the most challenging player for me to connect with. Although she performed well in the CYO league, she had difficulty adjusting to the higher level of play at the AAU level. Her body language on the court was often negative, and her attitude could be described as moody. It's possible she felt envious of my daughter Nicole, who excelled on our team and was also recognized as the top player in the entire league. Another factor could be that her father is no longer the coach, which may have affected her mindset. Of course, it could also just be typical teenage behavior.

Finley's performance at practices and games gradually declined as the season progressed. She started missing more practices and showed no signs of being a leader on the court. There were times when she acted immaturely, like lying on the ground during team huddles while her teammates paid attention. I would kindly but firmly remind her to stand up and join the group. In scrimmages, she would sometimes fake an injury after getting her shot blocked by another player, claiming it was a foul. However, her teammates would call her out and say it was a clean block, which would upset her. Looking back, I wish I had put more effort into building a stronger relationship with Finley. Despite her occasional disinterest and mood swings, she wasn't a bad kid and had moments of being a committed teammate.

Facing Blessed Sacrament in the championship game would be our toughest challenge yet. We didn't play them during the regular season, and both teams had similar statistics regarding points scored and allowed. This game would put our abilities to the test, especially since we were considered the underdogs. Blessed Sacrament had a talented team and a size advantage over us. To have a chance at winning, Nicole needed to continue her impressive scoring streak, but she couldn't do it alone. Her teammates, who had struggled with shooting in the playoffs, also needed to step up and contribute.

As we approached the highly anticipated championship game, we dedicated part of our practice time to mastering the full-court press and developing a strategy for breaking it if our opponents attempted it. We knew Blessed Sacrament had scouted us and that we rarely used this defensive strategy during regular season or playoff games. But by catching them off guard with our press secret weapon, we could gain an advantage. I handed out a concise one-page guide outlining each player's specific role and responsibilities in executing a diamond full-court press and how to counter a press on offense. During the week, I emphasized the importance of staying calm and enjoying themselves during the game, which was expected to draw a large crowd. This was their chance to celebrate a successful season as one of the top two teams in their grade level for CYO varsity middle school basketball.

The atmosphere was electric as the teams stepped onto the court for their pre-game warmups. The prestigious private high school's gymnasium was filled to capacity with over four hundred enthusiastic fans, all eager to witness the intense matchup between Riverside and Blessed Sacrament in the CYO eighth-grade varsity championship game. The top-ranked in-state Riverside High School girls varsity basketball team sat among the spectators, showing their support for our middle school team and cheering them on. However, something seemed off when we saw our opponents warm up. Blessed Sacrament usually had a full team of twelve players, but today only seven were present. Their weakest five were noticeably absent, raising suspicion that they intentionally left them at home to increase their chances of winning. Although I couldn't prove it, it seemed like a brazen move by the opponents to avoid having their least talented girls play at least a quarter as mandated by CYO rules. It was clear that Blessed Sacrament was pulling a BS stunt. Meanwhile, our team had nine out of ten players present, with the only missing player being Lexi, who had recovered from her injury but was participating in an out-of-state soccer tournament. We knew her absence would be felt on the court as she was an amazing athlete who could have effectively shut down one of their top players from scoring.

Before the game, four players approached me individually to discuss their full-court press roles and responsibilities for offense and defense. However, once the game began, neither team pressed much because each team had skilled ball handlers who could efficiently break a press and create easy scoring opportunities. Despite the other team rarely pressing us, the team was confident and ready to break a press if needed. The players did an exceptional job in game preparation. Their focus and determination were evident. They were locked in and ready to compete.

As was becoming a recurring theme in the playoffs, we fell behind again and were faced with a six-point deficit, the score standing at 9-3. Nicole continued to dominate on the court despite being constantly double and triple teamed. She scored an impressive 13 points and made three more three-pointers. However, Finley's performance was noticeably lacking as she played recklessly and refused to pass to her open teammates. This caught the attention of our bench players, who questioned me about her behavior. During timeouts, I stressed the importance of teamwork and ball movement, specifically directing my words towards Finley. But it seemed to have no effect as she played selfishly throughout the game. Frustrated, I made the decision to sub her out early in the fourth quarter. "Why are you taking me out?" she asked incredulously as she walked to the bench. "Just take a quick break for a few minutes," I replied calmly.

Despite Finley's antics and the clear difference in talent between our teams, the Lady Eagles showed grit and resilience throughout the game. We managed to cut the lead to four points midway through the third quarter, but it wasn't enough in the end. The final score was 38-30, leaving us with a bitter feeling, knowing that one small factor could have changed the outcome.

Maybe if Finley had played to her full potential and shared the ball more, or if Lexi had played, or even if a couple of the less skilled Blessed Sacrament players had shown up for the championship game, the outcome could have been different. However, it wasn't meant to be, and we were left to wonder "what if?" as we gathered our equipment and returned home. Even though we lost, our team was proud of what we had achieved that season, and the seventh graders were determined to come back even stronger next year.

The team's performance impressed me. Despite being up against physically stronger and more experienced eighth graders, the four seventh graders showed remarkable maturity and skill on the basketball court. Together, they contributed ten out of the team's thirty points, with three out of four players scoring. Chelsea confidently made both free throw attempts and a difficult ten-foot bank shot. Kaitlyn sank a fourteen-foot jump shot with an assist from Nicole. Paige scored twice in the key despite being aggressively defended by taller, more skilled Blessed Sacrament players. I had been encouraging her to take more shots when she had open opportunities, and I was thrilled that she scored four points in the championship game, matching her previous individual game-high.

Paige was honored with the esteemed Katy Branch award two days before the big championship game match-up. The award was named after a highly respected coach who had led Riverside High School girls varsity teams to five state titles. Several players on our team could have been nominated for this prestigious accolade based on their exceptional skills and accomplishments. However, after careful consideration, I chose Paige as the most deserving candidate. The entire middle school student body gathered at an assembly where the athletic director presented her with the award, reading my words of recommendation aloud.

"Paige always tries her best and puts in maximum effort to improve every day and develop her basketball skills. She is always positive in supporting her teammates and shows compassion and respect for her opponents. Paige is a "glue player" who does a lot of important little things to help make the team successful. She always hustles back on defense, does an excellent job passing the ball and effectively moves without the ball. In one game when the team was short-handed, she played point guard and effectively brought the ball up court against full court pressure defense. Paige always has a smile on her face and has fun competing on the basketball court both in practices and games."

That evening, Nicole shared with me that Paige was caught off guard about receiving the award and had a huge smile on her face. Nicki couldn't resist getting a jab at her coach dad, saying, "I was worried when the athletic director started reading what you wrote for her. I thought it would be a never-ending novel and we'd miss out on lunch."

I was also proud of Nicole. She was the best player on the court in the championship game. She carried the team on her back and kept the score close with her impressive skills. Not only did she lead in scoring, but she also blocked shots, defended against the opposing team's top scorer, grabbed rebounds, made remarkable passes to her teammates, and served as a vocal leader to encourage them. In the three playoff games, Nicki scored an incredible 73 points and amazingly made 11 out of 15 three-pointers.

My daughter was fuming after the championship game, disappointed with Finley's performance. "Why did she constantly take those crazy shots instead of passing to our open teammates?" I nodded in agreement with Nicki's assessment and listened attentively. I comforted her by reminding her that she had played outstanding basketball throughout the season and had been a fantastic leader and teammate.

Following the game, Samantha Brooks - a senior basketball star at Riverside High School with a full ride D1 college scholarship - texted Nicole to congratulate her on her performance and urge her to continue honing her skills and dominating on the court. This boosted Nicki's spirits and instilled confidence in her abilities. News was already circulating about her talent, and even the varsity girls team and coach were well aware of her potential to make a significant impact as an incoming freshman next year.

When the season ended, Allison's mother came up to me to thank me for coaching her daughter. She expressed how proud she was that Allison contributed to a winning team and played in a championship game for the first time in any sport. During our conversation, Allison's mother mentioned a humorous incident involving Allison studying the one-page press strategy document I had given to the players. She was sitting at the dining room table with her younger brother, explaining its contents to him. When her mother pointed out that the paper would get ruined during dinner, Allison confidently responded, "It won't get ruined. It's laminated."

In the championship game, Nicole passed the ball to Allison while she was open in the key, and she almost made a shot. Unfortunately, her 12-foot jumper hit the back of the rim and narrowly missed. She did get fouled on another attempt but missed each shot when both free throws bounced off the rim, "unlimited shot" near misses. Allison will always have fond memories of playing basketball for the Riverside Eagles, even if she never plays on another hoop team again.

With each passing week, the players improved their basketball skills and ability to work together as a team. It was a delight to witness their excitement during the trophy presentation. They cheered each other on, exchanged high-fives, and shared hugs while reveling in their achievement. As they stood side by side on the court, arms raised in victory, it was evident that this is what middle school sports should be about: teamwork, friendship, and unadulterated happiness. The trophy they received was just the cherry on top of an already delicious cake.

At the start of the season, Tatum and Molly were considered the weakest players on the team. Tatum, in eighth grade and on the lacrosse team, and Molly, a seventh-grade soccer player, struggled with fundamental skills like dribbling and shooting during their first practice. It was evident that both lacked experience in competitive basketball, but they were natural athletes and excelled in other sports. As the season progressed, Tatum's growth was extraordinary. She quickly became one of the top rebounders on the team, effortlessly grabbing difficult rebounds even in crowded situations. Her defensive abilities also vastly improved as she expertly shut down skilled offensive players. In the beginning, Tatum's shot was unrefined and often resulted in airballs. However, by the end of the season, her form was flawless: a perfect one-handed shot that consistently swished through the net.

She had become an integral part of the team and earned her spot in the starting lineup for the championship game.

During a late-season practice, I asked Tatum about her significant shooting development. "Your shot has really improved, Tatum. Your form is solid now, and you can shoot with just one hand. I saw you make three consecutive free throws just now; that's impressive. Did anyone else, like your dad, assist you with this?" I asked with curiosity. "Thank you, coach," she replied gratefully. "Actually, I've been studying how Nicki and other players shoot during our form shooting sessions and have been implementing your tips." It's remarkable what driven individuals can achieve in such a short amount of time.

During the season, Tatum's mother shared how much her daughter was thriving on the basketball team. Tatum herself could feel her skills improving each week and enjoyed the camaraderie of being part of a winning team. As an accomplished lacrosse player, she was tired of always coming in last place in her competitive club league.

Throughout the entire season, Molly proved to be an exceptional defender, eagerly taking on the challenge of guarding the opposing team's best scorer. She was a nuisance on the court, constantly disrupting the rhythm of even the most skilled players and throwing them off their game mentally. Despite scoring only two baskets, one of which was an impressive three-pointer from deep range, her teammates admired her. Molly's selflessness and commitment to the team were evident when she offered to play less during playoffs to increase our chances of winning. However, I declined her generous offer; she had earned her spot on the court and deserved equal playing time like everyone else.

The long season had finally concluded, and the streak had finally ended. But as I reflected in my office, surrounded by awards and memorabilia, I couldn't help but feel it was still a perfect season. My gaze fixed on a team photo hanging on the wall and I smiled at the memories of our journey together.

Though we fell short in the championship game, it doesn't matter to me. These girls are all champions, Eagle hoopers soaring and reaching great heights. They are destined for greatness in life, and it was an honor to have been a part of their journey.

I am ready to retire for good this time. I can't help but

reminisce. Every unlimited shot they took, every less-than-perfect practice session, and every moment of laughter and tears has led the players to this moment. These girls will go on to make a difference in the world, each of them a perfect swish through the basket of life.

The games may have ended, but the lessons and memories will stay with me forever. And I am grateful for every single one of them.

TRIPPED UP

The peaceful slumber that followed a day of raucous celebration and patriotic fervor was brutally disrupted by a shrill and unwelcome wake-up call in the early hours of July 5th. The blaring sound of the alarm sent shockwaves through my body, jolting me out of my pleasant dreams. The sounds of birds chirping and distant cars driving by were now drowned out by the urgent beeping. As I reached over to silence the alarm, I felt the cool sheets beneath my fingertips, a stark contrast to the oppressive summer heat.

We had spent the previous evening at Gas Works Park in Seattle, enjoying a dazzling fireworks show from our usual spot. Now, I was paying the price for my decision to stay up late before a long trip to Kentucky. It took all my willpower to force myself out of bed, groggily opening one eye at a time. My body felt heavy and lethargic, my muscles aching from lack of rest. Standing up unsteadily, I paused to admire my wife Gabby's serene sleeping face nestled into her pillow. Her name brings a smile to our faces – she's a "gabber," a non-stop talker, and the center of attention at any gathering. She is a sparkling firecracker of conversation, her words dazzling and explosive, igniting laughter and joy in those around her.

My name is Mike Smith. I don't like either of my names because they are so generic and common: nine letters, three vowels, six consonants, and two syllables that will inevitably fade into obscurity. At fifty-seven years old, I am a semi-retired accountant who spent most of my work career at a large financial firm. I'm short in stature with a receding hairline, though it never bothered me much. My life has been one of routine and predictability, filled with numbers and spreadsheets. Sometimes I feel discouraged when I think about what I have accomplished in life and imagine what will be written on my tombstone: "Here rests a mundane man with an unremarkable name and boring job."

Our family consists of Gabby, our daughter Natalie, and me. We are a small but happy unit living in a modest, comfortable suburban house. Gabby has long, brown hair that she often ties up in a messy bun, and her easy smile could light up any room. She is always making jokes and keeping us entertained.

Natalie is the spitting image of her mother. She has the same long brown hair and easy smile but with a hint of mischief in her eyes. Having just become a teenager, she is already wise beyond her years and has a curious mind that is always asking questions. She excels in school and basketball, making us proud parents. The only thing I would alter on

Nat's "resume" is her place of birth; she was born in Bellevue, not Seattle. My wife enjoys teasing me about my nitpicky nature and finds my fixation on this trivial detail endearing.

And then there is me, the quiet one in the family. I prefer to observe and take things in rather than be the center of attention. But I love my family more than anything, and they are my world.

Born and raised in Seattle, I have a deep sense of pride for my hometown. However, I dislike the official city nickname "the Emerald City" that is used by transplants. As a true Seattleite, I prefer to call it the "Jet City." Growing up near the highly acclaimed University of Washington, a renowned research institution, I am constantly amazed by the number of major global companies originating from our modest city. From Boeing (aerospace) to Microsoft (computing), Starbucks (coffee) to Amazon (e-commerce/books), these companies have left an indelible mark on the world economy.

The reason for our early wake-up was a trip to Kentucky, known for its famous 3 B's - bluegrass, bourbon, and basketball. My 14-year-old daughter and I were embarking on a week-long journey to Louisville, where she would compete in two consecutive AAU basketball tournaments. This was her second year on the Elite Lady Panthers team, and they had trips scheduled during the season to cities like Cincinnati, Las Vegas, Philadelphia, and Phoenix. I couldn't help but reflect on Nat's basketball journey so far, from the local rec league to now competing against the best players her age in the country. It was a testament to her hard work and dedication,

Playing on an elite travel team comes with a hefty price tag - club fees, travel expenses including flights, hotels, car rentals, food, and other miscellaneous costs quickly add up. After careful consideration, Gabby and I had budgeted $15,000 for the current season. It was a significant sum, but we didn't dwell on it too much. We chose not to focus on the fact that this amount could pay for an entire year of tuition at my alma mater, the prestigious University of Washington. We were willing to bear this expense for our daughter's love for the sport.

Thankfully, next season will be different. Natalie will be entering high school, and the costly year-round AAU travel season will be shortened to just six months during the spring and summer. This will allow for a much-needed break during the fall and winter when high school basketball takes place. It was a small consolation, but we would take whatever we could get to ease the financial burden.

Natalie was downstairs, her trusty basketball duffel bag hanging off her shoulder as she stood by the front door. She had pulled her chestnut brown hair back into a sleek ponytail, and her feet were clad in well-worn sneakers that bore the marks of countless games and tournaments. Even though it was an early hour, her eyes gleamed with eagerness and determination, ready to conquer whatever challenges and competition lay ahead.

Once our two suitcases and carry-on backpacks were securely packed in the trunk of our Subaru, we began our journey towards SeaTac International Airport - a bustling hub situated between Seattle and Tacoma. Our family calls Kirkland home - a lively suburban community known for its beautiful summers with mild temperatures and low humidity. On clear days, we could even catch a glimpse of Mount Rainier towering in the distance. The famous saying "the bluest skies you've ever seen are in Seattle" holds true, and it's no surprise that many people are drawn to the Pacific Northwest or choose to make it their permanent residence.

Gabby had offered to drive, and my mind drifted as I relaxed in the front passenger seat. As I get older and have dad responsibilities, random memories of old landmarks, now gone, occasionally surface in my head with increasing regularity. Sick's Stadium, where I watched my first baseball game with my father. The Kingdome, where I saw my first concert, was a teenage dream come true. The Fun Forest, where my friends and I laughed and screamed on roller coasters and ate cotton candy until our stomachs ached. The Twin TeePees restaurant on Aurora, where we would go for family dinners and make silly faces in the parking lot. And Chubby and Tubby, with their absurdly low prices and quirky advertising, a staple in the community.

It's mind-boggling to think how this once sleepy town in the Pacific Northwest produced musical legends like Jimi Hendrix and Kurt Cobain, each passing away at the young age of 27. First, there was Hendrix, whose electrifying guitar riffs and psychedelic lyrics still echo through the streets and bars of this town. His talent was undeniable, his passion for music unmistakable, but his demons ultimately consumed him. And then there was Cobain, the voice of a generation whose raw, emotive lyrics struck a chord with millions. His rise to fame was meteoric, but he couldn't escape the darkness that lurked within him. I had watched Nirvana's last local concert at the Seattle Center Arena a mere three months before the troubled musical genius took his own life with a shotgun. It's astonishing to consider how this ordinary city could give rise to such tremendous talent only to have it all disappear in an instant.

My parents often shared stories about the iconic 1962 Seattle World's Fair, where even Elvis Presley himself appeared and later starred in a movie titled "It Happened at the World's Fair." I heard stories about The Beatles' stay at The Edgewater Hotel on the waterfront, where they attempted to fish from their suite window. Despite my thorough research, I still couldn't confirm whether or not John, Paul, George, and Ringo actually caught anything.

Lost in nostalgia, my thoughts were suddenly interrupted by a notification on my iPhone. The memories disappeared without a trace, leaving me grasping for scraps of images, emotions, and details. I squinted at the small font, realizing I had left my reading glasses behind as I read the message aloud:

"Alaska Air: We're sorry – Flight 408 is departing late from Seattle (SEA) @ 7:30 am on 07/05 arriving Chicago-O'Hare (ORD) @ 1:27 pm, and Flight 4238, operated by Air Wisconsin as American Eagle, is departing late from Chicago O'Hare (ORD) @ 3:51 PM on 07/05 arriving Louisville (SDF) @ 06:10 PM on 07/05. Have questions? Visit the Alaska Air website. Reply STOP to opt out."

After a quick calculation, I realized that the first flight from Seattle was running ninety minutes late. Fortunately, the second leg from Chicago to Louisville was only delayed by one minute. It wasn't a big deal. I could have slept in longer but on the bright side, we could grab some breakfast at the airport now.

Natalie and I were stuck in a lengthy line at the airport's Starbucks, waiting to order our breakfast sandwiches and drinks. As an avid basketball fan and longtime season ticket holder for the Seattle Sonics, it pained me when they relocated to Oklahoma City in 2008. The billionaire owner of Starbucks, Howard Schultz, was also the local owner of the professional basketball team, which made his decision to sell the team to an out-of-town ownership group that moved them even more devastating. In solidarity with my fellow Sonics fans, I vowed never to step foot in a Starbucks again or give a single penny to the traitor Howard Schultz. However, my promise only lasted twelve days before my love for their Caramel Macchiato drink, my crack caffeine beverage of choice, lured me back in. I couldn't resist their overpriced but addictive specialty drinks, spending over $100 monthly on various Mochas, Lattes, and Fraps.

As soon as the Coffee Express faucet started working again, I couldn't contain my excitement. But for another household member, it was an even greater reason to celebrate. Our beloved dog, Brewster, had been sulking ever since his usual puppuccino "pup cups" filled with whipped cream were taken away. While it pained me to see him so dejected, I found some amusement in his dramatic reaction. The first time I returned home after the brief Starbucks boycott, I was welcomed by Brewster's wagging tail and happy demeanor. The magic powers of whipped cream had transformed him into a perfectly well-behaved pooch, sitting completely still after being instructed to. Without his favorite treat, he only followed simple commands like stay and sit occasionally. But as soon as he saw that white dollop of heaven, Brewster was turned into a best-in-show winner, ready to follow instructions perfectly.

Ordering coffee was no longer a simple task; now, customers enjoyed requesting elaborate and unconventional drinks. I found myself behind someone in line who asked for a "venti extra hot half-caf, half-decaf, chocolate almond shaken espresso with raspberry, sugar-free vanilla, hazelnut, and peppermint syrups topped off by a small ice cube with a dash of cinnamon." I tried not to be as excessive with my own orders, but I couldn't resist indulging in seasonal favorites like the Egg Nog Latte during the holidays. Brewster was the ideal patron, consistently ordering his pup cup to-go without any alterations. As a bonus, the puppuccino came at no cost, meaning my faithful dog wasn't supporting the wealthy person largely responsible for "Sonicsgate," the scandalous sale and relocation of the Seattle NBA team after 41 years in my hometown.

The flight from Seattle to Chicago was uneventful, as Natalie and I are seasoned travelers who don't mind flying. As our plane descended towards Chicago O'Hare Airport, Natalie tapped me on the shoulder with excitement in her eyes. "Dad, look at that view!" she exclaimed, pointing out the window. I followed her gaze and was amazed by the breathtaking sight below us - the city of Chicago sprawled out like a patchwork quilt of skyscrapers. After landing, Nat and I navigated the bustling airport to find our connecting flight to Louisville. The airport was filled with a mix of rushed travelers and families on vacation, creating a chaotic yet vibrant atmosphere. As we weaved through the crowds, I noticed the diverse group of individuals from different backgrounds and cultures, each with unique stories and destinations.

As we arrived at our connecting gate, Natalie and I quickly located seats to wait for our flight. She plugged in her headphones and lost herself in her music while I pulled out my Kindle, eager to dive into the historical novel I had downloaded for the trip. The time flew by as we were engrossed in our chosen forms of entertainment, the anticipation of the upcoming basketball tournaments heightening our excitement for the journey ahead. After killing twenty minutes browsing through magazines at the newsstand, we easily made our way onto our connecting flight from Chicago to Louisville and settled into our assigned seats.

Before long, we were informed that the Chicago area was about to experience severe weather conditions, and our plane might not be able to take off before the storm rolled in with its thunder and lightning. Five minutes later, the pilot informed us that the plane needed to be refueled, and he wasn't sure where we were in line for this service. What started as a five-minute wait turned into ten minutes, then twenty minutes, and finally one hour. A woman in row 22 started reciting the Lord's prayer and, after no response from God, decided to take things up a notch. She started uttering an expanded list of prayers and fingering the Rosary beads she bought at the Vatican gift shop. The beads were supposedly blessed by the pope himself and made of precious gemstones, Venetian glass, and a sterling silver crucifix.

The plane was sweltering and lacked any air circulation. The flight attendants, now reduced to "waitresses in the sky," walked up and down the aisles with small plastic cups of tepid water. Feeling anxious from the uncomfortable conditions, passengers eagerly gulped down the liquid like parched camels. I peered out the window and saw dark clouds on the horizon, steadily growing larger each minute.

The plane had been sitting on the tarmac for what felt like hours. Passengers were growing increasingly agitated and restless, their mutterings and sighs creating a palpable tension in the cabin.

Finally, the pilot's voice crackled over the intercom a final time, his words both dreaded and expected.

"I'm sorry, folks, but we will not be able to depart due to the current weather situation. It's for your own safety. We will be de-boarding shortly. I apologize for any inconvenience and thank you for flying with American."

As we exited the plane, I checked the flight status of our plane on the reader board: CLOSED. This was a new one for me. I was used to seeing ON TIME, BOARD-ING, DELAYED and CANCELED. Natalie and I talked it over and decided to stay in the gate boarding area. Seeing the CLOSED status gave us hope that the delay would be short, and we'd soon be on our way to Louisville. But after an hour, boredom set in. Our flight status remained unchanged on the airport flight board, but I noticed that the status of more flights was now showing as CANCELED – a troubling trend. We went to the American Airlines information booth, where there was already a lengthy line. After waiting for forty minutes, a customer service representative explained that while the weather was clearing up in Chicago, it was worsening in Louisville. Our flight to Louisville, with a status still showing as CLOSED, would not be departing today. Fortunately, we had the option to fly to Lexington, Cincinnati, or Indianapolis and then drive a rental car to Louisville - all three cities were roughly equidistant from our final destination. Since I had been to Indianapolis for work previously and Natalie had an upcoming AAU tournament in Cincinnati, we ultimately settled on Lexington - known for its Kentucky bluegrass and the renowned University of Kentucky basketball team.

We received our new boarding passes and headed toward the updated gate, hoping for an uneventful flight. However, at 6:20 pm, our new flight status suddenly changed from DELAYED to CANCELED. My worry grew as I remembered that Nat's first basketball game was tomorrow morning at 09:00 am. Quickly making a decision, I chose to rent a car and drive from Chicago to Louisville. After a short search on my iPhone, I calculated that it would take approximately five hours to get there, and we could arrive at the hotel by 1:00 am if we left by 8:00 pm. Hopefully, Nat could rest during the drive and not be too tired for her early morning game.

While walking towards the rental car sign, Natalie received a text from her teammate Ava Cooper, whose connecting flight from Chicago was also canceled. Ava asked if she and her father could share the rental car with us, which I agreed to since it would be good to have another adult for company, and it would help out a nice kid like Ava.

Ava gave Natalie an update on their progress, explaining that they were currently in line to retrieve their luggage. She said they would meet us at the rental car counter. Natalie and I hopped on a train to get to the Hertz location, relieved to find no line upon arrival. However, our relief quickly turned into disappointment when we heard the price for a week's rental - $2200. This was a drastic increase from the initial reservation cost of $600 (which I had just canceled) with pick-up and drop-off in Louisville. Now, on top of today's travel delay, I was facing an unexpected expense of $1600, a surprise kidney punch to my financial body.

Eventually, we settled on a Nissan Rogue as our rental car. We returned to the counter and waited for the Coopers... and waited...and waited. Every ten minutes, Natalie received a text from Ava stating that she and her dad would arrive soon. Forty-five minutes had passed before I finally got a call from Jackson Cooper.

"Hey, buddy - should we meet you at the rental car place, or can you pick us up after we grab our bags? We should be getting them any minute."

My anger boiled over, and I couldn't believe that I was being asked to drive aimlessly around O'Hare Airport, trying to find two people in a sea of faces. I was already doing a favor for the Coopers, and I responded sharply, unwilling to comply with such an unreasonable request.

"No, let's just meet here. It's much more convenient that way. Just follow the signs to the rental car center, hop on the monorail train, and take the escalator down. It doesn't take long at all, and it's a short trip to get here."

After another half hour went by, I spotted Jackson Cooper rolling towards us in a wheelchair. An airport staff member pushed the chair, and Ava walked alongside them. As they got closer, Big Coop struggled to stand up and declared in a booming voice:

"We never got our luggage, and now I'm hungry. We'll have to grab a bite to eat at some point. My medication was in my bags, and I really need that. I have health issues, including blood clots. Can you drop us off at our hotel? It's only five minutes away from where you're staying. I looked it up. We could take a cab or Uber, but it would be easier if you just dropped us off. How've you been, buddy?"

I couldn't believe the stream of words coming from this large man dressed in basketball shorts and a dirty sweatshirt. Jackson Cooper was a giant, standing at 6'6" and weighing over 300 lbs. He could have played the role of Goliath in a biblical epic. He was a towering figure with an even bigger mouth. I wasn't exactly sure what JC did for a living; my

guess is that he worked in sales and could close a deal by persuading clients into submission with his rapid-delivery bombastic speech.

His legs were swollen and aching, a constant reminder of an unforgiving medical condition that had plagued him for years. It was a struggle to keep moving, especially since his medication had gone missing, and the flight had only exacerbated the pain. With each shuffling step, time seemed to stretch on endlessly. The risk of blood clots, a constant threat, seemed to taunt him with each slow, labored movement.

After a lengthy delay waiting for the Coopers to arrive, we finally left the airport and merged onto the highway. On my left, the "L" train line ran parallel to us, the constant hum of the tracks providing a steady backdrop to the unending concrete scenery. It was difficult to focus as the rain pounded against the windshield, thunder rumbled in the distance, and lightning illuminated the darkening sky.

As we drove, I let my mind wander. The storm's intensity reminded me of a scene from the movie Divergent, where a post-apocalyptic version of Chicago served as the setting. The thought made me shiver, wondering if I had somehow been transported into the film through a futuristic time machine.

I shook my head, trying to clear my mind of these fantasy thoughts. I needed to focus on the present, on the road ahead of me. I couldn't afford to let my mind wander to the past or the future - not now, not when every second on this road was crucial. The weather was treacherous, with driving rain and low visibility making the drive more challenging than usual.

I took a deep breath and reminded myself of the task at hand. I had to make it to my destination safely, no matter what obstacles the weather threw my way. I adjusted my grip on the wheel and pressed down on the gas pedal, determined to push through the storm and reach Louisville safely.

As we traveled further away from Chicago, I noticed an exit sign for Gary, Indiana. The name brought me a bit of joy as I hummed one of my favorite Jackson 5 songs, "ABC." The Jacksons hailed from Gary; this was my only association with the city. I was unaware of its history of riots in 1968 or its current state as a decaying rust belt city with significant issues, including high unemployment, a decaying infrastructure, abandoned downtown buildings, and a significant drop in population. To me, Gary equaled the magic of Motown rather than its current struggles.

As we passed through the city's outskirts, I wondered how different things could have been if I had grown up here instead of in Seattle. Would I have still fallen in love with music? Would I have joined a band and toured the country? Or would I be struggling to make ends meet like so many of the residents of this forgotten city?

Lost in thought, I was jolted out of my tranquil state by Big Coop's booming voice: "Are your lights on? I can't tell if they are on or not." His abrupt interruption shattered the stillness of the evening, and I felt my heart jump in surprise.

I quickly adjusted the headlight knob, hoping that the lights would brighten and appease Big Coop's concerns. But to my dismay, the lights did not appear to be working properly. The dim glow they emitted was barely enough to light the road ahead.

Gritting my teeth, I tried to remain calm and composed as I fiddled with the knobs and switches, hoping to fix whatever was wrong. But the lights remained stubbornly dim as if mocking my futile attempts to fix them.

I made the decision to stop at the nearest rest stop in order to address the issue with the car's lights. As I pulled into a parking spot, the rain continued to slam against the windshield, creating a noisy distraction. The occasional sound of thunder added a deep bass note to the already chaotic symphony. The air was thick and humid, like trying to breathe through a damp wool blanket; each breath felt heavy and difficult, causing sweat to collect in my clothes. JC emerged from the car, his large figure looming over me.

I popped open the hood and began to inspect the headlights, trying to determine what was causing them to be so dim. Cooper hovered beside me, his presence looming large in the confined space under the hood.

"Let me take a look," he said, his voice much gentler than normal. And before I could protest, he had disappeared under the car's hood, his bulky frame bent over the engine as he tinkered with its inner workings.

As I observed his work, I felt a sense of gratitude towards this man who always seemed so intimidating. Yet here he was, sweat glistening on his forehead as he fixed the car without complaint. It made me wonder what had caused this change in his demeanor.

After a few moments, Big Coop emerged from under the hood with a triumphant smile. "All done," he announced, gesturing to the now brilliantly lit headlights. "It was just a loose connection that needed fixing. Good as new." I was amazed. With just a few simple adjustments, Cooper had restored the car's lights back to working condition.

As we settled back into the car and resumed our journey to Louisville, the mood inside the vehicle transformed. Cooper's upbeat demeanor was a refreshing shift. He entertained us with anecdotes from his time as a college basketball player, capturing the attention of both Natalie and Ava with stories of last-second shots and victorious championship games.

As the miles ticked by, the rain outside slowly began to subside, giving way to a clear night sky dotted with stars. The highway stretched out before us, illuminated by our now bright headlights and the soft glow of the moon. Natalie had drifted off to sleep in the backseat, her head resting against the window as Ava listened intently to her dad's stories.

I also found myself drawn into Cooper's tales, getting lost in the nostalgia of his glory days on the court. For a moment, the stress of the canceled flight and the unexpected rental car cost melted away.

"Hey man, I'm starving. Can we stop for food?" Cooper asked. I let out an annoyed sigh. I had finally found my driving groove, which would now be interrupted by a pit stop. The two teenagers in the backseat were probably hungry, too. "Of course, Jackson. Let's find a place to eat," I responded, scanning the highway for any signs indicating a nearby food venue. As if on cue, a neon sign loomed in the distance, announcing an upcoming exit with various dining options. Cooper let out a whoop of excitement, his booming voice filling the car with energy. We ended up three miles from the freeway exit at a sketchy-looking 24-hour Burger King with ten cars in the parking lot. It seemed like two businesses were operating on the premises: the fast-food restaurant and an open-air drug market. We walked to the front door to eat inside, but a sign informed us that the dining area was closed due to flooding and water hazards. Disappointed, we returned to the car and ordered our food at the drive-thru window. The two girls each got a chicken sandwich, fries, and a coke, while Big Coop ordered a Double Whopper Meal, two orders of eight-piece Fiery Buffalo Nuggets, five orders of Buffalo Dipping Sauce, and a large chocolate shake. I wasn't feeling hungry and settled for orange juice and fries, a strange combination for a strange day of traveling.

Back on the highway, we were greeted by many warning signs on I-65 about an upcoming detour and potential delay. We pressed on with our journey. It was past midnight, and the darkness outside was all-encompassing, making it difficult to see more than a few feet ahead. I held onto the hope that the reroute wouldn't be in effect so late at night. But my hopes were shattered when we were suddenly forced off the highway.

Our Nissan was surrounded by a sea of semi-trucks, all crawling along the detour path at an excruciatingly slow pace. We passed through unfamiliar small towns that we had never planned on visiting. We could only follow the endless line of trucks and hope that we would eventually find our way back to the freeway. We were a small fish in a sea of snarling metal giants, the detour path twisting through desolate towns with no purpose but to prolong our journey. For now, we were trapped in this late-night limbo, surrounded by the monotonous hum of engines and the eerie stillness of the night.

We finally reunited with the main highway after the long and winding detour that had us doubting our sense of direction. The delay was not helpful, especially with the girls facing an early game in the morning. But as the pavement stretched out before us, I felt a glimmer of hope that we could make up for some of the lost time.

I glanced at Big Coop to see if he had dozed off or was awake. "I have to take a leak," he announced, discomfort apparent in his voice. "Can we stop soon?"

I let out a sigh, knowing that we couldn't afford any more delays. But I nodded, relenting to the urgent needs of my co-pilot. We would have to make another quick pit stop and then push through the night.

I pulled off at the next exit. The highway sign promised a gas station and a diner, but I didn't see either. Cooper needed to do his business quickly, so I took the next turn onto a quiet, unpaved dark road, with only occasional stars peeking through the clouds providing any light and pulled over next to a large farm field. Cooper got out of the car and disappeared into the darkness, leaving me alone with my thoughts. He returned a few minutes later, looking relieved after relieving himself.

"That was a much-needed piss," he declared. "It was pitch black out there...I was half afraid a farmer would shoot me. I usually pack when I travel, but I didn't take my gun this time. I feel much more comfortable when I have it with me. Pissing on that field reminded me of when I was a kid and got hit by birdshot when trespassing with some buddies. It hurt like hell, but we can laugh about it now."

A wide grin spread across my face as I glanced over at Big Coop in the passenger seat. In my mind, I pictured a farmer catching him in the act of urinating in their field and chasing him with a pitchfork. Cooper noticed my expression and chuckled, asking, "What's up, man? You look like you've seen a ghost or something." I shook my head quickly, trying to push the thought out of my mind. Cooper's laughter filled the car once again, dissipating the image from my head.

Once we had merged back onto the highway, the road stretched out before us once more, shrouded by the darkness of the night. The highway detour and piss pit stop had set us back both in time and spirits, but Cooper's jovial nature was like a beacon, guiding us through the hurdles of our journey. Natalie and Ava, exhausted from the day's events, had fallen asleep in the backseat, their soft teenage snores blending with the hum of the engine. Fueled by his late-night fast-food meal, Cooper showed no signs of slowing down. He continued to prattle on, easily changing the subject and keeping the one-way conversation flowing.

Cooper never missed an opportunity to boast about his two basketball-playing daughters, Ellen and Ava. As we drove, he rambled on about Ellen's basketball skills, claiming she could have played professionally if she was a little taller. I could barely muster a response, the constant chatter draining my energy and blurring into background noise as we passed endless mile markers. He went on to talk about how great Ellen was in high school, especially on defense.

Next, he launched into a tale about how she had once "temporarily" fouled out of a game due to questionable calls by the referee. According to Cooper, Ellen had played an outstanding game and dominated on defense. However, the referee seemed to have it out for her, calling fouls at every opportunity. Even the opposing team's coach had commented on the bias of the calls. As the game entered its final minutes with their team barely leading by two points, Ellen went in for a steal and was called for her fifth foul. It was a clean steal with Ellen avoiding contact as she flicked away the opponent player's dribble. Cooper said he could see the frustration and disappointment etched on her face as she reluctantly left the court after fouling out. But then, something unexpected happened. The referee acknowledged his mistake and apologized to Ellen for his incorrect calls against her throughout the game. And to everyone's amazement, he reversed his call and allowed Ellen to continue playing.

I couldn't shake the feeling of doubt as I listened to the story. It sounded too good to be true, almost like something out of a movie. Given Cooper's tendency to stretch the truth and add dramatic details, I was convinced that at least some parts of the story were made up by him.

Cooper continued with tales of her college basketball success. After mentioning that she had once dropped 36 points in a game, my interest was piqued. I wondered if his oldest daughter played for a top D1 team in a major conference. Maybe she had played in March Madness. Maybe she had played for Gino Auriemma at Connecticut or Tera VanDerveer at Stanford. My curiosity got the best of me, and I asked, "Where did Ellen play her college ball?"

Without much enthusiasm, he muttered, "South Forks Community College." It wasn't the answer I had hoped for, but it wasn't unexpected either. After all, South Forks wasn't exactly renowned for its athletic program. Community colleges were typically associated with lower-tier basketball teams made up of players with noticeable flaws in their game. It was a far cry from the glitz and glamour of Division I universities with their huge arenas and high-caliber talent.

Cooper quickly pivoted and shifted his focus to his youngest daughter, who was asleep in the back seat.

"Ava is going to be something special," Cooper said proudly. "For the last few years, she has been working with the best personal trainer in the world. When she first started working with him, she could barely dribble. Now look at her. Next year, she will be going to Taylor High School, which has a good chance of winning state. She is already practicing with some of the varsity players, and the star junior picks her up for informal workouts. She is like a big sister to her."

My interest was again triggered. The best personal trainer in the world? That was quite a bold statement. I wondered what made him so special. I was eager to watch the greatest trainer in action. Ava had the potential to become a talented player, but her skill development lagged far behind that of her AAU teammates. Standing at 6 feet tall with a sturdy build and commanding presence, she certainly looked the part. However, her shortcomings in dribbling and shooting were obvious. Coops's "best trainer on earth" claim seemed like another in a never-ending series of fabrications.

As I drove through the outskirts of Indianapolis, I realized that we still had around 90 minutes until we reached Louisville. Cooper's voice was a constant drone in the otherwise peaceful car. He turned to me, his eyes boring into mine, and launched into a litany of his health problems.

"Type 2 diabetes, high blood pressure, blood clots, and back pains," he recited, a hint of resignation creeping into his voice. I gritted my teeth, knowing that this was just the beginning. He would go on to describe every medical appointment in excruciating detail.

I listened attentively as he detailed each doctor's visit, each diagnosis feeling like another heavy stone added to the burden he carried. His voice wavered at times, betraying the fear and uncertainty that lurked beneath the surface. I watched him closely, his eyes clouded with worry and fatigue as he spoke. But amidst all the medical jargon and grim prognoses, I saw a gregarious individual enjoying life.

"And to top it off, my essential medication is in my lost luggage," he lamented, his tone dripping with bitterness. I resisted the urge to roll my eyes, instead offering him a sympathetic smile.

"Maybe your luggage will arrive tomorrow," I suggested, trying to be helpful. But he shook his head, his frustration palpable. "I doubt they'll be able to find it in time. I need those pills daily to manage my condition," he explained, worry lines creasing his forehead.

The man's legs were even more swollen, a clear sign that the long drive had taken its toll. It was no wonder he was in pain, especially with the altitude changes and extended periods of sitting. As he tried to stretch his legs in the cramped passenger seat and ease the discomfort, I could see his dilemma.

"Waiting for your luggage to arrive might not be an option if you're in that much pain," I said, offering a small smile of understanding.

We were having a normal two-way adult conversation for the first time.

He looked at me with a mixture of gratitude and skepticism. "What do you suggest?"

"Call your doctor's office tomorrow and tell them it's an emergency," I replied. "They can send your prescription to a pharmacy here in Louisville and have it filled for you. In the meantime, get some compression socks. They might help with the pain and reduce the swelling."

The man shook his head vehemently. "No way, man. Those socks are for sissies. I only wear white athletic socks."

I laughed too loud, even as I sympathized with his stubbornness. "Trust me, those socks will help. Try them, and you'll thank me later."

He nodded, "Thanks for listening, man." Then, he was quiet for the first time since the rental car had left Chicago.

As we got closer to my hotel, I asked Big Coop which one he and Ava were staying at. JC replied that it was just a little further down the road. As we passed my hotel, I cursed internally as we continued on. The drive to the hotel the Coopers were staying at was torturous, each passing mile feeling like a half hour rather than a minute. My frustration and exhaustion grew with each passing ten-mile interval. It seemed that Big Coop and Ava's hotel was always "just a little further down the road," according to his repeated responses to my inquiries.

After finally dropping the Coopers off at their hotel, I drove back to our own hotel, annoyed that we had sacrificed valuable hours of sleep for no reason. Big Coop didn't even offer to chip in for the rental car expenses or express any thanks for the ride, which only added to my frustration. Reflecting on the trip, I realized why I had chosen the Nissan Rogue as our rental car - it was a hint at the rogue behavior I would have to endure from my unruly front-seat passenger. After a mechanical repair, a fast-food stop, a highway detour, a piss pit stop, and an inconvenient hotel drop-off, Nat and I

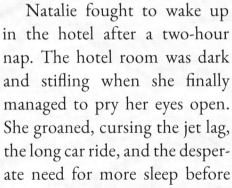

finally arrived at our destination shortly before 5:00 am.

Natalie fought to wake up in the hotel after a two-hour nap. The hotel room was dark and stifling when she finally managed to pry her eyes open. She groaned, cursing the jet lag, the long car ride, and the desperate need for more sleep before the early morning game. She felt disoriented and not her usual cheerful self as she stumbled out of bed and made her way to the bathroom.

Despite being exhausted, Natalie still managed to score four points during the game. News of Big Coop and my travel adventures spread like wildfire amongst the other Elite Lady Panthers. JC, never one to shy away from attention, had eagerly given a blow-by-blow recap of our late-night rental car ride, adding even more fuel to what was becoming a legendary tale. Nat and Ava were the only kids playing on a few hours of sleep. The other families had taken direct flights from Seattle to either Cincinnati or Indianapolis, where they had rented a car and driven roughly two hours to Louisville. None of the parents had any travel delays or issues, and their kids slept soundly while I was driving last night in challenging conditions. But amidst my frustration, I appreciated the lesson I had learned. In the future, I will always do my due diligence before embarking on a trip to avoid any potential headaches on the back end.

After the game, Natalie and I returned to our hotel room to catch up on some much-needed sleep. Before going to bed, I updated Gabby on our travel adventure the previous day. As a favor, I asked her to contact the airline and inquire about our two missing suitcases.

As Nat and I slept, Gabby tirelessly made numerous phone calls, switching between American Airlines and Alaska Airlines in an attempt to locate our lost luggage. The first flight had been with Alaska Airlines, but the second scheduled flight, which ended up being canceled, was supposed to be operated by Air Wisconsin under the name of American Eagle. My wife didn't even have all the details for the rebooked flight to Lexington, which also ended up being canceled. Despite her persistent efforts and attempts to explain the situation, each airline kept pointing fingers at the other for the missing baggage. After a frustrating ninety minutes of being transferred between different calls and getting disconnected twice, Gabby finally got on a conference call with representatives from both airlines to resolve the chaos. It was determined that American Airlines was ultimately responsible for our misplaced luggage, which could take some time to find due to numerous cancellations and lost bags during the busy post-holiday season. However, Gabby was assured that our belongings would eventually be returned either to our Louisville hotel or back home in Kirkland within a week if it took longer than expected.

An Alaska customer rep also told Gabby that her call was timely as Nat and my return flights from Louisville to Seattle via Chicago had been in danger of being canceled. Because we did not fly on a second flight from Chicago, we were accused of hidden city ticketing - a practice where travelers book a flight with a layover as the final destination, bypassing the final leg of the journey. The airline considers this a violation and will cancel all subsequent flights on the same ticket. Gabby was outraged and demanded an explanation. The representative tried to explain the complex rules of airline pricing, but it didn't make sense to her or most travelers. Airfare isn't solely based on distance traveled; it depends on the demand and supply of flights between two cities. For example, there may be higher demand for flights to one city but more availability of flights to another, leading to different prices. In some cases, booking connecting flights through a more competitive route may be cheaper than a direct flight on a less competitive route. After the lengthy explanation, Gabby was still confused but was reassured that an exception had been made for us and that our return tickets were valid and would not be canceled.

She called me later that night to update me on our luggage situation and explain hidden city ticketing - even though I'm an accountant, I, too, found it confusing.

The following day, Natalie and I made a quick trip to Target to purchase essential items like clothing and toiletries. We split up and grabbed a few necessary items but didn't go overboard as we weren't sure if our luggage would arrive anytime soon. If needed, we could always return another time. Since the weather in Louisville was blazing hot during the summer, we picked out t-shirts, underwear, socks, and shorts to last us for a few days.

After our shopping excursion, we headed to the gym where Nat's team beat a tough New York opponent by eight points. She scored fourteen points, and I beamed with pride as I watched her from the stands. Just two days ago, we had endured a grueling travel experience to get here, with delays, lost luggage, cramped airplane seats, and a rental car drive from hell. But all of that was forgotten as I witnessed her make an incredible play worthy of a highlight reel.

It started with a chase-down block, executed with perfect timing and precision. The ball soared into the air, propelled by her long arms and powerful jump. It seemed to hang there for a moment, suspended in time, before she snatched it out of the air and took off towards the other end of the court. Her strides were graceful yet determined, each step bringing her closer to the basket.

As she approached the hoop, her focus never wavered. She weaved around defenders, her dribble low and controlled. And then, in one swift motion, she rose up for the layup. The ball left her fingers and ended with a satisfying swish as she landed gracefully on the ground, a smile breaking across her face.

The crowd erupted in cheers and applause, but at that moment, I could only see my daughter, a fierce and skilled competitor, achieving something remarkable.

Around 06:00 pm, my phone began to ring. I glanced at the screen before answering and saw an unfamiliar number with area code 615. I hesitated momentarily, wondering who could be calling me from that area code. The caller quickly introduced themselves as Amanda and informed me that the airline had found my lost luggage. It would arrive in Lexington, Kentucky within the next thirty minutes, and Amanda kindly offered to bring it to my Louisville hotel tonight at 09:00 pm. I gratefully accepted her offer, relieved to have my belongings returned.

After confirming my hotel address and phone number, we agreed to meet at the designated time. I arrived in the lobby promptly at 08:40 pm and waited anxiously for my luggage to arrive. Unfortunately, 09:00 pm passed without any sign of Amanda or my luggage. Feeling frustrated, I decided to wait another twenty minutes before giving up hope. Just as I was about to return to my room, my phone rang again, this time from a different area code. A deep voice on the other end introduced themselves as Georgia and explained that she was Amanda's backup. Amanda's car had broken down, but Georgia would pick up my suitcases and make it to the lobby by 10:30 pm. She assured me that she was on her way.

Reluctantly, I agreed to the new meeting time and left the lobby in search of something to occupy my time while Natalie slept upstairs, resting for tomorrow's early morning game. Feeling daring, I ventured into the bar and ordered a Mint Julep - one of Kentucky's famous B's. This iconic drink, synonymous with the Kentucky Derby, was a mix of mint syrup, bourbon, and fresh mints. As I sipped my drink, I realized that today I had indulged in all three of the famous Kentucky B's: basketball by watching the Lady Panthers play, bourbon through my drink, and bluegrass associated with horse racing. After finishing my drink, I returned to the lobby and waited for my luggage to arrive. A heavily tattooed woman entered wearing flashy pink clothes and neon yellow sneakers, lugging two suitcases behind her. I tipped her $20 as she handed me my bags, and she thanked me before departing, revealing a frog tattoo above her exposed butt crack from her too-tight pink shorts and crop top.

During out-of-town tournaments, the team often coordinated meals with players and their families. After narrowly winning against a California team, the Lady Panthers decided to celebrate at a local brew pub. The tired girls sat around the table but were more invested in their phones than each other, communicating through text instead of talking face-to-face. To an outsider, it might have seemed like they were a group of zombies staring blankly at screens. Meanwhile, the parents' table was lively and chaotic, with Big Coop and Bob Simpson leading the conversation with their booming voices. They both considered themselves "foodies" and bonded over their love for meat and friendly competition to find the best deals on high-quality meals. These two human carnivores always tried to outdo each other in the quest for the ultimate title of meat foodie champion.

Cooper started the game off with a rapid-fire burst of words: "Dude, I had the most amazing steak at Ralph's - perfectly cooked medium rare, and the ribs were to die for. The baby back ribs just melted in my mouth." Simpson jumped in with equal enthusiasm: "Have you tried that new wing joint on James? Their BBQ sauce is out of this world, and their buffalo wings are incredible." But Big Coop didn't acknowledge the question and continued talking about BBQ places: "Speaking of which, there's a spot by Lake Union that serves unbeatable burnt tips and brisket. I tried to get their secret rub recipe, but they wouldn't give it up. And don't even get me started on their sides - the baked beans and potato salad are top-notch." Simpson shared his own food story: "I went to Vegas last month and loaded up on an all-you-can-eat buffet at Caesars. It was heaven for meat lovers - steaks made to order, prime rib, sausages, bacon. I never wanted to leave!" Cooper chimed in again: "Personally, I'm all about T-Bone Steaks cooked medium rare with juices dripping down as I savor every bite." Despite their animated chatter, all I could hear was "blah blah blah."

Their opinionated discussion reminded me of the countless food challenges I had watched on TV, where participants would devour excessive amounts of food within a set time limit. The thought of gorging on so much meat made my stomach turn, but the enthusiasm in Cooper and Simpson's voices was undeniable as they relived their meat-eating conquests. As they debated over the top burger joint in town, Natalie sauntered over to me with a smirk on her face. "Did you catch that, Dad? They're like children in a candy store, except it's all about meat," she said with a playful shake of her head. I chuckled and nodded, grateful for Nat's presence to break up the overwhelming discussions about protein. With her by my side, I felt grounded amidst the frenzied chatter about food. And just as quickly as she appeared, Nat returned to the teen table, the fortress of solitude.

I was the only one at the adult table not drinking alcohol excessively. Jenny's mother, Kate, ordered two drinks of hard liquor simultaneously. She seemed to love vodka, holding a tonic in one hand and a screwdriver in the other, alternating between sips from each glass to prove her impartiality as a drinker. It became apparent that many of the parents had drinking problems. Despite feeling the disapproving stares of some of the other parents, I resisted peer pressure and ordered a root beer, savoring it slowly during the meal. For dinner, I chose a large Caesar salad, trying to ignore the occasional glances from Big Coop and Boisterous Bob that made me uncomfortable. As the adults at the table grew more rowdy fueled with alcohol, I quietly picked at my salad, stealing looks at the clock and hoping for a speedy end to the meal.

As the evening progressed, the discussion at the table remained fixated on different types of meats and the optimal locations to savor them. Cooper and Simpson were now engrossed in a debate about the merits of dry rub versus wet marinades for ribs, their voices growing louder with each point made. Kate was now on her third round of drinks, and her laughter rang out above the others as she regaled the table with stories of her crazy college days. I sat back and observed the scene unfolding before me, feeling like an outsider in this group of boisterous and spirited individuals. The aroma of sizzling steaks and spicy barbecue sauce filled the air, making my stomach growl despite having just finished a large salad. Fueled by Kentucky bourbon shots, Big Coop got carried away bellowing "screw vegetarians. I am a proud meatatarian."

Just then, Natalie's coach, Coach Thompson, stood up and clinked his glass with a fork, signaling for everyone's attention. The table fell silent as all eyes turned to him.

"Alright, everyone listen up," the coach began, his voice commanding the entire table's attention. "I just want to thank all of you for your unwavering support of the Lady Panthers. Tonight's victory was a team effort, both on and off the court."

A round of applause erupted from the table, with cheers and whistles accompanying the clapping hands.

"In particular, I want to give a special shoutout to Mr. Smith and Mr. Cooper here," Coach Thompson continued, gesturing towards me. "For traveling all this way to support Natalie, Ava, and the team, even during a chaotic luggage situation and a canceled flight."

I felt my cheeks flush with embarrassment as all eyes turned to me.

"To Mike and Big Coop!" Coach Thompson raised his glass, and the rest of the table followed suit. "Thank you for being loyal fans and supporters of the Lady Panthers. Here's to many more victories together!"

Finally, the check arrived. This sparked a new complication as the parents debated how to split the cost fairly by family and factor in their teenage daughters' orders. One inebriated mother attempted to use a recently downloaded app on her phone called "Figure it Out," advertised as a convenient tool for calculating individual contributions at a group dinner. However, she struggled to use the unfamiliar app, and other tipsy parents chimed in with their own "assistance," prolonging the process by another fifteen minutes. Big Coop found this amusing and joked that there should be another app called "How Does it Work" to help users understand the "Figure it Out" app. After much back-and-forth and questionable calculations, the parents reluctantly agreed upon individual amounts to contribute towards the total bill. The slightly intoxicated adults gathered their children and left in rental cars to return to their respective hotels.

The next team bonding activity for players and parents was a trip across the Big Four pedestrian bridge, which stretches over the Ohio River and connects Kentucky to Indiana. The players walked fifty feet in front of the adults, taking turns dribbling and passing a couple of basketballs. The parents walked slowly. As we continued our march across the bridge, I noticed the stark contrast between the teenagers and the adults. The girls were energetic, their laughter and banter floating back to us in snippets as they played with the basketballs. It was a stark reminder of my own youth, carefree and unburdened by the responsibilities and worries that adulthood brought.

Big Coop, true to his name, lumbered along at a snail's pace, his heavy footsteps echoing loudly against the metal grates of the bridge. Bob Simpson, always one to rise to a challenge, attempted to keep up with the teenagers, but his wheezing breaths and flushed face gave away his struggle.

As the adults reached the center of the bridge, the sun began to dip below the horizon, casting a warm orange glow over the water. The teens up ahead found an empty court and were engaged in a lively basketball game, their laughter echoing in the open space.

"Quite a view, huh?" Kate remarked, pausing to take in the sight of the river stretching out before us. "It sure is," I replied, nodding in agreement. Despite my initial discomfort at the team dinner earlier in the week, I found myself enjoying this more relaxed setting with the other parents.

Suddenly, Natalie sprinted back towards us, her face flushed with excitement. "Dad, come join us for a quick game!" she called out, beckoning me to the basketball court. I couldn't resist her infectious energy, so I picked up my pace and headed over to join the group.

The sound of bouncing basketballs filled the air as we formed teams and began a friendly game. Laughter and friendly banter mixed with the steady rhythm of sneakers squeaking on the pavement. I found myself caught up in the moment, relishing the simple joy of playing alongside my daughter and her teammates.

As the game progressed, it became clear that the parents were no match for the younger, more agile players. But that didn't dampen our spirits; it only fueled our determination to score a point or two against them.

Underneath the starlit sky, with the lights from the bridge casting a soft glow around us, we played on. The competitive edge was softened by camaraderie. Each missed shot was met with good-natured ribbing and high-fives for every successful basket.

As the game wound down and as the group began to disperse, heading back towards the Kentucky side of the bridge, I lingered behind with Natalie. The cool breeze off the river ruffled our hair as we walked side by side, the lights of Louisville twinkling in the distance.

"Dad, thanks for playing with us tonight. It means a lot to me," Natalie said, her voice soft.

The Lady Panthers had a successful week on the basketball court, ending with a 6-3 record while competing against tough teams from various regions. Their hard work and dedication had paid off, with each player giving their all on the court. Coach Thompson was proud of how far they had come since the beginning of the season, but he knew there was still room for improvement. As they gathered in the hallway after the last game, he commended them on their performance but reminded them to stay focused and keep pushing themselves in practice.

Natalie's performance stood out, as she scored in double figures in all eight games after her initial lackluster sleep-deprived four-point game. Coach Thompson took notice and pulled her aside to congratulate her. "Natalie, I have been thoroughly impressed with your progress," he said with a slight smile. "I believe it is time we discuss making you a captain." Her heart jumped at his words, feeling a mixture of excitement and nerves. This was the opportunity she had been striving for, a chance to demonstrate her leadership abilities.

One of the most unforgettable moments of our trip was when we visited the burial site of Muhammed Ali. Natalie, who had initially been hesitant about going, only knew of Ali and found the concept of visiting a cemetery unsettling. However, with the help of GPS coordinates, we easily found our way to Louisville's Cave Hill Cemetery, where Ali was laid to rest surrounded by stunning scenery. Driving along the winding roads, we passed by majestic mausoleums and towering monuments, leaving us both in silent awe. The cemetery was filled with picturesque views of lakes, trees, flowers, birds, deer, gardens, and fountains.

When we reached Ali's grave site, I noticed how modest it was compared to the extravagant ones we had seen before. Then I realized that it perfectly captured his spirit as a man of the people. Standing at his grave, I felt humbled by the legacy he left behind.

For me, Ali was not just a boxer; he was a poet who danced in the ring, taunted opponents, and converted to Islam. He was a polarizing figure - a hero to some and a villain to others, depending on which generation you belonged to. Which camp you were in often depended on your age, with members of the younger generation usually viewing Ali as a conscientious objector and a leader of the 1960s counterculture, while the older generation predominately viewed him as a draft-dodging loudmouth who illustrated all that was wrong with America.

I was in the camp that saw him as a hero. As I stood in front of his grave, memories came rushing back - from his legendary fights against Joe Frazier to his surprising victory over George Foreman in "The Rumble in the Jungle." I also remembered watching him light the Olympic Cauldron at the 1996 Atlanta Summer Olympics with trembling hands due to Parkinson's disease. And who could forget the iconic banter between him and Howard Cosell? - two hyper-talkative showmen, a great athlete and broadcaster who are forever linked together, forming a must-see TV partnership.

Standing there in silence, my mind flooded with emotions and memories of this remarkable man who will forever be remembered as "The Greatest."

Throughout his life, Ali was known for his memorable quotes. The loquacious Louisville Lip shared his thoughts on assorted topics, including his most famous saying that described his athletic abilities in the boxing ring:

"Float like a butterfly sting like a bee – his hands can't hit what his eyes can't see."

I wish more people were aware of another one of his profound statements:

"I am America. I am the part you won't recognize. But get used to me. Black, confident, cocky, my name not yours. My religion, not yours; my goals; get used to me."

Sadly, fate had a different plan for the great athlete. As he aged, his body began to fail him, replacing his grace, strength, and eloquence with shaky hands and slurred speech. However, even as his physical abilities diminished, his legend only grew stronger. He became a household name around the world. When my daughter and I visited his gravesite, we were able to spend twenty uninterrupted minutes paying our respects in our own way. Later, I found out that this was unusual; people from out of town often made the trip to visit Ali's resting place and it was usually crowded.

That night at the hotel, Natalie revealed she had silently said a prayer at the grave. She couldn't explain why, but she knew the person buried there was someone special who had left a significant impact on the world. I pulled her close in a tight hug.

Rest in peace, Champ.

Natalie and I decided to visit the Louisville Slugger Factory during our trip. Nat wasn't keen on the idea, as she wasn't a big baseball fan. As we arrived at the factory's entrance, we were greeted by "The Big Bat," which holds the title of being the largest baseball bat in the world.

The tour exceeded my expectations, and even Natalie, who wasn't initially interested, ended up loving it. We were taken through an operational factory where we witnessed every step of the bat-making process, including a machine that produced the final product. It was interesting to learn that only top-quality wood is used for bats in Major League Baseball (MLB), while slightly lower-grade wood is used for amateur youth players and consumer markets. I was also surprised to discover that Louisville Slugger's main focus is now on producing aluminum bats rather than wooden ones. This shift makes sense given the popularity of aluminum bats in college and lower-level baseball games, but I had always associated this company with their iconic wooden bats. Furthermore, they hold a mere 15% market share in MLB, with companies like Marucci and Victus taking the lead - two brands I had never heard of before. It was disappointing to hear that such a legendary company, responsible for creating bats used by some of baseball's greatest legends like Babe Ruth, Joe DiMaggio, Ted Williams, Ty Cobb, and Jackie Robinson, was losing its foothold in the market.

Strolling down memory lane, I fondly remembered my high school days as a Seattle All-Metro League outfielder. My trusty Louisville Slugger bat was a key factor in my athletic success. One standout moment was when I made perfect contact with an incoming fastball, sending it flying over the outfielder and landing 350 feet away from home plate for a sensational home run.

During our visit, Natalie and I had fun taking practice swings with actual bats used by MLB players. There was a close call when a youngster almost hit me in the head with his practice swing. The tour ended with a trip to the gift shop, where we received complimentary miniature bats and personalized bat pens engraved with our names as souvenirs.

Our last excursion was a trip to Churchill Downs, the renowned racetrack that hosts the Kentucky Derby, known as "the most exciting two minutes in sports." Natalie, who loves horses despite being from the city, couldn't wait for this tour. She was an experienced rider and felt comfortable around these majestic animals. Unlike our previous trips to Muhammad Ali's grave and the Louisville Slugger factory, she had been looking forward to this one for weeks.

Once, Natalie and Gabby had gone horseback riding in St. Lucia, riding skinny horses crossing a shallow stream and waving to locals as the horses trotted through backyards. After the two-hour ride, 10-year-old Natalie excitedly re-counted how one grumpy horse had bitten a French tourist, causing her ankle to bleed. The tour consisted of six riders: a French family of four who were inexperienced with horses, along with Natalie and Gabby. Nat kept a safe distance from the Europeans, who struggled to control their horses. At one point, the mother even fell off her horse but, fortunately, did not get hurt.

The first thing that struck me about Churchill Downs was its run-down appearance. Despite its prestigious reputation, the entire facility seemed outdated and in need of repair. In contrast, our local minor league racetrack, Auburn

Downs, appeared more modern. We were fortunate enough to tour the VIP section where wealthy bettors watched the Kentucky Derby unfold, but I couldn't hide my disappointment. It seemed like any other average bingo hall you might come across in middle America.

A wave of memories washed over me as I continued the tour, my eyes lingering on the pictures and mementos adorning the walls. I could vividly recall watching Secretariat's iconic victory in 1973, propelling him towards the Triple Crown. Another memory came flooding back - collecting $340 from a local bookie after my filly Winning Colors won the 1988 Kentucky Derby against all odds, much to the disbelief of my doubtful friends. The first-ever Kentucky Derby was held in 1875, and as I closed my eyes and let my mind wander, I could almost feel the thundering hooves of past champion horses racing down the final stretch.

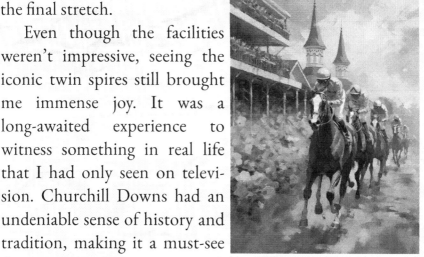

Even though the facilities weren't impressive, seeing the iconic twin spires still brought me immense joy. It was a long-awaited experience to witness something in real life that I had only seen on television. Churchill Downs had an undeniable sense of history and tradition, making it a must-see for Natalie and me.

The following morning, it was time to depart. Natalie and I were ready to go, but our hotel room reflected Gabby's absence during the past week. Clothes were haphazardly strewn about, and some crushed potato chips littered the floor. My daughter and I hurriedly threw everything into our suitcases without folding or arranging anything neatly. If the bags could close and zip up, we would be happy. It took some effort for me to shut one of the suitcases, and a noticeable bulge protruded from the top. Nevertheless, we managed to squeeze everything in. Before leaving, we combed through every corner of the room to ensure that we hadn't forgotten anything in our rushed packing process. Satisfied, we headed to the airport and returned our rental car without any issues (though seeing the $2200 charge on the receipt wasn't exactly pleasant).

After having breakfast and checking the flight board, we made our way onto the plane and settled into our assigned seats. I was fully immersed in my detective novel, flipping the pages and reaching the end of chapter ten, when the pilot's voice interrupted over the speakers: "Ladies and gentlemen, we are experiencing a delay for refueling. We apologize for the inconvenience and hope it will be resolved shortly. As of now, we are fourth in line." Refueling delays again, I sighed. Is there a shortage of gas? Did OPEC declare an oil embargo that I missed?

Twenty minutes dragged by before another announce-ment: "Good afternoon again, folks. We have some good news and some bad news. The good news is that we have been refueled. The bad news is that there is a minor issue with one of the lavatory lights, but maintenance is on their way to fix it. We will keep you updated as we receive more information." Another thirty minutes ticked away before yet another update: "Good afternoon, ladies and gentlemen. The lavatory light has been fixed, but unfortunately, we have discovered a problem with one of our engines that needs immediate attention before we can take off. We appreciate your patience and understanding during this time."

The third announcement from the pilot elicited groans from disgruntled passengers. We were seated on an Embraer 175, a smaller regional jet designed for short to medium flights. I had a scolding window seat towards the front of the plane, and my mood was quickly deteriorating, helped by a mischievous three-year-old boy behind me. He seemed like an innocent angel, but his actions were more devilish. He relentlessly kicked my seat and slammed his window shade up and down nonstop. Normally, I could handle these annoyances with ease, but this time it was wearing me thin. The pressures of traveling coupled with the unruly child were pushing me to my breaking point. Despite his father's attempts at scolding the boy and apologizing to me, the parent seemed unable to control his son's disruptive antics.

I'm not a particularly religious person, but at that moment, I hedged my bet and offered up a silent plea to anyone who might be listening, asking for the plane to take off soon. And while I was at it, I also begged for the restless toddler behind me to settle down. The plane was uncomfortably warm and stuffy, with poor air quality. The flight attendants, different waitresses in the sky, walked up and down the aisles, offering lukewarm water as their only beverage option. To my relief, my prayers were answered. The suspected engine issue turned out to be fine, and we had a smooth flight from Louisville to Chicago. Our second flight from Chicago back home to Seattle was equally uneventful.

As Gabby approached us at the airport, her arms extended for a warm family hug.

"Hey Nat," Gabby said, pulling away from our embrace and turning to our daughter. "How was the trip?"

Natalie replied with her typical teenage deadpan expression, "Same old, same old, nothing special."

I rolled my eyes at her response but couldn't help but smile at the unwavering bond between mother and daughter.

"Well, I'm glad you're back," Gabby said, beaming warmly at us both. "Let's catch up over some coffee, yeah?"

I eagerly nodded, excited to share all our travel stories.

Plus, Brewster was really in the mood for a pup cup.

THE GAME

The routine is familiar, played out countless times. Two best friends, Ryan Thompson and Xavier Washington, shooting hoops on the school court, laughing and having a good time. Little 8-year-old Ryan, with his blonde hair and blue eyes, makes a perfect shot from 10 feet away. His best friend, Xavier, an African American boy half a foot taller than the other second graders, cheers him on. They attend the same school: Carson Elementary. The two boys are inseparable, joined at the hip. Xavier impresses Ryan by making three baskets in a row, ending with a smooth jump shot. At such a young age, he's already showing signs of natural athleticism, and adults are taking notice. After goofing around for a while, taking turns shooting baskets, they decide to play two rounds of one-on-one until someone reaches ten points. As expected, Xavier wins both games easily. Although Ryan puts up a scrappy fight, he can't compete with Xavier's superior talent. The boys pedal off on their bikes when their basketball game ends to start a new adventure.

They race down the familiar streets of the neighborhood, the wind tousling their hair as they chat animatedly about their plans for the afternoon. "I heard there's a new ice cream shop that just opened up on Maple Street," Ryan exclaims, a wide grin spreading across his face. Xavier nods enthusiastically, his eyes lighting up at the mention of ice cream. As they turn the corner onto Maple Street, the sweet scent of freshly made waffle cones wafts through the air, leading them straight to the colorful little shop at the end of the block.

Excited chatter fills the air as they scan through the menu, finally settling on double scoops of their favorite flavors. Ryan goes for classic vanilla with rainbow sprinkles, while Xavier opts for a decadent chocolate fudge swirl. They sit on a nearby bench, savoring each creamy bite as they watch the world go by.

Their close friendship ended abruptly when Ryan's family relocated to the gated suburban community known as "the Plateau" just before sixth grade. They settled into a spacious 3000-square-foot house with a meticulously maintained lawn, complete with a half-court basketball court. Ryan spent countless hours practicing on the court, fine-tuning his signature outside shot and eventually extending his shooting range to an impressive 25 feet over the years.

The two boys made the usual pact of remaining best friends forever but drifted apart. They found new circles of friends and had different interests. They still crossed paths playing against each other in AAU basketball games, but it was not the same. Their once inseparable bond had been broken, and they were now mere acquaintances, exchanging casual nods and hellos as they passed each other by.

One sweltering afternoon the summer after he moved, Ryan found a weathered basketball tucked away in the corner of his garage. The memories of his carefree days with Xavier flooded back as he dribbled the ball on the famil-iar court in his backyard. The sound of the ball hitting the pavement echoed through the empty court, a stark contrast to the laughter and cheers that used to fill the air whenever Xavier was around.

As he took shot after shot, Ryan couldn't shake off the nostalgia that engulfed him. He missed the easy camarade-rie he shared with Xavier, the way they used to push each other to improve, not just on the court but in life. Despite their diverging paths, Ryan realized how much he cherished those memories and how much he missed his best friend. He quickly snapped out of his trip down memory lane; that part of his life was over.

Xavier also occasionally thought of Ryan. One time, Xavier sat on his bed, staring at an old photograph. It was worn and creased from years of being tucked into a wallet or taped onto a mirror. It showed two young boys grinning at the camera with innocent joy.

How had they drifted so far apart? Xavier thought back to first grade when they had been inseparable. They were always together, playing and exploring and laughing. But as they grew up, their interests diverged, and they drifted apart. Xavier couldn't even remember the last time he had spoken to Ryan.

But he kept the picture, a bittersweet reminder of the friendship they once had. Sometimes, Xavier would imagine what their lives would be like if they had stayed close. But he knew it was pointless to dwell on what could have been. The present was all that mattered, and in the present, Ryan was just a distant memory.

Xavier folded the photograph back up and tucked it back into its hiding spot. He had a feeling he would always keep it close, a reminder of the bond they had shared in their youth. And maybe, just maybe, their lives would intersect again. But for now, they were strangers, living separate lives, connected only by a faded photograph.

Academically, Ryan struggled at his new school. He was surrounded by privileged students whose parents had jobs in high-tech, academia, or other white-collar professions. In comparison, he felt unintelligent. His dyslexia and difficulty concentrating made it hard for him to keep up in class. Math was a particular concern, as numbers and shapes did not compute correctly in his brain.

One evening, as Ryan sat at the dinner table with his parents, the tension in the air was tangible. His father, Derek, was in a sour mood after a long day at work, and his mother, Elise, looked weary from trying to keep the peace. Ryan picked at his food, feeling the weight of their unspoken troubles pressing down on him.

Suddenly, Derek slammed his fork down on the table, causing Ryan to jump in his seat. "You need to focus more on basketball, Ryan," he barked. "Enough with this school nonsense. You're never going to make a career out of your smarts."

Elise constantly fretted about her son. She knew he was a sensitive boy who worried about his slipping grades and the tension within their family. Lately, she and her husband had been arguing increasingly, and during one heated confrontation, he had even struck her in the shoulder. Although his parents didn't think Ryan was home, he had witnessed the incident. Ryan felt a surge of guilt and helplessness as he watched his father raise his hand against his mother. The image was seared into his memory, haunting him even in the quiet moments of the night. He knew this wasn't right, that no one should ever lay a hand on another in anger. But what could he, a young boy, do in the face of his father's temper?

The unhappy couple had started going to counseling sessions together, although Derek attended begrudgingly at her insistence. He often accused her of using the threat of divorce as a weapon against him. Elise was also concerned about the pressure Derek put on Ryan to excel in basketball; she didn't believe it was healthy for their son.

One evening, as the sun dipped below the horizon and cast a warm glow over the neighborhood, Ryan was once again on his backyard court, practicing free throws under the watchful eyes of his father. Derek stood on the sidelines with a stern expression as he observed his son's every move. The tension between them was noticeable, hovering in the air like a thick fog. Ryan could feel the weight of his father's expectations bearing down on him as he missed shot after shot, the clang of the ball hitting the rim, breaking the tense silence between them.

Derek's face was furrowed with concern, his lips were drawn tight, and frustration was evident in his eyes. His voice was gruff and commanding, echoing off the court and piercing through his son. "Ryan, you need to focus. You're better than this. You have the potential to be great, but you need to work harder." "I am working hard, Dad. I'm trying my best," he said, his voice steady despite the nerves bubbling under the surface. Derek's expression softened slightly, a flicker of doubt crossing his features. "I know you are, son. But trying your best isn't always enough. You have to push yourself beyond what you think is possible if you want to succeed." Ryan nodded, the resolve hardening in his eyes as he lined up another shot.

As the ball sailed smoothly through the net, a sense of determination settled in Ryan's heart. He knew that he had to find his own path, separate from his father's expectations and the shadow of his past friendships. The realization dawned on him like a beacon of light in the encroaching darkness - it was time to forge ahead, to carve out a future that belonged to him and him alone. With newfound purpose fueling his every move, Ryan continued to shoot hoops well into the night, the rhythmic sound of the ball against the pavement becoming a soothing lullaby that echoed through the quiet neighborhood. Each shot he made felt like a step towards liberation, a declaration of his independence from the constraints that had held him back for so long.

As he made shot after shot, a sense of clarity washed over him. Deep down, he knew that he needed to confront his fears and insecurities head-on, to break free from the self-doubt that had plagued him for far too long. With each dribble and each jump shot, he felt a surge of confidence building within him, propelling him forward on his journey of self-discovery.

Ryan had mixed feelings about his father. Despite the constant criticism, Ryan admired and respected him. He knew Derek had achieved great success in basketball and business - running a successful company specializing in sports equipment - and he wanted nothing more than to make him proud.

Derek Thompson, a man in his forties with a tall and strong stature and unruly dark hair, was once a star player on his college basketball team at the state university. A passionate fan, he would often berate referees and never seemed to be satisfied with Ryan's performance on the court. Even if Ryan scored fifteen points, Derek believed he should have scored twenty. Although he knew he needed to improve as a father and husband, he struggled to figure out how.

Megan Taylor, a quiet teenager with long blonde hair and piercing green eyes, had struck up a friendship with Ryan in high school. The initial introduction took place during their sophomore year when she started tutoring him in geometry. But as they spent more time together outside of tutoring sessions, rumors started to spread that they were dating. Of course, they were just good friends, but it didn't stop the whispers from circulating. One evening, after watching Casablanca at the local theater, Megan decided to ask Ryan why he hadn't tried to kiss her yet. She wanted to know if he was attracted to her. His response caught her off guard; he said she was intelligent, beautiful, funny, and amazing. But he didn't want to risk ruining their friendship by making things romantic. After pondering his words for a moment,

Megan let out a giggle and replied: "You're such a good person, Ryan Thompson."

Ryan often confided in Megan about his anxiety while playing basketball. He felt uneasy performing in front of a large, crowded audience during home games: "My friends are there, my dad is there, the place is packed. What if I mess up?" Every time, Megan offered words of reassurance: "Just focus on doing your best and enjoy the moment. Don't forget that it's just a game. Many students at Oakcrest would love to be in your position." Despite his nervousness playing in front of packed houses, Ryan scored 23 points in his first senior year quad game - a major improvement for him.

Ryan only shared the details of his parents' fights with Megan. Sitting together on a park bench, he found solace in her presence. Her gentle demeanor and comforting words always had a calming effect on him. "You seem relaxed today," Megan remarked with a grin, giving him a playful nudge in the side. Ryan laughed softly, looking down at his hands. "I suppose I am. It's a relief to escape from all the turmoil at home."

Megan felt a pang of sadness as she reflected on their conversation from the night before. Ryan had opened up to her about the constant bickering between his parents and how it was affecting him emotionally. The latest fight had turned violent, with plates being hurled against walls. Starting off as a trivial disagreement, it quickly escalated into a battle of hurtful words and destructive actions. She could see the weight of it all on his face, but he always tried to stay strong. "I wish there were something I could do to make things better," she murmured empathetically. "Just having you here with me means a lot," Ryan replied sincerely. "It's nice to have someone to confide in about this stuff." Megan smiled appreciatively and rested her head against his shoulder. In that moment, they both found comfort in each other's presence.

After a few minutes of peaceful silence, Ryan broke the stillness. "Sometimes I can't help but think it's my fault," he confessed, feeling guilty for unloading his problems onto her. "Maybe if I were a better son or a better player, my parents wouldn't fight so much." Megan shook her head adamantly. "No way. You are an incredible person and an amazing athlete. Don't ever doubt yourself like that." Ryan felt a sense of relief wash over him as he gratefully smiled at her words. He was lucky to have such a supportive friend by his side through tough times like these.

Being a basketball player at Grant High School meant being treated like a celebrity, and Xavier was no exception. Located in the heart of the African American community, the school's reputation for producing exceptional basketball teams was well-known. They had won 22 state championships in the largest school classification. It was no wonder that the pressure to win every game was immense, and only bringing home the state title could make the season truly successful. This high level of expectation weighed heavily on Xavier's shoulders, as it did on all the players of the Grant basketball team. But for Xavier, it was even more intense. As the star player, he was constantly in the spotlight, with fans and media alike scrutinizing his every move on and off the court. Xavier had dreamed of playing for Grant High since he was a young boy, watching their alumni go on to become NBA stars.

Grant had been state runners-up for the last two years, and in Xavier's freshman year, they had finished fourth. There was no room for anything less than a state title this year. But Xavier was ready for the challenge. He had dedicated his entire life to basketball and was determined to bring the state title home to Grant High School. He knew it wouldn't be easy, but he was willing to work hard and sacrifice to make his dreams a reality.

On occasion, doubts crept into his head. He sometimes grew weary of how everyone just wanted to talk about basketball - his classmates, adults at the barber shop, neighbors, even the mail carrier. No one took an interest in his academic pursuits or knew that he had a 3.8 GPA and made the honor roll. At Grant, it wasn't considered cool to be smart.

Xavier's girlfriend Alicia Johnson, an outgoing African American girl with curly hair and a bright smile, often encouraged him to stand up for himself and show that he was more than just a stereotypical jock. Alicia had always believed in Xavier's potential beyond the basketball court. She admired his dedication to the sport but knew there was so much more to him than his ability to make flashy dunks and block shots. As they sat together on a bench one evening, the sun setting behind them casting a warm glow over the lake, Alicia gently took Xavier's hand in hers and looked into his eyes.

"Xavier, I know it's tough being in the spotlight all the time," Alicia began, her voice soft but determined. "But you have a voice, a powerful one, and you can use it to show everyone who you truly are."

Xavier gazed at her, feeling a surge of gratitude for her unwavering support. He squeezed her hand and nodded, a sense of purpose stirring within him.

"You're right, Alicia. It's time for me to make a stand," Xavier said, his voice filled with conviction. "I'm more than just a basketball player. I want to make a difference in the world and inspire others to dream big and reach their goals."

Like many teenagers, Xavier was confused about who he was despite his words to his girlfriend. Sometimes, when he heard his friends talking about their favorite players or watched them reenact game-winning shots, he wondered if he was missing out on something. Was he defined solely by his skills on the court? Did anyone even see him for who he truly was? Walking to class, he shook off these thoughts and refocused on his upcoming game. Basketball was more than just a sport to him; it was an important part of who he was, and he wouldn't let anyone or anything make him question that.

Like Ryan, Xavier's home life was far from ideal. His parents divorced when he was just three years old, and his father moved to Florida to start a new family with his stepmother and her children. For most of his childhood, Xavier had no relationship with his father until he became a high school star and started receiving college scholarship offers.

His first high school meeting with his father occurred during his sophomore year, and it was a surprise to him. One day, a car pulled up to the curb as Xavier was shooting baskets outside on the blacktop. A tall, imposing figure stepped out of the driver's seat and approached him. His heart pounded in his chest as he struggled to make sense of the sudden appearance of this man who was supposed to be his father but had been absent for so long. "Xavier," his father's voice was raspy, but there was a hint of forced affection. "I've been keeping up with your games online. You're quite the player."

Xavier stood frozen, unsure of how to react. Years of resentment and longing battled within him as he looked into the man's eyes. His mother had always been the one cheering him on from the bleachers, wiping away his tears after tough losses. What did this stranger know about his struggles, his triumphs?

Ever since that first encounter in high school, father and son maintained some level of communication. However, there was always a distance between them, and Xavier doubted if he could ever fully trust a man who had not been there for him during his formative years. His mother had always been his rock, providing unconditional support and pushing him to be his best self. She worked tirelessly to provide for their family and took immense pride in his successes both on the court and in the classroom. But despite her love and dedication, there were times when Xavier yearned for the presence of a trustworthy male figure in his life. With senior year approaching and the goal of winning a state championship on his mind, he didn't need any additional complications.

Ryan's confidence grew each game during his senior season, fueled by his determination to play for himself and find joy in the sport rather than seeking validation from others. Megan's steadfast support and insightful advice became pillars of strength for him, guiding him through challenges on and off the court.

One brisk winter evening, as the leaves danced in the wind and the sky blazed with fiery hues, Ryan sat on the porch steps with Megan after a particularly intense game. The sounds of nature around them created a tranquil backdrop for their conversation. Ryan turned to Megan, a soft smile playing on his lips. "You know, I couldn't have done it without you," Ryan said earnestly. Megan returned the smile, her green eyes reflecting the warmth and sincerity in his words. "You give me too much credit, Ryan. You're the one out there on the court, putting in the hard work and pushing yourself to be better every day," she replied, her voice gentle yet firm. Ryan shook his head, a look of appreciation in his eyes. "Maybe so, but having you in my corner makes all the difference. Your belief in me when I didn't believe in myself has been a game-changer." Megan reached out and squeezed his hand reassuringly. "That's what friends are for, to offer support during tough times and celebrate with you during good times." As they sat in companionable silence, a sense of peace settled between them, the unspoken bond of their friendship stronger than ever.

Powerhouse Grant High School and their senior sensation Xavier Washington were set to play surprise finalist Oakcrest High, featuring senior Ryan Thompson in the state title game at the downtown arena. Before the game, the typical cliches were used to describe both teams - Grant with their high-powered offense and talented individuals from the inner city, facing off against suburban Oakcrest from the plateau with their disciplined teamwork and smart coaching. These buzzwords even extended to the individual level, labeling Xavier as an athletic prodigy and Ryan as a cerebral player who relied on assistance from his teammates to get open and score with his deadly jump shot. However, in reality, both teams and their star players were more alike than different. They all played with determination, discipline, and a strong understanding of basketball strategy. Ryan had underrated athleticism with a thirty-inch vertical and quickness that often went unnoticed, while Xavier was a student of the game who carefully studied opponents for any weaknesses he could exploit.

Marvin Williams was Grant's coach, a middle-aged former pro player with a powerful presence. He was invested in his team's success but also emphasized the importance of sportsmanship. He strived to teach his players about teamwork and overcoming difficulties. During his twelve-year tenure coaching at Grant, he had led them to six state titles. Some accused him of recruiting talented players, but he defended himself by saying he coached anyone who made the team from those enrolled at the school. Others claimed his teams only won because of their natural talent, but Williams argued that his coaching also contributed to the squad's success.

Oakcrest was coached by Fred Anderson, a former Navy SEAL with graying hair and a stern expression. He pushed the team hard in practice and demanded that his players be in peak physical condition. Known for his intensity and meticulous game plans, he was considered a master tactician. Anderson had coached at Oakcrest for fifteen years, slowly building up the program from perennial losers in the beginning until now when they were on the cusp of winning the school's first state championship.

The entire state was tuned in for the highly anticipated game, and the announcer kicked off the broadcast with an electrifying intro. "This matchup is a dream for basketball fans! Twenty-two-time state champion Grant High, led by the consensus state player of the year, Xavier Washington, will face off against underdog Oakcrest High, hungry for their first title and led by sharpshooter Ryan Thompson. Get ready for a thrilling game!"

With the hype finally over, the game was finally ready to start. As they walked on the court, Ryan lightly bumped into Xavier, eliciting a steely glare from him. "You ready to get your butt kicked?" taunted Xavier. Ryan boasted with confidence, "You can't hold me."

Xavier's jaw clenched at Ryan's trash-talking, his competitive fire burning brighter than ever. As the referee tossed the ball up for the opening tip, Xavier leaped with determination, securing possession for Grant High. He raced down the court, his eyes locked on the basket. Receiving a return pass, Xavier rose up and flushed the ball through the hoop for the game's first points.

Ryan, undeterred by Xavier's skill, matched him step for step, weaving through the Grant backcourt press with finesse. After crossing halfcourt, Ryan planted his feet and launched a three-point shot from the logo. The crowd held its breath as the ball sailed through the air, swishing through the net cleanly.

Xavier felt a surge of adrenaline at Ryan's impressive shot, knowing that Oakcrest High was not to be underestimated. With a steely gaze, he dribbled the ball down the court, his mind focused on one thing: victory. He drove hard into the lane before dishing the ball to a teammate for an uncontested layup.

Ryan smirked as he saw Xavier's assist, his eyes narrowing in determination. He knew he had to step up his game if Oakcrest High was going to stand a chance against the powerhouse that was Grant High. As the clock ticked down in the first quarter, Ryan orchestrated a flawless pick-and-roll play, leaving him open for another deep three-pointer that sliced through the air and found nothing but net.

The crowd exploded in cheers as Oakcrest closed the gap, their energy radiating outwards and reaching every corner of the arena. Xavier could feel the pressure mounting with each possession, his rival proving to be a formidable opponent. Determined not to let his team down, Xavier called for the ball and drove hard to the basket, executing a perfect spin move that left his defender stumbling.

With a graceful layup, Xavier scored another two points for Grant High, matching Oakcrest's intensity with his own skill and prowess. Ryan countered with a half-court pass to a teammate filling the lane for a fast break layup. But it wasn't just about these two star players. Both teams showed incredible teamwork and hustle, diving for loose balls and sprinting back on defense. It was clear that both coaches had instilled a strong sense of togetherness within their teams.

As the halftime buzzer sounded, Grant held a slim 35-32 lead over Oakcrest. The locker rooms were energized as both coaches gave passionate speeches to their players.

"You guys are playing great out there," Williams said to his team. "But we can't let up now. We need to keep pushing and stay focused if we want to bring home another state title. Focus on defense and run the three-point shooters off the line."

Meanwhile, Anderson reminded his players of all the hard work they had put in throughout the season. "This is our moment. We have worked too hard to let this game slip away now," he said, his voice firm and confident. The team gathered around him; their eyes locked in on their coach: "We have to get the ball out of Washington's hands. He is killing us. Make somebody else beat us."

The second half was a continuous battle with multiple lead changes, the largest margin being a five-point lead by Grant. Witnesses said the quality of play might have been the best high school championship game ever played in the state. The game was fast-paced and intense, with both Xavier and Ryan displaying their incredible skills on the court. Xavier's athleticism was unmatched as he soared for dunks and blocked shots with authority. Meanwhile, Ryan's quickness 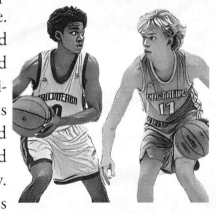 and sharpshooting ability kept Oakcrest High in the game, his range seemingly unlimited as he drained three-pointers from all over the court.

As the final seconds of the game ticked away, the score remained tied, and everyone's attention was on the star player of each team. With dogged determination, Xavier maneuvered down the court, each move calculated and precise. Ryan shadowed him on defense, refusing to let the offensive player outsmart him. The two opponents collided, and the crowd held their breath as the referee blew his whistle, waiting for the call that could potentially decide the game. The referee announced: "Block on # 11, two shots for # 0." Grant High was in the bonus, and as Xavier walked past Ryan on the way to the free-throw line, he elbowed his former friend in the midsection. In frustration, Ryan threw his arms up in the air, embellishing it by flailing backward, hoping to get a technical foul called on Xavier.

Derek Thompson sat fuming in his courtside seat, glaring at the action unfolding on the court. His mood was dark and angry, and the earlier argument with his wife before the game only heightened his frustration. Elise had made an innocent comment about the upcoming championship game, saying that it didn't matter if their son Ryan won or lost as long as he played hard and did his best.

But Derek couldn't stand such complacency. Winning was the only option. Ryan had to have a huge game and be the star – anything less would be a disappointment. Plus, his wife's words implied that she didn't share his intense passion for their son's basketball career, which made him even more irritated.

Upset with his wife's stupid comment, he slammed the door and went to the Green Lantern, the neighborhood tavern that he frequented.

As he entered the dimly lit pub, the familiar smell of alcohol, old wood, and cigarette smoke enveloped him. He made his way to the bar, feeling the eyes of the regulars on him. They knew him well, as he came here often to drown his sorrows.

"Three bourbons over ice," he said to the bartender without looking up. He could feel the man's curious gaze on him, but he didn't care. He just needed to drink.

As he sipped his first bourbon, his mind raced with thoughts of his wife's comment. It was a small thing, really, but it stung him deeply.

With each sip of the strong liquor, he felt himself grow increasingly bitter. Bitterness towards his wife, towards his son, towards his own life. He wanted to escape, to run away from it all. But he knew he couldn't. He was stuck here in this miserable town with his pestering wife and ungrateful son.

So, he drank, his mind clouded by the alcohol, until he could barely remember why he was upset in the first place. As he stumbled out of the pub and headed to the arena, he pondered that maybe, just maybe, drinking was the only way to survive this life.

Derek made the drive to the game by himself, a sense of unease gnawing at his gut. The weight of past wrongdoings seemed to linger in the air, waiting to strike. As he pulled into the parking lot, he could feel the tension building within him, like a coiled spring ready to snap.

He made his way up the stands, choosing a spot high enough to see the entire court. His eyes scanned the players warming up on the court, searching for his son Ryan among them. He spotted him easily, his tall frame standing out amongst his teammates. Derek's heart swelled with pride as he watched Ryan practicing jumpers.

Next, his gaze landed on someone else: George Foster, the referee for tonight's game and widely known as one of the best high school refs in the state. The sight of him brought up a mix of emotions in Derek - anger, resentment, and frustration. He and Foster had a history, one that stretched back to his son's freshman year. In Derek's eyes, Foster had been unfairly targeting Ryan, constantly calling fouls on him while turning a blind eye to the opponent's defensive fouls. It seemed like every game was an uphill battle with Foster determined to make things difficult for his son.

As the game progressed, Derek's agitation grew, fueled by the intensity of the contest and the growing number of his son's missed shots that Derek believed should have been made. To make matters worse, the referees seemed to be making biased calls in favor of Grant.

"You're terrible, Foster!"

"Open your eyes, you blind zebras!"

"Foster, you suck!"

His anger bubbled just under the surface, waiting for any excuse to explode. During the game, he scanned the court, scrutinizing Ryan's every move, hoping to see some spark of brilliance that would prove his worth as a player.

But all he saw was his son, a boy no more than seventeen, running around and chasing a ball like a puppy.

The game had been a blur for Derek, fueled by alcohol and raw emotions. He had started in the high seats, but as the game progressed, he moved closer and closer to the court. Finally, he ended up in a second-row seat, precariously perched on an illegal "stair seat" to watch the final minutes.

When the critical block/charge call was made against Ryan, sending Xavier to the line, Derek lost all sense of rationality. He leapt from his seat, screaming at the referees.

"Foster, you're blind! That was a charge, you moron!"

Derek's alcohol-induced fog was thick, clouding his thoughts and judgment. In his mind, Xavier had committed a blatant offensive foul, and Ryan had drawn a charge. Then, Xavier delivered a vicious cheap shot elbow at his son. Derek was convinced that the referees were conspiring against his son's team.

Derek had never trusted Xavier, not from the moment he had first met him as a kid. Even in those early days, when Xavier and Ryan had been inseparable, there had always been a part of Derek that doubted him. There was no denying that Xavier was a talented basketball player, a natural on the court, a phenom. But there was something about him that rubbed Derek the wrong way. It wasn't just his cockiness or his arrogance, though both of those traits were certainly present. It was something more, something that Derek couldn't quite put his finger on.

As they grew older and Ryan's basketball talents blossomed, the rivalry between him and Xavier intensified. Derek viewed Xavier as a direct threat to Ryan's future in the sport.

The combination of events pushed Derek over the edge, causing him to act impulsively like a windstorm snapping power lines. He rose from his seat and charged towards George Foster on the court  with single-minded determination. It was as if Derek was controlled by an unseen force, his body moving without his conscious consent. He could hear the roaring of blood in his ears, could feel the thumping of his heart, but he couldn't stop himself. Derek's fist clenched at his side as he stared into Foster's surprised eyes. Like a robot controlled by remote control, he lunged forward, his hand cocked back ready to strike. At that moment, he knew that whatever came next would change everything.

The official's head hit the ground with a sickening thud, described later as reminiscent of a grapefruit splattering against concrete after being dropped from a high balcony. Pandemonium erupted in the gym as chaos ensued. Derek's mind was a blur, his actions unfathomable even to himself. The weight of what he had just done crashed down on him like a ton of bricks as he looked at the fallen official, blood seeping from the wound on his head. Panic set in as he realized the magnitude of his actions and the irreversible consequences that would follow. He knew there was no going back now; his life would never be the same again.

The players on the court froze, their expressions a mix of horror and disbelief as security rushed in to restrain Derek. Ryan stood motionless, stunned by his father's sudden outburst, unable to comprehend what had just unfolded before him. The game came to a screeching halt, and the atmosphere in the arena shifted from excitement to tension and fear.

Derek's face was contorted with rage, his voice booming and erratic as he shouted obscenities at no one in particular. The spectators in the stands were equally stunned, some standing and pointing, others covering their mouths in shock.

Ryan's mother, watching from the stands, buried her face in her hands. She knew this outburst would have serious consequences for her husband's reputation and their family.

As the cops dragged Derek away, Elise appeared at the edge of the court, her face a mask of anguish and embarrassment. Ryan, still numb from the shock of his father's violent outburst, watched as she approached him with tear-filled eyes, silently pleading for understanding and forgiveness.

He felt a surge of conflicting emotions wash over him - anger towards his father for his reckless and selfish actions, shame for the spectacle unfolding before him, and concern for his mother caught in the middle of it all.

Elise reached out to touch his arm, but he recoiled.

"I'm sorry, Ryan," she whispered, her voice barely audible over the noise of the crowd. "I never thought it would come to this."

Ryan wanted to believe her, but he couldn't shake the feeling that she was somehow partially responsible for the situation. He couldn't understand why she had stayed with Derek all these years, enduring his volatile temper and explosive behavior.

But as he looked into her eyes, he saw the same pain and fear that he felt. At that moment, he realized that she was just as much a victim of his father's actions as he was.

The once raucous crowd had fallen into stunned silence, the tension thick and suffocating. Ryan watched in a daze as paramedics worked tirelessly to stabilize the fallen referee. As he watched the medics attend to Foster, Ryan's mind remained a jumbled mess of emotions and thoughts. He couldn't believe what had just happened, how quickly the game had escalated from a tense competition to an unprovoked attack by his father.

As he stood there, rooted to the spot in shock and disbelief, Ryan's attention shifted to Xavier. The look of disdain on Xavier's face cut through him like a knife, a stark reminder of the rift that had formed between them over the years. But beneath the mask of animosity, Ryan could see a glimmer of something else - pity or even a trace of understanding.

In an instant, Ryan made up his mind. While he couldn't alter the past or his father's behavior, he had control over his own actions and choices moving forward. Taking a step towards Xavier, he lifted his hand in a peaceful gesture, hoping for a ceasefire in the midst of turmoil.

Xavier's initial reaction was one of skepticism, his eyes narrowing as he regarded Ryan's outstretched hand. Years of pent-up resentment and bitterness surged within him, threatening to drown out any flicker of hope for reconciliation. But as he locked eyes with Ryan, he saw a vulnerability that mirrored his own.

A tense silence hung in the air before Xavier finally relented, slowly extending his hand to meet Ryan's halfway. The simple gesture spoke volumes, bridging the gap that had divided them for so long. At that moment, they both understood the weight of their shared history and the possibility of a new beginning. As they stood there, hands clasped in solidarity, the chaos around them seemed to ebb away,

The local community was reeling from the end-of-game pandemonium, quickly gaining widespread attention and becoming a heated topic on ESPN Sports Center. Videos of the final play and punch went viral on social media, gaining millions of views. Critics from across the nation condemned the increasing violence in youth sports. As they tried to understand what transpired on the court that day, both boys were forced to confront their own prejudices and biases. The media frenzy surrounding the altercation between

Ryan's father and the referee cast a dark shadow over what was supposed to be a thrilling championship game. The two boys, once fierce rivals on the court, now united in a different battle - one against public scrutiny and condemnation. The press hounded them for statements, trying to pit the teenagers against each other, while parents and fans alike debated who was truly at fault for the shocking incident that had marred the state championship game.

Despite the chaos unfolding around them, Xavier and Ryan shared a silent understanding born out of years of competition and camaraderie. They knew that the events of that night would forever change their lives, intertwining their fates in ways neither could have predicted. As they navigated the fallout together, they found an unlikely bond forming between them, forged in the crucible of adversity.

In the following days, the two teenagers stood side by side as they faced the consequences of that fateful night. They attended court hearings together, their once bitter rivalry giving way to a shared sense of solidarity. Ryan's father faced serious charges for his actions, and the weight of the situation hung heavily over both families. Torn between her loyalty to her husband and her concern for her son, Elise found solace in Xavier's unwavering support and understanding.

The two former best friends became friends again and attended community events to raise awareness about sportsmanship and respect in athletics, using their platform to advocate for positive change. The once bitter rivalry between Grant High and Oakcrest High had evolved into a partnership rooted in mutual understanding and a shared commitment to making amends for the past.

Together, Xavier and Ryan visited the injured referee in the hospital, offering their apologies and support as he recovered from the traumatic incident. Their goodwill gesture made headlines, restoring faith in the power of redemption and forgiveness amidst a storm of controversy.

The game was declared a tie, and Grant and Oakcrest were named state co-champions. Xavier and Ryan, the captains of their teams, joined Coach Williams and Coach Anderson at a press conference, where it was announced that an annual unity basketball game would be played between the schools on Martin Luther King Day.

After the successful press conference, Xavier and Alicia stood side by side taking in the breathtaking view of the moon. They could finally relax, their hands tightly intertwined symbolizing their unbreakable bond.

"You were amazing up there," Alicia whispered admiringly and with happiness in her eyes. I'm so proud of you, baby. You are truly making a difference."

They stood there quietly, basking in the peaceful moment under the soft glow of the moon. These moments alone, away from their busy lives, were rare but cherished whenever they could escape.

Xavier and Alicia had been dating for nearly three years now, and every day their love grew stronger. Despite coming from different family backgrounds - Xavier raised by a single mother in a low-income household and Alicia from a wealthy family with both parents present and supportive - they never let those differences get in the way.

"I love you," Xavier whispered into Alicia's ear, inhaling her sweet scent.

Alicia smiled and turned to face him completely. "And I love you too," she replied, tilting her head up to meet his lips in a gentle kiss.

Xavier wrapped his arms around her waist and pulled her closer as they continued to share an intimate moment under the moonlight. It was as if he were pulling her into an embrace that spanned centuries, a lover's knot tightening and loosening with the rhythm of their hearts. In this tranquil space, under the enchanting glow of the moon, they were the only two beings in the world.

They had been through so much together - from late nights studying for exams to supporting each other through tough situations - but nothing could ever compare to moments like this.

Xavier's voice overflowed with wonder as he softly exclaimed, "I can't believe how far we've come."

"Me neither," she replied, a hint of awe in her voice. "But I know we can conquer anything together."

They stood there, basking in the warmth of each other's embrace, knowing that no matter what challenges came their way, they would face them together. Finally, after sharing one last passionate kiss, they turned and made their way back, ready to take on whatever life had in store for them.

Bathed in the warm glow of the afternoon sun, Ryan and Megan strolled along the riverbank. The water flowed calmly beside them, gently rippling with each passing breeze. They shared a peaceful silence, enjoying each other's presence. As they neared a bend in the river, Ryan stopped and turned towards Megan. He took her hand in his and looked into her eyes, his heart fluttering with anticipation.

"I have something I want to share with you," he said, his voice barely above a whisper.

Megan held her breath, anticipation building inside her as she waited for him to continue.

"I've wanted to do this since the moment I met you," Ryan said, his eyes never leaving hers. And without another word, he leaned in and pressed his lips to hers.

The world seemed to fade away as their lips met, and all Megan could feel was the warmth of his touch and the beating of their hearts. Time stood still as they kissed, lost in the moment and each other's embrace. The gentle murmur of the river served as the perfect soundtrack to their first kiss.

"I've been wanting to do that for so long," Ryan whispered, his voice filled with emotion.

Megan's heart swelled with happiness, knowing that Ryan felt the same way she did. "Me too," she replied, her smile shining in the fading light.

They stood there for a few more minutes absorbed in their own little bubble of happiness. Eventually, Ryan broke the embrace, and they continued strolling along the river, hand in hand, immersed in lively conversation and carefree laughter.

As they reached a secluded spot, Ryan pulled Megan close and rested his forehead against hers. His hand gently caressed her cheek, and she closed her eyes, savoring the warmth of his touch. Ryan turned towards Megan with a playful smile. "There's one more thing I want to share with you," he said teasingly.

Before Megan could even ask what it was, Ryan reached into his pocket and pulled out a small box. He opened it to reveal a delicate silver necklace with a small charm shaped like a heart.

"I know this is a surprise gift, but I wanted you to have this as a symbol of how much you mean to me," he said sincerely.

Tears pricked at Megan's eyes as she took the necklace from him. "Thank you," she whispered, feeling overwhelmed by his thoughtfulness.

"I hope you'll wear it always," Ryan added with a smile.

Megan nodded, unable to find words to express her gratitude for this simple yet heartfelt gesture. She leaned in and kissed him again, grateful for the unexpected love that had blossomed between them.

As they continued their stroll hand in hand, Megan knew that this would be a day she would always remember.

Ryan invited Xavier over to his suburban home one evening, a gesture of true friendship. They both silently made their way to the basketball court, each with a ball in hand. The soft glow of twilight filtered through the trees as they warmed up with a few layups and dribbling drills.

Without a word, they began a one-on-one game, each determined to prove themselves on the court. Xavier, with his athletic build and effortless grace, sank five jump shots in a row before finally missing one. Ryan, with his sturdy frame and unshakeable focus, calmly made four three-pointers in a row, each from a slightly farther distance.

As they played, the noise and havoc of the outside world faded away, swallowed by the mesmerizing thumping of the ball and the rhythmic rippling of the net. For these two young men, the court was a sanctuary, a place where their differences and struggles disappeared into the timeless simplicity of the game.

As the sun gradually descended, the streetlights flickered on, signaling the end of their game. Xavier and Ryan walked back to the house, both smiling and panting from the exertion. No words were needed to convey the bond they had formed on the court that evening.

Two best friends shooting hoops on a court, laughing, and having a good time.

COSTLY FREE THROWS

Bounce, Bounce...the steady rhythm of the basketball hitting the hardwood echoed through the arena, competing with the roaring crowd and coaches yelling out instructions. We were down by a single point, and I was standing alone at the free-throw line. This wasn't just any game. It was the highly anticipated state championship, held in a sold-out arena in the heart of the bustling city. With only 1.2 seconds left on the clock, it all came down to this moment. As I prepared to take my shot, the referee blew his whistle and signaled for a timeout. The other team's coach had called the timeout to try and mess with my head while their star guard stood in front of me, blocking my path to the bench. She sneered and muttered, "You're going to choke," as she purposely bumped into me, trying to throw me off my game. It was all just a strategic move to gain an advantage, but I wouldn't let it get to me.

My name is Rory Dawson. I am the starting shooting guard for the Silver City Spartans, and I have become a household name in my small town. Despite its name, my town is just like thousands of other towns scattered across the country - unassuming, ordinary, almost invisible. But one thing that sets Silver City apart is our high school girls basketball team.

Silver City's basketball program is the town's crown jewel, a constant source of pride and joy for our residents. We have won sixteen state titles, including three of the last five, making us the state's winningest high school basketball program. I am the second-leading scorer on the team, averaging about thirteen points per game. Everywhere I go, people stop me to talk about the latest game or to congratulate me on my performance.

The high school girls basketball program is a point of honor for our town and defines us. The boys high school basketball team has never been successful, and it's been more than twenty years since they've made it to the state championship tournament. Their games at home are sparsely attended, while our games, both home and away, usually sell out and always draw large crowds of passionate fans.

Our coach, Candy Cook, was most likely named by her parents after a night of drinking and trying to come up with an eccentric first name. She is an imposing figure patrolling the sidelines. Standing six feet tall, with a lean, muscular frame and sharp, angular features, she commands respect and fear from us players. But beneath her tough exterior is a heart of gold, a love for the game that surpasses all else. She is a legend in our small town, already inducted into the state high school Hall of Fame for her ten championship wins as head coach.

Coach Cook has a way of making us feel both invincible and vulnerable at the same time. She pushes us to our limits, both physically and mentally, but always aims to make us better players and people. She is tough but fair, and we all know she deeply cares for us.

She also uses corny food-related metaphors and laughs as we groan at them. I still vividly remember her speech to our team after this year's first practice when she pulled out a menu and placed it on the table in front of us.

"Welcome to the new season, ladies," Coach grinned. "As you can see, I've prepared a special menu for us. The basketball schedule is the main course, with all the regular season games carefully planned out. The post-season is our dessert, a sweet reward for all our hard work. And winning the state championship, well, that's like putting a cherry on top of the cake."

We groaned and rolled our eyes, used to Coach's silly food references, but we couldn't stop smiling.

"And you all are my ingredients," Coach continued. "Each and every one of you brings something unique to the team. And just like a good recipe, we need every single one of you to "blend" into a successful team. Practice is our blender molding individuals into a "smoothie," a cohesive unit."

As the season wore on, we exchanged glances and stifled giggles whenever she brought up another food analogy.

"Oh, here comes the rotten tomato," we would whisper to each other, stifling our laughter as Coach launched into another motivational speech.

Or "Looks like we've got a loaf of stale bread on our hands today," we would joke when she imparted another round of food-related basketball wisdom.

Since I first held a basketball at the tender age of six, I dreamed of making two crucial free throws to win a state championship. I still remember holding a basketball in my early childhood. The leather felt cool against my palms, and I marveled at how it bounced and flew through the air. From that day on, I was hooked. I spent countless hours practicing in my driveway, shooting hoops until the sun went down and my fingers grew numb from the cold.

But it wasn't just about the love of the game for me. It was also about proving something to myself and others. In Silver City being a successful athlete is almost like a rite of passage. In a small town, sports are a big deal. Every young girl dreams of making two crucial free throws to win a state championship. And now, with a second left on the clock, that dream was real for me.

As I reached the bench, Coach Cook immediately pulled me aside. "Listen, Rory, don't let that other coach get in your head. You've been practicing free throws all season, and you can make them with your eyes closed. Just focus on your form and tune out all the noise. Be the secret ingredient."

Her words calmed me down, and I took a deep breath. My teammates huddled around us as our coach gave the team instructions for the final play.

"After Rory makes both free throws," she said, looking at me pointedly, "we need to make sure we don't foul them. We have to trust our defense to stop them without giving up a desperation basket. Katie, you guard the inbounds passer, wave your arms, and jump up and down. Remember, no fouls. We are about to put the cherry on top of the cake. Spartans on three."

"Spartans!" We all yelled in unison before taking our positions on the court. With the weight heaviest on a single player, myself, I wearily walked back onto the court, weaving towards the free-throw line. Hundreds of competing thoughts fought for my attention.

There was a sense of tension in the air, a palpable weight that seemed to rest on a single player, a burden that one person alone must bear.

That player was me.

As I slowly approached the free-throw line, my mind was in turmoil. Random thoughts raced through my head, each one competing for my attention.

Take a deep breath...and exhale.

Relax, you've got this.

But then another voice whispered doubtfully.

You're going to miss both shots.

Visualize making the shot.

And yet, the negative thoughts persisted.

You're a choke artist. You'll shoot two airballs.

Despite my nerves, I was confident. I had practiced thousands of free throws and knew that I was a 75% shooter for the season. As someone who loved math, I knew I would likely make both shots. And even if I didn't, there was still a nearly 100% chance that I would at least make one shot, forcing the game into overtime.

Unfortunately, the logical part of my brain couldn't quiet the doubts that crept in. These free throws weren't like the ones I practiced in the gym or my backyard; this was the state championship game, and all eyes were on me. The pressure was immense. The stands were packed with thousands of spectators, waiting to see if I would make these shots. My mind raced with thoughts of failure and ridicule. If I missed both shots it would be a lifetime of humiliation. I remembered how even Lebron James, considered one of the greatest players of all time, missed both free throws in last night's game. The crowd didn't care about his greatness then; they only cared about winning free fast-food chicken meals from a promotion if an opponent missed both free throws.

My inner self battled, torn between confidence and doubt. I knew this moment would decide the game's outcome, and I desperately wanted to make these two shots.

My dad's words about free throws came to mind, one of his many basketball life lessons. "Rory, never underestimate the importance of free throws. It often comes down to who makes or misses those shots in close games. And don't forget; it's called a free throw for a reason – they give you points for free; there's no defense, and it should be an easy shot. No matter where you play, the dimensions of the court are the same: the rim is 10 feet high, and it is 15 feet from the basket to the free throw line. It's all about muscle memory; if you practice enough, it becomes second nature."

My father also emphasized the importance of having a routine when shooting free throws. Whether it was spinning or flipping the ball, the key was to have a consistent ritual and never stray from it. My own routine was not impressive or showy, just two precise right-handed dribbles before taking the shot. My pre-shot routine was so dull and basic Coach Cook referred to it as "meat and potatoes."

As the referee tossed me the ball, his instructions echoed in my ears: two shots, take it easy on the first one. I caught the ball and stepped up to the line with confidence, but heavy pressure weighed on my shoulders. The crowd was roaring, the stakes were high, and my teammates' eyes were fixed firmly on me. Correction - every single person in the arena had their attention on a teenage girl poised to shoot a ball towards a basket. Thousands of eyes were trained on me, unblinking and intense.

I could feel the sweat forming on my palms. I took one more deep breath and bounced the ball twice before setting up for my first shot. My mind went blank as I brought the ball up to release it. For a split second, I couldn't remember what came next. Do I bend my knees? Do I push off with my toes? My confidence wavered as self-doubt crept in.

Luckily, my body instinctively took over. All those hours of practice and repetition paid off as I easily shot the ball. It flew through the air with precision, and I could already hear the satisfying swish called "string music." However, my confidence was shattered when I saw the ball barely graze the front rim. The once-hushed crowd erupted into cheers from the opposing team's supporters. The same opposing star guard had the audacity to taunt me in a voice just loud enough to be heard: "You, see? Bitch - Gag City. You're nothing but a choke artist, pretending to be something you're not...you can't keep up."

I was rattled. Nailing the first free throw was crucial; it would relieve all the pressure for the second shot. If I made the first, there were only two possible outcomes, and both were positive: a win for our team or overtime if I missed. But after missing the first shot, the pressure on my next one was overwhelming. The entire season rested on this single shot, and if I missed, my teammates, coach, the school alumni, and the entire town would be disappointed. It would all be on me.

The taunts from the opposing team's guard rattled in my ears as I stepped back to the free-throw line for my second attempt. A wave of doubt and frustration washed over me. I was shocked I had missed such a crucial shot, especially with all the confidence and preparation I had going into it.

I took a deep breath and tried to push away the negative thoughts. My teammates gave me encouraging pats on the back and words of support, but it was hard to block out the negative energy radiating from the other team and their supporters in the stands.

My overactive mind again took over.

Chill out...breathe.

Relax. You've got this.

You are such a failure.

Bet those mean girls from school are laughing.

You are a great shooter. Be confident.

What is my boyfriend thinking? Will he dump me if I miss?

The stage is too great. Pressure, pressure, under pressure.

I tried to fake a semblance of composure. I trusted my routine: bouncing the ball twice, bending my knees, flicking my wrist, and following through. I concentrated on nothing but the rim and my form.

When I released the ball, it felt like time slowed down, the way it sometimes does in moments of high pressure or intense focus. I watched as it sailed through the air, the perfect rotation a sign of its trajectory. It was going in. I was sure of it.

But then, in an instant, it was not. The shot was halfway down the hoop before it boomeranged out, an in-and-out shot, the cruelest kind of miss. My heart sank as I watched the opposing center corral the rebound and run out the clock, their team erupting into cheers as they realized they had won the state championship.

I stood frozen on the court, my eyes fixed on the now empty hoop, as the onslaught of emotions threatened to overwhelm me. I had dreamed about this moment for years, pouring endless hours into honing my skills and sacrificing time with friends and family, all for this one shot at glory. And now, in a split second, it was gone. When the final buzzer sounded, signaling the end of the game and our season, I felt utterly defeated. My teammates surrounded me, their voices blending together in words of encouragement and consolation, but it all sounded distant to me.

As we lined up for the post-game handshake, I felt a sense of dread wash over me. But to my surprise, the opposing team's players greeted me with hugs and pats on the back, offering words of encouragement as they passed by. Even their star player with an advanced degree in trash-talking came up to me with a smile. "You played great out there," she said, shaking my hand. "Don't let this loss get you down. You've got a lot of talent."

During the mid-court second-place award presentation, I stood in front of the crowd, feeling the weight of their expectations and my own disappointment. My eyes remained fixated on the gleaming hardwood floor, and I could not make eye contact with anyone. I was an ashamed and defeated girl.

As the presenter began to speak, I swayed slightly, my mind still reeling from the loss. The words he spoke were a blur, the clapping and cheering of the audience a distant hum. My entire being was consumed by the feeling of failure, the bitter taste of defeat lingering on my tongue.

As the tournament official handed me the second-place trophy, I accepted it with trembling hands and a forced smile. With every step I took leaving the court, the trophy felt heavier and heavier, a constant reminder of my shortcomings.

As we walked to the locker room, I mentally replayed the game and analyzed every move I made, thinking about how I could have done things differently. Every opportunity I missed, every missed shot, every errant pass, played through my mind like a broken record.

My head hung low as I sat in the locker room before a voice broke through my negative thoughts. It was Coach Cook. She stood at the front of the room, addressing the team with a solemn yet comforting tone.

"Girls, I know this loss hurts. But this is not the end. We still have a chance to come back stronger and win the championship next year. And you know what? I believe in every single one of you. I've seen the hard work and dedication you've put into this season. We finished second in the state out of 85 girls high school teams. That is an amazing accomplishment. Be proud. Don't let this defeat define you. Let it fuel your fire. Let it push you to be better."

The coach left the locker room, leaving us alone with our disappointment. The sound of slamming lockers and anguished screams echoed throughout the small space, reflecting the raw emotions of my teammates. Tears streamed down some faces while others pounded their fists against the metal locker doors in frustration.

But amidst the chaos, I noticed something surprising. Not one of my teammates blamed me for our loss. This was truly remarkable in a group of teenage girls where shifting alliances and frenemies were the norm. One day, a girl would be my best friend, only to give me the silent treatment the next day for no apparent reason. But at this moment, our shared defeat united us. We were a team, and we would stick together through the highs and lows of the game.

As I changed out of my uniform, I couldn't shake the feeling of defeat and worthlessness. And as I walked out of the locker room, I knew this was only the beginning of the long road ahead. How would I ever recover?

I slept at most an hour that night and did absolutely nothing Sunday. My room was messy, with clothes strewn across the floor and random pieces of paper scattered on my desk. I had no energy to face the outside world, so I stayed in my room the entire day, moping and wallowing in self-pity. My faithful dog Duncan, an energetic 8-year-old family member, lay at my feet, his warm body providing a comforting presence. I absentmindedly stroked his soft fur, finding solace in his unwavering loyalty. Duncan earned his unofficial therapy dog certificate on that day by never leaving my side.

My alarm rang at 6 am the next day, waking me from a restless night. I had barely slept, tossing and turning in a cold sweat, haunted by a recurring dream. In the dream, hundreds of unrecognizable faces surrounded me, their arms outstretched, pointing accusatory fingers at my bound body. I could feel their judgment and contempt pulsing through the air as they circled closer and closer, their individual features merging into one frightening sight. And then, in unison, they began to sing, their voices rising in a chilling chorus: "You are the one to blame. Here is your sentence..."

The nightmare started last night and always ended abruptly before I could hear the verdict, leaving me in a state of anxious unease. I shook off the remnants of my disturbing dream and forced myself to get out of bed. As a light drizzle tapped against the windowpane in my room, I felt a dull sense of gloom settling over me. The room was filled with drab grayness, which matched my mood. But there was no time to dwell on it - today was the first day of school since I was responsible for losing the state title game, and I had to get ready. I tried to push away thoughts about my strange dream last night. It was probably just stress from losing the game. I will need a therapist at this rate, which is ridiculous considering I'm only a teenager.

Despite my best efforts, the dream lingered like a stubborn stain. I couldn't shake off the feeling of unease, the nagging sense that something was amiss. My heart was pounding with nervous energy, a drumbeat that refused to fade. I tried to push it all away and focus on my morning routine.

I hastily dressed in a faded college sweatshirt and a pair of khaki pants, the unofficial high school uniform of my small town. My unruly hair defied my attempts to tame it, so I settled for running a brush through it in a half-hearted attempt. My mom had already left for her shift at the diner, so I grabbed a granola bar for breakfast before heading out the door.

The weather had changed. The sun was shining brightly as I walked to school, but it did little to lift my spirits. The dream had seemed so real, so vivid. It was like a memory that wasn't mine.

As I entered the school gates, I saw familiar faces sprinkled among students I rarely talked to. But the atmosphere was different this morning. An underlying tension seemed to emanate from every student.

I went to homeroom, where I saw some of my teammates sitting at their desks. A knot formed in my stomach as memories of our heartbreaking loss came flooding back.

The first period of the day was Spanish class. As I walked into the room, the students' chatter stopped, and all eyes were on me. I felt uncomfortable and sat down at my assigned desk, trying to ignore the stares and whispers behind my back. I looked up at the board in front of the room and saw three words written in Spanish—ahoga, mordaza, and perdedor - all surrounded by mocking doodles and insults.

Chris Mills, a bully who found himself amusing and had asked me out to a school dance freshman year, stood up from his seat and announced loudly, "Rory, these three words are your Spanish vocabulary word assignments today to memorize. They should be easy for you to learn."

The three Spanish words translated to choke, gag, and loser. The rest of the class tittered and snickered at Chris's cruel joke, and I could feel my face flush with embarrassment and anger. I clenched my fists under the desk, determined not to let them see how much the words hurt me.

The Spanish teacher, Mrs. Rodriguez, walked in, and her no-nonsense demeanor silenced the room. Without a word, she erased the offensive words from the board and began her lesson for the day.

When class ended and everyone filed out of the room, Chris walked past me and whispered, "Good luck with those vocab words," with a smirk on his face. I can't believe how cruel some teenagers are.

It was a mixture of emotions all day - anger, empathy, pity to name a few. Some of my close friends tried to cheer me up and comfort me by exchanging hugs and talking about any topic besides basketball. Others were not as kind. I felt that I was being stared at and pointed at by students, punctuated by shadowy whispers that went quiet as I walked down the hallway.

The rumors had already spread like wildfire, enveloping me in their burning embrace. The embarrassment, humiliation, grief - all of it weighed heavily on my shoulders, burdening me with an unbearable weight that threatened to crush my spirit. I couldn't shake off the feeling of being exposed, raw and vulnerable, to the prying eyes of my peers.

As I made my way to the next class, I wondered if this was my new reality - a pariah, a fallen hero, a cautionary tale. The thought of facing the basketball team in the coming days, once my sisters and closest friends, now filled me with dread and shame.

English class seemed to go on forever, but it wasn't as traumatic as Spanish class. My classmates occasionally gave me curious looks but didn't interrupt my thoughts. I felt like a discarded student sent off to a desolate fortress of solitude. Maybe this was my "dream" sentence: living a life of loneliness, exclusion, and isolation.

After second period, I had the early lunch period. Sitting down at the lunch table with my boyfriend, Bobby, I felt a bit relieved. Being alone for most of the day was starting to wear on me, and having someone to sit with made things a little easier. Bobby and I had been friends since kindergarten and had recently started dating about two months ago. It wasn't anything too serious in my mind, but our classmates considered us a couple.

Bobby smiled at me as he took a bite out of his sandwich. "You played great in the championship game," he said, trying to cheer me up.

I sighed, poking at my salad with a plastic fork. "Thanks, but it doesn't really matter. We lost, and I missed the key free throws at the end of the game."

Bobby's expression turned into a frown. "But you still were one of the top scorers. You're in great company."

"What do you mean?"

"You're just as skilled as Lebron James. I saw him miss both free throws during the Lakers game the other night."

At the same time, we blurted out: "And the crowd went wild for free chicken meals!"

We laughed uncontrollably, two teenagers finding humor in something seemingly insignificant and silly. It was a much-needed break from my unusual day back at school.

Bobby left the lunch table to use the restroom. As I ate alone, lost in thought, someone suddenly pulled up a chair across from me. It was Mrs. Rodriguez. She sat down without saying a word and started eating her own lunch. After a few moments of silence, she finally spoke up.

"I saw what happened in Spanish class today," she said softly.

I didn't know how to respond, so I just nodded silently.

"I want you to know that those words do not define you," she continued. "You are so much more than what some bully says about you."

As I looked at her, my eyes filled with tears. Her kindness was welcome, yet her words of reassurance only made me feel more fragile and powerless. Not only were my classmates talking about me, but also the faculty and possibly the entire community. I felt like everyone was scrutinizing me making me feel exposed and defenseless.

I could feel the tears welling up, ready to burst at any moment. I quickly made a beeline for the bathroom, trying to control my emotions. My hands trembled as I turned off the faucet and grabbed a towel to dab at my eyes. Despite my efforts, the tears were pricking at my eyes, threatening to fall. I had almost lost control in front of everyone in the school hallway on my way here, but somehow, I managed to hold myself together...until now.

I let out a shaky breath, trying to regain my composure before leaving the relative safety of the bathroom. But as I turned to make my way back out, I was met with an unexpected obstacle.

Barb, the queen bee mean girl, stood in front of me with two of her loyal followers, all sporting smug expressions, blocking my path to the door.

Barb laughed as she applied a fresh layer of lipstick in the mirror. "I caught you gagging during the game," she sneered, enjoying my discomfort. "That explains your gag reflex when giving Bobby blow jobs."

My stomach dropped at the cruel words, a mixture of shame and anger bubbling up inside me. I wanted to say something, anything. I tried to defend myself, but my voice caught in my throat. They were right; I had gagged, and everyone had seen it. And now, they were using it against me to humiliate me even further.

I struggled to control my emotions. I wanted to storm past them and leave, but I knew it would only worsen the situation. So, I stood there, my head held neither high nor low, refusing to give them satisfaction.

The fluorescent lights of the high school bathroom flickered above us, casting an eerie glow on our faces. I stood there, trembling, as Barb and her minions towered over me like three sharks circling a schooling fish.

"At least I made the team and am playing," I feebly countered in a stammering, soft voice.

Minion #1, a thin girl with a sharp nose and small beady eyes, piled on: "You blew it using the same weak form as when you blow your boyfriend."

I felt my face flush with embarrassment as tears stung at the corners of my eyes. Barb, with a doctorate in cruelty, grew bored of the game. I was no match for the team she captained named "Three Mean Girl Bullies."

The trio of tormentors exited the bathroom in their matching plaid preppy outfits, coordinated daily in a morning conference where only ringleader Barb was privy to the agenda. As the door slammed shut behind them, I crumbled to the hard tile floor, crying uncontrollably. I couldn't handle this any longer. The constant teasing and humiliation were too much for me.

Usually, the day's final period was a welcome relief for me. Honors Precalculus was my favorite subject, and I found solace in the elegant equations and logical solutions. But on this particular day, my heart was heavy with anticipation and dread. I just wanted the school day to be over. I entered the classroom with a mixture of nervousness and apprehension, greeted by the sight of Ted, the resident genius and resident social nerd, waiting for me at my desk.

"Hey Rory, I watched the game Saturday night. Statistics and probability are passions of mine. I looked at your season statistics and saw you are a 75% free throw shooter. I ran the calculations, and there was a 56% chance of you making both shots, a 38% chance you would make 1 of 2, and only a

6% chance you would miss both. I can show you the formula if you are interested."

I remained silent, refusing to give Ted the satisfaction of a response. I knew he meant no harm, that his analytical mind couldn't resist breaking down my failure on the basketball court into a quantifiable equation. But it stung, nonetheless, to have my emotions reduced to a mere mathematical problem. I felt dehumanized, reduced to mere numbers on a page.

Ted continued to scribble furiously in his notebook, his brow furrowed in deep concentration. I could see the numbers and symbols dancing before his eyes as he tried to make sense of my failure in clutch time. But he failed to realize that my free throw percentage was not the only factor at play. My mental state, confidence, and focus were all intangible elements that couldn't be captured in a mathematical equation.

No number of calculations or theories could fully explain what it means to choke under pressure. It was a feeling, a state of being, only understood by those who have been through the experience. And I knew that Ted, with all his mathematical prowess, would never truly grasp it.

Feeling utterly drained and disheartened, I struggled to gather my scattered thoughts. Even Ted, who was usually more interested in video games than sports, had watched the missed free throws that cost our team the state championship. It was an embarrassing moment. And to make matters worse, my conversation with Ted was just as uncomfortable as the one I had earlier with the clique of mean girls. It seemed like every student and social group in school was taking a shot at me.

I somehow made it through the school week. The week of school, classes, and social obligations had been a blur. Each day was a struggle, but somehow, I managed. The constant weight on my chest and the knot in my stomach never seemed to dissipate fully, but with each passing day, they became slightly more bearable.

Monday had been the worst, with the heavy burden of the title game failure still fresh in my mind as well as my classmates. I could barely concentrate in class, my thoughts consumed by regret and self-doubt. Tuesday was marginally better, as I was able to distract myself with assignments and group projects. Wednesday and Thursday passed in a similar fashion, with each day bringing a little bit more relief.

Days were bad, but nights were even worse. I did my best to stay awake and avoid the torment of my recurring nightmare. The circle of the repeating dream was cruel, and at night, the haunting vision tightened around my head like a noose.

The strange dream continued to torture me, twisting and changing as time passed. At first, I struggled to recognize any of the faces surrounding me. But gradually, some became vaguely familiar, only to morph into someone else in the next iteration. One night it was Barb, then Mills the next. And once, I even saw Coach Cook extending a long, bony finger toward me while I screamed in terror and was trapped by restraints like a mummy. The worst part? I still didn't know what punishment awaited me. The voices singing accusations always seemed to wake me up suddenly, leaving me drenched in cold sweat with no hope of falling back asleep. And the singing itself was unlike anything I had ever heard - a disturbing sound that echoed in my mind long after waking up.

Finally, it was Friday, and I couldn't have been more relieved. The weekend didn't offer any real respite from my troubles, but it at least allowed me to escape the constant pressure of school and social judgment by my peers. As the final bell rang and I exited the crowded hallway, I felt a small glimmer of hope that things might get better.

I walked home alone, lost in my thoughts. The cool winter air nipped at my cheeks, but I welcomed the distraction from my internal turmoil. When I finally reached my front door, I took a deep breath and pushed myself through it, ready to face whatever the weekend had in store. Duncan excitedly greeted me, licking my face, tail wagging fast and furious.

I slept deeply through the night for the first time since our heartbreaking loss at the championship game. The endless stretch of restless sleep was gone, replaced by a peaceful slumber free from the faceless, vaguely familiar accusers that had plagued me. Being the weekend, I didn't bother to set an alarm and instead allowed my body to wake up naturally. When I finally opened my eyes, the sun was already high in the sky. I stayed in bed for a little longer, relishing the feeling of being fully rested after a grueling and exhausting week.

As I stirred from my sleep and stretched out my limbs, my eyes were instantly drawn to the lone poster in my room featuring Michael Jordan. The black-and-white photo captured him mid-air, ready to make a shot on the basketball court. But the words beneath the image caught my attention the most: "I've missed more than 9,000 shots in my career. I've lost almost 300 games. 26 times, I've been trusted to take the game-winning shot and missed. I've failed over and over and over again in my life. And that is why I succeed."

I have always been a fan of Michael Jordan, not just for his incredible talent on the court but also for his strong work ethic and determination to never give up. Even as a young girl, I found his words inspiring, but they held even more weight now as a teenager facing my own struggles.

I knew what I had to do. In a flash, I was out of bed and grabbing my basketball from the corner of my room. Silently, I made my way to the backyard, where a lone basketball hoop stood tall and proud.

Basketball had always been my sanctuary, my escape from the stressors of everyday life. As I bounced and handled the ball, its comforting weight and texture in my palms, all else faded into the background. My mind was consumed with the flow and cadence of the game as I took shots and grabbed rebounds. It was the only time I could find true serenity and mental clarity. And after days of feeling displaced, I finally

felt like my true self again. My mind was clear as I focused on my form and technique. I released the ball and watched it swish through the net. It felt good, like an old friend I had been neglecting.

My dad and Duncan joined me in the backyard, assuming their normal basketball roles. My dad was my designated rebounder, ready to retrieve any shot and pass the basketball back to me. And my dog, as always, was my unofficial coach, observing my every move and taking mental notes.

I continued to practice shooting, moving to different spots on the court. Duncan barked encouragement at me as my dad retrieved shots. Usually, I would be in competition mode, trying to beat my previous score or impress my dad with my skills. But today, it was different. Today, I was just enjoying the game.

I tried some reverse lay-ins, pretending to be MJ or Kobe making a clutch shot in the final seconds of a game. My dog watched intently; his head cocked to one side as if he understood what was happening.

Next up was the Mikan drill, which involved alternating lay-ins with each hand while moving around the basket. It was one of my favorite drills because it required focus and precision.

After completing a few drills, I went back to shooting jumpers from various distances and locations on the court. Invisible imaginary defenders contested some, while others were wide-open shots that any NBA player would make in their sleep.

But for me, it wasn't about impressing anyone or proving anything. It was simply about getting lost in the game and finding joy again. And that's exactly what happened.

With each successful shot I sank, my mind started to feel lighter and more at ease. The pressures of school, the opinions of others, and my missed free throws all faded away as I focused solely on the game of basketball, the sport I loved.

My dad noticed the change in expression and smiled proudly as he rebounded for me. He has always been my biggest supporter, but today, it was more than that.

After working out for forty minutes, I finally stepped up to the free-throw line.

Bounce, Bounce, bend the knees, flick the wrists, follow through, swish.

Dribble, Dribble, bend the knees, flick the wrists, follow through, money,

Bounce, Bounce, bend the knees, flick the wrists, follow through, nothing but net.

Dribble, Dribble, bend the knees, flick the wrists, follow through, another pure shot.

I stood at the foul line, the ball snug against my fingertips. My dad's clapping echoed in the still air, a metronome for my rhythm. I breathed deeply, taking in the scent of freshly mowed grass and the distant sound of children playing. Closing my eyes, I visualized the ball gliding smoothly through the air, swishing through the net.

With a flick of my wrist, the ball soared towards the hoop. It nestled over the front part of the rim, circled twice, and dropped gracefully into the basket. 5 out of 5. My dad cheered as I retrieved the ball and returned to the line.

I took my time, bouncing the ball twice before releasing it with a satisfying flip. 6 out of 6. The symphony of swishing nets continued; each shot a perfect note in the sweet string music being composed in my backyard.

Duncan, my loyal pup, wagged his tail in excitement. He celebrated by doing dog zoomies on the grass. Was he cheering me on and celebrating, or simply enjoying being a dog? It didn't matter; his presence was enough to make me smile.

As I drained my fifteenth consecutive free throw, the sun beat down on my back, warming my skin. I looked up at the sky, a perfect shade of blue, and sighed contentedly. This was the essence of life, simple moments filled with joy and the comfort of companionship. I soaked in the warmth surrounding me and couldn't help but feel that, in this moment, life was perfect.

If my team ever finds itself in a crucial situation requiring a free throw or clutch shot, there is only one person I have complete faith in to take it and make it - myself.

There are more dreams to chase and more championships to win, and I am ready for all of them.

I am a Spartan - spirited, courageous, determined, resilient, and proud.

PACK LEADS THE PACK

Outside, it is unusually warm, and inside it is sticky
Brought a jacket anyway. Seattle weather is tricky
Excitement builds, there is a buzz in the air
The Sonics can't lose wouldn't be fair
On display will be the best basketball players in the world
This is the truth, not nonsense words being hurled
The league is the National Basketball Association
The game has the undivided attention of the nation
Matchup is between the visiting Nuggets and Sonics
If the home team loses, there will be histrionics

Game location is the Seattle Center Coliseum

Crowd before the game quiet like a mausoleum
Venue built in 1962 for the World's Fair
Elvis filmed a movie showing off his iconic hair
Fans arrive at the game via the Monorail
A few have been drinking smelling of ale
Seattle Sonics best team during the regular season
This will be a championship year using reason

Memorable day falls on the seventh of May
A win is coming, but a few fans still pray
For the team to win the deciding game five
Beg the creator for the Sonics skills to revive
The fateful year is 1994
This game will be a war
Stakes are high win or go home
Nerves hit me before the game. I start to roam
Walk the concrete concourse passing the concession line

Become concerned are the Hoop Gods sending a sign?
The Sonics team is more talented on paper
Games played on court expectations taper

No hiding on the floor - it's five on five
In a deciding game, the goal is to survive
After four games, the series is even
Are the Sonics still a team to believe in?

Seattle's starting five is Payton, Gill, Kemp, Schrempf, and Cage
Won league-best 63 in the regular season all the rage
Key reserves McMillan, Perkins, and Pierce
Series should be over instead competition fierce
Colorful nicknames like The Glove and The Reign Man
Both popular all-star players known in Iran
One player has 4 monikers - Big Smooth, The Big Easy, Sam
I Am, & Sleepy Sam
How many more were tested but ended up going to spam?
Sound like names from a children's book by Dr. Seuss
A player with four nicknames should dominate like Zeus

Denver Nuggets, a mediocre regular season team
But in this playoff series, they have a scheme
Game performances have accelerated
Basketball skills have been elevated
How this happens, nobody knows
Fate or random luck I suppose
The team does not have a star
Series tied 2-2. They have already gone far
Past what was reasonably expected
As a team, they must be respected
Starters are Ellis, Mutombo, Abdul-Rauf, Williams, and Stith
Not easy names to recite like Jones, Brown, or Smith
Exotic names like an alphabet soup
Make no mistake, these guys can hoop

So far in the series, their play has been inspired
Meanwhile, Sonic shot after shot has misfired

Denver center is Dikembe Mutombo
The whole series he put on a show
Over seven feet tall, born in the Congo
Great performance wish he would go go
Violently swatting shots out of thin air
In a twenty-second span, blocking a pair
After another failed shot, wagging a finger
A warning to dejected Sonic shooters, the images linger
Snatching rebound after rebound after rebound
Leaves the crowd gasping, an unusual sound

It is time to introduce one Robert Pack
The Nuggets player who broke the Sonics' back
Attended college at USC, nicknamed the University of Spoiled
Children
After this game, he should be comped an extended stay at
the local Hilton
Pack played on eight NBA teams, a basketball vagabond life
Today trash talking with fans slicing their hopes like a knife
Over his career, he was no better than average
Today, for 36 cruel minutes, points were coming in a barrage
He even played as a pro in Lithuania
Luckily, this game was before social media mania
He certainly aced the game five test
For this one crucial contest, the best of the best
Came off the bench and wasn't even a starter
His marvelous performance made him famous like a martyr
Born in New Orleans, a city known for voodoo

Sonic home fans sobbing like a child's boo hoo
Robert Pack, a journeyman bouncing from team to team
Why did he choose the deciding game to fulfill a dream?

It is Seattle, so inside it is raining
Smooth jumpers by Pack, all of them draining
Finishes with 23 points, many of them difficult
One high-arching swish launched from a catapult
Busting Gary Payton, aka The Glove
On this day, his defense resembles a dove
GP a top-five league defender for years
Sizzling shooting display reduces him to tears
Legendary Sonics Hall of Famer
On this day, his play is lamer
Than an overmatched bench-warming rookie
Shouldn't have wagered with a local bookie
Try another defender, try Det the Threat
The result is the same - nothing but net
Pack was on a hot steak, locked into a zone
Every time he shot, the crowd would groan
This is getting beyond ridiculous
Is our defense this atrocious?

Second game in a row decided in overtime
The talent level of players is sublime
Final play of the extra period crowd in a hush
Will spectators explode with joy or feel a crush?
Denver center Mutombo falls down basketball in his clutch
Home fans start to cry; this is entirely too much
Overtime periods are random, a speculative coin flip
Sonics lose games 4 and 5 in OT, title dreams disappear and slip

Trudge outside, blinded by sunlight
Why didn't our team win or put up a fight?
Some fans head straight to bars to get drunk
Championship aspirations completely sunk
How did we lose is the familiar refrain
On a day like this, where is the Seattle rain?
Predicting a sure win is an example of overconfidence
Proceed with caution; the declaration is ominous
This truth was learned by every Supersonics fan
Part of the Basketball God's master plan

HOOP HARMONY

The sport is basketball, also called hoops
Teams five per side or smaller groups
A simple game, score the most baskets
Not life or death, no guns or caskets
The game has evolved over the years
Debate the best era of all time over beers
Larger-than-life characters & personalities
Global sport, many nationalities
Every player has an interesting story
Deserves some pub, some lasting glory
Some players unknown, and others reach fame
Clever fans drum up a monicker, a nickname
Without any further ado
Meet the All-Name crew

Julius Erving introducing *Doctor J*

Try to guard him, better pray
Swooping and soaring
Buckets galore, always scoring
Basketball surgeon carving up
opponents
Fans applaud & remember those
moments
Gravity-defying slam dunk champion
Delivers a powerful hoop sermon
Played for the Sixers & the Nets
Reduced defenders to cold sweats

The Hick from French Lick
Could perform a trick
On basketball courts
Exposing weaknesses & warts
A skilled all-around player
An opponent slayer
An all-time great
Not open to debate
Larry Bird is his real name
A legend with serious game

Here cometh *the Iceman*
Impossible to stop without a ban
Given name George Gervin
Tricky moves leave them swervin'
Trademark shot the finger roll
Result is two points, a field goal
Physique tall and giraffe-like skinny
Popular player a legend in the city

Earl Monroe, *The Pearl*
Twist, turn, whirl and twirl
Noted for flamboyant flashy play style
Fans ate it up, watching with a smile
Revered in African American community
A hero due to his on-court ingenuity
Second moniker *Black Jesus*
Invent brand new moves to tease us
Crazy stutter steps and a spin move
Basketball genius who could groove

Giannis Antetokounmpo
A beautiful name, a flow
The Greek Freak
A cool cat, not a geek
Crazy blocks and rim-shattering dunks
Helpless defenders swerving like drunks
Won a title for Milwaukee Bucks
Defeated opponents muttering fucks

Sidney Moncrief aka *Sid the Squid*
Popular player in Spanish capital Madrid
Played college ball for Arkansas Razorbacks
Team reached final four, players not hacks
A top defender known for tenacity
Versatile player use in any capacity
Tremendous leaper whose knees gave out
Career cut short, future in doubt
Sad day when he had to retire
A class act, a competitor to admire

Tim Duncan, *The Big Fundamental*
Deadly bank shot makes defender grumble
A stoic figure on the court
Opponents give up, choose to abort
Played entire career for San Antonio Spurs
Basic player, no smoke and mirrors
Famous teammates Parker and Ginobili
A winner, one of the best, have to agree

Metta World Peace
Volatile figure call the police
Charged into stands during a game
Inducted into Melee Hall of Fame
Incident is known as Malice at the Palace
Showed little remorse, attitude callous
Given name Ron Artest
Lucky man avoided arrest

Up next is Gary Payton, *The Glove*
Seattle fans shower him with love
Always played, a true gamer
A superstar, a Hall of Famer
Known for a timely steal
Opponent ballhandlers squeal
A magician, a pickpocket
Quick hands, a bottle rocket
Teaching a course in defensive pressure
Master of D a tenured professor

Gary Payton II, *The Mitten*

Father the cat, son the kitten
Elder one of the greatest of all time
A trash talker supreme - kid quieter, a mime
Junior and senior went to Oregon State
Both all-conference, a fact no debate
Each played guard position like father like son
Youngster also played in NBA, watching a rerun

Lloyd Free morphed into *World B. Free*
A mad gunner on a shooting spree
Disinterested in playing defense
Lack of effort sure to incense
Fans who paid top dollar for a courtside seat
Didn't bother *All-World*, marched to his own beat
Briefly a Golden State Warrior
Flamboyant player deserves an editorial

Shawn Kemp, *The Reign Man*
Played on instinct, no plan
Soaring above the rim for Alley-Oops
Frustrated defender calls out whoops
As another bucket is dunked with velocity
Opponent posterized a humiliating atrocity
A blow to one's ego, never live it down
Defender retreats, head facedown
Fathered seven children with six different women
Multiple Thanksgiving celebrations that's a given
After retirement owner of pot shops
No longer a need for basketball high tops

Joe Barely Cares

Tepid game elicits stares
Given name Joe Barry Carroll
No effort might as well sing a XMAS carol
Result is the same as his on-court contribution
No season ticket refund, no retribution
For his disinterested play
Trade him, don't let him stay

Arvydas Sabonis, a Lithuanian great
Magnificent talent spoiled by fate
Tragic Achilles tendon injury
Caused him to play gingerly
Played on Soviet team and later came to USA
Finally allowed to play in NBA hip hip hooray
A Trailblazers fanatic in an alcohol-induced haze
Developed a Portland fan favorite catch phrase
"He's not your *vydas*. He's not my *vydas*. He's *Arvydas*!"
Catchy saying, witty words topped with special sauce
Son Domantas is a triple-double machine
Happens so frequently call it routine
Number one basketball father-son combo
Better than *Jellybean* and *Black Mamba*

Not to be confused with Matt Bonner, *Red Mamba*
Deadly shooter sends defenders crying for Mama
Moniker given by Kobe Bryant
Picked up a new nickname client
An upgrade from *Red Rocket*
Store it away in a coat pocket
First NBA player born in New Hampshire
Cold weather there must hamper

The odds of making it to the league
How he made it, a story full of intrigue

Nate Robinson aka *KryptoNate*
Short in height spectators can relate
Player with an amazing vertical jump
Fueled by leaping rocket fuel from a pump
Honed his skills in Seattle at Rainier Beach & U Dub
3-time NBA dunk contest winner, an exclusive club
Epic block of Houston Rocket Yao Ming
Replay viewed by hoop junkies, a big thing
Owned a chicken & waffle joint in his hometown
A joyful player always smiling, never a frown
Gimmick boxing match against Jake Paul
Nate Rob knocked out in round 2 I recall
Career spanned 8 NBA teams plus overseas
Traded often, diagnosis a frequent flyer disease

Marvin Barnes known as *Bad News*
Drinking problem, attracted to booze
Snorted cocaine during a game
A tragic figure, nobody to blame
Talented player facing a demon
Get it together or career will be done
Free spirit played for Spirits of St. Louis
Short career balloon pops, elicits a hiss

The Round Mound of Rebound
Powerful moves sure to astound
Given name Charles Barkley
A gift for gab, full of malarkey

A wide body, a tremendous leaper
Occasional skirmishes, not a peacekeeper
Colorful character, now an announcer
Amusing stories could have been a bouncer

Detlef Schremp, *Det the Threat*
All-around talent, skills heaven sent
Before coming to States played for Bayer Leverkusen
Scouts noticed his skill, except for the few snoozen
Gifted trash talker, second language German jive
Opponent responds to taunts, stirs up a beehive
Referee intervenes, and hands out a technical
Riled-up fans scream & curse creating a spectacle
Key contributor on great Sonics teams
Should have won one title or so it seems
Starred in Seattle, a popular player
Beloved by all, should run for mayor

Next up another German Dirk Nowitzki
A trend developing, easy to see
Bavarian Bomber, Dirk Diggler
A great player, a popular figure
The Germinator, The Berlin Tall
Nicknames multiply, a moniker sprawl
One of the all-time great jump shooters
Torched defenders commiserate over beers at Hooters
Signature move is a one-legged fadeaway
Create space for a shot, keep opponents at bay
Scored baskets in a variety of ways, quite clever
Many consider him the top international player ever

Alaa Abdelnaby aka *Alphabet*
Parents named him after losing a bet
In college a Blue Devil, a Dukie
Cameron Crazies are quite kooky
Average player best known for his name
1st time inductee in Moniker Hall of Fame
Repeat his name fast, a mouthful
Pronounce it correctly - doubtful

David Robinson, *The Admiral*
Graceful giant who could twirl
A basketball & sink left-handed shots
Played on dream team, connected the dots
Attended United States Navy Academy
Never saw active duty, never faced an enemy
Won two championships with San Antonio Spurs
Fun team to watch, ball movement purrs

Karl Malone aka *Mailman*
Internationally famous even in Japan
A power forward who played bully ball
Blasted defenders, causing them to fall
Rural kid from a small Louisiana town
Beat long odds to earn a crown
As one of the best hoopers ever
Made game simple, not clever
Starred with HOF guard John Stockton
Perfected pick and roll, a Utah Jazz doctrine

Dennis Rodman, *The Worm*
Flamboyance makes one squirm

Once dated the singer Madonna
The two ended up in a sauna
Often changed his hair color
Crowd reaction oh brother
Great timing as he soared
In pursuit of another board
Member of Detroit Bad Boys
Dirty team played with poise
Skinny physique never fat
To sum it up a strange cat

Bill Walton aka *Big Red*
Huge fan of the Grateful Dead
Played college ball at UCLA
Won 2 titles there, part of his DNA
Pro career cut short due to bad feet
Pain intense no longer could compete
At age 28 overcame a bad stutter
Eccentric personality, a loveable nutter
Became an announcer, told funny stories
Went on tangents, switching topics with ease
Died too early because of cancer
Must find a cure, need an answer

Paul Pierce, *The Truth*
Big ego like Babe Ruth
Played for the Boston Celtics
Serious game silenced skeptics
Stabbed 11 times in the face, neck & back
A scary incident, everything turned black
Recovered and became part of the "Big Three"

Great players who starred in a winning spree
Culminating in a hard-fought championship
A tremendous accomplishment, not a mere blip

Shaquille O' Neal aka *Diesel*
Highlight film drawn on an easel
Named himself *Big Aristotle*
Active imagination switched on full throttle
Starred in the terrible movie Kazaam
Panned by movie critics, a slam
Clashed on the Lakers with Kobe
Over who was better, fans can't agree
Heated debate turns contentious
No chance of ever reaching a consensus
Now stars with Chuck, Ernie, and Kenny
Hit show generates cash, a pretty penny

Here comes *Big Shot Bob*
Clutch performer, a heartthrob
An average player, stature elevated
By late-game heroics, celebrated
Given name Robert Horry
Another dagger, never sorry
7-time champion, a winner
Cool customer, not a beginner

Freddy Brown aka *Downtown*
A great shooter, hands down
Was an Iowa Hawkeye
The star player, the guy
His physique is a bit chubby

Some would say tubby
Unlimited shooting range
Smooth release will never change

Hakeem Olajuwon, *The Dream*
Fierce competitor, never out of steam
Signature move the dream shake
Off-balance defender forced to brake
Attended the University of Houston
A college that produced one
Of the basketball all-time greats
leaving opponents in dire straights

Meet Dwyane Wade aka *Flash*
Would win an NBA 100-yard dash
Attended college at Marquette
Schooled defenders causing them to fret
Played for Miami Heat, a super team
Many fans upset, dubbed it a scheme
To corner the market on top talent
Stay with original team more gallant
Married actress Gabrielle Union
High demand for a basketball reunion

Chris Anderson, *The Birdman*
A strange bird, needs a firm hand
Body covered in outrageous tattoos
Colorful figure often in the news
65% of body is covered in ink
Start a poll, what do you think?
A popular player, not much talent

Will never make a Hall of Fame ballot

Eric Floyd aka *Sleepy*
Smooth game other team is weepy
Not one of the dwarfs in Snow White
Trash talkers tried that line, led to a fight
In college, a Georgetown Hoya
Defeated teams feel paranoia
Once scored 29 points in a quarter
Must-see action - turn on a recorder
Glides up the court for another deuce
Opponents surrender and plead for a truce

Bill Cartwright, *Medical Bill*
Pedestrian player, rarely a thrill
Nickname a jab at his injury history
Who gave him the name is a mystery
Played college at University of San Francisco
Methodical game, not a hit at the disco
Claim to fame is played with Michael Jordan
Dollar Bill an inmate, MJ the prison warden

Rafer Alston, *Skip 2 My Lew*
Clever nickname, known by few
Standout streetball player from New York
Smooth, silky game ready to uncork
On an unsuspecting, overmatched defender
Left hapless & helpless, shaken in a blender
Played college ball for *Tark the Shark*
Before turning pro and leaving his mark

Gus Williams aka *The Wizard*
Sure to produce a blizzard
Of points in bunches
Take out your sack lunches
Marvel at the incredible performance
That will be talked about for months
A short guard with balding hair
Game so good it is unfair

Bernard King, *The Texas Massacre*
A superstar, a basketball ambassador
Back-to-back road 50-point games
Virtuoso performances announcer proclaims
Starred for NY Knicks, born in Brooklyn
Hometown hero, a native son
Unstoppable scorer with a quick release
Defenders mutter leave me in peace
Wore jersey number thirty
Consistent game always sturdy
Destroyed Pistons in playoffs despite dislocated fingers
A trip down memory lane, the vivid image lingers

Never Nervous Pervis
Witty nickname hard to dis
Starred at the University of Louisville
Frequently injured, buy more Advil
Drafted by Sacramento Kings
Big contract signed, buy lots of things
Eleven seasons as a pro
Quiet career time to go

Darryl Dawkins aka *Chocolate Thunder*
Some of these monikers make you wonder
Name given by Motown great Stevie Wonder
His original thought, or did he plunder
The unconventional nickname from another source
Maybe from an acquaintance or a talking horse
Sir Slam claimed to be an alien from planet Lovetron
An embellishment, a yarn, a humorous con
When he slammed over hapless defender punks
Assigned colorful names to his powerful dunks

Marvin Webster, *The Human Eraser*
Loved his mother, rushed to embrace her
Attended a small college Morgan State
Not a hoop phenom, blossomed late
Main skill was blocking shots
Happened often, lots and lots
Played for Supersonics and Knicks
Limited scorer, no offensive bag of tricks

Earvin Johnson aka *Magic*
Contracted HIV could have been tragic
Briefly retired before returning
Not ready to quit fire still burning
The greatest point guard of all time
A pleasure to watch him in his prime
Bullet passes, a blind no-look assist
Descriptive words fail. Call a linguist
Starred for showtime Lakers
Impossible to guard, any takers?

Vernon Maxwell, meet *Mad Max*
Volatile temper, showing some cracks
Won two titles as a Houston Rocket
Plug rage bulb into the nearest light socket
Used a free weight as a makeshift weapon
Not right in the head, the first impression
Deadly accurate, a clutch outside shooter
Stole opponent dreams, a basketball looter

The Owl with a Vowel
Can't top that, throw in the towel
An awesome nickname might be the best
Hard to prove, no deciding test
Given name Bill Mlkvy
Pronounce slowly. That is key
Played a single season in the pros
What happened next, nobody knows

Gilbert Arenas aka *Agent Zero*
An odd fellow, not a hero
Played for the Washington Wizards
A bad team all things considered
Brought guns into the locker room
Teammates scattered went vroom, vroom
Eccentric star with numerous superstitions
Actions performed over and over, repetitions

The Microwave
Cool nickname, a fave
Given name Vinnie Johnson
A true talent, the one

Won games by himself
Without any help from a Santa elf
A dangerous streak shooter
See his highlights on a computer

Chairman of the Boards
Appeals to the hordes
Given name Moses Malone
With a name like that never alone
Battled for position, a great rebounder
Relentless work ethic, a pounder
Skipped college & went straight to the pros
A wise and profitable decision history shows

Allen Iverson aka *The Answer*
Controversial figure, a team cancer?
High volume shooter
A scorer, a basketball tutor
Famous for practice rant
Said practice 22 times, a chant
Hero of the hip-hop generation
Popular figure for the youth nation

Damian Lillard here comes *Dame Time*
Sensational scorer can also deliver a dime
Attended little-known college, Weber State
Few envisioned him as an NBA great
Effortlessly makes shots from the logo
Waves at defenders time for you to go go
Clutch player sends teams home in postseason
Don't piss him off. Don't give him a reason

To eliminate your team, vacation time starts
Championship dreams end, rips out hearts
Points at an imaginary watch on his wrist
A trash-talking expert who can't resist

Wilt Chamberlain, *The Big Dipper*
Likely had sex with a stripper
Slept with over 20,000 women
True or false unsure if it is a given
Scored record 100 points in a game
Became a larger-than-life name
Even played for the Harlem Globetrotters
A basketball genius, graduating with honors

Saving best for last here comes *His Airness*
The perfect basketball player, a fact to prepare us
Best of all time, not up for debate
Larger than life, bigger than Kuwait
Acronym City, 5-time MVP & GOAT
Even goats agree if they could vote
Michael Jordan, *Air Jordan*
Perfect name is better than Gordon

Endorsements pour in
Where to begin
Be like Mike
What's not to like?
Starred in Space Jam
Stole the show, a ham
Scenes with Bugs Bunny
Looney Tunes cast funny

Off the expressway floor, over the river
Crazy HORSE shot attempt sends a shiver
Shooting game pits MJ vs Bird
Shot goes in, this is absurd
It's gotta be the shoes
Great ads, now old news
Over 100 million sneakers sold
Had a blueprint, the plan was bold

A quick sample of basketball players
Brief biographies, strip away layers
Of fluff and meaningless details
Colorful descriptions make great tales
Skill and talent amaze, a beautiful symphony
Words blend together into Hoop Harmony

Fifty stories in total
Some anecdotal
Thousands more are left untold
Narratives unwritten, some pure gold
Some players are mediocre; others are superstars
Easy to categorize talent, few debates needed in bars

Next time you see a kid make a hoop
Think about a nickname, deliver a scoop
Add flavor to a simple basketball game
Consider name options, and I'll do the same

PART 7
TICK TOCK BEEP BEEP BOOM

PANDEMIC BLUES

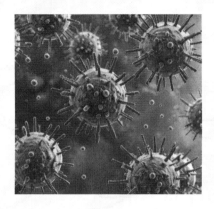

Can anyone inspire us?
Along came a virus
It started slow and picked up steam
Some think it's all a scheme
Numbers blurred as the pandemic purred
Disregarding orders, spreading across borders
Impacts individuals and families alike
Can't tell COVID to take a hike

Trapped in our four walls, narrow halls
Lucky ones can stare out the glass
At the overgrown grass
Social distancing leaves one bristling
Wash hands, wash hands, six feet, six feet
Rinse, repeat, forget to eat
Doesn't matter there's no food
Always in a terrible mood

Time to put on a mask
Just another repetitive task
Trudge to the food bank
Expression completely blank
No money for rent
Next stop is a tent

Remote monotonous learning
Leaves students and parents yearning
Bring back old-fashioned school
Accelerate the knowledge fuel
Youth are a total mess
Trying to survive with less
Should be laughing and hanging with friends
Hope beyond hope the damage mends

Look at the crooked politicians
To them we are a bunch of minions
Info always changing, words rearranging
Vaccination confusion is not an illusion
People are dying, another child crying
They don't care

Life ain't fair

Send an urgent fax
Kids need a Vax
Will play a Sax
To celebrate
And recalibrate
And rid the hate?
Call it fate

People be trippin'
Too much alcohol sippin'
Virus talk makes one crazy
Deep thinking becomes hazy
Must not think a bad thought
Or living will be for naught
Best thing to do is chill
Before despair starts to spill
Which allows hatred to grow
And become a river overflow

COVID crisis a tsunami
Has you running to mommy
But mama not around
Buried deep in the ground
Another impersonal pandemic stat
Snap, snap - poof she gone like that
More than a number, should have a shrine
Just want to drop out and resign
From this world gone mad
Did I mention never had a dad?

No faith in God or humanity
My sad eyes just see a calamity
Human life doesn't matter
People die, family members scatter
Preacher sermon titled "God's will"
Burn that nonsense on the grill
Oh God, why don't you intervene?
Probably laughing sight-unseen
Do you exist at all?
No response to my call

Another day, another month, another year gone
Another day, another month, another year wasted

When will it end?
When will it end?
It MUST end.

TO A SMILE

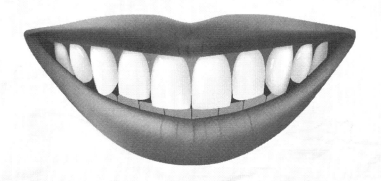

Walking through a school hallway looking left and right.

Pearly white teeth being flashed from every side.

Fast forward to now only seeing you through a computer screen.

Wishing I could reach through and finally see you.

Oh, how I miss your beaming, lighting up the room.

Cloth fabric only showing eyes, like you are wearing a disguise.

It seems as if a cloud of darkness has swept through the room making you vanish.

The mask masking emotions. Is that laughter or pain?

If only I could go back to the time when just seeing you could express a thousand words.

I declare I hold you dear.

HEADED FOR A MELTDOWN

Sad, sad summer of '23
Forest fires are rampant on a spree
Impacting much of the United States
Destroying homes including gates
Many fires originate in Canada
Impossible to contain, hard to manage a
Timber dry condition that destroys acre after acre
Wish destruction could stop by tripping a breaker

Some blazes are accidental, and many are intentional
No matter the cause, nothing is conventional
A lightning strike, a human-made spark

Result is the same - no kids playing in the park
Competing culprits are people and weather
Time to get our act together

Air pollution is unhealthy
Harmful particles acting stealthy
Monitor the air quality index
Dangerous levels make for bad sex
No need to sugarcoat or rephrase
People wander about in a daze
Contributing to a general malaise
Because of an out-of-control blaze
Proud forests are made to suffer
Life's a bitch and is getting tougher
Habitats and ecosystems are destroyed
One fire started by a man named Floyd

Smoke and heat, heat and smoke
Sick of this jingle need a joke
But what is happening is not funny
Journey outside leaves nose runny
Hard to breathe, start to gasp
Throat constricted by an Egyptian asp
Might suffer a heat stroke
Worst case some will croak

Reconsider and retreat back inside
Movement slow, hard to glide
Trapped inside walls and doors
Stare ahead at outdated drawers
Should be frolicking, enjoying nature

Too hot inside; visualize a glacier
No AC, not even a fan
Imagine a forest fire ban

Need to bring back Smokey the Bear
Help make the population aware
That only you can prevent a forest fire
To some message would be preaching to the choir
For others, this might be a new announcement
A modern call, a fresh pronouncement
An effective public service campaign
Becoming addictive like cocaine
Causing people to be more careful
One can hope and be prayerful
That the message will resonate
Must try something can't leave it to fate

Hundreds of fires over the summer
Overall quality of life is a bummer
What is the reason for this dry season?
Do some research, find the reason
On one side are the environmentalists
Preaching like religious fundamentalists
On the other side climate change deniers
Trying to sway opinion and find new buyers
Unsure which viewpoint is right
Heated discussion sure to incite
Two opposing factions at odds
Might be decided by the nature gods

Raging inferno visits picturesque Maui

Terrible destruction stops by for a howdy
The historic town of Lahaina destroyed
Community devastated, leaving a void
An economic and cultural hub
Reduced to a misery and sorrow club
Maui wildfires create publicity
Media buzz and electricity
Human toll overwhelming
Punctuated by panicky yelling
Legs and arms frantically in motion
Attempt to flee jump into the ocean

Scene on the ground is surreal
Not a joke the real deal
Death by drowning or burning
Hell of a choice, stomach-churning
Hundreds of poor souls die
Many of them completely fry
Dead bodies found beyond recognition
Wildfires a grim war of attrition

Homes and shops are gone forever
Can't stop an inferno too clever
Everywhere one looks, nothing but ruins
The only hope is to build new ones
Will take financial contributions
A small part of long-term solutions

Tone-deaf tourists complain
Vacation ruined a constant refrain
What are you saying?

You should be praying
For the poor islanders who lost everything
Ring the bell - ding, ding, ding
Get over yourself and your beach rental condo
There are dead people ID'd as Jane Doe
Your dream vacation is irrelevant
Be kind and caring, act intelligent

Blame game begins soon
Many at-fault nobody is immune
From poor response accusations
Anger builds heart palpitations
Siren alarm system not activated
Residents pissed aggravated
Why did alarms remain silent?
Hard not to become violent
Emotional feelings of rage
Can't just turn the page
Power company facing scrutiny
Residents contemplate mutiny
Emergency management chief resigns
A scapegoat sacrifice in the headlines
Other theories gain traction
Each with a call to action
Politician lip service pledges rotten
Empty promises are soon forgotten

Predatory vultures circle overhead
Easy money make some bread
Greedy opportunists initiate land grabs
Real estate hucksters keep tabs

Take advantage of people with trauma
Witness a real-life sickening drama
Voices whisper sell me your land
Sign here complementary pen in hand
Human greed has no limits
Contract signed property gone in minutes

Will this dreadful summer be repeated?
Debate continues to grow heated
The planet is dying
Time to start trying
To fix this considerable mess
Need to make progress
Strive for success
Reduce the distress
Of humans, animals, and nature
Before we build too deep a crater
That is impossible to fix
And leads to more conflicts

No matter what side of political spectrum
Conservative or liberal select from
More and more people agree
Reach a consensus, a guarantee
Maui wildfires are an example
Of increasing destruction, a sample
Planet Earth is in bad shape
Easy to see roll the tape

What is going on?
Call to action come on

Only reasonable reaction
Take the plunge spring into action
Before it is too late
Decide now I'll wait
Quit waffling and jump in
Facing long odds, we must win

Human survival is at stake
Better not make a mistake
As the quality of life melts down
The Doomsday Clock counts down
Time is running out
Now or never use your clout
Tick Tock Tick Tock
Figure it out we are on the clock

PART 8
FAMILY AFFAIR

HARMONY WITHIN THE FAMILY

My family is concise and compact. Mom and Dad. The two people I can rely on the most. Our tiny family is made up of different voices. Some are quiet. Some are loud. Some are not even voices at all.

My voice is uncomfortable. A blessing and a curse. In the mornings, it cracks like pressing the wrong key on a piano. Other times, it is smooth, like the melody of a cello. A freshly polished hardwood table. My throat will lock itself up like a prison cell. It doesn't listen to my brain or its feelings. My voice is a hit or a miss. I hope the next time I speak, the words will soothe like falling rain rather than shock like a morning alarm clock wake-up.

My father has a booming voice that could make the steep hills of San Francisco rumble in fear. He could be Zeus up on Mount Olympus with a dashing yellow lightning bolt and I wouldn't even bat an eye. My father's voice is gruff, Brad Pitt mixed with Dumbledore, a rattling clang of dishes placed randomly in the dishwater. Under the hardness of the snowball is the softness of fresh snow. He is the strong one in the family. I've never seen him shed a tear. My father lifts us with toughness and love.

My mother is a people pleaser. I feel bad for her dentists because they will never be able to keep her mouth closed while working on a filling. She speaks with fluidity. Her words make crashing waves turn into still water. An airy and gentle voice with a hint of an accent. Although she speaks fluent English, I can still hear her Romanian tones. Spice mixed into steaming chili. An aspiring artist whose art never made it out of the studio. Arguing with her feels like a sack of potatoes being slammed against your spine. Sometimes, I think she debates with me just for the sake of proving that I was wrong. Despite her talent for embarrassing me, my mother is the most caring and thoughtful person I know.

My dog is the one person who will never talk back to me. I used to get lonely and try to convince him and myself that his speaking English would be our ticket to fame, but it never worked out. A midsized dog trying to be a Doberman, his barks are secure and tough. An intimidation factor against all things evil - including squirrels. The woof after the battle. My dog is a protector, always putting our family first.

The rest of my family lives in Europe, scattered sifting grains of sand forming a beach. I do not get to hear their voices often. Instead of family reunions, we have Skype calls to avoid phone bill charges. We rarely use video; the words run together like an old-fashioned fireside radio chat. In my life, their voices are on low volume. Some of us have voices that sound like the morning song of a dove. Some of us have voices that sound like the squawk of a crow rummaging for garbage scraps. Regardless, even when living on different continents, I imagine our voices combining and creating harmony. We are family.

HARPER'S HALLOWEEN

Harper looked out the window dreamily. She was thinking of happier days when Daddy and Mommy loved
each other and the three of them were a family. Her
parents had been divorced for over two years, and shortly
after the divorce, her mother remarried and moved with
Harper to Hoquiam. Harper's natural father, Michael, still
lived in Aberdeen, a dying blue-collar community on life
support whose best and brightest residents fled as soon as
possible, never to return. Aberdeen and the rest of Grays
Harbor once had a thriving timber and fishing industry,
now replaced by the cash is king Methamphetamine industry. A state highway dissected the sister cities of Aberdeen

and Hoquiam, and local comics liked to say that all of the late-night speeders were on speed.

Aberdeen was known as the "Birthplace of Grunge," and many doctoral theses had been written at Evergreen State College in Olympia, analyzing the life of Kurt Cobain in comparison to the town's history. Nirvana's rise to fame mirrored the town's past prosperity from the timber industry, while Cobain's tragic death represented Aberdeen's subsequent decline. Some academics even argued that Cobain's DIY approach to his music career was similar to local amateur chemists in meth labs, with both producing remarkable results in their respective industries.

Michael, who was picking up ten-year-old Harper in Hoquiam for the Halloween weekend, was already over an hour late. Her mother's angry voice pierced Harper's calm, soothing, trancelike state, "Where's your father? It's just like him to be late!" Harper didn't answer her mother but turned away from the window. Why are things so confusing? she thought. She loved her father, but her mom said mean things about him. Her mom said Michael drank too much and was an irresponsible, good-for-nothing bum. Harper didn't like it when mommy said mean things about daddy, but what could she do? She was small, and mommy was big.

Ten minutes later, Michael arrived in his beat-up used black Ford and entered the living room. While her parents argued, Harper eagerly eyed the bag in Daddy's hand, which she knew had her surprise Halloween costume. All week, she had thought about going trick-or-treating door to door dressed up as either a princess or a witch. Michael handed her the bag and said, "Here you go, honey. I hope you like it." She raced up the stairs, floating up the individual steps without touching them like a most happy, friendly Hallow-een ghost. In the privacy of her bedroom, she slowly opened the box, trying to extend the anticipation and joy like an early Christmas gift-opening celebration. She blinked. She blinked again. Harper saw a plastic tiger mask and an orange and black tiger body. She felt tears forming in her empty blue eyes. Why did Daddy buy me this? she thought angrily. A tiger costume is for a boy. Tony the Tiger in that commercial is a boy tiger. I want to be a princess or a witch.

Harper, a most unhappy tiger, climbed into the passenger seat next to her father and silently brooded. The distance between the two seemed like an ocean rather than a few feet. Finally, Michael broke the stifling silence.

"I'm sorry about being late, honey. It wasn't my fault, and traffic was really bad."

A child's piercing accusation followed a brief silence.

"Whose fault was it then, Daddy? You're the adult, and I'm a kid."

"It's no one's fault. Anyway, I'm sorry, but we're going to have fun. Let's stop and get something to eat."

Michael pulled into the nearest Golden Arches and ordered a Big Mac, a strawberry shake, fries, and an apple pie for Harper.

"I'm not supposed to eat fast food," Harper announced. "Mommy says it's bad for you."

"Forget your mother. Damn, kids are supposed to love hamburgers. For Christ's sake, eating a Big Mac is part of being a kid."

"Mommy says you swear too much and says it's a bad influence on me."

"Well, your mother's not here now, so let's try to have fun. Please, princess. What other bad things does your mom say about me?"

"Mommy doesn't talk about you anymore," Harper lied.

The rest of the drive into Aberdeen was uncomfortable, the parent and child not recognizing the other's existence. It was getting dark and cold outside, and Harper passed the time looking out the window once again, dreaming of going trick-or-treating as a princess. She tried to forget that she was wearing a dumb boy's tiger costume. Once, Harper saw some kids trick-or-treating and asked Michael if they could stop the car and knock on a few doors. Her dad said something about them being bad kids, but Harper stopped listening when the answer was no and went back to ignoring him. She began to fixate on her ugly tiger costume, which now had a broken tail that drooped sadly, and the more she focused on it, the angrier and madder she got.

Harper and her dad finally arrived at the Aberdeen town hall, the site of the traditional local Halloween party. She entered the building and looked at the other kids, who were happily milling about in the center of the large room. Harper saw vampires, werewolves, witches, pirates, ghosts, and angels - not a single tiger. She was convinced that her costume was the worst of them all, and she felt tears form hidden by her sticky, uncomfortable mask.

Harper jumped when she heard the scream, "It's time for the costume judging contest!" She recoiled at the harsh sound of the familiar voice coming from Bill Bailey's mouth. Harper remembered Bailey as Daddy's boss, and he now bellowed, "Step right up, kids! Don't be shy. Form a circle in the center of the room."

Harper took a tentative step forward, then hesitated as if her blue Adidas Superstar sneakers were glued to the floor.

Michael said, "Go ahead, honey. You remember some of these kids. Go have fun."

Harper didn't budge. She felt her father gently nudging her, but she remained frozen in place. Bailey was motioning for her to step forward, but Harper was no longer an angry, confused kid. She was a caged baby tiger at the zoo, and everyone in the hall was staring. The grown-ups and kids had stopped talking and were pointing at the defenseless tiger cub. Bailey continued to motion for Harper, but the fingers on his hands were growing in size and reaching toward her neck as if he were an evil zookeeper who wanted to strangle the helpless baby animal.

Confused, Harper turned around, looking for Daddy. Michael was not in the hall, having gone outside in the parking lot to chat with friends.

Frantically, Harper searched the room for her father. Not seeing him, she circled the room in a daze, finally stopping next to a phone on a corner desk. Harper called her mom and cried that she wanted to go home. Her mom said she would leave the house in Hoquiam immediately and pick her up. The fragile girl exhaled and slumped against a nearby wall, trying unsuccessfully to rip off her entire tiger boy costume, an action that exposed part of her expensive ski sweater underneath. She kept the hated plastic mask on to hide the torrential tears streaming down the side of her face.

An undetermined amount of time passed, and Michael returned with the smell of alcohol on his breath. Remembering that smell, Harper stepped away from her father and timidly told him about the phone call to Mom. Michael angrily told her she was spoiled and could wait for her mom by herself outside in the cold. Relieved, the troubled girl said that would be fine.

The sad youngster stood in solitude near the hall entrance, shivering as the temperature quickly dropped, a bitter wind accentuating the piercing chill. Harper stared at the darkness and the oversized full moon, a warm milky glow in the sky. She was thinking of happier days when Daddy and Mommy loved each other, and the three were family. She was never a ferocious tiger, not even on Halloween. She was a timid little girl who wanted to be loved and protected.

GERVIN ICE

We were on our way to pick up our dog, Gervin, the newest addition to our family. As we drove over the Deception Pass Bridge, I knew we were getting closer to Oak Harbor, where the breeder was located. The Brittany breeder had assured us that all of their puppies had passed the test and reacted well to gunshots, which was important for hunting purposes. He also emphasized that they only ate nutritious puppy food and that table scraps and human food were strictly forbidden. After picking up Gervin and driving for a few miles, she got car sick and threw up red beets all over my wife Rachel in the back seat of our Nissan Maxima. And so began our introduction to Gervin.

We named Gervin after a legendary basketball player, George "the Iceman" Gervin, known for his signature "finger roll" move. On her official American Kennel Club pedigree certificate, her full name is "Gervin Ice Speeding Bullet." Her parents were named "Waldons Straight Shooten Bullet" and "Brew's Jackie Joy Maya." Her grandparents had equally colorful names like "Sir Ziggy of Kent," "Foxhill's Sara Andrea," and my personal favorites, "Maya the Moondog" and "Jumpin Jax Ah Nuts."

During our daily strolls or trips to the dog park, curious strangers often asked what my dog's name was. When I replied with "Gervin," I was met with puzzled expressions and confused reactions. Some thought I had said Kevin, while others questioned why a female dog would have a male human name. One older family friend even suggested we change her name to Gervina. But Gervin was proud of her unique name and waited patiently for the perfect moment to get her revenge. And that opportunity came at a festive holiday party, where she effortlessly jumped over the same family friend multiple times like an Olympic long jumper. The poor 85-year-old woman remained oblivious to this display of athleticism, much to the amusement of everyone else in the room, including Gervin herself. She always knew how to put on a show for an audience.

When our daughter Melissa was born, Gervin took on the role of a fiercely protective mother. She delicately sniffed the newborn during their first meeting at home after we had returned from the hospital. From that day on, Gervin was always by the baby's side, keeping a close eye on her as she rested or slept in her crib. Even when we went for walks, Gervin refused to leave the stroller's side and would dig her nails into the ground if we tried to take her away from the baby. It was clear that Gervin was determined to protect our daughter at all costs; she truly was the great protector.

Melissa and Gervin were inseparable best friends. They had a special understanding: Melissa would purposely drop crumbs off the table for the dog to lick up, causing them both to erupt in fits of giggles. Missy caught on quickly, realizing it was a win-win situation for her and her furry companion, as it meant she could avoid eating icky vegetables altogether. On the few occasions when the dog was in her crate, Melissa would crawl over and gently touch one of its paws with her tiny fingers, a sign of their special bond and solidarity.

Just two weeks before Missy was born, my wife and I had a terrifying experience that we would never forget. It was a quiet Sunday evening, and we were both cozied up on the couch, watching an old movie on TV. In her third trimester, Rachel had developed a sudden craving for soup and had gotten up to make herself a bowl in the kitchen.

I remember the moment distinctly as if it were a scene from a horror film. Suddenly, there was a blood-curdling shriek coming from the kitchen, piercing through the peacefulness of the evening. Instinctively, I jumped up from the couch and ran to the kitchen, where I found Rachel leaning against the counter, her hand clutched tightly to her chest.

At first, I couldn't see what was wrong, but then I saw the blood. It was everywhere, pooling on the countertop and dripping onto the floor, with a few streams trickling down the walls. My heart nearly stopped as I realized what had happened. Rachel had cut her thumb badly with the can opener while opening a can of soup. Gervin sprang into action and began licking up the blood as we rushed to the emergency room. She diligently set about her task, her tongue darting out like a precision instrument to cleanse every last drop of blood from the scene. Her eyes sparkled with an unwavering loyalty, embodying the essence of a protector who would stop at nothing to keep her loved ones safe.

Hours later, as we stepped back into our house after returning from the hospital, there was no sign of any blood. Our dog Gervin panted happily and wagged her tail, seemingly proud of herself for a job well done. She had eagerly cleaned up all traces of evidence, mimicking the tactics she'd seen on crime shows with us. As always, she was our devoted protector.

Gervin lived a vibrant and fulfilling life, often taking leisurely strolls around Green Lake. Her go-to spot for swimming was always the same, and we would sometimes walk her on the outer path where she couldn't see it. But Gervin was clever and could sense when we were near "her spot," dragging us there for a refreshing doggy dip. She also loved visiting the dog park, where she would play and get covered

in mud in the off-limits area. Occasionally, she'd reunite with her friend Johnny, a fashionable Brittany sporting a red bandana and shock collar to keep him from escaping the park perimeter like Houdini.

When Gervin turned eleven, we decided to add another Brittany to our family, a puppy named Barkley. As parents, we thought it would help lessen the pain for Melissa when Gervin eventually passed away. However, we didn't consider consulting Gervin beforehand. She was not pleased with the new addition to our family. "Who is this crazy little creature that keeps interrupting my sleep? I can't get any rest." Of course, the energetic puppy meant no harm and just wanted to play. Eventually, the two Brittanys reached a truce and became fast friends as they spent more time together. As Gervin grew older, Barkley was always by her side, and they would snuggle on the couch together. Gervin taught Barkley all her tricks; sometimes, the apprentice surpassed his master's skills. While Gervin would nibble on a corner of a bagel, Barkley perfected the quick strike half-sandwich gulp maneuver.

Gervin was known to cause trouble occasionally, and my wife would jokingly threaten to send her back to her original home using the Oak Harbor Freight Lines truck, which we frequently spotted driving on the nearby highway. Gervin knew this was not going to happen. Rachel loved Gervin.

Gervin's fourteenth birthday had come and gone, leaving behind a noticeable decrease in her energy levels. No longer able to bound down the stairs to play or relieve herself outside, we now had to carry her up and down the stairs. Her appetite had also diminished. One day, she lay still on the floor and looked at me with tired eyes. I gently picked her up and cradled her in my arms as we sat on the couch in

the living room. We stayed like that for an hour, a close-knit family finding comfort in each other's presence. Gervin was completely at ease and peaceful. It would be the last time I held her like that.

During my daughter's basketball practice that evening, my phone began to ring. I saw it was Rachel calling, and when I answered, she was crying uncontrollably. "Gervin is gone," she choked out between sobs. It turns out that during an emergency visit to the vet, they had discovered an inoperable tumor in our dog. My wife had to say her final goodbyes before Gervin was put down. I couldn't hold back my own tears as we ended the call. I found myself seeking solace in the hallway outside of the gym at the community college where my daughter practiced, letting out all the grief and memories that rushed over me at the loss of our beloved pet. My wife and daughter claim they have never seen me cry, but on this day, it was simply impossible to contain the flood of emotions and hold back the waterfall of tears.

When Melissa returned home, Rachel and I sat her down and delicately told her the news. She immediately sprinted to her room, where she cried for hours on end. Not just a few tears, but an entire storm's worth of raindrops, creating an ocean of sorrow. Her breathing was ragged and uneven, each inhale sounding like a gasping wheeze and each exhale a shaky sigh. She made small whimpering noises, unable to control the shock and sadness ravaging her body. We held her tight and tried to soothe her, but she couldn't be comforted. That night, our daughter had trouble falling asleep and once again broke down into heavy sobs that never seemed to cease.

"Why? Why? I miss Gervin."

I hugged her and tried to comfort her.

"Gervin is in a better place watching you from dog heaven and bragging to all her dog buddies about what a great kid you are. She is your guardian angel and protector just like she was here."

I fought to keep my composure, trying to stay calm for my daughter. That night, I woke up several times and retreated downstairs to be alone. Tears poured down my face as I wept uncontrollably. My family was wrong; I do cry...a lot.

My eleven-year-old daughter the next day wrote a eulogy and a letter without any prompting:

"Don't cry because it's over. Smile because it happened."
In loving memory of Gervin Ice Murphy,
2/21/2020
14 great years but now you are in a better place.
Heaven is a place on Earth for you.

Dear Gervin,

Currently there is something called the coronavirus going around. I miss you <u>so</u> much but I know that you are here with me. I pray for you each night so that you can get bananas and carrots! Here are some memories for the day:

- Belly rubs and "You're not so tough"
- How I accidentally lost you once
- One time mom wasn't watching you and there was a hole in the fence. We thought we lost you forever but instead we found you peeing in the front yard. You're so smart!
- Giving you my veggies. We need to find a way to transport my vegetables up to you on doggy heaven (Barkley's no help).
- Doggie ice cream, salmon, sardines, carrots, kale, bananas

I love you to the moon and back!

Best Buddies Forever,
Melissa

COOL CAT

Four-year-old Danny Newton woke up crying and shaking. "I miss Lit. I miss my buddy."

The boy had been inconsolable since his beloved black cat left for his new forever home.

A few weeks ago, Mr. Wilson, the neighbor next door, knocked on the door and told the Newton family that he and his wife had just bought a new house in a neighborhood eight miles south of their current one.

Mr. Wilson knew Danny was close to Lit and tried to break the news gently.

"Danny, you are welcome to visit Lit anytime. You will always be friends."

The boy tried to be a big boy and fight back the tears. He was mostly successful except for an occasional rogue drip streaming down his cheek.

Lit had two families, the Newtons and the Wilsons. The black cat and the young boy were inseparable, the feline following the child like a loyal dog rather than an indifferent cat. Lit loved suntanning on the Newton porch windowsill waiting to be let into the house by Danny. The cat would follow the boy on his many backyard adventures, peering over his shoulder as he lifted a brick underneath the porch to see the insects underneath. Lit loved to sit on the boy's lap purring contentedly, the soothing sound calming Danny.

The boy, an autistic only child, was often withdrawn and lonely. The cat had a therapeutic effect on the youngster, who had problems making friends and interacting with other kids his own age. Lit was his best friend, his kitty. Danny would often talk to Lit and was sure the cat understood.

Danny's parents were certain that the pain he experienced when the cat left would subside within a few days. Instead, the hurt intensified, the child becoming even more withdrawn and staring aimlessly straight ahead. His parents were becoming concerned. Should they send him to a therapist? Does the boy need professional help?

Danny woke up early Saturday morning after another night of little sleep. He started walking to the front door to get the newspaper for his dad. He paused, rubbing his eyes. It couldn't be. His kitty was on the porch windowsill, staring at him. Lit was back! Danny hugged the cat and placed her on his lap. The black cat purred, and the two friends reunited.

Later that night, Mr. Wilson stopped by the house to pick up Lit and take her back to his new house. He thanked Danny for taking such good care of the cat during the day and again extended an open invitation for the boy to visit

Lit any time. Danny watched his friend drive down the hill in the Wilson station wagon.

Danny felt the same feeling as the first time his buddy had left for good. He was sullen and in a zombie-like state with lifeless eyes. Two days later, he ran to the door after waking up. He knew somebody special was waiting for him. How did he know? It is a mystery, but what is clear is that a close bond between a child and a special pet is a mystical experience. It was Lit! His kitty had returned.

The cat looked a little thinner and had a scratch on his back paw, caked with dried blood. The tabby contentedly sat on the boy's lap, purring and snuggling, two old friends catching up.

Danny strained to hear the adult conversation in the kitchen. He heard the sooth-ing, distinctive voice of his mom and dad alternating:

"How did Lit make it back."

"How did the cat know the direction? How did it cross either of the long bridges and avoid all the car traffic without getting run over?"

"Equally amazing how did it know the direction back here without getting lost? It is eight miles."

"How did it not get eaten by coyotes or attacked by a dog?"

"So much for the black cat bad luck superstition. You can rename her Lucky Lit for surviving that journey twice."

"Who names their cat Lit? What kind of name is that?"

Danny remained silent but knew the answer to all the questions. Lit was his cat. Lit sensed his sadness and saw how unhappy the boy was. The bond between him and his cat was stronger than anything. They are family, and family must always be together.

Danny picked up Lit and put her on his lap. The tabby closed her eyes and purred loudly, a steady hum of contentment filling the room.

The Wilsons and Newtons decided that Lit would stay in the old neighborhood with the Newton family. Lit was a remarkable, determined cat and the tabby had made the decision for them by completing two remarkable journeys, using up six of her nine cat lives in the process.

The cat, aptly named Lit, turned towards the boy and beamed, "lighting" up the room. The child always knew how the pet got her name, but they shared a special connection that kept it just between them. Danny returned a knowing smile, like the Cheshire cat, as he looked at his best friend.

A FINAL DANCE

(Nancy is crying in her room next to a ripped-up home-coming proposal sign. Suddenly, her favorite lamp starts to flicker.)

NANCY: Hello? Who's there?!

JEREMIAH: I am. It's...complicated. Please don't be afraid.

NANCY: I could never be afraid of you - even as a ghost.

JEREMIAH: Doesn't my hair look great translucent?

NANCY: For sure. I've missed this. I've missed us.

JEREMIAH: Me too. (Pause.) But that's why I'm here. You need to move on with your life. I think rejecting Henry's homecoming proposal was a mistake that I don't want you to regret.

NANCY: But how can I move on when all I think about is you?

(Nancy and Jeremiah are silent for a few moments. Jeremiah is lost in thought.)

JEREMIAH: Are you hiding something?

NANCY: No, no. I'm fine. Don't worry about me.

JEREMIAH: Nance, I can tell when you lie. Your bottom lip starts to tremble slightly.

NANCY: Oh Jer, you know me so well. I don't even have to speak, and you can read my mind. It is downright spooky, which makes sense now that you are a ghost.

JEREMIAH: Oh, yeah? Your favorite color is purple, you hate ketchup and love mustard, and you are trying to convince your dad to get you a corgi. Is there anything else I am forgetting?

NANCY: Actually, I'm starting to lean more towards golden retrievers. They run faster.

JEREMIAH: Welp, I was close enough.

NANCY: Not really, but I'm still flattered you remembered.

JEREMIAH: As much as I love talking about silly things with you, we need to get serious. I don't know how much time I have left.

NANCY: Alright. I can explain why I was crying. Remember what happened last year? It was five days before the winter ball. You. Me. Our first dance. We were both so excited.

JEREMIAH: Of course, I remember.

NANCY: You were driving to the store to pick up your tux when...when...well, you know. The accident happened. I guess I rejected Henry because I've been longing for the dance we would have had together. Our special first.

JEREMIAH: (Attempting to lighten the mood.) Maybe the acne medication I applied before getting in the car was special vanishing cream makeup. At the winter ball you had no BODY to dance with. Nance, if I'm being honest, the first day I saw you talking to Henry, I think I died a second time. Now I've learned to accept that you deserve to be loved and cared for by someone else even if it hurts my ghostly heart. You shouldn't feel tied down to me.

NANCY: I will never feel tied down by you. If anything, you help me break free from my shell and be myself.

JEREMIAH: (Thinks for a few seconds.) Wait a minute! I think I know how to give us both closure. (He clears his throat and announces in a regal voice.) Madame Nancy Hill Winger, will you have this first and last dance with me? (He offers one of his flickering hands to Nancy.)

NANCY: (Chuckles) Why, of course, Sir Jeremiah of Locke-field. I would be honored to.

(She interlocks her hands with Jeremiah's. The couple start to slowly dance with each other.)

NANCY: How can I feel you right now? Aren't you supposed to be a ghost?

JEREMIAH: I have no idea.

NANCY: I guess this dance was fate.

(Nancy and Jeremiah keep dancing together, hoping the moment will never end.)

JEREMIAH: Henry's a good guy.

NANCY: Yes, he is.

JEREMIAH: I'm sorry for being so judgmental.

NANCY: It's alright...I love you.

JEREMIAH: I love you too.

NANCY: Even in the afterlife...

JEREMIAH: You will always be the one.

(In comes a large gust of wind and Jeremiah disappears. Nancy is left standing happily by herself in the ballroom.)

PART 9
FUNNY BUSINESS

CORPORATE CUBICLE CLONES

The cubicles formed a labyrinth, each one indistinguishable from the next in the drab uniformity of the workspace. The men, all dressed in the same white shirts and ties, were required to be clean-shaven, their faces sculpted into conformity.

Art Patton, the office manager, was a tall, broad-shouldered man with conservative, short-cropped hair and a military bearing. He took great pride in his last name, often joking that he was directly related to the famous American World War II general, George Patton. Whether this was true or not, Art liked to imagine himself as a distant, yet worthy, descendant of the renowned leader.

As a tribute to his possible ancestor, Art had watched the movie "Patton" countless times. He could recite many of the famous lines, such as "No bastard ever won a war by dying for his country. He won it by making the other poor dumb bastard die for his country." And "I don't want to get any messages saying, 'I am holding my position.' We are not holding a goddamned thing. Let the Germans do that."

Art often channeled General Patton's fearless and un-yielding spirit in his daily life. He ran the office with strict discipline and unwavering leadership, earning both respect and fear from his employees. His office was always spotless, his desk organized, and his schedule meticulously planned out. No detail escaped the manager's keen eye, and he prided himself on running a tight ship.

Patton was known as the hair police chief behind his back. He regularly patrolled the office floors, ever vigilant for any sign of deviation from the prescribed corporate dress code. If a man's hair was deemed too long, he would be tapped on the shoulder and given a deadline to rectify the situation. Failure to comply would result in immediate termination.

The strict regulations within the office created an atmosphere of tension and unease, as the employees constantly monitored their appearance and behavior. The slightest misstep could lead not only to a reprimand but also to losing one's livelihood. As a result, the men moved with a sense of urgency, their faces etched with worry and fear.

It was a far cry from the creativity and freedom many had imagined when they first walked through the doors with their freshly pressed resumes and polished shoes. But in this cutthroat corporate world, conformity was king, and individuality was a threat to be stamped out. The company's success relied on the employees being interchangeable cogs in a machine, all working towards the same goal with no room for personal expression.

As the day wore on, the men sat at their desks, staring at their computer screens and filling out spreadsheets with robotic precision. Any hint of personality was suppressed, and the only sounds were the clicking of keyboards and the hum of the fluorescent lights above. The monotony was only broken by the occasional phone call or meeting,

Offices like this were a dime a dozen, each filled with disillusioned employees who had traded their dreams for a steady paycheck.

But amidst the sea of dreary cubicles and stifled personalities, some dared to dream of something more.

Owen Anderson sat at his desk, trying to ignore the stares and whispers that followed him. He had spent years suppressing his individuality to fit in and climb the corporate ladder, but it had all been for nothing. As he typed away at his computer, pretending to be engrossed in his work, Owen felt a sense of rebellion building inside him. He had always been a rebel at heart, and now he was finally ready to let it show.

He slowly removed the bald cap from his head, revealing long locks of thick brown hair. A few gasps and shocked murmurs could be heard around him as he ran his fingers through it, relishing the feeling of freedom.

The hair police chief noticed immediately and made a beeline toward Anderson's cubicle. As he approached, Owen stood up with a determined expression on his face.

"Mr. Anderson," Patton said sternly. "I see you've decided to disregard our strict grooming policies."

Owen held his ground and looked the manager straight in the eye. "Yes sir," he replied defiantly.

Anderson felt a sense of unease wash over him as the old school manager stood behind his chair, casting a shadow over his desk. The man's eyes were hard and cold, his perfect short hair a stark contrast to Owen's unruly curls extending past his shoulders. His hand reached out tentatively toward Anderson's hair, the air heavy with unspoken tension. Yet before his fingers could touch it, Owen's swift reaction pushed the hand away. The pounding of his heart reverberated in his chest, but he remained resolute, refusing to back down.

"I like my hair the way it is," he declared, his voice surprisingly steady despite the nerves fluttering in his stomach. Patton raised an eyebrow, clearly taken aback by his boldness. The other workers held their breath, waiting to see what would happen next.

After a moment of tense silence, the manager let out a chuckle. "I like your spirit, Owen," he said with a smirk. "But rules are rules here. You'll have to follow protocol like everyone else." Anderson's heart sank as he realized he had no choice but to comply if he wanted to keep his job. However, as Patton turned to leave, Owen had an idea. With a mischievous glint in his eye, he reached into his drawer and pulled out a pair of scissors. Before anyone could stop him, he gathered up his long locks and defiantly snipped them off, leaving behind a rebellious mess of jagged edges that framed his determined expression. The manager turned back in shock as the discarded hair floated to the ground like a soft, silent rebellion.

"You wanted me to cut it, didn't you?" Owen asked with a sly smile, holding up the scissors as if they were a victorious weapon. The other workers gasped in surprise, some stifling laughter behind their hands at the audacity of his actions.

The hair police chief's stern facade cracked into an unexpected grin. He let out a hearty laugh, the sound echoing through the office's sterile atmosphere. "Well played, Anderson," he admitted, impressed by his creativity and nerve. "You certainly know how to make a statement."

When he got home, Owen locked himself in his bathroom and began dying his hair a bright shade of blue. He had always been drawn to bold colors, and this was just another way to express himself.

As the dye set in, Anderson wondered what would happen if he took things even further. What if he dyed his hair different colors? Or shaved parts of it off? The possibilities were endless and exhilarating.

The next morning, he was startled when he looked in the mirror. His freshly cut hair had uneven edges and a choppy texture, evidence of his self-made haircut. As he ran his fingers through it, he noticed the shorter length and the new vibrant blue hue that now covered his strands, a stark contrast to his natural brown color.

An hour later, Owen walked into the office with a new-found confidence. He could feel the curious stares and whispers from his coworkers, but he didn't care. This was who he was, and he wouldn't hide it any longer.

As soon as he sat down at his desk, the hair police chief stormed in with a scowl on his face. Anderson braced himself for what was to come next, but to his surprise, Patton just stood there sputtering incoherently.

"You...you...you..." He struggled to form a sentence as he pointed at Owen's head.

Anderson smirked. "Do you like it?" he asked innocently, knowing full well that the manager would not approve of his new hair color.

Patton's face turned an alarming shade of red. "This is unacceptable!" he finally managed to yell out. "I can't have my employees looking like circus clowns!"

But Anderson wasn't bothered by the manager's outburst. He knew that there were strict regulations regarding hair length in the company manual, but there was nothing stated about hair color. And so, with a smug expression on his face, Owen shrugged and went back to work.

As expected, the other workers were all talking about his new look during their lunch break. Some were impressed by his boldness while others were taken aback by his rebellious act. But overall, everyone seemed to be enjoying the change in atmosphere that Owen had brought about with his short uneven blue hair.

As the days went by, Anderson continued experimenting with different hair colors and styles. He would come into work each week with a new look that would leave everyone speechless and wondering what he would do next.

Owen's coworkers began to look forward to seeing what his new style would be. Some even started asking for his advice on how to style their own hair in more unique ways. Owen was happy to share his knowledge and passion for self-expression through hair with others.

But not everyone was pleased with Owen's new persona. Patton grew increasingly frustrated and threatened to fire him if he didn't conform to the dress code. But Anderson refused to back down, knowing that he hadn't broken any rules.

Despite the tension with the manager, Owen's work performance remained stellar. He had even started receiving compliments from business clients about his hair. This only fueled his desire to push boundaries even further.

One day, Anderson decided to shave part of his head and dye the remaining hair bright pink. He wasn't sure how his coworkers would react, but he was excited nonetheless.

As soon as he stepped into the office, all eyes were on him. But instead of disapproving looks or whispers, Owen was met with cheers and high-fives from his colleagues.

"You look amazing!" one co-worker exclaimed.

"Yeah, I wish I had the guts to do something like that," another chimed in.

Many of his co-workers began to question the rigid rules of the office and, one by one, they too started to find small ways to express their individuality. The once uniform rows of cubicles began to show signs of life and personality, with colorful trinkets and personal touches appearing on desks.

The changes in office culture were subtle at first, but they were noticeable. Owen's bold choice to cut his own hair and dye it a brilliant shade of blue sparked a wave of individuality among his work peers. Suddenly, people were wearing crazy socks and wild ties, their previously tidy hairstyles now tousled and unconventional. They were still careful to stay within the official dress code and personal appearance regulations, but these small acts of rebellion brought a new energy into the office.

At first, the higher-ups seemed uncomfortable with this sudden burst of self-expression. They would sniff disapprovingly and purse their lips, muttering about professionalism and conformity. But as the days went on, they couldn't deny the boost in morale and productivity that came along with the eccentric changes. Soon enough, even they were sporting colorful socks and experimenting with new hairstyles.

One day, quiet Sarah from accounting showed up with a bright purple streak in her hair. She had always admired Owen's courage and decided to show her support by joining him in his colorful rebellion.

The hair police chief was starting to lose control over his perfectly manicured office space. He tried reprimanding Owen and Sarah for their unconventional choices, but it only seemed to make things worse. After weeks of trying to maintain the strict corporate image, the manager finally gave up. Productivity was up and he couldn't deny the positive effects that Anderson's act of rebellion had on the office.

The once rigid and oppressive environment had transformed into a lively and diverse workspace. Patton slowly began to embrace the changes happening around him and even started to loosen up himself.

He stopped giving warnings for unconventional hairstyles and instead started complimenting them. He even made a bold move, by his terms, by wearing colorful ties instead of his usual plain ones.

After closing the door to his office, Patton motioned for Owen to sit down. The only sound in the room was the faint buzzing of the fluorescent lights above, creating a dull hum that added to the already tense atmosphere. Anderson's heart raced as he waited for the manager to speak, the silence becoming almost suffocating.

"Something has been on my mind," Patton said, breaking the lull. "Why did you decide to cut your own hair in the office and dye it blue before the next day?"

Owen took a deep breath before answering. "Because the unnecessary regulations were making me BLUE," he replied.

RANDOM BUBBLES

O ur supervisor, George Hansen, was a large man, his two most striking physical attributes being the biggest butt in history accompanied by short non-muscular arms, resembling a cross between a hippo and T. rex. His cantaloupe-size ankles, which had a discolored purple hue, were swollen. A pungent smell sometimes emitted from his privates, and we speculated that he would need at least a full roll of toilet paper to wipe himself clean. On one occasion, he had returned from the restroom with a long piece of toilet paper trailing from his pant leg all the way down to his shoe heel, leaving a five-foot trail on the unvacuumed rug. It was like watching and observing a rare human creature hybrid, an endangered Tyrannopotamus shuffling through our workplace, completely oblivious to our fascinated gazes.

Prioritizing his own health and well-being was never a priority for George. His meals consisted mainly of unhealthy fast-food options, lacking essential nutrients like fruits, vegetables, and whole grains. Our team was shocked when he started bringing a lone green apple to work each day for lunch, attempting to make a change in his diet. However, this short-lived effort was soon abandoned as our boss reverted back to his usual fast-food habits.

His go-to snack was a Butterfingers candy bar, filled with unhealthy ingredients like corn syrup, sugar, and vegetable oil. George would chomp, devour, and attack three candy bars during each eight-hour work shift, leaving a trail of chocolate and wrapper fragments scattered along the office floor. It was almost as if he intentionally left these behind to help him navigate the maze-like cubicles back to his own office without getting lost.

Although he was an IT manager, George often struggled with personal computers. On one occasion, he was trying to hire an entry-level employee. While going through his emails in front of our team, he suddenly exclaimed, "What the hell is she talking about? There's no resume attached!" Fred, a knowledgeable computer operator, noticed George's frustration and offered to help. "Boss, what's the issue? Do you need some assistance?" George replied, "Barb from HR keeps sending me these emails with resumes attached, but there are no resumes!"

Fred leaned over to see the open email on George's screen. "George, scroll down," he suggested. "Scroll down? Why?" "Just do it. Click on that little elevator-looking thing on the far right. You're getting warmer... colder... now scroll in the opposite direction. See? Let me show you." Fred took control of the mouse and scrolled down to reveal the bottom portion of the email message. George snatched the mouse back to show who the boss was. But Fred remained unfazed and calmly instructed George to double-click the paper clip icon at the bottom of the message. After a few failed attempts, George was able to open the resume. He squinted at the small type and grumbled, "The text is too small. I can hardly read it." "Why don't you just print it out? It'll be easier to read like a book." In a loud voice for all our staff to hear, George declared, "I'm going to print out these resumes and review them at my desk." And miraculously, he was able to click on the print icon without needing any more help. Feeling triumphant, George marched off to solve another pesky problem - all in a day's work.

Having successfully navigated the thorny missing resume crisis, George moved on to conducting candidate interviews. Two days later, during the team check-in at the start of the shift, he was asked how the interviews were going. Without hesitation, the boss eagerly shared, "I had an interesting interview this morning with a broad who looked like Sherman with huge tits." Some of my colleagues chuckled, trying to imagine what a 300-pound woman resembling a former high school jock would look like with large breasts. Sherman Brown himself, who had gained over 100 pounds since his football days due to his love for beer and barbecue, didn't take offense and even joined in on the laughter with the rest of the team. In today's times, such a comment would be considered grounds for immediate termination, but back then, it was just seen as George being George.

George had been Sherman's boss for over six years, and they were both large individuals. One time, Tim Fisher hip-checked Sherman into George, the two super heavyweights performing "The Tango Sumo" dance, which was finally interrupted when the boss regained his balance and shrieked, "What's your problem, Sherman? Get your act together." Duane, the least senior member of our IT group, later described the scene as reminiscent of two hippos performing a mating ritual celebration in sub-Saharan Africa.

George was well-liked by his crew, including myself, and we were all loyal to him as a supervisor. He had a reputation for being fair and advocating for salary increases for those who worked under him. Our team consisted of a diverse group of IT "professionals," all working the overnight shift in a large financial services company's data center. We monitored a mainframe computer that hosted critical applications and processed important transactions. The entire team was male, and we started our shifts at midnight and finished at eight in the morning.

During our annual review meetings, my colleagues and I would compare the notes written by George. We noticed a pattern: after informing us of no raise or only a small salary increase, he would always add a comment suggesting that "insert name could always use more money." These reviews were still done by hand, with George crossing out lines and jotting down indecipherable notes during the discussion. Once an employee signed and submitted their review, George would make additional notes, leaving us curious about what other cryptic words and phrases were being added to our personnel files.

Once a month, we would receive our paper paychecks. Many of my co-workers were young revelers who enjoyed partying after getting paid, indulging in booze, good food, clubbing, and skirt chasing. By the last week before payday, they'd usually run out of money and would resort to eating lots of cheap ramen noodles until the next paycheck came. George had a solution for this issue, which he shared at a staff meeting: "Here's what you do. Split your monthly paycheck into four equal parts and put each part into an envelope. If you run out of money for one week, that's it - you can't use the next envelope until the new week starts." Someone raised their hand and asked, "Boss, a month doesn't divide evenly into four weeks. What about the extra days in the month? Also, Is there a special strategy during a leap year?" George, who had little patience for details and complications, replied curtly, "Figure it out yourselves. Stick to my plan, and your financial problems will be solved." We didn't follow George's financial advice or his generous suggestion. Math and division gave us headaches, and the allure of local coeds and entertainment was too strong to resist.

Every month, we went to the bank to cash our paper checks. The bank didn't open until 9:30 AM, an hour and a half after our shift ended. On payday, we would eagerly gather around George, much like hungry baby birds begging for food from their mother, as he handed out our hard-earned paychecks. One day, I arrived at the bank way too early at 8:30 in the morning and decided to take a quick nap in my car. But I ended up sleeping for five hours, waking up feeling disheveled and sticky from the hot ninety-degree temperature. Thankfully, the off-duty cop working in the bank lobby didn't investigate me.

One of George's employees once accidentally washed his paycheck in the laundry. When the employee informed George about it, he shrugged and said there was nothing he could do. He suggested that the employee should view it as a learning opportunity. After making the dejected young man wait for a few moments, George finally announced triumphantly, "I'll see what I can do. Consider it taken care of." A new check was issued a few days later, much to the employee's relief and appreciation for his boss.

George had a weekly meeting with other managers after our graveyard shift ended. The other shift supervisors tactfully informed the human hippo that he had an unpleasant body odor and suggested he "freshen up" before attending the meeting. George's solution was to apply deodorant directly over his white shirt's armpit area at precisely 7:30 AM, eventually leaving his white dress shirt permanently stained with two faded yellow circles, resembling an expanding flood zone under his arms. He stored his Old Spice deodorant in an overhead bin in his cubicle, and one of us always hid it an hour or two before his weekly meeting.

"Have you seen my deodorant?" George would anxiously bellow.

"No idea what you're talking about," we'd reply.

Muttering incoherently, the Tyrannohippo waddled back to his cube, and by the start of the next graveyard shift, his missing deodorant mysteriously reappeared in the bin.

On April Fools' Day, George gathered our department together and delivered a grave announcement: "Team, I have some major news. And there's no easy way to say this: the data center is moving to Sioux Falls, South Dakota in six months." The room was filled with shocked faces and hushed whispers. "I can't believe it. I just signed a lease on an apartment. Where is Sioux Falls anyway?" Sherman quickly grabbed an atlas to locate South Dakota on the map.

As our manager stood up and exited the room, a mischievous grin spread across his face. Our team had fallen for his prank completely. George had expected someone to see through it, but everyone was fooled. The idea had come to him just moments before as he walked from his car into the building.

After spending thirty minutes at his desk, George called another meeting. "I know the announcement about moving to Sioux Falls was a shock," he said. "But let's try to stay positive - we still have jobs. Sometimes, change can lead to growth and opportunities. And there's one more big announcement."

We leaned in eagerly, some still dazed from the previous news. Enjoying the suspense, George paused before revealing his final bombshell: "Gentlemen, the move to Sioux Falls was just an April Fools' joke." As he got up and left the conference room, ten mouths dropped open in unison—half relieved that they weren't relocating and the other half wishing they could throw sharp objects at George's departing figure - perhaps a dart aimed at a huge can't miss target, his rotund buttocks.

The following year, our team plotted to get our revenge and play a joke on George by having everyone call in sick on April Fools' Day. However, George was always vigilant about avoiding pranks on this day and quickly figured out our plan when the third caller, who pretended to have the flu, turned out to be "never miss a day" Teddy. To get the last laugh, the boss stationed himself at the data center entrance at the beginning of our shift, personally greeting each employee as they arrived for work.

During the rare lulls in our work shift, the staff would amuse themselves by pulling pranks on our easily fooled manager.

"Did you see that?"

"What are you talking about, George?"

George's eyes were fixed on the community computer monitor in the shared workspace, but soon he retreated to his cubicle where he could doze off discreetly. It was all part of his job as a manager, pretending to be productive while actually getting some much-needed rest. The following night, he returned to his new favorite spot, once again intently staring at the large display screen like a hawk spotting its prey from high above.

"There! Did you see it?"

"No. Are you feeling alright? Are you hallucinating?"

"Right there, that bubble! Did you see it on the monitor? And look, another one! It moved to a different spot."

"Maybe you should take a break. You are working too hard. Rest your eyes."

George had no idea, but two nights prior, Mike Miller had installed a Bubbles Window screensaver on the computer with the intention of playing a prank on George by reeling him in like a marlin at sea. The other employees were in on it and found it entertaining to see if they could trick their boss. It became a nightly tradition to watch this "fool-the-boss" game and add some amusement to our mundane work routines. My co-workers kept things interesting by altering the frequency and duration of the bubbles on the screensaver each night, and sometimes, they even skipped turning it on during their shift for a change of pace.

Night after night, George would plop his ample booty on the too-small chair, positioning himself directly in front of the monitor for the best view. He constantly asked us if we saw the bubble or the vanishing wave on the screen, but everyone always replied no and questioned his sanity. Even if there had been a major outage with all systems and critical applications crashing, Curious George wouldn't have noticed or cared. This bubble mystery was his top priority, and he was determined to unravel its secrets. The back-and-forth between us continued for weeks, with George enthusiastically yelling whenever a bubble appeared while we insisted that nothing was there.

One morning, George convinced another supervisor to look at the monitor ten minutes before the screensaver had been programmed to turn off. Excitedly, the human hippo pointed at the screen and exclaimed, "Do you see that bubble?"

His colleague, clearly annoyed and unimpressed, brushed off George's excitement with a dismissive gesture. "George, it's just a screensaver. You're overreacting."

Detective George waddled off, pleased that he had finally solved "The Case of the Random Bubbles." He could hardly wait to share his discovery at the check-in meeting later that day. His team would be amazed and grateful for his keen detective skills. He would finally be recognized as the great detective he knew himself to be.

That night at our staff meeting, George confident-ly shared his new findings with his usual know-it-all atti-tude. "Remember what you were worried about? It's just a screensaver."

He left the meeting feeling pleased. A celebration was in order; he reached into his back pocket and pulled out a slightly melted Butterfinger, relishing the moment of "sweet" victory.

ALSO BY MITCH OLSON

PANDEMIC BLUES & OTHER VERY
SHORT STORIES (2023)

WIN TODAY DIE TOMORROW & OTHER VERY SHORT
STORIES (2024)

HOOP HARMONY & OTHER VERY SHORT
STORIES (2024)

ABOUT THE AUTHOR

Mitch Olson is a renowned author recognized for his impactful poetry and short stories. His writing delves into the complexities of flawed characters and their range of emotions, from despair to hope. Born in 1962, just two weeks before the opening of the Seattle World's Fair, he has been a lifelong resident of the Seattle area. Currently, he resides in Washington State with his wife and daughter.

Throughout his life, Olson has cherished his local roots, although he regrets never seeing the legendary hometown hero Jimi Hendrix in concert. However, he did manage to attend Nirvana's last American performance at the Seattle Center Arena. Despite the passage of time since the publication of his first book, some things have remained constant. Olson eagerly awaits the return of his beloved hometown basketball team, the Supersonics. And he still finds joy in his playful Brittany, Barkley, who occasionally behaves like a cat.